NIGHTHOPE

GREGORY N. WHITIS

PAGE PUBLISHING, INC.
Conneaut Lake, PA

First originally published by Page Publishing 2021

ISBN 978-1-6624-2404-5 (pbk)
ISBN 978-1-6624-2405-2 (digital)

Printed in the United States of America

ACKNOWLEDGMENTS

Above all, my loving parents, Peter and Martha Whitis, of Eau Claire, Wisconsin. They probably thought I had lost my mind when I said I was moving to Alabama to work on a catfish farm.

My wife, Karen. The endearing arguments about alienating specific segments of society, "Can't you wait until we retire and move before you publish this one?" And my rehearsed reply, based on a poster that hung in my dorm room at Iowa State, "A ship that stays in the harbor isn't really a ship." Then I would try to change the subject, asking permission to get another implement for my tractor.

The rest of my esteemed review team, Anne Weston, Christie and Jay Haffner, Joe Campbell, Robert Dewitt, and David Teichert-Coddington. Particular thanks to Kristie Taylor for polishing the final revision.

For all my fellow struggling writers, follow the advice of Stephen King: get friends who will throw humbling punches during the review process. If you can't take criticism as a writer, find something else to do.

All my Alabama catfish farmer-friends and law enforcement colleagues who read my debut novel, *Blue Green,* decreeing that I should keep on writing since I knew what the hell I was doing. Specifically I want to acknowledge Chief George Cooley, retired director of Tuscaloosa's Alabama Law Enforcement Academy. His words of encouragement spurred me onward. And Willard Powe, for sharing the comical story about sinking a truck in a catfish pond.

The following people provided technical assistance along the way: Stephen May (Army stuff), Beth Ezell (legal matters), my son Andrew (medical stuff), Jay Seale (tires and trucking), Charlie Seale (airplanes), and Jordan, my daughter-in-law, an elementary school-teacher, on the attributes of five-year-old boys.

All the dedicated, author-friendly folks at Page Publishing and, in particular, Gretchen Wills.

This book is dedicated to my writing mentor, Aileen Kilgore Henderson. Twenty years ago, she encouraged me to write my first novel. Damn near took me twenty years too. She never gave up on me. She'll always be in my heart.

CHAPTER ONE

Stuart Baron's bright quest for the good life dimmed again as he gazed through his windshield. He was parked in the middle lane on the Santa Ana Freeway. For the third day in a row, the daily commute made it absurdly clear: he couldn't go on living like this. At this rate, he calculated, he'd spend three years of his life watching one cluster after another, between two dashed white lines, staring at the towering skyline of Los Angeles. Making it worse, he could barely make out his corner office on the thirtieth floor of the US Bank Tower, two miles away, in the lifting brown smog. He could get there quicker running in his Nikes, but he'd probably get robbed, assaulted, or killed. Inhaling the damned smog would probably shorten his life span another three years.

California happens.

The typical morning chaotic commute continued to unfold all around him. The heated argument between a middle-aged interracial couple on his right turned into an animated verbal beatdown by the obese black woman. The skinny white man stared straight ahead, his pockmarked, bony hands clenching the wheel. He let his partner vent while silently praying she wouldn't knock out the rest of his teeth. It was hard enough maintaining dental hygiene with a meth habit.

Just off Baron's left front quarter panel was a half-ton Ford Ranger, loaded with over a ton of rusted scrap metal, loosely bound with a rotten hemp rope. A pointed five-foot-long steel spike was precariously scrunched between a half-ass knot and a duct-taped fender. One good bounce going down the freeway, and it would morph into a human shish kebab. The three Hispanic males shared a fat joint. The familiar sweet smell of burning grass reminded Baron of his crazy college days at UCLA in the seventies.

And directly in front, an agitated businessman squirmed restlessly in a shiny black Mercedes-Benz 190 Turbo D. He repeatedly slapped the black leather cover on the steering wheel while looking constantly to his left and right. Pall Mall butts, smoked down to the filters, littered the area outside his driver's door.

The rocking in the lime-green Chevy conversion van behind him finally stopped. A hand appeared out the side window, dropping something squishy and rubbery onto the pavement. The driver climbed back behind the steering wheel. The shit-eating grin on the youngster's face made Baron smile.

Los Angeles never ceased throwing the occasional brushback pitches. Abnormal gradually morphed into normal. He wondered when he would finally become emotionally numb to the darkening humanity of Southern California. The state's name being the first clue. It had something to do with getting screwed. Even the governor was quirky at the time—they called him Moonbeam. Baron grew up in the north woods of Minnesota and landed in UCLA after high school. The culture shock of college was an almost imperceptible series of tremors, lasting for nearly four years. The psychic stone by stone adjustment to life in LA was now callousing his soul.

He was parked on the elevated Los Angeles River Bridge. He could see Dodger Stadium up the interstate on his right. His exit was two miles farther west, onto Cesar Chavez Avenue. Then he'd head south on Grand. The US Bank building was almost in the middle of the downtown's two dozen skyscrapers. Thirteen miles further west was the Pacific Ocean. It was clearly visible in the wintertime from his corner window after the seasonally dry west winds blew the smog out of the city.

He hadn't moved an inch in the past hour. He checked his gas gauge. The needle had barely moved since leaving the house an hour ago. The new 1997 Isuzu Trooper sipped gas. He had traded in the thirsty Toyota Land Cruiser. Both sported four-wheel drive, but the Trooper featured more cargo room. The family had recently taken up car camping and needed a tad more space. Their recent encounter with a mama black bear and her cub up in Yosemite forced them to grab their sleeping bags and retreat through the rear hatch. He grinned. It'd be a cherished family memory.

The Trooper still had that new car smell. A few more farting contests with his five-year-old would take over the virginal aroma. His only complaint was that the air conditioner was too small for the boxy interior and the extensive glass windows. He should have opted for the extra tint. The Trooper's excellent visibility did come in handy for negotiating the craziness of rush hour traffic. The salesman had quipped that he could probably grow pot in the rear after its useful life on the road.

He turned on the radio, punched the preset for KXLA, endured the latest undecipherable hit song, and waited for a traffic report. Major Delay, the station's traffic guy, was hovering in a helicopter between the stadium and Alpine Park. The misnomered greenspace was a mere topographical bump with its less than endearing elevation of 322 feet and could abruptly change with the next jolt from the southern tip of the San Andreas Fault.

"Listen up, all you Angie Leenos, if you're going westbound on the Santa Ana before the Alameda exit, you need to be patient. Our boys in blue are involved in some kind of skirmish."

There was a perceptible pause in the vocal transmission, followed by static, and indistinguishable babble in the cockpit.

"Captain, did you see that?" Major Delay was talking to the pilot, not realizing his microphone was hot. "That cop just went down. Oh, man, this is turning into a cluster."

"Folks, there's a gunfight right now on the Santa Ana. Four police units have surrounded a panel van. They're shooting at it. Oh, thank God, the cop that went down, he's staggering back to one of the cruisers. He's nodding his head. Man, I hope he's okay."

Stu Baron could see the Alameda exit. He was within range.

He heard the popping of distant gunfire.

An intense firefight involving semiautomatic AR-15 patrol rifles, now standard equipment for street officers, echoed along the concrete barriers lining the freeway. The almost-constant shooting briefly going staccato as twenty round mags were tactically dumped to the pavement.

The distinctive *whap, whap, whap* of helicopter blades beating the still brownish air overhead grew louder. The shadow of the helo passed over Baron's moon roof.

Major Delay, his normal vocal pitch much more elevated, "Oh no, I can't believe this. The rear doors of the van just opened, and there are men scrambling out with fully automatic AK-47s, returning fire."

The cops were outgunned.

"Where's SWAT?" the pilot was yelling over the noise in the cockpit.

Baron stared straight ahead, searching for the mayhem happening less than a mile away. Car windshields directly in front of him and to his left and right shattered. Bullets continued their way through numerous cars, exiting rear windows. The man ahead of him in the Mercedes took a round to the head. Blood and pink tissue splattered the rear window. In effect, the man had stopped the bullet in the line of fire with Baron.

Baron ducked over the center console. He heard glass cracking. A stray bullet came through his windshield. A whisper of air grazed his left cheek. The round thunked into the back seat.

"Lord, I've had enough," Stu Baron whimpered.

*****

The crime scene included Baron's vehicle. The all-too-familiar yellow police tape extended two vehicle rows behind him. Shattered safety glass littered the Santa Ana. Two police officers killed. Six more wounded, their five-hundred-dollar bulletproof vests had slowed down the rifle rounds enough to make the wounds survivable. The drug gang was ripped apart by SWAT's Black Hawk helicopter, the thirty-caliber machine gun on the side rail finally outmatching the AK-47s.

"The militarized LAPD had lanced another societal blister. The city's deepening acne was nearing the incurable stage. Los Angeles was festering. Today, the relief was hot lead," the lead editor would write in the *Los Angeles Times*, wondering if a cure was even possible.

Baron leaned against the median's concrete barrier while the police investigators photographed and diagrammed bullet trajectories. A bloodstained white sheet covered the poor guy in the Mercedes.

He stared off toward the east. The enigmatic Los Angeles River, confined in solid concrete, was bone-dry again. Hollywood loved to use the Big Ditch for action films. They should have been shooting today—they could have stayed under budget.

The din of the constant blaring of ambulance sirens and the Angel choppers leaving the scene finally numbed his senses. Becoming surreal. Shifting into slow motion. He was transfixed on a new glossy billboard. Never noticed it before.

It read "Fresh from Their Ponds to Your Plate." Four middle-aged men, three clad in dark-blue jeans and brown leather belts adorned with nondescript belt buckles, stood, seemingly nonchalantly, with the fourth man, the trimmest, wearing baggy khaki chinos. They were wearing open-collared knit T-shirts, the unmistakable sheen of new fabric, freshly freed from plastic wrap and recently ironed.

They weren't strikingly handsome. Looked like real salt of the earth types one might find at a Hole 19 in a less-than-swanky golf course. Not like that buffed-up model with a two-day stubble on his chin, advertising Drakkar Noir cologne on the billboard up the road. They were smiling comfortably, not in the least bit forced. They appeared to be completely at ease. Living the good life. The men stood in front of a squared-off blue pond with a strange-looking machine floating in the water. The machine's blurred paddles appeared to be spinning, throwing sparkling water several feet into clear air.

Baron squinted into the rising sun and made out the wording under each man, Denny Mosses, Brandon Laring, Joey Oglethorpe, and Townsend King, Catfish Farmers of the Year from Arkansas, Louisiana, Mississippi, and Alabama. Underneath them, inside a football-shaped logo, read a nicely curved line, "US Farm-Raised Catfish." In the lower left-hand corner, a stoneware plate showing off a perfectly grilled fish fillet, artistically covered with a dainty serving of black bean salsa. Vividly orange-pinkish, thinly shredded carrots balanced out the plate. They were almost the same color of the brains splattered on the back window of the Mercedes. The smell of bile wafted through his nose. He fought back a twinge of nausea.

He had never eaten a farm-raised catfish. They were cousins of those bloody-red bullheads he used to catch and toss on the bank in Minnesota. He recalled seeing farm-raised catfish on the menu at the Red Lobster. The billboard tweaked his interest in trying it. He turned around and gazed at the four farmers. He studied each face. No hint of apprehensions. Lack of tension in the eyebrows. He was good at reading faces. He had interviewed hundreds of people for his company.

He wondered what their mornings were like. *They sure as hell didn't waste their time in urban gridlocks. Endure all this freaking carnage.* A police officer yanked off the yellow tape stretched between two signposts. He shrugged as he meandered back through the bullet-perforated vehicles.

He glanced at his Timex Ironman. It read 11:48. *Damn*, Baron said to himself, *this day's shot to hell*, wincing at his choice of words.

He was so late for work they'd be worried about him. He hadn't missed a regular day of work in years. His administrative assistant, Margo Sue Follor, had probably called his house and alarmed his wife, Tabitha, to his unscheduled absence. They would be terribly anxious about his whereabouts. Especially if they were watching the news. The reporting of the civilian fatality compounding their anxiety.

Baron noticed the news crew edging their way closer to the Mercedes. He walked over, positioning himself behind the pretty brunette holding the microphone. He gave a thumbs-up gesture. His partner, Ross Whitestone, at Coast to Coast Trucking, and maybe Tabitha would be watching the noon news. Two birds, one stone.

Stu Baron's efficiency mode was still in high gear. But his normal thirst for life and adventure was throttled back as the past several hours sank in. The chaos that had unraveled before his eyes made him realize he needed to shift gears or die in LA.

He stared at the bullet hole under the rearview mirror and then at himself. He knew it was purely imagination, but it seemed he had visibly aged since leaving the house. It dawned on him he'd be half a century old in less than four years.

Stuart Baron's midlife crisis started when he slipped the transmission lever into reverse, aiming for the concrete gap in the median. He waited on the eastbound traffic to clear. The rubberneckers still at sloth speed. Wrecker crews were still hooking up disabled vehicles.

He gazed at the sign posted in the median, "Emergency and Official Vehicles Only." The catfish billboard was in front of him.

He smirked back at the four farmers. The water scene brought back vivid memories. He recalled growing up in Minnesota. Relaxing on the deck overlooking the lake. Listening to the loons. Fish slapping the surface.

I bet they know where the bears shit in the buckwheat. Don't need a sign for that.

He crossed through the concrete barrier and pointed the Trooper back east.

CHAPTER TWO

Baron drove home, deciding he needed time to decompress. He contemplated moving from Southern California. He could help Ross run the company from the Atlantic coast. They had discussed opening an eastern administrative hub in Jacksonville. But it was similar to Los Angeles. In terms of populated sprawl, Jack city was almost as spread out without the people. He needed a change. More green. Less concrete.

Peeing behind a tree in the backyard without pissing off the neighbors. He got away with it at his parents' lakeside home in northern Minnesota.

He pulled into his double-wide cobblestone driveway and parked in front of the twin-bay garage. His neighbor, Donny Jones, a retired firefighter, rumbled to a stop on his new sparkling-green John Deere riding mower. The model was the largest riding mower on the planet. Donny loved machinery with lots of horsepower. The twenty-eight-horsepower twin-cylinder uncatalyzed grass eater spewed more emissions than the four cars in both garages. Their combined yards were barely big enough for a decent bout of throw and catch. The hell with the emissions. The environmentalists dancing around the sequoias could kiss his hairy ass. Jones thrived on teasing his tree-hugging neighbors.

A skinny can of his favorite Union Free Coors was nestled in the convenient can holder. Drinking while mowing was Donny's latest deviation from law and order. The U-turns in their cul-de-sac on the wheeled monstrosity surely violated something in the largesse of California codes. He shut the mower down and sipped on his beer.

"Hey, Stu, we saw you on the noon news. Some crazy shit, huh?"

"Yeah, just another day in LA. I never did hear the final body count."

"We lost two LAPD officers, six more wounded but all the wet-backs got their Christmas cancelled. Bajalistas. That damned cartel again. Assholes had two hundred kilos of blow in the van. Oh, and one civilian killed."

"Donny, I saw him die. Poor guy was in the car in front of mine."

"Damn, Stu. Hate you had to see that." Donny had seen his share of mayhem in his twenty years as a firefighter and rescue medic. "Looks like you took a round, too." He pointed to the front windshield of Stu's Trooper with the beer can in his hand, his pinkie finger pointed straight out.

"Hope my insurance covers it. I remember reading a clause about insurrections not being covered. The war on drugs might be considered one, huh?"

"Lock and load, dude. Lock and load." Donny guzzled the rest of his Coors and fired up the mower. He disappeared into his double garage. Stu stared at the shattered right half of his windshield. He'd have to call his insurance agent and get it replaced before the cops cited him for defective equipment. Bullet holes in windshields still merited quizzical looks from the LAPD.

Get it fixed, bud. Next time, no warning citation.

Stu thought about buying a gun. At least one he could keep in the house. His Daisy BB rifle, a cherished present when he had turned thirteen, was locked away in a dusty wood chest somewhere in his garage.

He rang the doorbell on his house. Tabitha and Win always kept it locked. He could have used his door key, but the standard welcome-home kiss from the wife was a better option.

"Oh, Stu, I've been worried sick. You okay?" Tab tightly hugged him.

"I aged ten years this morning." He dug his keys out of his front pants pocket and threw them in the turned mahogany bowl from Costa Rica, a welcome-to-the-neighborhood gift from Donny. Sometimes when he used the bowl, the introductory retort from his opinionated neighbor flooded back, "Damn the tree huggers. After we cut down the mahoganies, the sequoias are next, buddy."

"Tab," Stu looked at his watch, "I know it's only one o'clock, but I need a shot of the good stuff right now."

In their fifteen years of marriage, Tabitha Baron had rarely seen her husband drink before six. And when he did, it was always just one to unwind and relax. If he needed serious decompression, a five-mile run into the San Gabriel's was the preferred stress reliever. And the postshower sex would further ease the tension of living in his never-ending rat race.

"Go sit in your chair, and I'll get your drink. Have you eaten?"

"No. Normally I could eat the bunghole out of a camel right now."

"That's totally gross. You've been hanging out with your truckers too much."

"Tab, I watched a man die. Don't have an appetite right now."

Tab sat down next to him, grabbing his hand. "What happened, Stu?"

Stu filled her in. Tab wrapped her arms around him and gave him another hug and a kiss. He gazed into her vivid teal eyes. They always reminded him of gemstones.

"You going to be okay, Stu?" She squeezed his hands.

"I'll be all right."

She walked into the kitchen and lifted a crystal tumbler out of a cabinet.

Stu asked about their five-year-old, Winchester.

"It's Rhonda's week for hauling kids. He should be home by three."

Stu looked at his watch. It'd be another couple of hours before a typhoon of boyish energy descended on the Baron household. He wanted to be home when Win arrived. He'd forego the afternoon run. Spending quality time with the family might help him deal with the morning.

He wanted to close his eyes and put the recliner all the way back. But the urge to call work was overwhelming. He reached for the cordless phone on the end table and dialed.

"Good afternoon. Coast to Coast Trucking. How can I help you?" The new voice on the other end was pleasant and friendly. Stu didn't know her name.

"Hey, good afternoon to you too! This is Stuart Baron." He attempted to match her effusive enthusiasm for good customer relations.

"Mr. Baron! We've been worried about you. Are you okay?"

"I'm fine, thank you. Just another day in the city, right?" Stuart was kicking himself for not knowing her name. "Hey, let me talk to Ross."

"Yes, sir, Mr. Baron. Please hold."

Ross Whitestone picked up right away. "Stu, you okay, dude?"

"Yeah, I'm okay. Added some gray today, but I'll make it."

"Where are you?"

"I went on home, Ross. Retreated to the loving arms of Tab. Didn't figure you'd be french-kissing me when I popped in your office."

"Hell no, but I did have a jigger of your favorite scotch waiting on you. I had to drink one myself after seeing you on the noon news. They didn't give us any details about the dead guy. You know, I can't run this place without you."

"Ross, I'll see you in the morning. I'm going to try getting to the office by six. The seven-o'clock plan isn't working too swell."

"Okay, bud. I don't know about the six-o'clock shit though. We're too old to be putting in twelve-hour days again. We've been through too much and paid too many dues. You just plan on knocking off around midafternoon, we'll get it done. No problem, okay?" Ross paused.

Stu rubbed his forehead, thinking about Ross's idea for changing up the daily grind. It wasn't meshing with his new plan.

"Stu?"

"What?"

"Nooner."

They both laughed. Ross and Stu not only were co-owners of Coast to Coast Trucking. They were best friends. They had been college buddies and roommates since their freshmen year. Their wives were the best of friends too. Their friendships knew no bounds. They were like brothers and sisters. The men would die for each other if it came down to it. The wives had their sixes.

"Hey, Ross, who's the receptionist now? I can't for the life of me remember her name."

"She's new. She started last week. She replaced Gayle. Gayle's in a rig now. She's the crew leader for our first female team. New girl's name is Marcela Quiroz. Why?"

"Good hire, Ross. She's good on the phone. She's got a voice that could melt a trucker after hauling ass for a week. How about putting me back on with her?"

"Sure, see you tomorrow." The phone went silent momentarily.

"Good afternoon. Coast to Coast Trucking. How can I help you?"

"Marcela, this is Stuart Baron again. I hope you have a wonderful day."

"Thank you, Mr. Baron."

"Looking forward to meeting you, Marcela."

"Me too. Glad you're okay."

"Bye, Marcela." Stu hung up.

Three times he said her name. He wouldn't be forgetting it anytime soon. He put the phone down and looked out the big picture window toward his dinky, almost-laughable yard. The in-ground pool filled in most of the space inside the head-high red cedar board fence. The push mower was overkill. A weed whipper would have been sufficient.

The hummingbird feeder on the back deck was nearly empty. They were out there, three different species this time, about a dozen or so birds, fliting and dive-bombing one another, fighting for a spot on the feeder. The larger Annas, with their crimson heads and throats, were keeping the smaller Allens at bay. A lone male Costa, with its brightly glowing amethyst helmet, rested on the hanger waiting for an opportunity.

Stu envied the patience of the male Costa. His time would come.

He slipped his loafers on and headed for the refrigerator, hoping Win had remembered to make another jug of nectar.

CHAPTER THREE

The 6:00 a.m. commute worked much better. Traffic in all three lanes heading into downtown was steady. Thousands of downtown office commuters had figured out the same strategy. It wasn't bumper to bumper yet. Baron made steady progress toward the Chavez exit.

The sun rose directly behind him in his rearview. He noticed that the rays softly illuminated the catfish billboard. All the other billboards seemed dim in comparison. The realistic blueness of the pond was especially eye-catching. It reminded him of Sacagawea Lake up at his parents' home in Minnesota. As he drove past the billboard, he again noticed the plate of fish. The grilled white fillet glistened in the early morning sunshine.

Man, that looks good. He wasn't a big fish eater, but the delectable image was more appealing than the mushy, brown-spotted Guatemalan banana and stale Zone protein bar he just forced down.

The corporate office for Coast to Coast Trucking was located on the entire thirtieth floor of the US Bank Tower. It was the logistical nerve center for the nation's largest perishable freight trucking company. Six hundred eighteen wheelers were headed to one of the company's four cold-storage lockers. They were in Long Beach off I-710, in Jacksonville at the last eastern exit for I-10, in North Chicago near the lake, and the Port of New Orleans. The company only hauled perishables—Asian frozen shrimp, Alaskan salmon, Hawaiian pineapples, Japanese tuna, and vegetables from California's Imperial Valley and Mexico. The Jacksonville locker loaded out trucks laden with Florida vegetables, Carolina pork, Georgia chickens and Indian River citrus. The company never dead headed. Most of the rigs stayed on I-10 headed between the west coast and the east coast lockers. A spur route from New Orleans to Chicago supplied the country's midsection with fresh avocados, bananas, papayas, and mangoes from Central America. Coast to Coast had nearly 5 percent of the nation's perishable trucking business.

The company had grown from one truck, co-owned by Stuart Baron and Ross Whitestone. They started off catering to graduating UCLA students moving to their first jobs. Their first truck, a 1979 Mack, was a five-million-mile beater with the mechanical personality of a flea-ridden burro that wasn't worth the bullet. Now they orchestrated a frenzied fleet with two thousand employees. Coast to Coast's competitive edge was the fastest continental delivery time in the trucking industry. They were faster and cheaper than a freight train. Their three-man teams could go ocean to ocean in two days, guaranteed. Their standard routine was forty-one hours of driving time at a company-mandated limit of sixty miles per hour, allowing for six hours of NASCAR-style pit stops for fuel and tire checks, hot showers, meals, and pee breaks.

Coast to Coast also had a secret weapon, subsidized by the US taxpayer and expertly maintained by the Department of Defense. All their trucks were outfitted with GPS trackers. The Army had ridiculed the Navy, in front of Defense Secretary Cohen and President Clinton, bragging that they could build a better tracking system. The Army's would be better, the generals boasted. Faster. Capable of tracking more motorized units. Besides, compared to the Army, the Navy didn't have a big enough fleet to thoroughly test a prototype system. The Secretary of Defense issued a challenge to each of the branches: develop a prototype and field test it for three years.

The Navy had recognized that outfitting supply ships with GPS while they lumbered in the open ocean at a top speed of thirty knots would be comedic relief for a room full of generals. The Navy, with its share of the three-way split of one and a half billion dollars, was determined to demonstrate their technical savvy. They would design a combined nautical terrestrial system and flaunt it in the face of the landlubbers. The US Navy's entry in the race to perfect a military satellite tracking system was launched during a very fortunate golf game with Rear Admiral Brian Rompton and Ross Whitestone, proud co-owner of a fleet of seventy-foot-long banana haulers hauling ass through America's southern corridor at one mile per minute. The system would be on temporary loan for research and development purposes, but the Navy would "forget" to decommission the system. The admiral's weeklong family vacations at the company's retreat on Lake Tahoe would ensure further forgetfulness. Ross never hesitated picking up the admiral's tab at Hole 19 at the Links in Palo Verdes. The fleet trackers and dedicated satellite hookup were worth a third of a billion. That could buy boatloads of the admiral's favorite scotch.

Stu and Ross were discussing a new system for fleet refueling along I-10 when Margo, Baron's administrative assistant, knocked and entered Whitestone's plush corner office facing the Pacific. The day's ozone alert and smog warning precluded any chance of viewing the endless expanse of blue water.

"Mr. Baron, we have a situation in Wisconsin." Situation was code for a cluster involving a rig.

Ross looked at Stu. "Glad it happened today and not yesterday."

Stu handled the situations. Ross didn't do well with emergencies. Deviations from the status quo were not his forte. His business acumen was top-notch, but dealing with human nature down on the ground level was better left to his partner. Baron's graduate degree in psychology and Ross's MBA were a perfect blend for managing a league of long-haul truckers.

Margo followed Mr. Baron into the situation room. She gently closed the door behind him. The dimly lit room was off-limits to everyone but Stu, Ross, Glenda, his administrative assistant Margo, and the admiral's sailor nerds. They hadn't seen the Navy guys in years. One other person also had blanket permission to enter, the company's chief of security, Terrance "Terrible" Benson. He was on the way.

Facing Stu and Margo was a large display board one might see in the SITCOM room in a fortified bunker below the Pentagon. An illuminated navy-blue board took up an entire wall, ten-feet high and thirty-feet long. The United States with all the states boundaries were highlighted in white. Interstate 10 and Interstate 55 were highlighted in a thick light-blue line along with thinner-lined state highways that connected, looped, and paralleled the two interstates. These were designated detours the teams could use in emergencies. None of the minor routes strayed from the interstates by more than fifty miles. All the rigs in service were indicated by solid green dots. Most of the green dots were moving almost imperceptibly on the board. Solid green indicating they were moving or temporarily stopped for less than thirty minutes for refueling or crew breaks. Green blinking dots indicated rigs were stopped for more than a half an hour but less than an hour. Yellow indicated stops of one hour to four hours. Trucks getting unloaded and loaded were usually yellow. Bright yellow conflagrations lit up the board at the lockers in Jacksonville, New Orleans, Chicago, and Long Beach.

A red blinking dot indicated a rig had been stationary for more than four hours. This meant a serious accident, a major, major traffic jam, a breakdown, or a security issue.

Each dot was assigned a number from one to six hundred.

Red dot, number 273, was flashing just north of the Illinois-Wisconsin state line, a long way from I-55 in Chicago. It wasn't anywhere near a highlighted blue line or a minor detour line. It appeared to be sitting in southern Wisconsin all by itself in utter vastness. For all they knew, looking at the wall, it could be in the middle of a pasture, surrounded by black-and-white Holsteins waiting on the milking bell.

"Okay, Margo, what in the hell's going on in Wisconsin?" Stu asked.

Margo Sue was one of those confusing woman types. Most men had a hard time visualizing her ever wearing a cocktail gown. She was a no-nonsense dresser, always in a dark pantsuit that conservatively covered her stout medium-tall frame. If she ever took the inclination to wear high heels, she would come nose to nose with her six-foot-tall boss. Her butch hair, square face, double-A flat chest, and meaty arms would make for more confusion in a dark tavern.

Her fourteen years of long-distance trucking was replete with lots of pleasant and unpleasant memories. She knew the country inside and out, especially all the choke and pukes along the I-10 corridor. Some of the locales she had holed up in were so remote that crime didn't even pay. But America's Dairyland was foreign territory to her. She had a ready excuse if asked. Lactose intolerance. The farts were paint peelers.

Margo replied, "Here's what we know. The truck was loaded out in New Orleans with fifteen thousand pounds of live crawfish and forty thousand pounds of bananas. Remember, we got a new guy down there. Leroy Beauregard. At the border, Wisconsin DOT pulled the truck over for routine inspection. They called in Game and Fish. The truck's been confiscated and our team is sitting in the pokey right now."

"You're kidding?" Ross asked rhetorically. Margo didn't kid.

"Get Beauregard on the line. I wanna know why the rig is in Wisconsin and why Game and Fish has my fricking truck," Stu said. His demeanor had shifted out of surf boy mode into a hard-ass executive calling the shots. Ross stared at the board, hoping red dot number 273 might move just a little.

"Yes, sir," Margo replied.

"If he needs the standard riot act read to him, do that also," Stu said, his hands on his hips, staring at the flashing red dot in Wisconsin. "Crawfish? How long have we been hauling around live seafood anyway?"

"Mr. Baron, we've been hauling live lobsters for years," Glenda volunteered reluctantly. She had approved that first bill of lading back in the early nineties.

"This is the first time, I think, we've ever hauled crawfish," Ross added.

"Yeah, it may be the last time too." Stu grimaced.

Margo left the room, gently closing the door. It would take an earthquake to rattle her. She was unshakable most of the time.

Stu studied the board while he waited on her intel. Green dots were evenly spaced all along I-10. About a dozen green dots were making their way along the Mississippi River up I-55 in Missouri. The new Midwest spur line was a good move for the company. The teams could do the New Orleans-Chicago route in a day. Finding full loads to haul south was a problem at times. Wisconsin cheese and Iowa pork filled most of the southbound trucks. Once in a while, cranberries from Michigan and Door County cherries would round out a load. The locker was located near the shore of Lake Michigan.

Damn, it gets cold up there, Stu recalled. North winds coming off the Lake in mid-January were brutal. His Cajun truckers didn't waste any time getting back on the road after getting loaded at the Chicago dock.

Terrance Benson, chief of security, entered the room. He removed his Ray-Bans and hooked them in the v of his tight military-green polo shirt. His eyes adjusted to the dim light in the room. Glenda gave Benson a quick recap. Benson walked over to the board and gazed at the blinking dot.

"Shit fire, it's thirty miles north of the warehouse," Benson remarked.

"Yeah, and it's in freaking Wisconsin with all those cheese-heads," Ross quipped, trying to ease some of his partner's anxiety. There wasn't a Packer fan in the room. The LA Rams always had a hard time up at Lambeau Field.

"Boss, heard you got into a firefight on the Santa Ana," Benson said as he stood next to Stu and Ross in front of the map.

"Yeah, you should have been there. It would have been like the good ole days."

Terrance Benson was a Vietnam War Navy vet. But unlike most of his Navy brethren, safely protected by the two-inch-thick steel of a destroyer, he had served as a Swick or SWCC, Special Warfare Combatant-Craft Crewman, delivering SEAL teams deep inside the Mekong delta. Team extractions were often accompanied with fierce firefights. He had mowed down acres of river cane with his deck-mounted fifty cal. The utter devastation Swicks could leave behind were legendary.

He still maintained the military look, a high and tight butch haircut, trimmed weekly, and a physique that could deliver a hundred push-ups any day of the week. He was as fit and trim as a Marine drill sergeant, narrow-waisted with broad shoulders. His reputation in the company was summarized by his middle nickname, Terrible. He protected the company's assets like they were his own. He lived for the occasional bare-knuckle slugfests with the intimidating Teamster union reps. They preyed on CTC's new trucker recruits. Benson could send the union thugs scurrying like rats in a barn.

Margo entered the room. She barely acknowledged Benson with an emotionless glance. It had been a short office romance. He was still too military. She wasn't into spending every weekend at the local gun range, hanging out with all his gun nut buddies.

"What you got, Margo?" Stu asked while he stared at the blinking red dot in Wisconsin.

"Beauregard says the man up in Chicago screwed up letting the team deliver the crawfish to Kenosha. Kenosha is the first town inside the state line. Wisconsin's got regs on importing nonnative crawfish. The crawfish were going to be used for a boil at the Playboy resort in Lake Geneva. They were supposed to be picked up at the Chicago locker."

"Playboy Resort? Boss, how soon can we get there?" Benson deadpanned.

Stu cracked a hint of a smile.

Margo stifled a retort aimed at Terry. *Those bunnies are way out of your league, Benson.*

"How about our team?" Stu inquired.

"They're still sitting in the Kenosha County Jail."

"Okay, let's move. Terry, we're going to Kenosha. Margo, get CTC One ready to go." Stu grimaced and left the room.

Margo walked to the door, dutifully following her boss.

"Hope he likes bunnies," Benson quipped.

Margo turned around, staring at him. Her scowl could have melted a platter of lard. "I doubt he has the urge to pet a bunny, Benson. He's married to one."

"Yeah, he got the only one around here, didn't he?"

She flipped him off and left the room.

"Bitch," Benson said under his breath as her flat trucker's butt disappeared through the doorway.

*****

The Alabama welcome center outside Grand Bay was occupied by a few eighteen-wheelers and a church van. The magnolias were in full bloom. Bumblebees darted in and out of the palm-sized white blossoms. A portly old black man, the rest area's assigned groundskeeper, pruned the red teacup rose bushes at the front entrance. The church kids were in front of the life-size, Heisman-posed steel statute of Bo Jackson, taking their group photo for the day.

CTC Team leader Hugo Sanchez checked the idling *Thermo King* unit between the trailer and tractor. Team members Mandy Ruiz and Jose Medina were in the restroom. Their breakfast two hours ago in Ponchatoula, Louisiana, had evidently introduced a new bug to their hardened truckers' stomachs, requiring an unplanned stop. Sanchez looked at his watch. They had ten more minutes, and then the green light would start blinking on the big board at corporate. Sanchez took pride in maintaining his stellar record of on-time deliveries. He'd pee in his favorite tumbler before turning into a green blinker. His team members were also invested in the mission. They each had a urinal bottle.

Fred Willing, owner-operator for Willing Trucking in Atmore, Alabama, noticed the large upside-down shiny steel bowl centered on the roof of the Coast to Coast Peterbilt. The bowl's antenna, a wrist-thick black rod, about six inches long, attached at the apex, pointed slightly backward toward the sky.

The fellow trucker walked up to Sanchez. He was looking at the front door of the Alabama welcome center. His hands on his hips. He debated about going inside, checking on his team.

"Hey, mind if I ask you a question?" Willing asked.

"No, go ahead. I'm just waiting on my team."

"Team?"

"Yeah, CTC has three-man teams. Our trucks only stop for fuel. One guy's usually sleeping while the other two are operating," Hugo replied.

"Teamsters know about that?"

"Oh, yeah. Drives them nuts."

"So how come you guys aren't union?"

"The company takes what the Teamsters would take out of our checks for dues and matches it with interest. Goes towards our retirement. CTC makes sure we're usually home for weekends too."

"What in the hell is that thing on your roof?"

Mandy and Jose exited the welcome center. They briskly trotted toward the two men conversing in the shadow of the CTC tractor trailer.

Hugo looked at his watch again. Three minutes to spare.

"That's a solar-powered CBR."

"CBR?"

"Coffee bean roaster. That black thing is a handle."

"Can I climb up and look at it?"

"Sorry, can't let you do that. Patent pending. Company's testing it out. Hey, man, nice talking with you. Gotta go." Hugo climbed in the rig, closed the driver's door, and snatched the seat belt over his shoulder. The rig roared down the ramp, steadily shifting through all thirteen gears. Jose settled into the sleeper cab, reading the latest issue of the Hispanic version of *Sports Illustrated*. Mandy had shotgun for the next eight hours.

"Coffee bean roaster my ass," the Alabama redneck shrugged. "Damn Guacamalans are using it to warm up their tortillas."

Team leader Hugo Sanchez chuckled as he merged into the right lane between a vintage VW camper van and a Buster Brown-, trucker's lingo for UPS.

"What's so funny, Hugo?" Mandy asked as he flipped the lap-sized worn road atlas over to the page for the Florida panhandle.

"One more gringo thinking he can cook food on his roof."

CHAPTER FOUR

CTC One touched down at 2:00 p.m. at DuPage Municipal Airport in West Chicago. Bill Durham, the Chicago locker manager, paced back and forth at the private hanger gate. He was as nervous as a fat tick on a hairless tomcat. He had been with the company for two years. He had only met Mr. Baron once, for his job interview in LA. Also arriving would be Chief of Security Benson. He was the company's terminator. Rumor was if he was on the way, one could go ahead and start packing. Durham contemplated looking for a small cardboard box for all his personal desk shit before he left for the airport. Statistically, the most likely day to get canned was a Friday. It was only Thursday. But then CTC wasn't run like most companies. It was more family oriented. Employees rarely left for other pastures. This was the greenest one in the trucking industry. He loved his job. He looked forward to going to work every morning. Then those damned crawfish showed up.

As the company's twin turbo prop Beechcraft King Air C90B was anchored down, the pilots asked the airport's ground crew where they could get lunch. They'd have to hoof it somewhere close. Baron wasn't popping for the crew's taxi on this trip. The crawfish fiasco was costing him way too much money. The pilots could eat stale Cheetos from a vending machine.

Baron and Benson briskly walked across the tarmac to the gate in front of the parking lot.

Durham outstretched his right hand. Baron gripped it firmly and gave him a decent shake. "Good to see you again, Bill. This is Terrance Benson."

Benson didn't offer a handshake. He looked off into the distance through his very dark sunglasses. It was part of the act. They didn't come to fire him unless they found something that really deserved it. They wanted to impart some seriousness into the situation. Rigs were never authorized to go off the grid. Durham was sweating buckets. His career, finally landing the perfect job, working for CTC admin, was flashing in front of his eyes.

Benson wanted to grin at Durham's obvious discomfort.

Baron got right to the point. "Why is my truck in Wisconsin?"

Durham stammered, "Sir, the reefer the resort folks had lined up for pickup broke down on the way to the locker. I had fifteen thousand pounds of live crawfish on my dock. The sons of a bitches were getting out of the sacks and crawling around everywhere. Shit, they were getting inside the lettuce crates. The banana boxes were already full of them. We had to the pop the lids on four hundred boxes. Bastards got pinchers, you know. One of my guys said they were like armored cockroaches fighting back."

Baron and Benson stifled a quick laugh, visualizing burly dock hands delicately picking them out, avoiding the outreached, menacing open claws.

Durham continued with his rehearsed story. "I told my load foreman to get them the hell out of here. The team that delivered them from New Orleans offered to take them to the Playboy Resort in Geneva. Next thing I know, the rig's been confiscated by Wisconsin DNR. I'm sorry, sir. I know it's company policy not to send rigs off the chart. I realize now I should have called corporate for clearance."

"DNR?" Benson inquired.

"Wisconsin's Department of Natural Resources. The twig pigs. Game wardens," Durham replied.

"Okay, what's their beef with crawfish?" Benson asked. Baron remembered the conversation with Margo. Benson hadn't heard it.

"They're not native. Wisconsin gets a hard-on about exotic species," Baron answered for Durham.

"Shit fire, some Cajun blood might benefit the species up here, reckon so, Durham?" Benson cracked a smile. The act was over.

Stu grinned at Benson's retort and gently cupped the wiry, short-statured Durham behind his neck. "We got the picture now, Bill. You screwed up not hiring an independent hauling the crawfish away, but we understand there was some urgency in the situation. Let's get our team out of jail."

The bail bondsman, Tricky Dick Martin III, took Stuart Baron's company check for $3,500 and posted three $1,000 bonds plus a quantity surcharge service fee of $500. The team would reappear in person back in Kenosha district court in one month. Baron assured the team that there would be a company attorney representing them if the case went to court. Transporting nonnative crawfish was a misdemeanor offense and in no way would it impact their truck driving credentials. Stu instructed Durham to buy the team members first-class tickets back home to New Orleans and they were to take Friday off. At double pay. The team was all smiles as they loaded up in a taxi summoned from Chicago. Coddling the team after spending the morning in jail would pay dividends in the future. The rest of the teams would appreciate that the home office had their backs. Baron knew when to spend money. Everything was in terms of costs and benefits. And human resources were never short-changed. He'd rather eat Cheetos with his pilots before opting for a three-martini lunch.

Baron looked at his watch. If they left soon, skipping lunch, they could make it back before sunset. Flying back into the Pacific Time zone would still make for a long day, but they could avoid the jet lag if they beat the sun before it extinguished into the ocean.

They arrived back at the airport in Mrs. Durham's recently detailed and hand-waxed Lincoln Town Car. She was driving around in his Chevrolet Silverado, a half-a-million-mile beater with a neck-jerking transmission, praying her husband still had a fucking job.

Benson parked his sunglasses on his forehead, firmly shook Durham's hand, looking him square in the eyes. "Durham, if I were you, I'd round up the rest of them mudbugs back at the dock, boil 'em up, suck some heads, and wash 'em down with a six-pack of Leinenkugel. Hey, turn some of the little buggers loose. Maybe they'll find some Wisconsin pussy before this place turns into a freaking glacier."

For the first time, Durham cracked a smile. "Sounds like a plan."

Baron gently admonished Benson and Durham. "Let's get the day shift over with before we pop any brewskies."

"Ten-four on that, boss," Benson replied.

Durham nodded.

Baron added, "Okay, Bill, we're all on the same page now, right? Only thing leaving the reservation from now on are horny crawfish. Got it?"

"Yes, sir, Mr. Baron," Durham said, realizing he still had a job.

"Durham, get our truck back as soon as possible. We'll fly the team into O'Hare when you get it back to the locker," Benson said.

"Yes, sir, Mr. Benson."

"Okay then. Benson, go find the pilots and let's head home."

CHAPTER FIVE

Two miles above a gargantuan dark-green cornfield in central Illinois, the copilot of CTC One advised the boss that, due to a severe line of tornadic thunderstorms rumbling over central Kansas, they'd have to divert from their charted westward course and head south, gradually making a right turn over central Alabama and flying over I-10 to get back home. This would add a couple more hours of flight time and a refueling stop at Phoenix Municipal.

The skies were clear over Tennessee and the upper Appalachian foothills of northern Alabama. A new 1997 edition of a Rand McNally truckers' atlas rested in Baron's lap, opened to the state of Alabama. He fixed his position on the map by studying the landmarks out of both side windows. Birmingham, known as Smoke City in CB lingo, appeared in the distance out his port window. Interstate 20/59 stretched out below, connecting the Steel City of Bessemer with Tuscaloosa, the home of Crimson Tide football. As they angled southwest, the Oakmulgee National Forest spread out beneath them. The forested, gently rolling foothills of the Appalachians were covered with dense, mixed stands of shortleaf and loblolly pines and occasional, more sparsely planted, longleaf pine groves. The longleafs were planted for an endangered bird. Stu had read about the red-cockaded woodpecker in his latest *Sierra* magazine. Their preferred nesting niche was a mature longleaf. Back in the 1800s, the nation's longleaf forests had been decimated by western expansion and the shipbuilding industry. The woodpeckers almost disappeared too.

To the south, square patches of water shimmered in the afternoon sun. He remembered the square pond on the billboard.

Benson was fully reclined in his leather seat, snoring in suffocating fits, occasionally waking himself up. He looked around, closed his eyes again, and resumed snoring, eventually reaching another rattling crescendo. The racket was driving Stu nuts. *No wonder he wasn't married. How in the hell could anyone get any sleep?*

He unbuckled his lap belt and crouched just behind the cabin, gazing out the windshield.

Baron asked Art Matthews, the pilot, if they could fly a little lower and maybe back off the speed for a better look at the ponds. He was curious about the growing patchwork of rectangular ponds stretching all the way to the Mississippi state line. Matthews obliged and descended to about three thousand feet and throttled back to one hundred twenty miles per hour, twenty miles per hour higher than stalling speed for the King Air.

Stu moved forward a little more and kneeled behind the center console. They were curious about the hundreds of glistening ponds laid out in scattered checkerboards of levees and water throughout the west central area of Alabama.

"What do you suppose they grow in them?" Art wondered.

"Can't be shrimp. We're too far away from the coast," Matt Jones, the copilot said.

"Guys, they could be catfish ponds," Stu responded.

"Only one way to find out," Art said.

"What you got in mind?" Stu asked.

"I see an airstrip dead ahead. There's a pond next to it."

All three looked straight ahead. Jones checked his chart and the compass bearing. "That's the Bellevue airfield."

They banked over the small airport and noticed several men tending to a bright-yellow crop duster parked on an oil-stained patch of concrete outside a steel panel-sided hanger.

"Let me notify Atlanta Center, and we'll set her down."

Art got on the radio with AC and assured them they weren't having problems. Just going down for a visit.

The Tuscaloosa tower's airport controller, a weekend recreational pilot, overheard the conversation.

"Hope they brought some Twinkies." He chuckled.

They circled around one more time and approached from the south into the wind. The landing gear locked into position. Baron retreated back to his seat and belted in.

Benson woke up, noticing the different tone of the engines and the whirring of the electric motor opening the wheel bay.

"What's up, boss?"

"Welcome to Bellevue, Alabama. Just taking a break. Thought we'd take a stretch here. Got a pond I wanna check out."

Stu had full confidence in his flight crew. Both were Air Force veterans. They never got to fly the expensive jet-powered stuff but had amassed thousands of hours flying prop trainers from base to base. Touching down at an unfamiliar airport was not a concern in the least. He was looking forward to getting out and stretching. He'd miss his late-afternoon run.

Jones and Matthews made final adjustments to the Beechcraft while approaching the 3,500-foot runway. The men on the ground, tending to the Grumman AgCat, heard the approaching aircraft. They stared at the expensive plane coming in for a landing. The tarmac sported several parked Cessna single engines collecting pine pollen at the rarely used airport.

Buster Seal, ace crop duster for Seal Crop Dusting, said, "Looks like we got visitors."

Homer Willkins, former lineman for the Auburn National Championship Team of 1957, and Buster's best buddy, asked, "Anybody seen Gus lately?"

Timmy "Skiprow" Gross, former crop duster, now half-blind, said, "Hope they brought some Twinkies."

They went back to work on the Ag Cat's cantankerous Pratt and Whitney engine. They were checking the compression on each of the nine radially oriented cylinders.

The plane was twenty feet above the runway on the southern edge, moments away from touchdown. The wind was light and dead on. There was no need to compensate for cross winds. The billowed-out windsock on the hanger's roof was flying in the same direction as CTC One. Stu could see the knotty trunks of the mock orange trees along the fence row as they whizzed by his starboard window.

*****

Gus loved the coolness of the four-foot-high culvert under the middle of the runway. The approaching airplane had interrupted his midafternoon nap. He stretched his neck high and backward. His massive curved horns scraped against the top of the ridged, galvanized-steel pipe.

It finally happened.

Gus's right horn fully impaled the hanging melon-sized paper nest. It ripped loose. Dozens of bald-faced hornets left their home, now mobilized, and delivered all kinds of grief to Gus, the three-hundred-pound Twinkie-addicted, feral goat and unofficial groundskeeper of the Bellevue Airfield.

Gus shot out of the pipe like a cannonball. The crop duster crew heard the crazed goat's nonstop bawling over the approaching silenced turboprops, the propellers feathering the wind at idle speed. They turned around. Gus was galloping down the center of the runway, toward the approaching plane. The nest still attached. Bucking and kicking. Shaking his head side to side. A dark cloud of stinging hornets buzzing around his head. The goat was now running flat out toward the approaching plane.

"What the hell is that?" Matthews yelled.

The two-headed critter headed straight for them.

"Brace for impact!" Jones screamed.

Baron and Benson's lives suddenly flashed in their minds. They closed their eyes, grabbed their knees, and prayed, waiting to be torn into a hundred pieces.

It was too late into approach to attempt a takeoff. Matthews locked up the tires. He maintained a straight squealing skid toward the approaching animal. The plane screeched as it stopped, inches away from Gus, rigidly standing his ground, facing the nose of the plane. The goat's chest muscles quivered after the all-out sprint down the runway. Gus had finally shaken the offending nest loose about thirty yards away. A cloud of hornets hovered above it.

Two skid marks, fifty yards long, indelibly marked the near collision. The acrid smoke from the nearly peeled Goodyears lifted into the hot, humid air.

Matthews grimaced as the blue smoke wafted over the nose. "I need to check the foreskin on my dick. May need to roll it back."

Jones rubbed his right breast. "The damned harness inverted my nipple."

In his last crazed move of the day, the goat delivered a solid head butt to the nose of the plane.

Baron and Benson heard the loud thump in the front. They unbuckled and darted toward the flight deck.

"What in the hell happened?" Stu then saw the goat, looking upward through the windshield, his head tilting from side to side.

"We just played a bout of chicken with a rabid goat," Art said.

"Welcome to Bellevue, Alabama," Matt added, wringing the tension out of his hands.

Gus sauntered off to the starboard side of the plane. They watched him through the side windows.

"Damn, that's a big goat. You ever seen one that big?" Benson asked.

"Shit no," Art replied.

Gus spied the edge of the wing.

"Oh, no," Matt said, shaking his head.

Gus leaped on the plane's wing and peered inside a window.

"Benson, get that damned goat off my airplane." Stu winced.

Benson opened the door. The goat stared at the two-legger.

Just then, Buster Seal arrived, driving an EZ Go electric golf cart with his two buddies, Homer and Timmy. Timmy was clutching the roof rack with both hands, standing on the rear bumper. Homer poked his greasy hand in the glove compartment on the right side.

He unwrapped a Twinkie, yelled "Hey Gus!" and waved it back and forth.

Gus promptly jumped off the wing and trotted over to Homer. The overpowering musky odor of the buck goat wafted into the cabin of the plane.

Benson was in the doorway. "Guys, you should check out this stench back here. Smells like pussy on a Saigon whore on a Sunday morning."

Gus delicately lip-snatched the stale pastry out of Homer's hand.

The four Californians exited the plane and met the three Alabamians. After introductory handshakes, pleasantries, and some good-natured back and forth about the four-footed welcoming committee, Stuart Baron got back to business.

"What's in the ponds, guys?"

"Farm-raised catfish. It's getting to be a craze around here. Folks taking out soybeans and corn. Going to fish. Looks like our crop-dusting days are coming to an end."

"Sorry to hear that," Stu commiserated.

"That's okay. My liability insurance was taking care of what profit I was making anyway."

"Mr. Baron, if you told him what your liability insurance cost last year, maybe he'd get to feeling better," Art added.

Baron laughed. It was in the millions. He remained humble and steered the conversation back to the ponds. "Catfish, huh. Is there any money in it?"

"Oh, yeah, takes a lot to get into it, but the payback's pretty good. Hell-a-va-of lot better than beans," Buster replied.

"What's that?" Benson asked.

They turned to see a flatbed pickup with a square-shaped hopper ascend a levee. It was slowly making its way down the side of the pond. A twin-cylinder gasoline engine cranked up. The slow whirring of a blower fan became a deafening roar. Marble-sized pellets shot out of a steel chute, arcing into the water. A six-inch wave of schooling fish, most of them about a pound, followed the truck down the levee. Smaller quarter-pound catfish were half leaping out of the water to get at the flying feed. The men watched for several minutes. Buster waved to the catfish farmer. He waved back and disappeared back down off the levee onto the paved road.

"That's how they feed 'em, boys," Buster announced.

"Mr. Baron, we better be getting back to LA," Art said.

"You're right, Art." He looked at his watch. "Hey, it was nice talking with you. Is there someone I can call around here to talk about catfish farming?"

"Yeah." Buster dug into his wallet and pulled out a business card. "Call them. My nephew works there." The card read "Brian Caine. Alabama Fish Farming Center."

Baron dug out his stuffed wallet and fished out a business card. He handed it to Buster.

"Damn, fellas." Buster looked at Homer and Timmy. "He owns Coast to Coast Trucking. I see your trucks all the time."

Baron stared at Buster. "Around here?"

"Oh, no, not here. I got a place on the coast. See 'em mostly on I-10 around Mobile."

Benson patted Baron on the shoulder. "You okay, boss?"

"Did I say something bad?" Buster inquired.

"No, you're good. Boss here has a problem with his rigs going off the reservation. Finding one up here would be like the end of the world as we know it, huh, boss?"

Stu looked at his watch again. "Let's get going. Bye, fellas. Take care of that crazy goat. Next time I'll bring my own Twinkies." They laughed and shook hands.

*****

CTC One banked into the eastern horizon and headed west into the midafternoon sun. They touched down near Los Angeles after nine.

Art stuffed the empty Cheetos snack bag into his flight briefcase and knocked a few orange flecks off his black tie. He always forgot to pack something to eat for the cluster missions. They usually had decent meals at the national trucking conferences and vendor meetings. When Baron was in firefighting mode, he could get tight-fisted with the company's travel account.

Benson flew down the steps to the tarmac and lit out for his Dodge dually. He was headed to his favorite Tex-Mex diner. A craving for carnitas de cabrito washed down with an ice-cold pitcher of Tecate had been on his mind since the refuel at Phoenix.

CHAPTER SIX

Winchester Baron loved Saturday mornings. Daddy was still home when he woke up. Mommy was usually in a super good mood first thing in the morning. He stood outside his parents' bedroom door, listening for the strange noises that he never heard outside their bedroom. He couldn't hear anything, so like he had been told over and over again, he knocked loudly before opening the door.

They were face up, their eyes closed. He snuggled in between, waiting for them to stir. Dad popped him in the shoulder. He whispered, "Isn't today sign-up for T-ball?"

"Yes, sir. Remember you said we had to buy a bat and glove?"

"Oh, yeah, I remember now. Guess we better get moving, huh?"

Win looked at his mother. She pretended to be asleep. Win tickled her firm left side. She giggled. Tickled him back.

"What time do Win and I have to be at the park for sign-up?"

"Nine, maybe? The flyer's on the refrigerator."

"I'll get it." Win hopped out of bed and disappeared down the hallway. They could hear him thump, feet together, down the carpeted stairs to the kitchen.

Stu peered at his wife. She gazed into his eyes. She longed for a little more Saturday-morning cuddling. Her satiny light-blue nightgown was still unbuttoned from last night's amorous activities. Stu traced the slight gap between her firm breasts with his index finger.

"Guess we'll have to pick up again where I left off last night," Stu said.

"I can't believe you feel asleep on me. What the heck did you do yesterday?"

"We had a situation in Wisconsin. Flew there and back, including a refuel in Phoenix. The crew was exhausted."

"Wisconsin? You and Ross expanding again?" Tab was well aware of the trucking kingdom the two were building. Family time was getting more and more precious.

"No, long story. Had a rig go way off the reservation. Everything worked out in the end. We touched down in Alabama on the way and stretched. Art almost hit a huge goat on the runway."

"Alabama. I would say that's way off the reservation for you too."

"We saw some catfish ponds. Folks actually making a living raising fish."

Tab turned on her side and propped her head up on her forearm, studying Stu's face for a second. He gazed at the popcorn ceiling, lost in thought. Her mind was locked on the words *Alabama* and *catfish*. She recalled the flashback of that Star Trek episode when Captain Kirk said, "Beam me up, Scotty."

Stu had his moments. He was coming up with the weirdest schemes. Since turning forty-five last year, he was becoming more and more restless. She kept reminding him of how good he had it now. For Stu, it wasn't enough. The world, he thought, seemed to be beckoning for more.

Winchester ran into their bedroom with the flyer. Stu and Tab straightened up on the bed. All thoughts turned to their rambunctious child.

"Daddy, Freddie's upside down. He's not moving."

"I'm sorry, Win. I don't know what else to do."

Freddie the Fourth was the latest victim of a long line of feeder goldfish to succumb to the peculiarities of Los Angeles tap water. Stu had a shoebox full of water conditioners that supposedly cured every ill in the aquarium trade. The stuffed box contained numerous plastic squirt bottles: pH Up, pH Down, pH Stabilizer, chlorine remover, Ammonia Tamer, pink and white sea salt, De-Foamer, EcoFix, TankZilla, Microbe Lift, VitaStim, NovAqua, and Stress Coat.

"Stu, should we be drinking this water?"

Stu looked out the master bedroom window at their pool. "Crap, I wonder if we should even be swimming in it."

"Mommy, I'm hungry," Winchester said. He disappeared down the stairway. Moments later, the downstairs toilet flushed and refilled. Freddy Four's chemically etched DNA was on the way to the Pacific.

"*Hasta luego*, Freddie," Stu sighed.

CHAPTER SEVEN

The assistant store manager at Academy Sports unlocked the glass doors exactly at eight o'clock. Stu exchanged "Good mornings" as they strolled through the doorway.

The baseball aisles were well stocked. Stu was amazed at the huge assortment of bats. He remembered back when he was a kid. One choice. A light-brown hickory Louisville Slugger. Now there were dozens of choices, all made with space-age alloys. If the country ever got into a race for Mars, they could melt down baseball bats for rocket frames. There wasn't a wooden bat in sight. Win picked out the one he wanted, a fluorescent-blue Mizuno with white sparkles.

Stu looked at the price tag. One hundred and forty-nine dollars. *Ouch.* Stu winced. "Son, that's too rich for your poor ole daddy."

"But, Daddy, all my friends say we're rich."

Stu looked at Win with one of those okay-my-five-year-old-just-kicked-my-brains-out-again look. "We'll talk about that later. Right now, let's stick with one in the fifty- to sixty-dollar range."

The precocious preschooler understood numbers. He could count to a hundred. The Montessori Academy's cloistered young sisters had anointed Win as one of the brightest kids to ever bless their school. Stu and Tab couldn't take credit for the genes. They had adopted him as an infant. Abandoned at the portico of Los Angeles General in a cat litter box. Tab was working that night as a volunteer.

Win picked out a Rawlings fielders' glove in the same price range. Stu grabbed a few practice balls. He looked at the prices of the adult models, deciding the Spalding mitt he had from his high school days could last another season or two. He opted to splurge a little, snatching a rectangular can of leather glove oil off the eye-level shelf.

"Win, I need to check out something over there." He pointed to the aisles of hunting equipment.

"Daddy, you going hunting?"

"No, son. Just looking."

"Good, 'cause Mommy hates guns."

"Yeah, I know Win."

Stu gazed at the various shotguns. Dozens were vertically racked behind the counter along the wall. He recognized the pump actions from the police dramas, short, black-barreled, with plastic stocks and sliding fore ends. He waited patiently for the clerk's attention. He had lots of questions. He'd never owned a real gun. Win peered through the head-high glass case at the hunting and tactical knives. Stu held on to Win's bat for fear he might start taking some practice swings too close to the glass cases.

The clerk was waiting on a twenty-something-aged thin short Latino wearing old out-of-fashion black Ked sneakers, dingy blue jeans, and a soiled T-shirt advertising a Tijuana cantina.

"No, you don't need a permit to buy or possess a pellet gun," the clerk politely answered.

The Latino was holding a package containing a .177-caliber pellet pistol. It looked like a real semiauto. It was in a hardened plastic case that would require a miniature crowbar to open.

He asked another question in Spanish. The bilingual clerk answered back.

"We are out of air cartridges for the pellet pistols. We're expecting them tomorrow."

Stu, fluent in Spanish, overheard the entire conversation. The clerk had winked at him. They shared the same thought. *Wish we could figure out a way not to sell this to him.*

Stu looked at his watch. He decided to come back without Win. They checked out at the front of the store. The Latino with his newly acquired purchase was getting into his beater, an extensively dented Toyota Camry. The side fenders were covered in dull Bondo piebald. Stu watched him through the plate glass windows.

I'll bet he isn't taking that home to his kid, Stu winced.

Stu and Win walked to their Isuzu Trooper. Win was now big enough to sit in the front seat. He couldn't quite see over the dashboard and across the hood unless he stretched really straight. He was big for his age.

"Win, I'm going to run in the store and get something for Mommy. Can you stay here for a minute? Keep the doors locked until I get back?" Stu rolled both front windows down about two inches. They were parked in the shade, and the morning was comfortably cool.

The Starz liquor store was next to Academy Sports. Stu peeked at the rest of his cash in his wallet after shelling out one hundred and fifty bucks for baseball equipment. He barely had enough to buy a bottle of single-malt Glenfiddich. He wanted Win to stay in the car. The upcoming discussion about their comparative social status after dropping some serious change on exorbitantly priced booze would be another complication.

"Sure, Daddy." Win punched his fist into his new glove. He stuck his face in the pocket and inhaled the aroma of new leather. It smelled a lot better than Daddy's car, but not as good as Mommy's Beemer.

"Oh, no," Stu said softly. The Latino from Academy had left his car and stormed into the package store. He nervously looked around. There were two other customers in the store, two cute coeds wearing tight midthigh shorts, running shoes, and cardinal red USC Trojan T-shirts.

"What's wrong, Daddy?" Win asked, still punching his new glove.

"Nothing, son."

The man approached the counter. He pulled his T-shirt up past his lint-caked belly button. The Middle Eastern clerk suddenly looked extremely agitated. He turned quickly and yanked the cash register drawer open.

"That son of a bitch," Stu whispered.

Win had good ears. "Who's a son of a bitch?" Win cocked his head sideways and looked up at his daddy.

"Win, listen to me. I want you to scrunch down and stay down until I get back, understand? I gotta go help with an emergency. I'll be right back, okay?"

Baron grabbed the baseball bat on the back seat, climbed out, and locked the car's doors. He darted to the Coca-Cola vending machine on the left side of the glass door of the package store. He figured the guy would exit and walk past it, back to his car. Stopping the robbery with a bat, considering the functionless pellet pistol, were pretty good odds.

He crouched behind the blind side of the machine. He waited with the bat cocked behind his shoulder. He turned, peered around the window side of the machine, and watched the man leave the counter area. The bell tinkled above the door. He peeked around the street corner of the machine. There he was as expected, trotting toward him.

Stu stepped around the machine. He swung as hard as he could, making a solid hit with the bat's trademark on the man's nose.

The thief flew backward to the ground, smacking the back of his head on the concrete sidewalk. He wasn't moving. Blood streamed out of the man's nose, now completely shattered. Squashed cartilage plugged the sinuous nasal cavities on the man's pockmarked face. Blood oozed out of the man's scalp on the back of his head.

The liquor store clerk appeared first. "The police are on the way."

The two coeds looked down at the man.

"Is he dead?" the shorter one asked.

The taller one callously replied, "Doubt it. See the blood spurting out of his nose? Heart's still pumping."

They could hear the sirens getting louder. The wailing stopped as the police cruisers entered the parking lot from three different directions.

Win ran up to Stu's side. "Daddy, why'd you hit him?"

The clerk chimed, "Your daddy's a hero. He stopped this bad guy."

Win was staring at the man at the ground and the growing pool of dark blood. Other onlookers started to crowd around, excitedly pointing and gawking.

"Son, I need you to get back in the car. Now!"

He hustled Winchester back to the car, locked the doors again, and anxiously stood in front, still clutching the bat, watching more onlookers gather around the incapacitated man.

Four policemen arrived on foot, guns drawn. The onlookers parted as they circled in. They looked down at the bleeding groaner. The clerk said something, and then he pointed at Stu. One of the officers got on his walkie-talkie and requested an ambulance. An older cop, bright-yellow sergeant bars on the upper sleeve of his navy-blue shirt, approached Baron. The bat was still in his right hand. He was shaking. Win was stretched as high as he could get, wide-eyed, listening intently.

"Sir, mind if I take that?" the sergeant asked.

Stu handed the bat to the officer, handle end first.

"Wanna tell me what happened?"

While Baron explained, the other officers bent down and mar-veled at the deconstruction of the man's face. One of the officers, a corporal, reached down and pulled up the man's shirt. Tucked inside the man's waistband of his beltless blue jeans was a semiauto 9 mm Taurus. The two other officers, not so gently, rolled him over on his belly and cuffed him behind his back. The man's dark-red blood con-tinued to pool on the sidewalk. The criminal evidently didn't merit any attempts at first aid. He could bleed out for all they cared.

The corporal inspected the thief's pistol. He removed the fully loaded magazine, pulled the slide back, and ejected a shiny brass cartridge.

Stu was just telling the sergeant about the thief purchasing a pellet gun at Academy and figuring the odds were pretty good about taking him out with a baseball bat.

The corporal approached. "Sarge, we found this on him." He showed him the Taurus. "There was one in the pipe."

Stu asked, "What's that mean, 'one in the pipe'?"

"Mr. Baron, he didn't use a pellet gun. He had a real one, loaded up too. You brought a baseball bat to a gunfight." The sergeant grinned.

One of the officers checked the Toyota Camry. On the passenger seat was the pellet gun, still in its hardened plastic adult-proof shell.

Stu was shaking again. He looked at Win. Win looked back.

"Mr. Baron, this one's going down in the good column. One of the officers will get some contact information from you. You may have to testify to a grand jury and then district court. He'll probably get locked up for first-degree robbery and illegal possession of a firearm. If he's already a felon, then it's three strikes and life. Poetic justice, isn't it? Three strikes and he's out after getting slugged by a baseball bat."

The sergeant stepped off the curb and walked over to Win's window. Win cranked it down with both arms.

"What's your name?"

"Winchester Baron, sir."

"Well, Winchester Baron, you should be proud of your dad. He helped us catch a bad guy." The officer looked at the new mitt in Win's lap. "Hope you have a good game today." The officer straightened up and lightly slapped Win's new baseball bat in his other hand.

"You got a good kid there, sir."

"Thanks, Sarge."

"Gotta keep this for evidence." He held the new bat up. "Could be a while before you get it back."

Stu shrugged and glanced back at Win. He mouthed, "Sorry."

A reporter for the *Los Angeles Times* arrived. She took several pictures of the scene and snapped one of Baron. He left after giving the rookie officer his contact information. Stuart Baron didn't have time to talk to a reporter. They were late for sign-up.

Stu and Win met Tab at the baseball park.

"Where have you been? I already signed him up." She bent down and admired Win's glove. "Where's your bat, Win?"

"The policeman took it." He darted off to meet his new teammates.

"Tab, it's been another glorious morning in LA."

46

CHAPTER EIGHT

Stu arrived at work right after six Monday morning. Margo already had the coffee carafe full of Columbian dark roast and brought him his first cup. She used his once favorite cup marked, "Happy Fortieth. Welcome to the decade from Hell." His morning ritual's first cup had a light splash of fresh half-and-half and a packet of sweetener, thoroughly stirred. Stu had given up admonishing her for bringing him coffee, making it abundantly clear that he was fully capable of getting his own.

She had a secret crush on the boss, and this was her latest strategy for edging her way into an affair. She would approach from his back while he was seated at his desk, touch him lightly on his shoulder, bend over, and let him get a fresh whiff of her Chanel No. Five. As far as Stuart Baron was concerned, taking any further physical interaction wasn't a remote possibility. He worshipped the ground his wife walked on. After fifteen years of marriage, he still found her emotionally and physically attractive. An inseparable pair. Their wedding day vows were as strong as covalent bonds, holding firm in a nuclear detonation. And given Tab's healthy appetite for exploring new carnal pleasures, he never felt the urge to stray.

"Have a good weekend?" she asked.

"I did, Margo." He recalled the liquor store incident, deciding he'd tell it once to everyone at lunch. "How about you?"

"Same old thing. Pigged out on frozen pizza. Drank cheap beer. Washed the dog. Watched *Laverne & Shirley* reruns Saturday night."

"Margo, you ever want to get back on the road, tell me."

"That's okay, boss. I don't miss the hemorrhoids."

"Jeez, Margo, that's a little too much information." His coffee suddenly didn't taste near as good. He detected a hint of stank ass in the dark roast. Images of bean pickers flooded his brain. Juan Valdez included, on a volcano slope, dropping their shorts, squatting down, taking care of business in the waist-high coffee, snatching beans with shit-soiled hands. Whole Foods, clueless to boot. *What the hell, it's still organic.* Stu focused again on the stack of papers awaiting his signature. Margo's lingering perfume replaced the stank undertones.

"I'm sorry," Margo replied.

"No biggie. You just let me know when the road is calling." Stu looked at his Ironman. "What time is it in Alabama?"

"Prehistoric, why?" Margo grimaced.

He laughed. "I gotta make a phone call out there, that's all."

"I think they're central time, so that'd be plus two. About eight thirty."

"Good time to call. He's had half an hour to drink coffee and check the hemorrhoids on his secretary."

Margo laughed.

"Hey, would you close my door on the way out?" He chuckled as he reached for the phone.

"Got it." She walked to the door and gently closed it. *The boss made a joke about anatomy. That's progress.*

Baron dug into his miniature file cabinet of a wallet and removed the Alabama business card. He looked at the phone console on his desk. One of the six outgoing lines wasn't red. He punched in the number and hit the speaker button.

"Good morning. Alabama Fish Farming Center."

"Good morning to you too. Who am I speaking with?"

"This is Destiny. And who is this?"

"This is Stuart Baron calling from Los Angeles, California."

"Well, Stuart Baron from Los Angeles, California, how can I help you today?"

Stu was sizing up Destiny. Friendly, courteous, nice, confident voice. Probably enjoyed working there. She didn't seem harried. At ease with herself. Given her voice, Baron imagined she was probably easy on the eyes too. Maybe she had a doting husband that loved to see her go to work in a good mood.

"Ms. Destiny, I would like to talk to a Mr. Brian Caine, please."

"Well, it's your lucky day then. Mr. Caine is actually in the office today. Please hold, Mr. Baron from Los Angeles, California." She was toying with him. He enjoyed the repartee.

"Hello, Brian Caine."

"Good morning. Stuart Baron."

"How can I help you, Mr. Baron?" Brian Caine's mind raced. Cold calls from unknowns could usually be classified in three distinct groups. The first group were salesmen. He dreaded those calls because nine out ten times they were either selling snake oil pond amendments or they had designed the ultimate pond aerator. They would want him to blow an afternoon watching it drown fish.

The aquashyster consultants fell into the second group. Kinda like the losers he ran into at his favorite college hangout. They knew fifty different sexual positions but didn't know any women.

And the third group were the lost souls who had read an article in *Newsweek* about aquaculture saving the planet from running out of food. They wanted in on the action. Brian Caine lived for this group. He loved bursting their ideological balloons. Depending on their arrogance, he could bust it with a needle or a cannonball.

"The other day I ran into an acquaintance of yours, a Mr. Buster Seal. He recommended I talk to you about catfish farming."

Caine's mind raced some more. *Okay, a friend of the family. Need to burst his balloon near the ground, not at five thousand feet.*

"Where are you located?"

"California. Los Angeles."

No way, Jose. Land's too expensive. Water's not plentiful. Too many damned regulations. This is gonna be a short conversation. He glanced at his to do-list for Monday. *Dump this guy gently and get back to work. My USDA grant is due at noon Eastern. I haven't even started drafting the dreaded logic wheel. Washington's grant geeks thrived on that bullshit...*

"Mr. Baron, I can think of better things to do in California than raise fish for a living."

"You're right. Besides, I don't think the water out here will grow fish."

Uh-oh. This guy's going to move here to raise fish.

"Mr. Baron, what line of work are you in?"

"Trucking. Why do you ask?"

"Oh, just making sure you weren't an engineer."

"What's up with the engineers?"

"They make terrible fish farmers. You see, engineers think in terms of black and white. For them, gray areas don't exist. They don't function well in an abstract world. Catfish farming is an unfathomable intergalactic gray universe, still full of unknowns. That's why there's an Alabama Fish Farming Center. There aren't chicken farming centers, hog farming centers, cattle farming centers. Montgomery put us out here in West Alabama to space travel with the lost souls that want to raise fish in a gray universe."

"Mr. Caine, I like the way you put things. Reminds me of my hazy days at UCLA."

Okay then, got me a college-educated hippie. Probably doesn't have two nickels to rub together. I can end this quick like...

"Mr. Baron, most folks don't realize this about catfish farming, but it takes an insane amount of money to get started. If you want to do this full-time and make a decent living, you're going to need, at a minimum, two hundred acres of water. Land out here is cheap compared to where you're at, about twelve hundred an acre, but the pond construction costs are about two thousand an acre. So now we are at almost three quarters of a million before you have stocked your first fish."

Stu wrote, "240,000 for land + 400,000 for ponds = 640,000."

"Mr. Caine, I'm still here, keep going."

"Okay, let's say you set your production goals at the statewide average of six thousand pounds per acre. The cost of production is sixty cents a pound, so that means you gotta have an operating note of roughly seven hundred thousand dollars."

Baron did the math. "6,000 @ 200 @ .60 = 720,000." He added some dollar signs.

Caine thought, *Okay, his bubble has finally burst. The enthusiasm in his voice will waver right about now.*

"Caine, we're up to almost one-point-four million. What kind of return are we talking?" Baron asked.

Jeez, what's this guy been hauling in his truck.

Caine swallowed hard. "Well, right now the producers are getting eighty cents per pound. Cost of production is sixty. That's twenty cents a pound profit times six thousand pounds times two hundred acres." Caine rapped some more on his black Casio calculator. Baron beat him to it.

Baron replied, "Two hundred forty thousand dollars. Initial capital outlay for the ponds is sixty-four hundred thousand. So return on investment is around thirty-five percent. That sounds too good to be true."

"Well, Mr. Baron, we've left out the gray. First off, you never get all the fish out. We grow 'em in ten-acre ponds and, if you're lucky, get sixty percent out in a harvest. Then you have the water quality killers like low oxygen, high carbon dioxide, brown blood disease, and ammonia. Then there's the damned fish-eating birds. And then the commodity market ups and downs on feedstuffs. The feed amounts to about sixty percent of the production costs. That eighty cents for live fish is an all-time high. I've been doing this for twenty years. I've seen the price of fish go below breakeven half a dozen times. Fish farming is still farming, boom or bust."

"Wow, sounds like a gray universe all right. How come folks get into it?"

"Well, most of them are born into it. They inherit the land, build a few ponds at a time, manage a cattle herd, maybe some beans and corn on the side. Very few get started off with two hundred acres from the get go. Like I said, you gotta be pretty strong to get your feet wet. We haven't even talked about all the specialized machinery it takes—aerators, oxygen meters, feed trucks, feed bins, tractors. You're going to need a tractor for every three ponds. Figure ten-acre ponds for two hundred acres, that's twenty ponds needing seven tractors at thirty Gs each. That's another quarter mil plus interest."

Baron's top page on his yellow legal pad was full of notes, dark arrows, and numbers punctuated with thick dollar signs.

"This has been very enlightening, Mr. Caine."

"You can call me Brian."

"Okay, Brian. Likewise, here, I go by Stu."

"Stu, promise me if you get into this, you don't mortgage your house or use your retirement fund on fish, okay?"

"Why?"

"This is risky business. Catfish die out here all the time. I've seen a veteran airline captain bawl like a baby after his pond of fish floated belly up. He hauled his Delta retirement to the landfill. Bankers don't mind lending money on hard assets like land and ponds. The boys get separated from the men on the operating notes. Lenders won't use live fish for collateral. Basically, first-timers float their operating notes, no pun intended, with hard collateral until they establish some cred with a bank. Please don't borrow on your house or retirement fund on animals with brains the size of watch batteries. I take a lot of pride in talking people out of this business rather than into it. No one's punched me in the nose for selling them false hopes. One thing's for sure, you get into it, I'll bend over backwards to give you the best advice out there."

"Sounds good, Brian."

"Okay, give me a call if you have more questions."

"Will do, Brian. Have a good day. Bye."

"Bye, Stu."

Brian Caine scratched the weekend stubble on his chin. *California. That'll be some culture shock.* He never had anybody get into fish past Texas.

Stu studied the figures. He refigured the 60 percent catch rate on the operating loan for two hundred acres. It came out to one million two hundred. He figured he could start with one hundred acres, learn the ropes, and expand another hundred acres. Six hundred thousand was still a lot but not out of reach.

Hell, he and Ross were spending that much on diesel every week.

Margo knocked on the door.

"Come in."

She stood in the doorway. She had that look. It wasn't good.

"We have a cluster in New Mexico."

Whenever Margo used the term *cluster* in lieu of *situation*, Stu was already sliding his chair back, heading for the door. And it was Monday. The worst clusters happened on Mondays. Most of the rigs were parked during the weekends. The teams were loaded and on the road by sunup the first day of the week.

"Now what?"

"Team leader Dan Higgins was shot at a Heart's. The shooter hijacked the truck."

"Damn. How's Higgins?"

"He'll live. Took one in the shoulder. The other two weren't hurt."

Stu remembered interviewing Higgins for the team leader position. Definitely type A. The one most likely to get in someone's face and take one for the team.

"The team called it in from the truck stop after notifying state police," Margo added.

Baron headed out the door to the situation room. Margo followed on his heels. He glanced over his shoulder. "Benson?"

"On his way."

They closed the door. The board cast a blue glow in the dark room. Stu walked over to the western end of the board and peered at the outline of New Mexico.

"Unit number?"

"Two eight seven," Margo replied.

"There it is." Stu pointed to the number on I-10.

Unit 287 was westbound on the edge of Las Cruces.

"Damn." Stu winced. "Son of a bitch is hauling ass too." The green dot was perceptibly moving on the board. Stu grabbed the plastic six-inch ruler on the bottom ledge. He measured the distance between two wax marks he had made tracking 287's progress and looked at the second hand on his watch again. "Shit. He's doing ninety."

Margo studied the board. "He's in between the Florida and Cookes Mountains, headed downhill into the Lost Comanche Valley. Right here at Deming." She pointed with her unadorned ring finger. "He'll be coming up on the pass. He'll be lucky if he can do forty over it with the load."

Benson entered the room and shut the door.

"Terry, here's your opportunity to immobilize a unit. We got a hijacked truck headed west on I-10. Margo says he's approaching a pass in about forty minutes. There aren't any exits for seventy miles. I'm thinking we take him out as he approaches this steep overpass at the top."

"Sounds good. Can we get State Police on the line?" Benson asked.

"One step ahead of you, Benson." Margo smirked.

The phone on the big conference table beeped. "Mr. Baron, Colonel Whitacre, New Mexico State Police, on line one." Benson punched the speaker button.

Stu answered, "Colonel Whitacre, Stuart Baron, Coast to Coast Trucking. Sir, that hijacked truck is going to be at Exit 82 on I-10 in approximately twenty-four minutes."

"Baron, how in the damned hell do you know that?" Colonel Whitacre replied.

Stu, Terry, and Margo had the same what-the-hell look.

"Sir, it's a long story. Let's save it for later. I'm absolutely sure our truck is coming up on an overpass at Exit 82. Right now he's doing about ninety miles an hour. We gotta get him stopped before he kills somebody," Stu replied.

"You know how fast he's going?"

"Please, for Christ's sake, sir, let's get him stopped. We'll talk about our logistics capabilities later."

"Okay, what's your plan?"

"I'm going to let you talk with my chief of security, Terry Benson."

"Terry Benson here, Colonel. You need to immobilize the rig as it approaches the overpass at Deming. It'll be grinding its way up the hill around forty. I'm sure you realize the danger of immobilizing it at a high rate of speed. This is our best opportunity to reduce danger to others."

"How do you propose we immobilize it? And what's it hauling?"

Stu and Terry looked at Margo. She studied a dot matrix print-out. "Mostly frozen Alaskan crab legs. Twenty-two tons of them."

"I heard that," the colonel replied.

54

Stu hoped they were still frozen.

Benson bent over the table slightly, like he was going to do an angled push-up, placing his meaty palms flat out in front of the speakerphone. "You can immobilize the truck by shooting directly at the center of the front radiator grill. A full metal jacketed round should crack the cast-iron water pump. All of our rigs are outfitted with water pressure relays. As soon as the water pressure drops to five pounds per square inch, the engine shuts down. He should come to a dead stop before he gets to the overpass. Tell your shooter to unload his mag on the front grill, dead center. You'll get him dead in the water. Get your shooter on that overpass. Remember, full metal jackets. You gotta punch through the radiator, the fan blades, and crack the pump. If you only get the radiator and not the pump, he gets down the hill with a stalled engine and no air brakes."

"Okay, let me get an officer there. What kind of time I'm I looking at now?" Whitacre asked.

Margo studied the map. "He's got two mountain passes to get over before exit eighty-two. I'd say twenty minutes, tops."

"Can we keep this line open?"

"Sure, no problem," Margo replied.

*****

New Mexico State Trooper Corporal Buck Heartsong, 100 percent proud Apache, and retired Marine, was sitting in his favorite booth, facing the front door at Lucky Lucy's truck stop, when the tactical channel on his portable radio squealed. Everybody in the café turned in the direction of the officer. Trooper Heartsong darted outside and climbed in his patrol cruiser, a standard-issue Crown Vic. He snatched the microphone off the metal clip on the dashboard's rim.

"Unit 77 to Base. Responding to Tact One. Sector Three. Go ahead."

"Unit 77. Standby for Colonel Whitacre."

Heartsong sat ramrod straight in his bench seat. He subconsciously positioned his official Trooper fedora squarely on his head, like he was expecting the colonel to genie morph from the radio's speaker grill. The only time he had ever spoken to the colonel was at his academy commencement.

Colonel Whitacre's godlike, booming voice resonated from the box speaker mounted on the transmission hump. "Trooper Heartsong, we have a tactical emergency in Sector Three. Need you positioned at the Exit 82 overpass with your patrol rifle. Use FMJs. Disable a Coast to Coast tractor trailer on westbound approach."

Colonel Whitacre had Heartsong's one-page service bio in his hands.

> United States Marine Corps.
> Three years infantry.
> One year Marine Recon.
> Honorable Discharge.
> New Mexico State Police Academy Bravo Class 1994.
> Graduated Top Gun.

Whitacre, also a Marine, with a meritorious Silver Star awarded during his third tour in Vietnam, gazed at Trooper Heartsong's official graduation picture in front of the furled flag of New Mexico, gem clipped to the upper left corner. The graduate's ruggedly sharp facial features, thick coal-black hair, and the piercing game-face scowl into the lens cast a squared-away aura of self-confidence. A melding of proud Apache heritage and the mystique of a warrior. Heartsong was the embodiment of operating on the tip of the spear. Wired the way Whitacre wished for in all his troopers. He realized that it would never happen. Standards were softening in order to make recruitment goals. Trooper Buck Heartsong's "mess with me and I'll kill you in a heartbeat" visage made Whitacre grin.

"Corporal, you need to disable the engine with multiple rounds to the center of the radiator grill. Intel says the water pump needs to be destroyed. The rig should shut down. Other units are in route. Driver's armed and dangerous. He shot the trucker. Get the truck stopped. Take control of the situation. Understood?"

"Understood. ETA for truck, sir?"

Colonel Whitacre looked at his Luminox. The timer feature was running.

"Approximately seventeen minutes."

"No problem, sir. I'm looking at the overpass now." The ramp for the interstate bordered the truck stop's parking lot. The remoteness of New Mexico had its advantages. Lucky Lucy's was the only option for diesel fuel for sixty miles. It was in the middle of Sector Three and the best place for slow food for a hundred square miles.

Heartsong flicked on the rocker switches for the roof and grille blues. He scratched out of the gravel parking lot, the four-barrel carb inhaling four hundred and sixty cubic inches of dry, hot air. He parked sideways on the overpass over the westbound lanes of I-10 and mashed the center dashboard button for the rear trunk lid. He hustled out of the unit and stood in front of the open trunk. Fastened securely to the bottom of the lid in a metal gun rack hung a Smith and Wesson M&P AR-15. It was very similar to the M16 Colt he had used in the Marines. The AR wasn't fully automatic but could still unleash twenty precision rounds in four seconds.

He deftly unclamped the patrol rife from the rack and inspected the loaded twenty round magazine. The first bullet in the stack was a soft lead jacket. After tossing the mag on the floor of the trunk, he reached for his duty bag and pulled out his tactical vest. In the front chest pockets were three more magazines, two were loaded with sixty-two-grain green-tipped Penetrator FMJs, and the third, hollow-pointed copper clads. He might need them for the driver if they got into a firefight. He threw the vest over his head and buckled it. It was snugger than usual.

Need to lay off those double cheeseburgers.

He grabbed the rifle, ramming a mag of FMJs into the lower receiver. He heard it click home. He tugged on it for further assurance.

Five minutes to spare.

Heartsong looked down the interstate. He could see a half mile down the slope. It would allow ample time to dump two mags. He'd start shooting at about two hundred meters, near the very beginning of the exit ramp lane and, if needed, unleash the second mag by time the truck approached the exit arrow sign, between the off ramp and the right lane.

He studied the metal workings of the overpass. The vertical gaps of the metal railings would allow for a prone position, the most stable of all the shooting platforms. In terms of placing shots in the front of a truck, that wouldn't be the problem. The problem would be inflicting catastrophic damage to the engine. The relatively small hardened bullets would have to slice through the slats in the grille, punch through the tight aluminum fins of the radiator, the radiator core, miss a spinning fan blade, and then penetrate or, at least, crack a cast-iron water pump. One round from the fifty-caliber BMG in the agency's tactical Hummer would be a more capable truck immobilizer. But it was two hundred miles away at headquarters in Albuquerque.

The traffic was light. Most of the motorists were staying in the right lane. He mentally focused on the what-ifs. An innocent motorist passing the truck on the left and merging back in the right lane in front of the truck was a possibility. He studied the angle down to the interstate. He might be able to shoot over a car, depending on the gap. He hoped he wouldn't have to make that call. If the truck exited the interstate, he'd attempt to block the exit ramp at the stop sign. It would become a complete FUBAR at that point. His cruiser would get T-boned.

He looked at his Luminox. *Any time now.*

A tractor trailer was lumbering its way up the incline. He squinted into the bright sun. He tried to recall the color scheme of the Coast to Coast trucks. He had never stopped and cited one because they were always the slowest trucks on the road, usually staying in the right lane. He was thinking they were bright banana yellow with cherry-red lettering. The truck approaching was dark brown and tandem-trailered.

Buster Brown. UPS.

Another truck appeared about a half mile away. He could hear the truck mashing gears as it downshifted. Plumes of black smoke billowed out of the dual stacks. The driver was rawhiding the heavily loaded truck. The high noontime desert sun reflected off the exposed bright yellow front of the trailer above the roof of the red Peterbilt sleeper cab. The red letters *CTC* on the front of the trailer were behind an upside-down steel bowl on the cab's roof.

Damned Chinese wok with three missing legs.

Heartsong proned out on the hot shimmering concrete of the overpass. He snatched back the bolt, released it, and a shiny brass cartridge slid into battery. He kicked his ankles outward, propping the rifle under his elbows. Despite his Ironman sunglasses, he still had to squint as he aligned the front blade and rear peephole on the center of the grille. The driver looked up at the blue lights of the cruiser. He wasn't braking. He mashed down on the other pedal. The rig's turbocharger roared.

Flipping the safety lever off with his right thumb, Heartsong aimed dead center at the grille, and pulled the trigger repeatedly.

PAH-ching.

PAH-ching.

PAH-ching.

He paused. No sign of damage.

Seventeen more rapid-fire *PAH-chings*.

Cartridges clinked as they hit the pavement to his right. The distinctive report of the AR-15 filled the still New Mexico air. Café patrons ventured into the parking lot, watching the scene a hundred yards away, hunkering behind their dusty pickups.

The truck was now at the beginning of the exit ramp. The rifle's bolt was locked open. Blue gun smoke wafted past Heartsong. He had fired all twenty rounds from the first magazine.

Come on, let me see something. Wait, what's that? He saw faint wisps of radiator steam roll out from the tight seams of the hood cowling.

Trooper Heartsong's muscle memory kicked in, allowing him to keep his eyes on target. He mashed the magazine catch with his right index finger. The empty mag clattered to the ground. He inserted another loaded mag from his front vest pocket. Smacking the bolt release lever on the left side with his palm, the bolt slammed shut, forcing another green-tipped round into battery. He cut loose again on the front grill, taking more careful aim, putting all twenty rounds dead center in a cheeseburger-sized group.

Thick plumes of steam billowed from the windshield wiper grate. The truck rolled to a stop about a dozen yards from the overpass. The driver looked up at the trooper, still prone on the bridge. Their eyes locked on each other. Heartsong pulled the last mag from his vest pocket, inserted, slapped, and aimed the rifle at the seated driver in the lifting fog of steam now mixed with black smoke. One of the rounds had ricocheted, penetrating the turbocharger. It squealed like a stuck pig as it seized. He could smell pungent hot antifreeze. The fluorescent-green liquid oozed out around the steer tires.

Give me a reason, asshole. Heartsong's index finger was firmly centered on the trigger. The open sights lined up on the driver's upper lip.

New Mexico's history was unfolding for another chapter. The tables turned. Down to one Apache. On the tip of a spear. And one desperate cowboy, seconds away from a cancelled Christmas in the lonely expanse of the Cooke's Range.

Bill Cassidy, sitting in a forty-ton dead horse, had made his mind up several miles back. When the cops found his wife with a bullet hole between the eyes, and his bitch mother-in-law, a hole in each eye, back in Las Cruzes and that mouthy truck driver at the truck stop, he'd be facing capital murder. He wasn't going back to prison. He was going out in a blaze of infamous glory. Death by cop. He'd take a few of them out too. *Bastards always screwing me since ninth grade after they killed Daddy.*

He kicked the driver's door open.

A white church van slowed down to walking speed in the left lane as it passed the stalled truck. Steam billowed out from the truck's hood. The van's passengers stared out the right side. Then a man leaped out of the truck with the big shiny pistol.

Cassidy stepped in front of the van. He pointed the gun at the driver.

The van abruptly stopped.

Cassidy ran to the side. He tugged violently on the passenger front door and side slider. They were locked. The van's driver made no attempt to speed away. Frozen in fear. Her foot firmly planted on the brake. Like the proverbial trembling lamb staring at a snarling hungry wolf.

Trooper Heartsong immediately recognized Cassidy's shiny semiauto as a Colt 45. Now the man was in between the van and the tractor, pointing the gun at the front passenger side window. Heartsong aimed at the man's side, high in the rib cage. He shot once. Cassidy staggered around, pointing the pistol up at the overpass. His knees buckled. The heavy pistol shook in his weakening arm.

He got one shot off at the trooper.

Heartsong double-tapped him. Center mass.

Cassidy crumpled to the ground.

Muffled screaming.

Fatally wounded, he twitched as foamy pinkish blood gurgled out of his mouth, indicating high lung shots. Blood pooled around his chest. It took two minutes before he bled out.

Trooper Heartsong yanked the mic off the dashboard. "Suspect down." He paused, still hearing the screams and cries for help from the van. The van driver was slumped over the steering wheel, out cold from fainting or possibly shock.

"Send an ambulance and a heavy wrecker."

*****

The team at CTC in Los Angeles overheard the radio traffic from the colonel's office.

There was some unintelligible chatter for a minute or so on the tactical channel between Whitacre and Heartsong.

Ross entered the room. Margo whispered in his ear.

"You guys still there?" Colonel Whitacre asked.

"Yes, sir, looks like our unit is stopped right at the overpass," Baron replied.

"Damn, Baron, I'm dying to know how you know that. The suspect is down. The truck's immobilized. No innocents hurt. We'll need several hours to process the scene, and then you can get your truck back. It needs a wrecker. My officer put forty rounds through it."

Benson smirked. "Those Peterbilts are tougher than I thought."

"The hell with the tractor. Let's save those crab legs," Baron moaned.

"Colonel Whitacre?" Ross piped up.

"Yes, go ahead."

"Can you make sure the reefer unit's still running? We've got a quarter million dollars' worth of crab legs on that damned truck. I'd rather not eat them at the company Christmas party." Benson was already thinking the opposite. Baron was staring at the speakerphone, hanging on the moment.

"I'll see what we can do. Thanks for your intel. We ended this without hurting any more innocents or officers. Sorry about your truck."

Margo listed out things to do in the aftermath on the backside of her printout. The crab legs were overdue somewhere. Higgins in the hospital. Filing workers' comp. The stranded crew at the truck stop. Insurance adjusters. Hauling the truck back to Los Angeles. Buying a new engine. Body work on the front. She was zoned out from the conversation between Baron and the colonel.

"Colonel, next time you're in LA, come by our corporate office. I'll show you around. I think you'd be impressed."

"Baron, I'm already impressed. I'll definitely take you up on that one."

"Thanks for the help, Colonel."

"You're welcome. Goodbye." The speakerphone clicked off.

Benson pushed it to the center of the table. Margo slid her list toward Stu. He looked at it and slid it back to her, nodding his head in the affirmative. *She was worth her weight in gold.* CTC wasn't just a job for her. It was her baby. She would protect the company at all costs.

Stu, Margo, Benson, and Ross were sitting on the same side of the conference table facing the board.

"Margo, how's Higgins doing?" Ross asked.

Margo looked up from her list. "He made it out of surgery okay. He'll be out for a couple of weeks. Took the bullet in the left shoulder. He won't be rolling up any windows for a while, but he swears he can still shift and smack his navigator."

"We got another A to fill in for him?" Stu asked.

All team members in the company were psychologically profiled by Baron at their time of hiring and classified as A, B, C, and D personalities. Ds were never put on the road because they couldn't work in team settings. They made good bean counters, though. Baron never put more than one A on a team. It took two Bs or Cs to keep the reins tight on the A. Put two As together, and the C ends up duct-taped back in the reefer.

"I'll check with HR. The other two are strong Cs. Definitely need an A to balance them out," Margo said.

Ross looked at Stu. "Those As attract the shit, don't they, Stu?"

"Yeah, they do. But you gotta have them around. Lotta gray out there on the open road. The B and Cs keep them from going off the reservation. They still end up poking the cowboys once in a while." Stu smirked.

As the board glowed in front of them, Ross noticed two green dots staying almost abreast as they steadily progressed up I-55 near Springfield.

"Hey, guys, check out units 561 and 598 in central Illinois," Ross instructed.

"Unit 598's our newest female team. Good ole Gayle's the leader," Margo replied.

"And 561?" Stu asked.

Margo flipped over the printout. "Max Simmons."

Stu and Ross smiled.

"Moon shot time." Margo grinned.

"Another one for the staff board," Terry said with a hearty chuckle.

*****

CTC units 561 and 598, both northbound for the locker in Chicago, loaded full of green Guatemalan bananas, were in the pool table flatness of central Illinois. The only change in topography being the elevated overpasses over creeks named after vanquished Native Americans, nameless county dirt roads, and railroad tracks, their rustless rails kept shiny from trainloads of Midwest grain. Deep borrow pits, now fishing ponds, gifts from the DOT to the farmers, were filled with shimmering spring water. They punctuated the boring landscape near the ramps. Thousands of acres of irrigated hybrid corn, seven feet high, stretched almost to the horizon, their yellow tassels bending to the east in the steady west breeze. Fluttering plastic grocery bags, impaled on the barbed wire fences, dotted the ditches. Their eventual watershed journey to the Gulf impeded until the breeze gusted and ripped them free.

Traffic was light. Gayle Bumpers had the wheel of CTC 598. Lucille Smythe fidgeted with her hair in the navigator seat. Maxine Knott was snoring in the sleeper. Gayle maintained a steady sixty in top gear. CTC 561 pulled out from the draft position, merged into the hammer lane, and came up abreast.

Max Simmons, team leader, strong type A, was in the navigator seat admiring Gayle's side profile. She was cute beyond cute. She turned and gave Max a nice smile. Rumor was she wasn't married. A loyal company girl, having worked in corporate directly under Mr. Baron.

Max turned to Greg Jones. Jones was six hours into his driving shift, bored absolutely shitless due to the damned corn scenery. "Corn, corn, and more corn," he lamented. "You guys in Illi-noise ever heard of sunflowers—"

Max interrupted his latest rant. "I bet she's never been company mooned."

Greg looked past Max at Gayle. "Go for it, dude."

Max unbuckled his belt and zipped open his blue jeans.

Lucille noticed Max squirming around in his seat. "Gayle, brace yourself, girl. You're fixing to get mooned."

"No way."

"Hell yeah, Simmon's the moonshot champion," Lucille squalled.

She grabbed the disposable camera off the center console, quickly rotating the advance film knob. "Look. Look. There it is."

Max Simmons firmly pressed his butt cheeks against the side passenger window.

"Damn. That's the hairiest ass in the world," Gayle said with laugh. The flash of the camera caught Gayle's platinum-blond mane centered in Max's pressed flat ass.

"This one's going on the board, girl," Lucille howled.

Max and Greg were also in bouts of side-splitting laughter. Luke Mann hollered from the sleeper, "What the hell's so funny?"

"Max mooned Gayle Bumpers. The girl from headquarters."

Luke groaned, "Damn, Max, how come you get all the good ones?"

CHAPTER NINE

Stu double-laced his new Nike cross-country trainers. He looked forward to breaking in his seventh pair of shoes after discovering the stress-relieving pleasure of long-distance running. It had taken him a year to shed the posthoneymoon flab from his thirties. The rutting years in his late twenties while dating Tab had kept him trim. Postrut had put on the pounds. It was either go up a waist size or get back in shape. Tab's playful pinching of his love handles was the last incentive he needed.

The first year of running came with plenty of anguish, finding the right shoes, learning how to dress for the weather, training in gradual increments, and coping with constant soreness in muscles and joints. His life as a runner after forty could flesh out a self-published memoir. It wasn't until he had worked up to running five miles nonstop that he experienced the euphoria of a runner's high. When his second wind kicked in, it was like he was in overdrive, labored breathing only returning on long uphill slogs through the shifting terrain of the San Gabriel's.

But the biggest pleasure, next to his newfound stamina in bed, was the mind-clearing effect of running. After the first half mile, getting loose and locking into his stride, the pressures of being a trucking magnate melted away. He wondered why more presidents hadn't discovered running. Jimmy Carter had run laps around the White House. Their homeboy, Ronald Reagan, managed to relieve stress chopping wood at his ranch. Clinton was currently giving the Secret Service fits about running around the reflecting pool at the National Mall.

Stu stood at the carport door. "Hey, Tab, back in an hour. Going up Yucca Hill."

"Okay. I've got steaks marinating for dinner. Win's at Benny's for a sleepover. Have a good one."

Stu bounded out the front door. He noticed Donny furiously yanking on a new Husqvarna weed whipper. The owner's manual, still in the sealed plastic wrapper, was buried in the bottom of the long box, under all the packing materials.

Damn engine was the size of a basketball. Big enough to blaze a bridle trail through the Amazon.

It finally roared to life, spewing plumes of thick blue smoke. The nylon string whirled. The screeching sounded like a mini tornado. Donny threw the black padded strap over his shoulder and proudly waved at Stu. He goosed the whipper. A shin-high green cloud of minced grass spewed upward. Stu recalled that movie Win liked when Rick Moranis shrunk his kids down to the size of bugs. He wondered what it was like being buried deep in the turf with all that mayhem overhead.

The morning's conversation with the fish guy made him think about those Alabama rednecks. The TV reporters always managed to find that one hapless, toothless tornado survivor with a chaw of tobacco in his lower front gum, saying it sounded like a freaking freight train. He'd be thinking more about the conversation with the man in Alabama during his run.

Baron took off slow, working the creak out of his left knee. He headed east, up Monterey Drive to the Yucca Hill trailhead. The parking lot was empty. The county park featured a four-foot-wide cinder trail. It was a winding, switch-backed four miles to the top. He could knock out the eight-mile run in sixty minutes, including time for a nature call.

He had given up competitive running after suffering a humiliating need to void number two at mile eight of a half marathon. His only choice that day was dart off course and leave a dump behind a palm tree in a neatly manicured backyard in seaside Malibu. No toilet paper. And a very pissed-off old woman in a nightgown with a hockey stick. He decided then and there, never again.

About three hundred yards from Yucca peak, a secret stash of TP and handwipes in a metal Folgers can was hidden in a boulder crevice. A near perfect outhouse.

As he climbed in elevation, the concrete sprawl of Los Angeles unfolded for fifty miles in three directions. The day's smog obliterated any hope of catching a glimpse of the Pacific. The dry eastern exposure of the San Gabriel's was dotted with fragrant sage scrub, stubby pinyon pines, and an occasional clump of prickly pear cactus. Toyon bushes were fruiting, their red berries attracting the crow-sized, gunmetal-blue pinyon jays. Creosote bushes were in full bloom, five petal yellow flowers adding color contrast to the brown-pebbled dirt. Creeping wild rye and knee-high mountain grasses gradually replaced sturdier vegetation as he neared the windswept four-thousand-foot peak.

The switchback leveled out between two valleys. The next mile allowed him to cruise and ruminate. He called it kinetic meditation at the runner parties. Tab hated the gatherings. They turned into verbal suffer fests, everyone bragging about their latest injuries. Of course, there wasn't a board-certified orthopedist in sight. The complaining in the huddle was as futile as a screen door in a submarine. On top of the usual moaning, half of them preached about the latest diet from hell. And they looked like holocaust survivors. The other half were certifiably nuts, trying to kill themselves while running a hundred miles through the Mojave desert. Tab usually poured herself a stiff one after they left. He admitted that the gatherings were a little on the crazy side.

Today, all body systems were in go mode. No painful distractions. His knees and hips felt good. No hotspots on his feet. The shoes were breaking in like the others. He performed a mental checklist for hotspots on his soul. He thought about that morning's cluster. He hated that someone died but his conscience was clear. The idiot had it coming.

His private mission control cleared him for takeoff. He could enter the realm, kinetically meditate, hopefully solving some personal issues in the next hour. He thought about the conversation with the man in Alabama. The financials didn't seem that scary. Ross could roll the farm into the trucking company. Maybe there were lucrative tax write-offs. The biggest problem would be dealing with Ross's feelings. Leaving headquarters. He could see himself locating a short day's drive from their locker in New Orleans. Dropping in for a couple days a week.

"They have telephones in Alabama," he chuckled. It'd be awhile before the internet, though. California was in the lead for being a wired state in more ways than one.

A plump Merriam chipmunk, both cheeks crammed full of pinion nuts, darted across the cinder path.

He'd have to invest in a decent home office with a multiline phone conference hookup. It'd take a minuscule investment for a new workstation, a new computer, spreadsheet software—Ross was addicted to Excel—and a fax machine. Hire a part-time secretary for the home office. Figure out a way to get an intel feed from the blue board. Ross could put a call into the admiral.

He thought about the major career shift from being a business executive to a catfish farmer. It really wouldn't be a complete shift, though. He'd still be doing both. He couldn't walk away from CTC. Tab wouldn't go for that. She was enjoying the lifestyle too much. Rich and almost famous or infamous depending on how one interpreted that sordid chapter in her life before she met him. She wanted to move to a more glamorous suburb. Selling the move to Alabama would be a challenge. It would definitely be a radical culture shock. She had never lived anywhere else but California. Never been to the Deep South. Not even Disney World in Orlando. And then there was Win's schooling. Alabama certainly didn't have a stellar reputation there. The state usually sucked a dry hind tit next to Mississippi.

She'd have me fitted for a white jumpsuit and committed to North Harbor with all the other loonys.

His thinking shifted back to the conversation with the Alabama guy.

"Raising fish can't be that hard," he said as he rounded the curve before the next switchback.

Uncle Phil owned a large turkey and hog farm in southern Minnesota. Tab and Win had visited his operation several times on the way to his parents' cabin. Phil was living the good life. Farming wouldn't be that alien to Tab. She didn't care much for the factory-style production and the overpowering ammonia stench of the hog houses but found some humor in the turkey buildings. Phil was always saying there wasn't anything dumber than a domestic turkey.

Catfish might be a close second. Baron sidestepped a basking lizard.

I need a sign. An omen. A genie materializing out of a gold lamp telling me to go for it. Something that would even out the fact that I can't keep a fricking goldfish alive for more than a week.

As he started to climb out of the last valley, he heard the helicopter. Its unmistakable *whap whap whap* of blades beating the air. It rose over the peak, missing it by less than a hundred feet, dust swirling underneath. Excited hollering in Spanish grew louder and louder. He stopped. Now the yelling was distinct and mere yards away. He heard feet pounding the trail up ahead.

The first Latino whizzed past him in full gait down the hill. His eyes were focused on the trail several feet in front of his sandaled feet. Stu wondered if the fleeing man even saw him.

The second man saw him. No doubt. A little heftier than the first guy, he was toting an AK-47. The distinct thirty-round clip curved back toward the stock.

He yelled, "*Quitate de el camino, culero!*" Stu translated quickly, "Get out of the way, asshole."

Then a third man appeared half-limping. He looked like pure evil. A deep scar ran across his face, starting at his right cheek and ending at his left ear. Half his scarred nose had been lopped off. His eyes didn't even match. One eye looked left, and the other stared straight ahead. He was armed too. A sawed-off twelve-gauge Mossberg was cradled in his arms as he shuffled down the trail.

He stopped and stared at Baron. His shifty beady eyes dark as coal. Coldly thinking. *Should I kill him or let him live?*

"*Gringo, quitate de mi camino, chingada madre.*" Get out of my way, motherfucker.

The helicopter roared overhead. Painted in white letters on the all-black side body panel were *DEA* and a tricolor decal of an

American flag. Three men armed with M-16s, their legs sticking out, were sitting on the deck of the copter, their rifles pointed at Baron and the Mexican. The agents fortunately saw the middle-aged male in running attire. They held their fire despite the drug runner now pointing the shotgun at them.

Baron could barely move to the side to let the man pass. He was frozen in fear. He hoped if he stayed in the view of the helicopter, they'd protect him. The Mexican brushed him aside with the short gun barrel and took off again down the path. The helo continued to track him down the hill. The agents knew where they were headed. The parking lot at the trailhead was supposed to be the pickup location.

As the helicopter roared away, Baron regained his senses. He wildly dashed uphill, wanting to put as much distance between the bad guys and himself as possible. From the peak, he'd be able to see the trailhead. He could watch the cluster unfold less than a vertical mile away.

As he approached the peak, the sudden urge to void overcame him. He was, in effect, scared shitless. His body instinctively wanting to get lighter, run faster. He fought back the sensation in his lower bowel. Fortunately, he had restocked his supply of TP when Tab, Win, and himself had hiked to the peak after mass last Sunday. As he dropped his shorts and squatted behind the boulder, he noticed an army-green, lumpy duffel bag under a pile of mesquite branches about fifteen feet away. Someone had made a half-assed attempt to hide it. He pulled off the red lid of the Folgers can, unrolled some Northern, and stared at the bag.

Finished with the task at hand, he walked over to the clump of branches and pulled out the bag. It was one of those military issues. The kind that servicemen toted over their shoulders in the airports. Very faint black lettering indicated it belonged at one time to a Sergeant Alan Schemak, US Army. It was about a third full. Stu surmised it was either money or drugs or both. The long green shoulder strap was clipped to a stout carabineer in a quarter-sized grommet. He unclipped it, spread open the top, and looked inside. He could see stacks of strapped one-hundred-dollar bills. He reached in and grabbed a stack. The paper strap read "$5,000." His eyes opened wide. His mouth gaped. Stu continued to stare inside the dark bag.

His mind raced.

There were easily a hundred bundles.

He quickly calculated.

Half a million.

He stood on the balls of his feet and looked around, shuffling twice. He turned a full 360. All alone.

Stooping down, he fastened the bag back together. He did a better job covering it with the branches. Sitting on his haunches, he contemplated his next move.

It's drug money. Whose is it? Was it the government's and used for a bust? Or did it belong to the drug runners? If it's the drug runners', it's finders' keepers, assholes. If it's the government's and I hear they're looking for it, I'll turn it in.

He looked over the edge at the crevasse next to his boulder. He jumped down on a rocky ledge about three feet from the foot of the boulder. There was a hole in the bank where another boulder had washed out in a recent deluge. He figured it would be a good hiding spot. He hopped back up, looked around again, and snatched the bag away from the branches. After dropping the bag down on the ledge, he jumped down and stuffed it in the hole, filling the entrance with fist-sized rocks and packing it with loose dirt. It was completely obscured.

He scrambled back up the bank and darted back to the trail. He jogged to the peak of Yucca Hill and looked down in the valley. The parking area at the trailhead was empty. The helicopter was long gone. He closed his eyes and concentrated on his hearing. All he could hear was the steady breeze as it blew through the rustling branches of scraggly pinyon pines scattered along the peak. A chipmunk squeaked on his left.

He was still alone. He looked down the hill at the area where he had hidden the bag.

Do I dare risk toting it down the hill now? Maybe wait. Or better yet retrieve it at night. Yeah, I'll come back for it. Wait a week. They'll be back looking for it, for sure.

This could be the omen he'd wished for. Use it for his new venture. Escape the tumultuous rat race of LA. Buy a farm. Raise fish. Giddiness mixed with apprehension. Getting caught by the smugglers. They would, in all likelihood, kill him over the money. Getting it off the hill would be the most stressful thing he had ever done.

So much for running being a stress reliever.

He took off downhill, much faster than normal, strategizing how he was going to get the money off Yucca Hill.

*****

DEA agent Cooper Adams rubbed the itch out of his new scar in his upper left leg from his latest gunshot wound. The twenty-five-caliber full metal jacket barely missed his femoral artery. It had smacked soundly into his femur, delivering a four-inch-long pencil-wide crack. Following a thirty-day healing period, the agency's doctor had ordered another thirty days of light duty, patrolling the immediate area around his battleship-gray steel desk, issue circa 1957. Sitting behind the monitor watching a green blip on some barren mountain in Southern California was extremely boring. The bullshit paperwork the special agent in charge dumped on him last week was ticking him off. The bimbo secretary was supposed to be doing it, but she was on the same vacation, sucking the SAC's dick on a Pacific island.

Adams couldn't wait to hit the streets again. He missed the adrenaline burns. Busting the scumbags selling death in America's back alleys. He stared at his Zenith monitor at headquarters in Arlington.

The cloudless sky above Yucca Hill allowed perfect viewing from the National Security Agency's geo-stationary Advanced Kennan satellite. The new video surveillance program, code-named Misty, fed directly into the DEA. The war on drugs had taken on new heights, about two hundred miles above the Mexican border. The fact that the bus-sized NSA satellite was peering down on the homeland, an unapproved violation of Congressional largess, would be summed up in the corridors of the Justice Department and NSA's big brother arm, the National Reconnaissance Office, with the unofficial statement, "Shit happens." In Orwellian speak, the joint investigation would be recreated using parallel construction. The field agents summed it up the usual way. Shit still happens. The Cuban agent in the cubicle next to Adams had translated it in his native tongue. *Mierda asi pasa.*

Near the top of the thick canvas bag, a poker chip-sized pinger pinged away in the hidden double-stitched seam underneath the cloth handle. The signal was weaker now since being placed under several feet of rock and dirt. The dual lithium batteries were fresh and would last for three more months. The undercover agent, now trying to keep up with the biker gang on his Yamaha 250 as they cut through the Santa Monica National Recreational Area, had installed the batteries at the Los Angeles district office a few days ago.

Agent Adams watched the middle-aged man dart through the parking lot. He lost him as he made his way down the busy tree-lined street in the northern affluent suburb of Hildago. He made a few notations in his logbook and resumed eating his twelve-inch honey oat turkey breast Subway. Sweat beaded underneath his nose. The sandwich artist had squirted an extra line of Sriracha. He zoomed back in on the dimmer green dot slowly flashing on top of Yucca Hill.

He wiped his nose again. "Damn," he muttered, "this Sriracha doesn't play."

*****

Near the quaint seaside town of San Peter in Baja California, cartel kingpin Jose Agosto slammed down the corded phone. He was not happy. He wanted to kill people but wasn't sure where to start. His mules just delivered one hundred kilos of cocaine to Los Angeles. This was in addition to the previous week's delivery of two hundred kilos on credit. That delivery was last week's front page news and locked away in LAPD's warehouse. Now his money was lost on top of some damned hill, his men chased away by the DEA. The dope was headed north to San Francisco, courtesy of the Los Serpientes. They were on dirt bikes churning through the Cholame Valley. The damned federales had invited themselves to the party again. Either his cartel or the Serpientes had an informant in the midst. The impostor was usually the newest guy hanging around. Snipping off a few fingers would eventually reveal their identity. The short trip down the stainless steel hopper into the industrial-sized meat grinder would put a gruesome end to the leak.

His uncle down in Chile preferred to feed chunks of his impostors to the vultures. They'd still be alive, begging for mercy, while their limbs were hacked off with a machete. Agosto preferred the meat grinder. The vultures in America were overfed and too unpredictable.

CHAPTER TEN

Baron ended his eventful run at Montezuma Circle, a cul-de-sac half-circled with million-dollar homes. He always walked the last fifty yards, allowing time to cool down. He contemplated his next move as he headed toward his house, a stucco-sided two-storied Spanish colonial. A terra-cotta-tiled roof matched the other four houses in the quiet neighborhood.

Should I tell Tab now or wait? Better wait. She could be tight-lipped, but the odds of her telling just one close friend was a dangerous risk. And if that one friend told another...

He stepped out on the patio and looked eastward at the ridge of hills bracing the Los Angeles suburb of Hildago. He picked out Yucca. He concentrated on the peak's cardinal directions. He could almost pinpoint where the bag was hidden. It was on the northern face. He was looking east, so it had to be to the left of the ridge. It was at least a mile away as a crow flies. He wondered if a telescope or a pair of good binoculars could spot the boulder and the ravine. He recalled seeing optical goods at Academy Sports.

"Have a good run?" Tab asked from the multipaned french door that opened up onto the red-bricked patio.

"One of my best ever. Set a new PR." It was a new personal record all right. Finding half a mil on top of a mountain. He wondered about Tab's reaction.

"That's great. How about firing up the grill before you take your shower?"

"Okay. Just two steaks, right?"

"Yeah, just two." She grabbed a bottle of Alto Moncayo, her favorite Merlot due to its light cherry flavor, out of the wine cabinet and closed the door gently. She was looking forward to the evening with only her husband. She felt like getting a little frisky.

Stu noticed the green tinge in the pool. The time and money he spent maintaining it compared to the time he actually spent in the pool was an unfavorable cost-benefit ratio. The few instances of satisfaction when Win invited his friends over and he served as a lifeguard, laughing at the antics of energetic five-year-olds. Tab liked to skinny dip in the moonlight after midnight. Watching her silky-smooth trim body emerge soaking wet, beads of water rolling down her breasts, never failed to arouse him.

He twisted the valve counterclockwise on the propane tank, listened for the regulator to click, and rotated two of the six stainless steel knobs on the Viking grill. The gas hissed. He waited a second or so and punched the igniter button. The grill responded with a *pumph* and a complimentary lid shake.

*****

Stu reached over and turned the brass lamp off on the night-stand next to their king bed. Tab nestled in next to him, playfully plucking at his chest hairs.

"Tab, I'm trying to decide what was better. The steaks or the sex."

"Just for that, you're not getting any more porterhouse. It's ground round from now on. For that matter, I hear La Tienda has a special on cabrito this week." Tab playfully pouted, admonishing him with a pointed finger to his defined left pec.

Stu laughed. "I'm sorry, girl. Didn't mean to compare you to a piece of meat. It didn't come out the way I meant it. Both were great. Guess all that red meat ignited my carnal desires."

"You want to make it up to me?" Tab asked.

"How?"

"Round two on the patio after a dip in the pool."

Stu peered at the clock on the nightstand. It read 1:15. The moon would be directly overhead. She wanted it again. On the patio recliner. She'd be riding cowboy.

CHAPTER ELEVEN

Stu strolled into Ross Whitestone's corner office, gently closing the door behind him. Ross looked up from a stack of papers taller than his coffee cup. When his partner closed the door, it was usually something serious.

"Is this going to be good or bad? I'm working on bad right now. Definitely need some good."

"What're you working on?" Stu came around the desk and looked over his shoulder.

"New proposed trucking regulations from the feds."

President Reagan had directed a major deregulation of some of the more onerous trucking rules issued by the DOT, making it easier for nonunion carriers to enter the market. Old labor regs mandated by the Department of Labor had threatened CTC's three-man-team business model. Bureaucratic regulatory creep threatened the trucking industry again under President Clinton.

"I think we should schedule some quality time with Senator Emory. Good thing he likes golf. You should learn how to play."

"I heard a good one about golf the other day at the barbershop. You know why old men play golf?"

"No, tell me."

"Because they find sex more frustrating."

"Well, I'm not old yet." Ross chuckled.

Stu walked over to the dark-walnut bar in the corner. He grabbed an ice-cold diet Mountain Dew out of the mini refrigerator.

"You want something to drink, Ross?"

"No thanks, still working on this coffee."

Stu plopped down in the plush chair in front of the desk.

Ross was about to swallow the last of his tepid coffee.

"I found half a million dollars in cash yesterday."

Ross choked, spraying the pile of papers.

"Say what?" Ross wiped his mouth with the back of his hand, looking at Stu over his reading glasses, teetering on the end of his sun-blistered nose. Coffee dribbled off his chin.

Stu yanked a Kleenex out of the box on the coffee table and handed it to Ross.

"On top of Yucca Hill while I was running. Well, not actually running. More like taking a dump."

Ross removed his readers, stood up, walked around his desk, and sat on its edge, moving the family photo out of the way.

Stu described his encounter on the hill with the men, the helicopter, and that he had told no one else.

"Tabitha doesn't know?"

"Hell no. You know how women are. They'll tell one girlfriend, and then that one friend tells another 'just one friend,'" Stu paused, using his arms for air quotes. "And all of sudden, crazed soccer moms are scouring Yucca Hill for the loot."

"What're you going to do, Stu?" Ross had left his perch on the desk and settled into the other plush chair. His elbows were on his knees, hands forming a tepee, looking at his best friend.

"I want you to help me get it off the hill. We'll split it fifty-fifty. One condition, we gotta swear our wives to complete secrecy."

"I don't know, dude. This could be dangerous. Drug cartels, you know. They'll kill over this." Ross wrung his hands and looked out the corner picture window southward, toward Mexico.

"Well, the way I figure it, we wait at least a week. I'll buy a telescope and take up astronomy, paying particular attention to the moon as it rises over Yucca Hill. Figure I could at least see if anybody's looking for it. Should be able to see flashlights, huh?"

"Yeah, that's about all you're going to see too. I earned the astronomy merit badge in Scouts. The light pollution around here is going to rule out looking at anything else."

"You know, now that you mention it, I can never see the stars anymore. Not even the North Star. Shit, some days we can barely see the sun."

"What's Tab going to say about your new hobby?"

"Ross, she loves moonlight. Makes her horny."

"Okay. Getting back to the money. What next?" Ross said.

"I'll be watching the hill at night from my place. Might even drive through the trailhead parking lot after dark. Check out the vehicles. I figure they'll be looking for it all this week."

Ross stood up and paced back and forth between the chairs and the door. "Stu, what are the chances they find it?"

"Not very. I hid it pretty good. It's a good ten yards from where they left it, hidden in a hole up under a bank. I covered it with rocks and dirt. When they find those branches scattered all over, they'll figure some hiker found it."

"How big, space-wise, was the stash?"

"I think I can get it all in my backpack. You still have your mountain bike?"

"Yeah, the tires may need some air. A good spray down with WD-40, and she's ready to rock and roll."

"Okay, let me do a week's worth of surveillance. We'll plan the mission next week."

"When should we tell the wives?" Ross asked.

"Let's get it off the hill first and count it."

"A half mill, you say…" Ross looked at Stu intently.

"At least."

"What'cha going to do with a quarter mil, Stu?"

"Use it for a down payment on a fish farm, dude."

"A fish farm? You can't keep a goldfish alive."

Stu winced. "Yeah, I'll have to buy several truckloads of Perrier to raise 'em in, huh?"

Ross laughed.

"What'cha going to do with your half, Ross?"

"Get a decent boat. Something we can all sleep on. Abigail loves the water, you know. That gentle wave action in the starlight. The waves lapping against the sides all night long. It puts her in a romantic mood. Guess what I'm going to name it."

"What?"

"Stu's Dump."

They laughed heartily and exchanged high fives.

CHAPTER TWELVE

Baron was spot on in his prediction. His new Meade 118-millimeter telescope was almost perfect for the task. On the second night, he counted four light beams flitting near the peak of Yucca Hill. *Giant lightning bugs on steroids*, he quipped to himself as he sipped on his neat scotch. Only problem was everything was upside down. Telescopes, unlike binoculars or spotting scopes, had this distinct disadvantage, the optical goods clerk said. Studying Yucca Hill with a pair of binoculars for a week, pretending to be an amateur astronomer, wasn't going to fly with Tab or Donny, his nosy neighbor.

On the third night, he counted two lights. On the fourth and fifth night, just one. And on the sixth and seventh, nothing. They gave up. The parking lot surveillance indicated the same thing. California plates on worn-out cars. Lots of Sierra Club, Trails to Rails, Vote for Jerry Brown, and No Nuke stickers on the rear windows. Never did he see a newer model that could pass as a rental or maybe even government issue.

Tab came out onto the deck with her Scotch and Seven after putting Win to bed. Stu deftly aimed and refocused the telescope on the moon as it breached Yucca Peak.

"Wow, full moon tonight," Tab said.

"Yeah, you should see this." Stu quickly centered the scope on the northeast quadrant, which was actually the southwest quadrant since he was viewing an upside-down moon. Tab handed her drink off and crouched behind the telescope, her tight running shorts riding up her NordicTrack butt. Her bent over form made Stu lose his train of thought for a second. She peered in the tubular eyepiece.

"Oh my gosh. I always wondered about that dimple. It's beautiful."

"It's called the Mare Crisium. They call it a lunar sea, but it's really a crater. It's 350 miles across. You're right, it's one of the few features you can see without a scope."

Stu was glad the clerk recommended the *Cambridge Guide to the Moons, Stars and Planets*. He perused the chapter on the Earth's moon.

"Any luck seeing anything more than the moon?"

"No, afraid we can't do that here. Too much background light. Need to go somewhere really dark."

"How about this Friday? We can take an evening stroll to Yucca peak and set it up there."

Stu looked at his wife, stifling a gasp. She looked at him quizzically.

"What's wrong?"

"Oh, Tab. Too many Looney Tunes running around here for that. I'm not taking my only child and wife out to some desolate place in LA these days. Sorry."

Stu hated not being able to tell his adoring and trusting companion the whole story. It was eating away at him. He looked into her vivid teal eyes. The evasiveness would be atoned for eventually. It was for her own good. They'd be sharing the money soon. He hoped the bounty assuaged this new dent in his shining armor.

*****

Stu strolled into Ross's office, closed the door gently, and plopped down in the chair facing Whitestone's desk. He was on the phone with a Bandag retread salesman in Long Beach.

"Sounds good, Jay," Ross said into the phone. He twirled a long pencil in his right hand.

Ross continued to listen. Stu neatly stacked the past issues of *Trucker's Digest* on the black walnut glass-topped coffee table in front of the chairs.

Ross spoke into the phone. "Jay, according to our tire guy over in accounts, we went a whole week without throwing an alligator using your retreads."

Stu chuckled at the truckers' term for shredded recaps littering the nation's interstates.

"That new recap process your company developed is really winning over our fleet teams," Ross continued.

Ross listened, the corded handset wedged between his cocked head and shoulder. He winked at Stu.

"Jay, can't do that, dude. We gotta stick with just retreading the drive and trailers. Stu and I promised the teams we'd never use retreads on the steers. The retreads stay behind the steers. There are attorneys itching to make the case that a retreaded steer caused a fatal accident. They'd claim it was done to save money. CTC doesn't need that courtroom cluster."

Ross listened again, gazing up at Stu, smiling. "That's really impressive. I'm writing it down as we speak." Ross scribbled some more on his yellow legal pad. He stuck the dull pencil in his "Welcome to the Forties Decade from Hell" coffee cup. Ross preferred drinking out of his "Greatest Father Ever" cup his son, Benny, gave him.

"Okay then. Looking forward to it. See you at the Truckers' National in Vegas. Bye, Jay." Ross hung up and sipped on his coffee. "Just made a deal with Jay at Bandag. They can retread for ninety-five bucks. We were paying one hundred and twenty-five." He rapped for a few seconds on his Canon desk calculator. "That's a savings of a quarter mill a year, reducing our delivery cost by almost one percent. And we get out of paying the fed excise tax on new tires and the waste tire fees."

Stu nodded. "Sounds good."

Ross continued. "Jay says their new process is yielding a cradle to grave average of nearly two hundred and fifty thousand miles."

"That's amazing. Hard to imagine a casing going that far with, what, three retreads?"

"Wait 'til I tell Retread Ted in accounts. We'll have to find something else for him to do in between counting the gators."

Ross made a note to himself on a sticky pad.

"Ross, let's go get the money."

"Dude, give me some intel."

"No activity for the past three nights. Tab thinks I'm obsessed with this astronomy gig. Staring at the moon for seven nights straight, she's probably wondering if I need to get checked out. No telling what my neighbor thinks."

Ross chuckled, "Hey, maybe we can send the old bachelor up there first. Kinda like a snipe hunt in the Boy Scouts. Tell him there's been reports of moon-worshipping nudists up on the peak at midnight."

"That's a thought. He'd be packing heat too," Stu said.

"Speaking of packing, think we oughta consider going up there with some protection?" Ross asked.

"No way, dude. We're not getting into a gunfight over money. Not with a bunch of professionals. Not enough money in the world for that shit. We see anybody up there, we'll turn around and head back down."

"So what's the plan?"

"I figure we bike up to the peak. You serve as lookout. Stay on the trail while I put the money in my backpack. We can book ass down the hill. Be out of there in ten minutes max."

"What stage is the moon in?"

"Almost full. To be exact, it's a waning gibbous."

"Waning and waxing, I could never keep those straight." Ross looked intently at his partner. "I do know this, if you give your eyes time to acclimate, you can see pretty damn good without a flashlight. Learned that in the Scouts. Bring a headlamp just in case, but we can probably get by without them, at least until we hit the pavement at the trailhead."

"What about the wives?" Stu asked.

"Hey, don't the boys have a soccer game tomorrow night?" Ross asked.

"Yeah, how are we going to explain missing a game, though?"

"Just tell them we're working late on a project with a hard deadline."

"This subterfuge with the wife is working on me. I'm gonna have to come clean soon or start confessing with Father Rex."

"Yeah, I keep wondering what Abby's going to say."

"Okay, so the match is at seven. Wives and boys will be gone by six thirty at the latest. Let's meet at my house at six forty-five. I'll load up my bike after they leave. We'll park the cars at the Walgreen's. Bike from there."

"How come you want to start from Walgreen's and not the trail-head?" Ross asked.

"Just in case we get followed off the peak or some federales are patrolling the lot at the trailhead. Racking the bikes elsewhere, getting out there as quick as possible, I reckon," Stu said.

"So when should we hit the peak?" Ross asked.

"Last night the sun set at eight ten. Let's be at the peak before sunset and hang out. We can watch the trailhead parking lot from there. By eight thirty, it should be almost dark. You keep an eye out on the top of the trail. I'll get the stash. Should be rolling through the parking lot by nine and back at my house by nine fifteen."

*****

Manuel Castillo, known as El Diablo, Jose Agosto's chief lieutenant in the Bajalista drug cartel, wasn't giving up. He was on the peak when the DEA showed up, noted where the panicked mule had dropped the money and then half-assedly covered it up. The helicopter had completely freaked out the new guy. He could have made it down the hill with the bag. Agosto's 9 mm bullet in the ear prevented the man from making that mistake again.

Diablo decided to look one more time. He would approach from the north flank of Yucca Hill. It'd be more of a trek compared to using the well-used south side trail. *Maybe a hiker discarded the bag along the trail on the other side of the mountain.* This would at least confirm the money was no longer on the hill. Jefe Jose Agosto was not a patient man. Diablo could be the next recipient of a well-placed bullet.

CHAPTER THIRTEEN

Ross and Stu unfastened their trail bikes hanging off their tailgates behind the Walgreens. The local pharmacy closed promptly at seven. The freshly waxed black BMW, parked next to Stu's dusty blue Isuzu Trooper, belonged to the pharmacist, a fellow church member.

Dr. Stanley Byrne headed in Stu's direction.

"Kinda late for a trail ride," Stanley stated as he inserted the key in the driver's door.

"Doc, we're doing a quick shakedown with the bikes before the weekend. Making sure everything's tuned up. First time we've had them out since last summer."

Ross was fiddling with the tie-down buckles attached to the rack on his Land Rover. He was within earshot. He politely smiled at the pharmacist.

Stanley noticed the thick layer of dust on top of the Stu's bike seat. "Might want to wipe that."

He climbed into the leather bucket seat, started up the car, and rolled out of the parking lot into traffic. Stu watched the BMW disappear down the street. He reached in the back of the Trooper, grabbing his empty Gregory internal frame backpack. He slid into the padded shoulder straps and buckled the plastic snaps for the hip and chest belts.

"He's kinda on the anal retentive side," Ross observed.

"Guess you gotta be a little anal, counting pills your whole life." He wiped the bike seat with his gloved hand. "Good to go, Ross. Let's do this."

They straddled their bikes, donned their helmets, and snapped their chin straps.

After giving each other a high five, they pedaled off to Yucca Hill.

*****

El Diablo looked up at the peak, swearing to himself that this was the last time he was climbing the *chingada madre.* Thirty years of sucking down Casa Dragones had taken a drastic toll on his health. There was a dull ache in his left lung. The occasional coughing spasms were hellish. Sometimes bloody. He headed up the northern face of the hill on the rarely used cinder trail. The shadows were getting longer. He kept his eyes peeled on both sides of the trail for the empty bag.

*****

Ross and Stu shifted into granny gear as they turned on the last sharp switchback before the peak. Ross was puffing hard.

Stu chuckled at his winded buddy. "You gonna make it?"

"Shit. Didn't realize I was this bad out of shape."

"It doesn't take long to get sorry at our age. You need to rest?"

"Nah, I'm good. Let's get to the top. I'll catch my breath up there."

As Stu passed the area near his boulder, he stared down the hill at the gully where he had hidden the bag. Everything looked like he had left it.

Except for that pile of branches. They were scattered all over the place.

He pedaled on, waiting for Ross at the peak.

"Well, you made it," Stu said.

Ross climbed off his bike and laid it down. He bent over and held his knees with his hands, taking deep exasperated breaths. "Definitely looking forward to the rendezvous with Mr. Gravity."

"Yeah, it'll be a coaster all the way down."

Ross straightened up and faced the setting sun. He put his right hand up in between the orange glow behind a high bank of cirrostratus clouds and the smoky horizon. The Pacific was obscured in brownish dinginess. His palm, at arm's length, fit in the gap of the horizon's edge and the bottom of the orange glow. "Looks like about thirty minutes before sundown." This was a tip on telling time he had learned in the Scouts. Ross drifted off, lost in thought, thinking back about his days as a Scout.

"Time to pitch the tents and gather firewood boys," his fearless scoutmaster, Looney Hayes, had barked to the troop.

He never made it to Eagle. The enticing sweet smell of perfume mixed with cheap gasoline, and the new drive-in movie complex two miles from high school, was a much more stimulating venue than lugging around heavy canvas tents. His intrepid scoutmaster soon learned that boys needed to earn the rank of Eagle before the driving age of sixteen, realizing his goals for the boys couldn't compete with raging titers of testosterone.

Stu stared at Ross. "Dude, back to Earth. Time to focus."

"Sorry, man. Thinking about my scouting days."

"We get the money off this hill, you can sponsor a troop at your church."

Ross studied on that for a second. "I like the boat idea better."

They peered over the southern edge of the peak, looking down toward the trailhead parking lot. Still empty. They listened for voices coming up from the valley below. Nothing except for the incessant squalling of two male pinyon jays reconfirming established territories. A slight breeze from the north rustled the pinyon tree branches, drowning out the footsteps of a lone man inching his way up the northern flank.

The last crescent of orange dipped below the horizon. Coalescing shadows instantly disappeared as if ordered by an invisible wizard. The men's eyes slowly acclimated to the developing darkness. A great horned owl swooped by Stu and Ross, its approach and departure completely soundless.

"Did you see that owl?" Ross asked.

"Yeah, they're amazing. That big of a bird being able to fly like that without making a sound."

"Wish I had their eyes right now," Ross whispered.

"It's time. Let's do it."

The men picked up their bikes, walking them down the hill about fifty yards. Both shifted into a whisper and stealth mode. Taking a hint from the owl.

Stu could make out his boulder on the left side of the trail.

"Okay, you stay here and hold my bike," Stu whispered.

"Got it," Ross whispered back.

"Anybody comes, you give out an owl hoot."

"What kind of owl?"

"Damn, Ross, a *who-who* will work."

Stu walked off into the dark. Ross concentrated on peering through the developing darkness. The moon crested behind their backs.

The breeze ceased. Ross heard pebbles crunch under Stu's feet.

To the far right, Ross thought he heard another set of feet slowly approaching. Then a branch snapped. *Probably a mule deer.*

El Diablo heard the scratching and digging sounds just off the summit trail. He, too, had adjusted to the dwindling light. Traveling at night without a flashlight was second nature to him, having crossed the Rio Grande into Texas countless times in his early years as a drug mule. He preferred the border tunnel at Imperial Beach City. Lots of scorpions but no snakes. He'd witnessed several men die from cottonmouth bites after fording the river.

Stu stood on the narrow ledge, digging out the bag with his gloved hands. He worked quickly, driven by the desire to get off the hill with the money as fast as possible. Dislodged rocks tumbled down the slope.

He reached in the dark hole, felt the stiff fabric of the bag, and groped for the strap. He yanked the bag out and was about to chunk it on top of the ledge. He looked up. A man, sitting on his haunches, looked down at him. It wasn't Ross. The moon was completely over the hill, silhouetting the short, stocky figure. He slowly waved a pistol at him with one hand. The satin chrome finish on the Llama .45 ACP semiauto reflected in the moonlight.

Stu's face was two feet away from the end of the barrel.

"*Yo me llevo el dinero,*" the gunman said. I'll take that money.

Stu remembered the voice. He stared at the man. His face was partially shadowed by the moon behind his head. *The nightmarish deep-jagged scar from one ear to the other.*

The man continued to point the gun at Stu's face. He moved his right thumb slightly, pushing the safety button in and off behind the trigger. Stu heard the click.

"*Dame lo, culero. Ahora!*" Hand it over, asshole. Now!

Ross saw the man approach Stu in the moonlight. He watched him pull the shiny pistol from his rear waistband. Picking up a bowling ball-sized rock, he held it above his head as he rushed forward. Ross hurled the rock as hard as he could, smacking the man squarely between his shoulder blades.

El Diablo and the pistol sailed over Stu. Stu ducked. The man's legs grazed Stu's shoulders.

El Diablo face-planted a boulder down in the ravine. He crumpled to the ground, motionless. The pistol discharged upon smacking into another boulder. The bullet soared into the night sky. The ear-splitting gunshot echoed through the valleys. The pistol clattered down the side of the boulder, finally lodging in a deep crevice.

Stu threw the bag past Ross. Ross stepped forward, grabbing Stu's hand in a fireman's grasp, yanking him up. Stu vaulted four feet of air. Adrenaline surged as they darted for their bikes.

"The money. Did you get the money?" Stu yelled.

"Shit, it's still back there!" Ross yelled back.

"Dammit, man."

"My bad. I'll get it."

Stu waited. He got down on one knee, trying to catch his breath. He was shaking down to his ankles. His heart raced. His eyes lost complete focus. Peripheral vision fogged over. Blood pounded in his ears.

Ross showed up with the bag moments later. He was also sucking wind, heaving and gulping. "Holy shit, I can't stop shaking."

"I know. It's a bitch. Did you see him?"

"No, but I heard him moaning."

Ross stuffed the bag in Stu's backpack, barely able to buckle the main compartment strap due to a loss of fine motor skills. He managed to slap Stu on both shoulders. "You're good, dude. Let's get the hell out of here."

They hopped on their bikes and took off down the hill. The moon was directly overhead, barely illuminating the cinder trail. It was enough light to keep from peeling off into the brush.

Minutes later, they whooshed through the trailhead parking lot, stopping on the other side of the street.

"We better go with lights from here. That'd be a hell of a note getting hit by a car after all that shit," Stu winced.

They fished out their Coleman headlamps from the front pockets of their cargo shorts and hit the street again.

They whirled into the Walgreen's parking lot. Both were still shaking. "The hell with the bike rack." Ross chunked his bike in the back of his Land Rover.

"I heard that." Stu did likewise and slammed down his rear hatch door.

*****

DEA special agent Joel Junkins was chewing on a mouthful of kung pao, liberally doused with Chinese hot mustard sauce, when the green blinking dot moved. At first, he didn't believe it. The sinus-clearing mustard clouded his eyes. His contacts were fogged over. Tears streaked down his cheeks. After wiping his face with the Panda Kitchen napkin, he watched the green dot zigzag down the dark hill. He quickly swallowed, almost choking.

"Holy shit, it's moving!" he yelled to himself. The janitor, thirteen empty cubicles away, looked up at him and went back to mopping.

He grabbed his desk phone and quickly dialed. It was thirty minutes past midnight, Virginia time.

Cooper Adams was in the middle of a vivid dream, harvesting a trophy bull buffalo with a spear. His Sioux ancestors on the Great Plains had hunted bison for centuries. Continuing the legacy was number four on his bucket list.

The phone rang on his lamp table. He fumbled for it in the dark. His right hand passed over his 10 mm Glock. He lifted the handset.

"Coop!"

"Damn. What time is it?" Cooper Adams squinted at the alarm clock.

"The son of a bitch is moving."

*****

Before Stu cleared the pharmacy's lot, he stopped abruptly. Ross slammed on the brakes to avoid crunching into Stu's Trooper. Stu trotted back to Ross.

"Thinking about that man up here," Stu said.

"Yeah, me too. Reckon we oughta call the police? I don't want it on my conscience that we left him up there to die."

"That bastard almost killed me. It's not going to bother me as much as it will you. But still, that's a burden we don't need. You're right, let's call the police. Call anonymously and report a gunshot." Stu looked at the pay phone in the parking lot.

"You want me to do it?" Ross asked.

"Yeah, go ahead. I'll wait."

*****

"Nine one one. What's your emergency?"

"I want to report a gunshot on Yucca Hill, near the top. One shot." Ross blurted into the mouthpiece on the steel-corded handset.

"Your name, please?"

"Ma'am, I'd rather remain anonymous. I was on the hill biking and heard it, that's all."

The dispatcher checked her screen. The call was coming from Hildago. She needed ten more seconds to pin down the address.

"Sir, can you give me an approximate time when you heard the gunshot?" She tried to stall the caller. If a unit could get there while he was still talking, it would help fill in the blanks for the authorities.

She was a hardened veteran. The LAPD appreciated her dedicated, quick-thinking service.

Her display blipped with a location. Pacific Bell pay phone on Jerome Street. Walgreen's parking lot. She silently dispatched a unit. Maybe they'd get there before Mr. Anonymous left.

"Ross, let's go!" Stu yelled. He had watched enough of his favorite television show, James Garner's *Rockford Files*, to recognize this stalling ploy.

"Ma'am, maybe about fifteen minutes ago. Gotta go."

The line clicked dead. *Well, his name was Ross.* She filled in a blank on the log sheet.

As they turned off Jerome Street to Monterey Drive, a police cruiser flew by. Stu shook his head. *If they had stopped, searched us, found a half million in the backpack, boy, what a goat rope that would have been.*

Ross and Stu parked on the cul-de-sac. Abby Whitestone's silver Mercedes sat in the driveway. The wives were chatting in the front yard. They stared at their husbands as they emerged from the vehicles. Both women sharing the look, "Okay, what's up with this?" Also wondering why Ross had showed up at Stu's.

"Tab, where're the boys?" Stu asked.

"Upstairs. Playing video games. Benny's spending the night."

"Okay. We need you two to come in the garage," Stu insisted.

"I thought you two were working at the office tonight?" Abby asked Ross.

"The garage, please." Ross winced.

Abby and Tab shrugged, looked at each other, and strolled into the garage. Ross followed. Stu walked to the back of the Trooper, retrieving his backpack. He met them inside the cluttered garage. He punched the garage door switch next to the doorframe and waited until the screeching door closed with a loud thump.

Ross walked over to the garage workbench, yanked the string for the overhead fluorescent work light, and moved stuff to the sides. Stu pulled out the duffel bag from his backpack and placed it on the bench. He cleared his throat.

"Girls, I found this up on Yucca Hill about a week ago. It's been up there the whole time—"

Tab interrupted. "So you've really been watching it instead of the moon?"

"Well, yeah. Actually both," Stu grimaced. Tab gave him the eye. There would be further discussions about the subterfuge.

"Tonight, Ross helped me get it down off the hill. We made a deal to split it fifty-fifty."

"Split what?" Tab asked.

Abby looked at Ross quizzically, tilting her head, then frowning, "What are you guys up to now?" She had plenty to go on. *These two were always hatching wild schemes. The latest one was renaming the company Three Men and a Reefer.*

Stu started pulling neatly strapped bundles of hundred dollar bills out of the duffel bag.

Ross took a bundle and showed it to Abby and Tabitha.

"Each bundle is five thousand dollars," Ross said, pointing to the wording on the paper straps.

Stu continued to yank bundles out of the bag. "Oh my god," Tab exclaimed softly. Abby's mouth gaped. When Stu finished placing the bundles in stacks of ten, there were thirty-four even stacks.

Ross, being the best numbers guy in the bunch, quickly calculated. "Damn, Stu, that's one million, seven hundred thousand dollars. That's a lot more than you thought."

Stu reached over and, in the middle of the seventeenth and eighteenth stack, separated the money into two distinct piles. "And half of it is yours, partner."

"Whoa, guys. I need way more information on where this came from," Tab asserted.

"We think it's drug money," Ross said.

"What makes you think that?" Abby asked, hands on hips.

Stu recounted the episode on the hill with the helicopter. He didn't mention the gunman less than an hour ago. Ross winked at Stu while standing behind the girls, silently condoning the abbreviated story.

"How do you know it's not the DEA's money?" Tab asked.

"We don't know that for sure," Stu said.

Stu took a moment to think things through. *That man on the hill was not DEA.* His weeklong surveillance of the parking lot suggested that the feds weren't looking for it. He was confident that the money didn't belong to the government. Circumstances prevented him from explaining more to the wives. The brush with death would have to remain a secret for now. It would just upset them. Spilled milk, in a way. *A freaking tanker load.*

"Well, I personally don't have a problem keeping money from some cartel, but I think we need to chill on it," Tab said.

"I agree with Tab," Abby stated.

"Ross and I thought so too. A cooling off period would be wise."

"Yeah, let's hold off for a while," Ross added. The overwhelming desire to take tomorrow off, be in the boat dealer's showroom at eight in the morning, purchase a new boat, and take Abby out for a sunset cruise in the Pacific would be scuttled for now.

Stu cleared his throat again. "Listen to me, please. We have to keep this a secret. If it belongs to a cartel and they hear any inkling of a rumor about some folks spending piles of cash, they'll come looking for it and us. Those people don't play around."

Tab, Ross, and Abby nodded.

"Let's get together in two weeks and discuss how we're going to spend it," Stu said.

Stu looked at his Sierra Club calendar above the workbench. He counted off fourteen days, flipping from June to July.

"Looks like Friday, July seventh."

Stu started packing Ross's half back into the duffel bag.

"Whoa, dude. I'd rather not use that bag. Someone may recognize it. Abby, you still have those Whole Paycheck grocery bags in your car?"

"Yeah. I'll go get one. One be enough?"

"I think so," Ross said as he stared at their share of the stash.

"Stu, where are you going to hide this?" Tab asked.

He looked at his Gregory backpack. He picked it up. "Reckon this will work for now. I'll keep it in our bedroom closet."

"Put it up high, okay? We don't need Win taking five grand to Bible study for show and tell."

Stu winced at the thought.

*****

Cooper Adams zipped up a wrinkled pair of khaki pants. He sniffed both armpits of his black tactical polo shirt, deciding it could go one more day. He inserted his Alien Gear waistband holster on his right hip and clipped his gold badge next to it on the thick brown leather belt. Grabbing his Glock off the nightstand, he shoved it firmly down into the holster. Adams inspected the top of the spare magazine for lint, declared it good to go, and slipped it in his mag carrier on his left hip.

Adams raced to headquarters in his government-issue Crown Vic, rolling through all seven stop signs on the way. He climbed two steps at a time to the second floor. His leg felt good, but he was a little winded from falling out of shape due to four solid weeks riding his desk. Damned government doctor had vastly overcompensated his recovery time, one more prime example of someone covering their ass. DEA was full of CYA. It was becoming part of the agency's creed. It might get incorporated into the oath at academy commencement. He was ready to get back. Fighting the war.

He stood over his desk and typed in his DEA password. The active video surveillance program icon appeared on his screen. He smacked the mouse button.

Agent Junkins strolled over and pointed to the blinking dot. "We got a location, 3131 Montezuma Circle, suburb of Hildago, north LA. Owners come back as a Stuart and Tabitha Baron. No criminal history. Not even a speeding ticket on either of them."

The blinking dot was centered on Baron's garage.

*****

El Diablo staggered to his feet. He lightly touched what remained of his nose. He lost half of it in a knife fight back in Nuevo

Juarez. Now the other half was swollen, full of coagulated blood and hurt like hell. He searched for his Llama in the bright moonlight. It was wedged down in a crack. He tried to fish it out with a mesquite branch. The distant *whap whap whap* of the approaching LAPD helicopter was getting louder. Off in the distance, arising from the south, it climbed in altitude in a straight line toward him, the blinding spotlight on the nose, moving from side to side. The helicopters were outfitted with heat detecting FLIR scopes. They'd spot his greenish thermal image if he hung around.

He took off down the northern flank, his shoulder blades shooting bolts of pain into his arms as he swung them from side to side. He limped and hobbled down the north trail, scattering small rocks as he negotiated the sharp switchbacks. He remembered a wooden shelter midway down. If he hid in the rafters, he could fool the FLIR. He recalled the shelter having a shingled roof. Good insulation. It'd be still hot from the day's heat, hiding his ghostly green image. His drug-mule experience was paying off.

He swore to himself he'd kill the gringos eventually. Get his boss's money back or at least bring back some fingers. He got a good look at one of them.

CHAPTER FOURTEEN

"Mr. Baron, you have a call on line four," Marcela's sweet voice from the speakerphone broke the silence in Baron's corner office.

Stu stared at the phone. He was muddling his way through a legal document from a law firm in Jacksonville. An environmentalist group was suing Coast to Coast about the roof-high pile of scrapped tires behind the mechanics garage at the Jacksonville locker. They were breeding clouds of mosquitos. Instead of simply asking the locker manager to remove them, they hired a billboard attorney looking for work. Stu needed to issue a quick memo to the other warehouses about waste-tire storage. Coast to Coast was generating hundreds of them, mostly old steer tires. Stu knew they'd eventually be an environmental problem. He was waiting for the next truckers' convention, hoping a vendor would offer the service of properly disposing or, better yet, a way to recycle them. He'd call the complainants personally, asking them to drop the lawsuit in exchange for compensation. Maybe his Sierra Club membership could unruffle some feathers.

"Marcela, who is it?"

Marcela asked the caller.

"Lieutenant Cooley from LAPD," Marcela said.

Oh shit. This is not good. I'm so screwed.

"Marcela, put him through." He took a deep breath.

"Mr. Baron, this is Lt. George Cooley, LAPD. How are you this morning?"

Stu rubbed his forehead as he held the phone. The voice had a friendly tone, not in the least accusatory or threatening.

"Sir, I'm doing fine considering someone's trying to sue me in Florida as we speak."

"Mr. Baron, just tell them what I tell them."

"What's that, Lieutenant?"

"Take a number. Get in line."

Stu forced a chuckle.

"I'm calling about that incident several weeks ago when you stopped that armed robbery. The perp pled guilty. He's been sentenced to twenty years at San Quentin. Thanks for getting him off our streets."

"You're welcome, sir. I was at the right place at the right time. Glad I could be of help."

"The mayor's office called. They want you to appear at our Annual Citizens Against Crime Recognition Dinner. You'll be getting a plaque. It'll be a meet and greet with the mayor and other dignitaries. We'll have a few Hollywood celebs there, too. Bring your family."

"Sir, that sounds good." Stu thought he'd really like to pass, but it'd be good for Win. Win loved new experiences. Of course, Tab lived for these occasions, meeting the righteous, hoity-toity denizens of Los Angeles. He'd just have to suffer through it. Maybe there'd be a fellow runner in the crowd.

"Okay, it's on July seventh at six p.m. at the Kimpton Hotel Palomar in Beverly Hills."

Stu recalled the other engagement scheduled for that night. He had 850,000 reasons to bow out. He figured they could meet later and discuss the discreet use of the loot.

"Lieutenant, that sounds good. I'll bring my wife and son. Thanks."

"No. Thank you, Mr. Baron. Oh, and by the way, if you ever apply for a pistol permit, provided you pass the background, I'll personally expedite it through the sheriff's department. That way, you can use something besides a baseball bat." Cooley chuckled.

"Thanks, I'll keep that in mind." Stu returned a chuckle.

"Have a good day, Mr. Baron."

Stu hung up. He glanced at his stack of papers and his cold coffee cup. He left his chair and walked over to the picture window. He stared out at the sprawling metropolis, a cultural cataclysm festering underneath the thousand-foot-thick layer of brown air. When he and Ross bought the entire floor fifteen years ago, the view was mesmerizing. The air weighed less back then.

Now all he wanted was out. Get as far away as possible. When he took a deep breath of air, he didn't want to taste it. Enough of this humanity gone amok. He was merely existing day to day on the wooden board of a loaded rat trap, skirting around the baited plate, the cocked coil spring flexed for an instant strike. The spoils of living in Southern California serving as the bait. The neck-breaking bar unhinging. Snapping down. Taking him out. His life ending with an involuntary spastic twitch. Living on borrowed time, the freeway bullet barely missing, the liquor store thief with the loaded gun, the mule brushing him aside with the sawed-off shotgun, the click of the pistol on the hill. Staring at that barrel.

How many more am I allowed before the bar finally found its mark?

CHAPTER FIFTEEN

The Los Angeles Times
July 8th, 1997

Armed Robber Thwarted by Bat-Wielding Citizen

Stuart Baron of Hildago, who wielded a baseball
bat to thwart an armed robbery, was awarded the
Citizens Against Crime Annual Award for his
bravery at the Annual Citizens Against Crime
Recognition Dinner hosted by Los Angeles
Mayor Richard J. Riordan at the Beverly Hills
Kimpton Hotel Palomar on Monday. Baron used
his son's baseball bat to take down an armed robber at the Starz Liquor Store in Altadena on May
15. The suspect, Hector Sanchez, of San Diego,
was briefly hospitalized following his arrest at the
scene. He later plead guilty to armed robbery and
received a twenty-year sentence that he is now
serving at San Quentin.

Tab cut out the article and Stu's picture while she sat at the kitchen
counter. Stu sipped on his morning joe from the highlands of Costa
Rica.

"This is a terrible picture." Tab winced at the image of her grinning husband as he held the wooden plaque with her and Win standing at his side. "Look at that huge stain on your tie."

"Yeah, that glob of caviar nailed it good. Look at that picture.
Do you really think people were paying attention to me? You're the

one they were talking about. Several people asked me why you weren't interested in films or modeling. And that black choker and gloves. You should wear them more often. Where did you get those gloves?"

"Abby lent them to me. She says gloves are the punctuation mark of a lady."

"Well, the way that Hollywood director was leering at you, I wished Terry had come along. I could have handled the pervert but would have needed his help with the bodyguards."

Tab walked over to the refrigerator. She attached the clipping to the refrigerator door at waist height with a colorful toucan magnet for Win.

"Win was excited about meeting Tom Cruise."

"I was excited too, especially after that peck on the cheek," Tab purred.

"Remember, he's an actor. I deck criminals in real life."

"I hope the days of taking bats to gunfights are over."

"Lieutenant Cooley suggested I get a gun permit."

"Oh, Stu. You know how I feel about guns. Especially with Win. You know how curious he is. They scare the crap out of me."

"I know, Tab." Stu sighed. Someday he'd have to flesh out why Tab was so opposed to having a gun for family protection.

"What are your plans about the money?"

"Let's talk about it on the patio tonight. We don't need Win to hear."

Stu kissed Tab on her forehead, grabbed his travel mug off the kitchen counter, fished his keys out of Donny's bowl, and dashed out the front door. He had a list of questions for the fish guy in Alabama.

As Stu turned left at the stop sign, he noticed the Ford Econoline van parked on the opposite side of the street. He didn't see any surveyors out and about. The light-blue magnetic sign on the side of the white van read "Fiber Optic Cable Survey Crew." Pairs of orange cones were in front and behind the van. He wondered why the waist-high cones were placed so close to the rear cargo door.

Surely the cones would be in the way every time they opened the rear door.

CHAPTER SIXTEEN

Stu bounded into Whitestone's office. Ross was sitting behind his cluttered desk, absorbed in a colorful brochure of inboard cabin cruisers. Stu half-circled the desk and peered over his partner's shoulder.

"You picked out your boat yet?"

"Getting there. Abby wants to save some for kitchen remodeling. My boat budget's down to six hundred grand, including a slip at the marina." Ross was nearly drooling over a picture of a glistening Chaparral 300 Signature cruiser with twin five-liter Mercury inboards. "Abby thinks she needs at least forty to redo the kitchen. Dang women come up with the craziest shit about spending money."

Stu was eyeing the pictures in the glossy brochures scattered over the desk. Pictures of shiny boats dashed over the glittering calm water of Lake Tahoe.

"Look at this one." Ross pointed to a twenty-nine footer. "Sleeps four."

"You won't be towing that with your Land Rover, fella. You're going to need a serious truck."

"Yeah, you're right. Been thinking about trading in anyway." Ross laid the brochure down, grabbed his coffee, and took a sip. "What're you going to do with yours?"

"I mentioned this a few days ago. I really want to escape the rat race and move. Relax. I'm not bailing on you. What do you think about me operating out of our New Orleans warehouse? I could spend a day or two in an office there every week. Set up a home office too. I'd keep the house here. Come back when you need me for special company functions and the like."

"What are you gonna do the other days?" Ross asked.

"Raise catfish in Alabama."

"Oh, dude. What's Tab think about that?"

"She doesn't know yet. I'm going to call this guy in Alabama again. He knows a lot about catfish farming. Get some more details. You know Tab. She usually supports my ideas but makes sure they're well-grounded. She's gonna put me through the wringer on this one, though."

"Dude, she's going to have you committed."

"No shit. I better have my facts down before I spring it on her. Might need you and Abby's help."

"Well, Stu, from a strategic standpoint, having you in the middle of the country may be a good move. You'd be closer to Jacksonville too. New Orleans definitely needs tweaking with management. Some stuff is hard to do over the phone, particularly the HR issues. Those Louisiana boys sure are hard on the women. I don't think a month goes by when we don't have a harassment issue."

"Well, look, I told HR not to relocate California girls in the New Orleans office with a bunch of Cajuns. I think we're down to two Valley girls." Stu walked over to the corner window. "Ten years ago, it never entered my mind we couldn't run CTC from LA. Now we've got assets in three other cities. It's time to get some upper management out there."

"I'm going to need someone to replace your duties here. Got anybody in mind?"

"Margo can do it. Make her our new senior vice president. She's loyal, dependable, and definitely qualified. The teams would approve the promotion. She's got the over-the-road experience. She can talk on their level. She's got more street cred than anybody on this floor."

"Yeah, Margo would be good. She's kinda rough on the edges, though. Still got that truckers' way about her. I don't see her doing well at cocktail parties drumming up new business. God, I bet she doesn't even own a dress." Ross winced.

"Yeah, I can't picture her wearing high heels. It's almost frightful thinking about it."

"We'll find someone for the public relations gigs. Abby and I may have to pick up the slack. Tab loved doing it. She'd make our customers melt."

Stu strolled over to the picture window. He gazed out at the smudged horizon.

"Guess we'll be entertaining a lot more in our new kitchen. Reckon I could deduct it as a business expense?"

"I wanna be that fly on the wall when the IRS agent asks where you got eight hundred thousand in cash to buy a new boat and a kitchen in the same year." Stu chuckled.

"Catfish farm? And just how long have you been trying to keep a goldfish alive?"

Stu put his hands on the steel ledge midway up the picture window. He peered out over twenty-five hundred square miles of concrete.

"Too damned long," he replied softly.

Ross walked up next to him, pulling Stu's shoulder sideways in a half hug. "Make me a promise, partner."

"What's that?"

"I get the first box of catfish off your farm."

CHAPTER SEVENTEEN

Stu poked his head in the doorway of Margo's office. He gripped both sides of the doorframe over his head. Margo was absorbed in a recent fax report, completely oblivious to her boss looking at her. He was afraid to interrupt for fear of startling her.

He feigned a shallow cough. Margo looked up. "Can you run interference for me while I'm on the phone? Tell Marcela to hold my calls."

"Yes, sir." She was studying a hot CTC incident report filed by the team leader, listing the who, what, why, when of a recent cluster. The company used them in case legal was pulled in. One hand propped up her right cheek. Her left middle finger was thumping the desk top as she read. Margo always did this when concentrating on something out of the ordinary. For the mundane crap, she squeezed her "Who Gives a Shit" stress reliever ball, uttering profanities to herself.

"What'cha working on?" Stu asked.

"Cluster for the day. Our female team had a little mishap at a truck stop in Springfield this morning. Some owner-operator got a little grabby with Lucille. Gayle kicked him in the plums. Maxine came along, finished him off with some kung fu shit. Asswipe ended up in the ER with cracked ribs and a rearranged face. Cops made a big deal out of it. Lucille and Maxine wanted to hit the road. The state police made them wait two hours during the investigation. Gayle pitched a fit. She's fretting about ruining her perfect delivery time record."

"The guy pressing charges?"

"Hell no. He's got outstanding warrants for domestic abuse in Iowa. Past due on child support too. A real piece of work. Asswipe is chained to the hospital bed as we speak."

"Trucking's fun isn't it, Margo?"

"Love every minute of it, Mr. Baron."

"That's good, Margo. I appreciate you too."

Stu turned to go to his door.

"I'll let Marcela know," Margo said as she looked up to admire her boss's backside. Baron still had that beach-god, lifeguard look. His sandy-blond hair was thinning on top. But she hadn't lost her desire to grind away on his boner. Her latest fantasy about doing it in the sleeper of a new Peterbilt resulted in a change of batteries for the love toy.

*****

Stu fished out the Alabama business card from the two-inch stack. The stack of cards needed to be filed in the almost-full Rolodex. He doubted he'd ever have time to do it. If he highlighted one word on each card, Win could file them alphabetically. Win had mastered the alphabet after his fourth birthday.

He dialed the number.

Destiny Peatman answered in her customary delightful voice. "Good morning, Alabama Fish Farming Center."

"Good morning, Destiny. This is Stuart Baron from Los Angeles again. How are you today?"

"Just peachy. How are you, Mr. Stuart Baron from Los Angeles?"

"Fine, thanks. Can I talk to Brian?"

"Sure, hold on just a second. He's headed to his desk now." Destiny winked at Brian. He was sorting the junk and good mail on the chest-high counter in front of Destiny's workstation.

Brian winked back. "Girl, what a stroke of luck this is." He darted down the recently waxed hallway.

He closed the door to his office and punched line one and the speaker button.

"Hello, Stu."

"Hello, Brian."

"Man, I'm glad you called back. I didn't write down your number. Destiny and I hoped you would call. We've had an interesting development since we last talked."

"What's that?" Stu asked.

"Well, it's tragedy for now and maybe good in the long run," Caine replied.

Stu sat up a little straighter in his chair. He fingered the smooth porcelain handle on his coffee cup. "Jeez, I hope this one ends well. I don't relish tragedies."

"We don't either. Anyway, let me fill you in. One of our producers was killed in a farming accident. He was bush hogging a pond levee and must have hit a hole. Maybe going too fast. The tractor flipped and crushed him. Killed him instantly. His wife found him after he didn't come in for supper. It's tragic because the tractor had a roll bar. He wasn't wearing his seat belt. He probably would have lived if he had been wearing it."

"Gosh, that's terrible. How's his wife holding up?" Stu asked, rubbing his forehead.

"Well, not good. The widow, Beverly Hopkins, is a close friend of mine. We graduated together in high school. I was a pallbearer at the funeral. She came up to me after the graveside service. Told me flat out to find someone willing to buy the farm. The quicker the better." Brian tapped a pencil on his legal pad. "Another pallbearer, a local real estate agent, agreed to handle the sale."

"How big is the farm?"

"It's three hundred acres of land and two hundred acres of water. I realize that's a little bigger than what you were planning on." Brian looked at his notes from an earlier conversation.

"What are some considerations from operating a farm that big?"

"Mostly labor. I know one farmer who used to operate a two-hundred-acre farm by himself. Come early August, he was a freaking zombie. Never got six hours of sleep at one time. He slept about three hours at night and took a three-hour nap after lunch. Worked like that from June through September. Wife and kids almost left him until he promised to get more help. That's no kind of life, man."

"Yeah, nuts on that. What are we looking at, labor-wise?" Stu asked.

"You're going to need an oxygen checker and a day laborer. The oxygen checker can work five nights straight, but he's gonna need weekends off. You may luck up, hire the rare soul who'll work two to three weeks straight. They're hard to find. Better plan on working weekend nights from May through September." Brian caught his breath. "There's only twenty ponds on the farm. Nice layout. All the ponds are in a tight grid, reducing travel time between ponds. You may get a two-, three-hour break during the night. It'll take a good hour to stick all the ponds on each check."

"Stick the ponds?" Stu asked.

"You ride along the levees in your pickup, stick an oxygen pole out the window into the top six inches of pond water, get an oxygen reading. Takes about two to three minutes for each pond. May have to hop out of the truck and turn aerators on and off too."

"And the day laborer?" Stu inquired.

Destiny knocked perfunctorily, came in his office, and poured freshly brewed coffee. Brian gave her a thumbs-up. She smiled. Brian gazed at her tight butt as she pranced out of his office.

She didn't mind the attention. Auburn's HR director could kiss her ass.

Brian sipped on the steaming-hot coffee. "Ah, the day laborer. Man, this guy is critical. You can get one that tears up shit just looking at it or someone who can tear down an engine and install new piston rings with a pair of vise grips. They have to be able to do it all, though—treat ponds, fix aerators, bushhog, run fish and water samples to the Fish Center. Basically help you manage the farm. You can call him a farm manager, but for a farm this size, a full-time farm manager may not be financially feasible."

"Okay, so what does the owner do in terms of daily work on the farm?" Stu asked, rubbing his forehead.

"You're going to do the number one job on the farm, which is feeding fish. This daily chore will make or break you financially. The feed conversion rate on the farm has the highest impact on profitability. Feeding the fish for this size farm is going to take you four hours every day from mid-April through mid-October. You can skip Sunday. When you're not feeding fish, you'll be helping your day laborer with two-man jobs like replacing aerator motors and gearboxes. Of course, you'll have to pull oxygen duty when your regular guy is off or sick."

"Sounds kinda relentless. I guess summer vacations are forbidden?"

"Well, it just depends how capable your day laborer is. If you trust him with the farm, you can make that call. The important thing is you gotta make time to look at the forest. Not just the trees. You gotta keep the cash flow going. Market your fish in a timely manner. Keep the banker happy."

"I guess now is a good time to discuss the money side." Stu grabbed another sharp pencil out of a cup and flipped to a new page on his legal pad.

"Man, you sitting down?"

"Yes, dude, bring it on." Stu chuckled.

"Well, like I said, it's three hundred acres of land with two hundred acres of water. Here's how it breaks down." Brian drew a deep breath. He moved his desk calculator closer to the phone. "The land is valued at eleven hundred an acre, so that's three hundred and thirty thousand. The ponds with all the infrastructure that goes with them—the feed bins, gravel roads, power supplies, and drain structures—have a value of six thousand per acre. The total pond value is one point two million, plus the three hundred thirty for the land, bringing us to a farm value of about one and a half million. Stu, you still there?"

"Yeah, dude. Still here. Just thinking what that amount of land would cost here in my suburb. Somewhere north of sixty million."

"Whew. Forget catfish farming out there, huh?"

"Only folks getting rich out here are the real estate agents."

"Now, there's a house, equipment shed, an old barn, and well house on the farm, valued at about a hundred grand."

Stu added up some numbers. "We're almost at one point seven now."

"Right on, bro. Now there's the equipment. I have a three-page list I can fax you. The top item being the pond aerators. There are thirty of them valued at two hundred thousand. The rest of the equipment is valued at another two hundred thousand. This includes all the tractors, trucks, tools, oxygen meters, boats, outboards, trailers, and emergency aerators. Equipment total is four hundred thousand. Bringing us to a grand total for the farm at two million and change."

Stu added up the exact amounts and wrote "2,030,000" on his legal pad in big bold numbers and circled it.

"So from what I hear you saying, I can write a check for two million dollars and start farming."

"Yeah, also saving hundreds of headaches from starting from scratch too. The farm's in good shape. It's only five years old. Ponds usually last about fifteen years before they need renovation."

"Anything else I need to know? What about the fish in the ponds?"

"Good question. Beverly wants to handle it this way. She appointed me as overseer. She's packing as we speak. Moving to Point Clear down on Mobile Bay. About as far away as she can get from here and still stay in Alabama."

"I understand that," Stu said.

"Each pond will be seined twice with a clean-out net. The net has a one-inch mesh and theoretically removes all fish over half a pound. Any fish remaining after the clean-out become full property of the new owner."

Stu thought for a few seconds. "Wow, I'm having a little trouble handling that data dump. We need to break it down. I'll be explaining this to my wife and business partner, so I need to get it right." He looked at her picture on his desk. She was settled down with Win on her lap in a lounge chair in the company's suite at the Los Angeles Memorial stadium.

"I'm sorry. Let me back up a bit. The ponds on the farm are managed in what we call a multiple batch system. What that means is you've got all sizes of fish in each pond. You could have fingerlings, these are anywhere from four to seven inches long. Stockers, which are longer, say around eight to twelve inches. And then your food fish sizes, from half a pound to four pounds. Hell, you may have freaking whales in there too, ten to twenty pounders. When the pond is seined with a clean-out seine, a long net with a one-inch mesh, all the fish smaller than half a pound work themselves through the mesh and escape. Most of the bigger fish are caught and hauled away to the processor."

Stu furiously scribbled. He hoped he could explain this to Tab and Ross. Ross was willing to roll the farm under the Coast to Coast umbrella.

Brian paused and sipped again on his coffee. "Stu, I can tell you this. Six of the twenty ponds were harvested in the last two months and restocked with fingerlings. You're getting over a hundred thousand dollars' worth of fingerlings, not to mention all the fish under a half pound. It's a pretty sweet deal for the buyer."

"Care to put a total value on the remaining inventory after the ponds are cleaned out?" Stu asked.

"Based on my experience with farm sales and leftover fish, my rough estimate would be a minimum fifteen hundred pounds per acre after a clean-out. For two hundred acres, you're looking at nearly three hundred thousand pounds of fish valued at eighty cents a pound. That's almost a quarter million dollars."

"Hopkins willing to leave that kind of money on the table?" Stu asked.

"Yeah, she is. I explained to her that we could seine all the fish up with a smaller meshed seine, basically catch all the fish, weigh them, and put them back in the pond. And then figure up their total value. Problem with that is stressing the fish and risk killing them in the process.

"Gosh, this is one hell of an investment. Like purchasing twenty-five new trucks in one swoop."

"Come again, Stu?" Brian Caine almost knocked over his half-empty coffee cup. A new tractor trailer cost eighty grand. His brother just financed one. He cosigned the note. He punched at his calculator. Two million dollars.

"Oh, my partner and I usually buy tractor trailers, Peterbilts usually, in large lots. We end up getting a pretty hefty discount that way."

Brian gulped. "What's the name of your trucking company?"

"Coast to Coast."

Damn, I've got the Bill Gates of trucking on the other end. Wait 'til I tell my brother.

Margo knocked and entered. She whispered, "Situation."

"Hey, Brian, I gotta run. Thanks. I'll go over all this with the wife and give you a call tomorrow."

"Okay, Stu. Looking forward to working with you."

They ended the phone call with pleasantries.

CHAPTER EIGHTEEN

Stu fixed Tab her favorite drink, a Long Island iced tea, while she put Win to bed. He nearly detested ordering the signature girly drink in their favorite bar, particularly when his bartender friend was slaving away filling drink orders, simultaneously keeping several hormone-infused, monthly synchronized barmaids from getting into the next catfight. The half jiggers of tequila, vodka, rum, and gin, a dash of triple sec, and a splash of Coke usually accompanied the harried expression, "Come on, dude. Can't you get laid with a rum and Coke?"

Stu didn't mind concocting them at the house. Tab would shed clothes after her second.

He took the drinks outside to the patio table. He sipped on his Guatemalan dark *anejo* as a gibbous moon crested Yucca Hill. The telescope was tucked away in the corner, covered with an old pillow case. The pool had taken on a darker-green sheen. The filter pump hummed in the fake hollow boulder next to the pool.

He contemplated the opening line for his self-admitted midlife crisis. It would be a doozy. He wondered if he made her drink strong enough.

Tab slid the patio door open. She had changed into a pair of white terry-cloth gym shorts and a tight pink T-shirt. The bra very evidently didn't make the wardrobe change. Her firm, perky, perfectly round natural Cs outlined the thin cotton. She smelled of coconut oil and lavender. Her hair was still damp from a steamy shower after her treadmill duel with a virtual Jillian Michaels.

Stu looked her over. He asked anyway, despite the super comfortable looking I'm-not-going-anywhere outfit. "Tab, would you come with me to the driveway?"

"How long is this going to take? I'm not dressed to get caught outside." She winked. "What if Donny sees me?"

"I wouldn't worry about Donny. I think he's gay."

"What makes you think so?"

"Just a hunch. Not ever being married. He never talks about women."

"Maybe I should go over. Ask for a bowl of sugar."

"Save it for another day. I need to show you something." Stu playfully swatted her *Nordic Track* butt as she slid the door open.

Stu opened the front passenger door of his Trooper and popped the glove box. He pulled out a thimble-sized piece of shiny metal, twirling it between his thumb and forefinger.

"What's that?" Tab asked.

"It's a rifle bullet. The window tech found it inside the back seat. He was curious if the bullet was still in the car after replacing the front windshield. Look here."

Stu pointed to the front passenger headrest. A grape-sized hole was centered in the headrest. The fabric was ripped open on the backside. Stu inserted a pencil through the front and back hole. The pencil angled slightly downward. It pointed to the middle of the back seat.

"The tech found it right here." Stu pointed to another tear in the fabric.

"Why are you showing me this?"

"That morning of the highway shooting was family day at the office. I was supposed to bring you and Win to work for breakfast biscuits. I completely forgot. If you had come, you or Win would have been shot. He always sits here when you ride up front, right?"

"Oh god, you're right, Stu."

"I want to move away from Los Angeles."

"What about the company?"

"I've already talked with Ross. He's okay with it. We think it would be a strategic move."

"Where?"

"Let's go back in the house. Our drinks are getting warm."

"I hope you made mine a strong one." Tab winced. She stared at the holes in the seats, her arms folded across her chest, tucking in the girls.

Stu savored his dark rum as Tab settled into the other padded wrought iron patio chair. She sipped on her tea.

"Okay, let me have it," Tab said, looking directly at him.

Stu took a deep breath. He peered into Tab's teal blue eyes, steeling himself for her initial reaction.

"I want to move to Alabama. Raise catfish on a farm."

She stared at him, gauging his seriousness. *He looked damn serious.*

She looked down at her drink, grabbed it, and took a good swallow. She stared out into the yard for a couple of seconds. And took another swallow, swirling the ice cubes as she gently placed the tall glass back down on the cork coaster.

"You can't keep a goldfish alive for a week. You can't be serious."

"It's gotta be the water."

"What do you know about catfish or, for that manner, farming?"

"To be perfectly honest, not a damned thing. But I've been talking to an extension agent in Alabama. He says he can help until I learn the basics. He's been very thorough. I've had some long discussions with him over the phone. He even found a farm for us, complete with a house and a swimming inventory."

"Okay. Let's back up some. What's an extension agent?"

"They work for a university. They're stationed in the field, away from campus. Mainly assist farmers with production problems." Stu took another sip. "Remember that show *Green Acres*? Mr. Douglas always asking that skinny guy, the ag agent, in the khaki pants, a farming question. He always shrugged his shoulders, saying, 'I'll get back to you on that.' Gosh, what was his name?"

Tab looked at him intently. She wasn't the least bit interested in Mr. Douglas or his idiot sidekick.

Stu returned the look. This was going pretty well so far. Tab hadn't recommended he see a shrink.

"Stu, let's back up again. Where in the Sam Hell did you get this idea about catfish farming?"

"Well, I guess it all started with a billboard advertising farm-raised catfish. And then I saw some ponds in Alabama on our trip back from Chicago. I called an ag agent in Alabama. Lots of people farming catfish in the southeast. You know, Red Lobster has it on the menu."

"Stu, you willing to give this up? Do you realize how good you have it here?"

"Give what up, Tab? Sitting on the freeway for two to three hours every day. The crime. Wondering if you and Win are safe during the day? I worry about that constantly. Look, I'm not abandoning anything here. Ross is okay with it. Like I said, he thinks it's a good move strategically. We'll keep the house. With CTC One, we can come back for quick visits and stay a little longer for Thanksgiving and Christmas. Hey, if it doesn't work out, we can come back to this rat race you call a lifestyle."

"This farm. Why, for God's sake, Alabama?" Tab's images of Alabama flooded her mind. That ignoramus governor standing in the schoolhouse door. The mugging of protestors on the bridge. And the standard interview of the hillbilly on national news after a tornado sucked his mobile home into the sky, leaving him in the bathtub with a chaw of tobacco in his cheek. She couldn't think of anything good ever coming out of Alabama.

"Alabama's a good place to raise catfish. Good water and a progressive catfish industry. My guy there says they're a close-knit group. They work together to solve problems. Mississippi and Arkansas have catfish farms, but they're in the delta. He says their living conditions are bleak as hell. Wanna hear something funny about their delta water?"

Tab finished off her drink, twirling the ice. "What's up with the water?"

"Those poor delta folks live with brown water every day. Something about the aquifers being full of organic matter. The water comes out of the ground looking like weak tea. The extension guy in Alabama says that's why the delta folks have a pissy attitude. They keep on flushing the toilet, and it stays shit brown. I thought it was funny."

Tab wasn't smiling. She studied her husband, wondering if he was truly serious, or better yet, this was all a dream.

She pinched her arm. *It wasn't a dream.*

Tab asked, looking into Stu's eyes, "What about Win? You know how smart he is. How's he gonna do there? Alabama isn't exactly known for strong education. Don't they usually rank dead last?"

"Well, yes, that's true. I checked. They share hind tit with Mississippi. I figure we'll have to fill in at home. You have an education degree, Tab." She stayed on the dean's list at UCLA until her senior year. He drifted off for a second.

"Stu, are you sure about this? Come on, give me the real reason you want to make this drastic change."

Stu focused back on the conversation. "Tab, Los Angeles isn't a place to raise a family. I see things on the way to work that makes me wonder if the human race is reverting backwards. The lack of respect for others. The callousness about life. The highway shooting capped it. Remember, if you had been there. God, it could have been the end for us."

Tab winced. Scratched her head. Regrouped. "I love you. I trust you want to do the best for me and Win. If you really think," she grabbed both his hands, squeezing them, "this is a good move for us and you're absolutely sure, we'll give it a go."

Stu and Tab's eyes met. They gazed at each other. The look of complete trust with each other's life. Stu blinked first. He needed to atone for the week of watching the moon.

"Tab, I'm sorry about my devious behavior pretending to be Galileo."

She looked at the telescope behind Stu's shoulder. "That stung a little, especially you springing it on me in front of Ab and Ross. Water under the bridge now. Don't make a habit out of it, okay?"

"I promise." Stu finished his drink. "I'm wondering. I expected a little more hysteria. You're holding back."

"Well, the way I see it, this could end up being a very expensive vacation from hell. You may decide it isn't what you bargained for. You can always sell the farm, right? I doubt it'll sink the company if it doesn't work out. Ross isn't stupid."

Stu nodded. "I'll use most of the loot for operations, so it's not that big of a risk. The company will actually own the farm. Ross said it'd be a good tax write-off due to all the depreciable equipment."

She continued, "We're keeping the house so we can always come back. We'll have steady income from the company. Win hasn't started school yet. This midlife crisis of yours may crash and burn. It's not like it's a huge gamble unless you're a fish and Stu Baron's in charge of your life." She grinned. "I'm up for the grand experiment."

She took a deep breath. "Seriously, though, I don't feel safe here anymore either. Besides the violence, it's getting too crowded. The other day I was thinking, what if the power or water went out for three or four days? What would people do? I read the other day that grocery stores would run out of food in less than a week if trucks couldn't get diesel. There would be absolute panic. People would turn into animals…"

She looked off into the night sky. She remembered the twinkling stars she slept under while at Girl Scout camp in the Sierra Madres.

"Tab, they're already animals. They just don't realize it yet. Benson says you can put people into three basic groups: sheep, wolves, and sheepdogs. Main problem, the way he sees it, there won't be enough sheepdogs when, not if, the shit hits the fan. Way too many sheep. The wolves eventually take over. He worries about having enough bullets."

"I need another drink," Tab said.

Stu got up and bent over, kissing Tab on her forehead.

"Can we see the stars where we're going?"

"Ten four on that, girl."

CHAPTER NINETEEN

Abby couldn't wait to show off her new kitchen. The going-away party for Stuart and Tabitha just had to be held at their house. Abby insisted. Ross pleaded half-heartedly for making a reservation at the private golf course's five-star restaurant. Her hands on the hips posture indicated it wasn't worth the theatrical revisit to the OK marriage corral. Ross had written a check for forty-one grand for stainless steel everything. Abby was very proud of her imported Brazilian teak cabinets. Ross marveled at the immense new double-doored refrigerator. It was big enough to hang the next feral goat that wandered into the yard. He loved the new pony keg dispenser and built-in beer tap at the wet bar. The oven was big enough to roast a harem of turkeys. The microwave reminded him of the MRI at the sports medicine clinic. He wondered if the lag screws attaching the power meter to the side of the house were long enough. He joked with Stu that Hoover Dam would keep one more turbine running just for Abby.

Their comfortable villa home, perched on a sheer cliff, overlooking the Pacific on the very top of Caballero Vista, was bathed in a gentle sea breeze. The aromatic smoke of mesquite charcoal from the new six-burner stainless steel Viking grill wafted into the air. The lingering aroma of blazing Angus porterhouse steaks wafted through the gated community of Torrance Estates.

Abby showed off her new kitchen to Tab and Margo. Stu, Ross, and Terry leaned against the deck's side railing, watching colorful sailing yachts ply the blue waters between Long Beach and Santa Catalina Island.

"Terry, Stu and I have something for you while the ladies are inside. We figured we'd tell you in private."

Terry Benson took a hefty sip of his Evan Williams and 7 Up. "Now what are you two cooking up?"

"We're promoting Margo to vice president for operations. Given your ability to work with her on a professional level and the equal amount of time served, we're giving you a similar promotion to vice president for security. Specifically, like you've already been doing, looking after our company assets. Now you'll be handling the clusters in Stu's absence. Of course, Margo will be asked to weigh in as appropriate. She knows this country inside and out. Being a former trucker, she has the respect of our teams," Ross said.

"We want you to find a security assistant to cover your current field duties since you will be working on the floor now," Stu added.

"You okay with that, Terry?" Ross asked.

"Sounds good. Who gets your office?" Terry asked Stu.

"Nobody," Ross interrupted. "That's always going to be Stu's office." Ross pointed the greasy, steaming steel meat flipper at Benson and then at Margo on the other side of the sliding patio door. "Stu knows he can come back anytime. He may decide this catfish farming gig is for the birds."

Stu laughed. "Ross may be right. My track record with goldfish makes me wonder if I can pull this off."

"Terry, we'll get you situated on the floor somewhere. Pick which one of the office girls you want for your AA."

"Marcela's off limits. I want her answering the main line. She still makes me melt when I hear her voice," Stu said.

"I need to pick one that can run interference when Margo gets hormonal," Terry deadpanned.

"Dude, I'd recommend Jaky Bostich. She's one of those Iron Maiden ultramarathoners. She's got more testosterone than the three of us put together. She could hold her own with the butch in there," Ross said, looking toward Margo. She had just twisted the pry cap off her second Olympia with her bare hand.

"What'da think, Stu?" Terry asked.

"Give her a shot. Messing with female dynamics on the floor is always unpredictable. Everything seems to be clicking right now. Promoting Jaky to AA can cause ripple effects we men can't even fathom. The VP at our auditing firm says she'd rather manage fifty men then twelve women. You think men can be cruel on a battle-field? They can't hold a candle to the shit that goes on in an office."

"Amen to that," Ross said as he flipped the burners off and placed the steaks on the top rack of the grill. "We're good to go here."

The ladies appeared with the platters of side dishes. Win and Benny lit the votive candles on the patio table and then disappeared back into the house. They were feasting on hot pizza out of the new stainless steel gas-fired pizza oven.

The adults grabbed a seat around the patio table. Stu, Tab, Ross, and Abby sat across one another. Terry and Margo were at opposite ends of the table, out of knife's reach but still within pistol dueling range. A seagull laughed off in the distance. An American flag motif wind sock billowed in the breeze on a corner deck post.

Ross popped the cork on the first bottle of Austrian Pinot Noir, stood, and poured glasses for everyone. He stayed standing, propos-ing a toast and a meal blessing.

"To Stu, Tab, and Win on their new Alabama adventure. Please, God, show mercy on their souls. Amen."

With that, Abby playfully punched Ross in his hip. Stu and Tab grinned at each other.

Ross sipped at his wine and the rest did likewise. "We wish you the best in your new adventure. In a way, I envy your desire to go somewhere where you can see the stars at night, listen to the whip-poorwills, dodge the armadillos, and watch the kudzu snatch your mailbox and drag it into the woods."

"Okay, my turn." Abby stood, pointing a finger at her husband. "Sit down if you can't be serious for once," she said, stiffly poking him in his chest. Ross playfully grimaced and sat down.

She raised her wine glass. "To the best friends in the world. You two are going to set the world on fire. And I can't wait to eat Baron Catfish."

Everyone chinked their wine glasses and sipped.

Ross said, "Okay, let's eat before it gets any colder."

As they ate, the sun melted into the ocean. Twilight gripped the sky in a mosaic of light blues, yellows, and orange hues. They watched the last sliver of crescent orange disappear below the horizon. Win and Benny reappeared with long-necked Bic lighters, lighting the cotton wicks of the half-dozen tiki torches along the railing.

"How was the pizza?" Abby asked.

"Mommy, absolutely fab-u-lous," Benny said, mimicking his mom's latest favorite phrase. Win nodded affirmatively. "We're going downstairs and play Nintendo."

"Okay, boys," Tab said.

"Those two are going to miss each other, aren't they?" Margo asked.

"They've become best buddies for sure. Hey, we're not disappearing forever. We'll have our home, and with CTC One, we'll be able to visit easily enough. CTC still has a skybox at the arena. Hopefully we can make it back for some of the home games later in the season," Stu said.

"Speaking of the company, Stu and I have good news for you and Terry," Ross announced, looking directly at Margo.

Tab smiled. She placed her hand on Stu's upper thigh under the table.

Ross said, "To our new vice presidents, Margo Sue Follor and Terry Benson."

Tab, Stu, and Abby raised their wine glasses, exchanged clinks, and sipped, waiting for the reactions of the newly named execs of Coast to Coast Trucking. Margo gasped slightly, wiping away a tear in the corner of her right eye. Terry feigned surprise, stood, and shook hands with Stu and Ross.

Margo and Terry looked at each other with forced smiles. It would be a cool détente, a warming of relations coupled with continued professionalism, maybe eventually overcoming their personal baggage from the failed office romance. They were, above all, fierce company loyalists. The dual promotion might become a forged bond of cooperative spirit.

"Both of you will be working closer to Ross and dealing with the clusters in my absence. Ross needs to spend more of his time looking at the forest and not the trees, concentrating on the changing world of trucking. Maintaining our competitive edge. We'll have a phone in Alabama in case you need to discuss pressing internal matters. I'll still provide input on selecting teams based on their personality profiles. I'll conduct interviews at the New Orleans locker."

Margo and Terry nodded. Mr. Baron wasn't riding off into the sunset. He was dividing up responsibilities, taking his main duty of running general operations, spreading it out to two capable individuals. One would be running operations, the other looking after company assets.

Looking to get away from all the talk about company business, Abby asked, "Have you two heard the story on how Tab and I met Stu and Ross?"

"No, I haven't," Terry replied.

"I haven't either, but I'd love to hear it." Margo realized how strong and devoted the bond was between Mr. Baron and his wife. The love between them was as deep as the water where the sun just disappeared. She also realized she wasn't in the same league with Tabitha Baron. She was nearly perfect in every respect. Loving life in general. Truly affectionate with friends. A compassionate listener. An adoring mother. Margo's troubled upbringing in a fractured, violent home hadn't honed many parenting skills. She realized her clock was ticking louder. The one-night stands didn't hold out much promise. That grandbaby momma wanted wasn't on the horizon. Maybe the promotion would entice someone down the road. Get some better digs. *Stop living like damned trailer trash.*

Stu started off. "Terry and Margo, this is what's known as the Deaf Parrot Story. Sure to go down in the annuals of how not to go about asking a girl for a first date."

"Amen, bro." Ross chuckled.

"Listen, while you two fill in Terry and Margo, I'm going to put up this food and pack it for your trip tomorrow. Eat in a picnic area instead of those nasty truck stops you men love for some godforsaken reason," Abby said.

"We like our truck stops because you never see neat tattoos in the butt cracks of women in picnic areas," Stu said.

Benson added, "You guys ever notice that a butterfly above a butt crack of a young girl turns into a damned cockroach when she turns gray? Happened to my sister." Tab and Abby stared at him, finishing their wine with a bottoms-up gulp.

"Well, on that pleasant note, I'll get started on putting this food up," Abby said.

"I'll help," Tab said as she rose out of her seat. "Those steaks were awesome, Ross." She bent over Ross's shoulder from behind, planting a soft kiss on his cheek. Ross reached over his left shoulder with his right arm and squeezed Tab's face against the side of his. "I love you, girl." This display of affection affirmed for Margo that love among friends existed outside the coveted bond of marriage.

Benson realized how tightly woven the friendship was between the Barons and the Whitestones. It was more than a business partnership. More of a brotherhood. He hadn't witnessed one this strong since Vietnam, bringing back badly wounded SEALs in his patrol boat. He drifted back in time, thinking about his days as a Swick, rescuing SEALs in the fog of the Mekong delta. He surmised that this was why Mr. Baron obsessed so much about putting driver teams together with the right personalities. If he could get a team working together, the bonding, the forging spirit of comradery, combined with the company mission, it would ensure that goals would be met and often surpassed. This was the creed of the elite teams in the Navy, without the blood, sweat, and tears.

Tab and Abby, each carrying plates of leftover food—jicama coleslaw, bacon-wrapped asparagus spears, boiled jumbo shrimp sprinkled with Cajun seasoning, blueberry pie—met inside at the kitchen island. Abby opened up an overhead cabinet, pulling out empty plastic containers and matching lids. Tab walked up behind her and put her hands around Abby's thin, rock-hard waist.

"I'm going to miss you, girl," Tab said softly.

Abby turned around and held Tab's hands in hers. "Hey, you call me whenever you feel like talking."

"You know I will. Abby, what do you think? Is this crazy or what?"

"When Ross first told me, I thought yeah, this is just about the craziest thing he has ever come up with. Farming, and then crazier yet, fish farming."

"Abby, he can't even keep a goldfish alive."

"I know. Listen, girl, he's your husband. Remember your vows. Through thick or thin, no matter what."

"Abby, what would you do if Ross wanted to do the same thing?"

"Probably shoot him. Put him out of his misery. Flush him down the john in pieces, like a goldfish," Abby deadpanned and then cracked a smile.

"Yeah, that's what I thought you'd say."

"Win going to be okay with the move?" Abby asked.

"Oh, he's excited about it. I don't think it's dawned on him that he's not going to see Benny all the time."

"Yeah, Benny seems pretty nonchalant about it too. Funny how young boys react to life changing events like this. It'd be a little more traumatic for a teenager in high school, though.

"Oh, definitely," Tab said as she rinsed off a plate under the stainless steel faucet.

"What are you worried about the most, Tab?" Abby asked as she wrote *shrimp* on a strip of masking tape.

"I guess Win's schooling. Getting started in first grade. Doing well. He gets bored easily, you know."

"You'll just have to fill in, Tab. Use that MRS degree we got through the grace of God." They both chuckled. "He'll be all right. Might turn into a farm boy instead of your nuclear engineer though." Abby giggled.

"Well, I agree with the boys in terms of being more strategic for the company. Having Stu closer to the hubs," Tab said.

"What about the farm? A house, I assume," Abby asked.

"Stu says the farm's only five years old, so I assume the house is still in good shape. He says the biggest difference will be not having any close neighbors. He thinks he'll be taking a wiz off the porch whenever he wants to."

"Pepper spray can fix indecent exposure in a hurry." Abby chuckled.

"Amen to that, girl."

"Tab, did you see the size of the latest partner draw?

"Yeah, I glanced at our bank statement before we came over."

"One point two for the past three months. Those guys set a new record." They looked outside toward the patio. Both Stu and Ross were waving their hands and talking back and forth, laughing at each other. Terry and Margo were eating up their bosses animated mannerisms. "That's another reason I'm not having major qualms about the move. Whatever they touch, it turns into gold."

"Catfish..." Abby winced.

"What color are they?" Tab wondered.

*****

Stu took a long sip of his wine, draining the crystal flute. Ross obliged with a refill.

Stu began, "As you know, Ross and I started with a 1979 Mack Midliner. It was the first model year for Mack van bodies. The serial number was double ought fifty. We always wondered if number fifty-one was also a piece of shit. We bought it with about two million miles on it. The engine had about five hundred thousand miles since the last rebuild. No way would that sucker pass an emissions test nowadays. That right, Ross?"

Ross quipped, "That sucker burned more oil than my two-cycle outboard. We debated about adding oil to the diesel just to keep it lubricated. Man, it could burn some oil."

Stu continued, "We started out moving students on our weekends to their new jobs after graduation. We'd pack them up on a Friday afternoon, drive all night if we had to, unload their stuff Saturday, and make it back Sunday. We made good money if we could haul for at least three students and do it as a circle route. We drove all over California."

"Found out quick like that this is a huge state. We didn't realize how big it was. It's freaking seven hundred miles from San Diego to the Oregon border," Ross said.

"About like Texas. Driving east to west. Takes all day to get anywhere," Margo added.

"I'd prefer stoned hippies in Northern California over Texas cowboys any day," Terry swigged his wine. "Them cowboys shoot back." He wiped his chin with the back of his hand.

Margo nodded and smiled at Terry. The wine was working on her. *Maybe one more time in the sack...*

"Well, we get this call from two roommates on the other side of campus. They were living in a university duplex. They both had been hired by a new elementary school up in Redding. Of course, this is a no-brainer for us. Same pickup and drop-off. They were sharing another duplex. We were hoping that we'd get a third moving to San Fran along the way. Glad we didn't. They had more shit than our truck could hold. We left their worn-out sleeper sofa sitting on the curb."

Stu took another sip. "Abby had a VW Super Beetle. No trunk space whatsoever. The front trunk was the gas tank and the four gerbils for an engine were in the rear trunk. The back seat was barely big enough for their overnight bags."

"No room for the parrot," Ross added as if on cue.

"Yeah, Tab had this pet parrot supposedly from the Amazon."

"What was his name, Ross? I keep forgetting."

"Chico."

"Chico, the deaf parrot." Stu chuckled.

"Deaf?" Terry inquired.

"Yep, deaf. Tab bought him at a pet store for a real good price. Seems no one wanted a deaf and dumb parrot. The pet store couldn't unload him. They were going to turn him loose in the city park. You buy a parrot so you can talk with him, right?" Stu asked rhetorically.

Terry and Margo nodded.

"Well, this parrot came with a big cage. Tab wouldn't let us put him in the back because it'd be too hot. So he ends up riding in the middle with us in the cab."

Margo scooted her chair back and crossed her legs, brushing her short dark-brown almost-butch hair back behind her ears, tilting her head to one side, trying to exude some delicate femininity. Benson offered a fleeting smile. She remembered that she hadn't shaved her legs in weeks. *Oh well, some more wine and he won't give a shit.*

Benson was thinking along the same lines. Margo had drifted again into the six-pack category. The two cocktails and wine brought back images of her thick patch of brown kinky hair, unshaved since puberty.

"Well, we're headed up the road towards Redding, which is like five hundred miles or so. Back in those days before the interstate, it was a good twelve-hour haul."

Ross noticed the eye looks between Margo and Terry. He filled both their glasses. *They were progressing well past the truce.*

"Okay, so it's me, Ross, and Chico, the deaf parrot," Stu continued. "Well, being guys, we naturally start talking about girls and specifically these two girls. Ross and I weren't dating anyone at the time. You can imagine what we were thinking. Abby and Tab didn't seem to be attached. They weren't wearing rings. No beaus hanging around when we left. They were moving to new territory, so we figured they were unencumbered. All the baggage they left behind was miles to the south."

Not all the baggage. Stu stopped talking, now lost in a new train of thought. Ross looked at Stu. He winced at Stu's familiar uneasiness at this juncture in the story. It wasn't about the damned parrot.

"Excuse me for a second." Stu got up and walked to the railing, peering out into the darkness of the ocean. The half-moon reflected off the rippled water. This juncture of the story brought back troubled times. It was a dark secret shared between the two couples. Tabitha Fuller's past still haunted their marriage.

"Stu, you good?" Ross asked.

"Yeah, go ahead, Ross. Just need a second, dude."

Ross picked up with the story. "I started talking about Abby. I was attracted to her smile at first. The way her dimples formed when she smiled. All through college, I had this thing for dark brunettes. I think Sandra Bullock is the prettiest actress ever. I lived for her movies."

Terry visualized the actress. She had a lot in common with the willowy Abby Whitestone. Long slender legs. Trim, athletic, lissome body. Dark long hair, doe-like brown eyes, and a gorgeous come-hither smile. Her movie *Speed* and the hijacked bus was Terry's favorite.

"Stu had taken up an interest in Tab. We double-dated a lot through college. Stu preferred golden blondes with flashy, showy manes like Farrah Fawcett. Tab's easygoing nature and bubbly personality was the major attraction then."

Stu was still gazing into the shimmering waters of the Pacific, flashes of diamond-bright light flickered with the moon's reflection.

He said to no one in particular, "It still is."

Ross continued. "So there we are, driving north in the Mack, killing major blocks of time being boys. Cutting up about sex, booze, and all the girls we had dated, talking some business, of course, and then the conversation would revert back to Abby and Tabitha. We decided to go for it. Shacking up with them for the night instead of a motel was the game plan. We'd ask them out for pizza and beer after we unloaded."

"And there sits Chico, every time I look at him, his eyes are closed. I remember telling Stu, 'Damn, this parrot sure does sleep a lot.' Stu was hoping Tab didn't pay too much for a stupid bird. You all know how tight Stu is. He didn't hang with girls with rich-daddy spending habits."

Stu grinned, sat back down, and glanced at Ross. They exchanged the-everything-is-cool look. Tab and Abby pranced through the patio doorway, giggling about Ross shelling out half a million in cash in front of the boat dealer.

"Well, boys, where are we?" Abby inquired.

"Ross got the bird post out of the truck and is hanging Chico's cage in the corner of the living room. The pizza delivery guy just left." Stu grinned.

"All right then, just in time for the best part," Tab said.

Terry and Margo leaned slightly forward in their seats.

"So the pizza has arrived. We're munching away, washing it down with Olympia. Stu and I are ravenous after unloading all that girly stuff. Our mouths are slam full. Tab and Abby are digging in. Starting to relax." Ross pauses, gulps the rest of his wine. "This high-pitched voice behind us shrieks, 'Abby. Nice ass.' Now I'm looking at Stu. His eyes as big as saucers."

"Then the voice shrieks, 'Tab. Perfect tits.'"

"Then three freaking times with squawks in between, 'Horny! *Squawk!* Horny! *Squawk!* Horny! *Squawk!*' Ross imitated the parrot squawks perfectly.

"Stu yells at the bird, 'Deaf parrot, my ass!'"

"'Deaf parrot my ass. *Squawk!* The bird answers back."

"Tab and Abby started laughing then. Then we start laughing, and well, the rest is history."

Margo bawled with laughter for a minute or so, wiping happy tears off her cheeks. Benson laughed until his side developed a cramp. He got up and walked it out. Margo left to find a bathroom and reapplied her discounted Kmart lipstick.

Win and Benny were summoned, taking turns with Abby's Nikon. They all stood for a picture with the moonlit ocean behind them using the timer function.

Terry and Margo left first after a few winks and whispers.

Stu, Tab, and Win pulled out of the driveway in their silver BMW. As they pulled past the ornate black wrought iron gate at the foot of the hill, Ross wiped a lone tear off his cheek.

"You can't ask for better friends." Ross sniffled.

Abby squeezed him around his waist with one arm, looking at her husband's wet eyes. "They'll be all right."

"I sure hope so. Alabama's a different world."

PART TWO

CHAPTER TWENTY

Nighthope Catfish Farm, Bellevue, Alabama

The Baron family rolled into the driveway of the Nighthope Catfish Farm around nine in the morning after spending the night in Meridian, Mississippi. The CTC truck and its uncooled reefer trailer was about an hour behind them, unable to keep up with CTC Two, Baron's darting, lane-nimble silver Beemer. Wingless but fast. The team stuck to the company-mandated sixty-mile-an-hour speed limit. They enjoyed the new territory. Leaving I-10 for I-59 at Slidell, viewing the rolling scenery of the interior of Mississippi was a nice change. The dinner with the family at Big Mike's Steakhouse, on Mr. Baron, was the highlight of their trip.

Leftovers from the twenty-four-ounce porterhouses were secured in foam clamshells inside the mini refrigerator purring away in the sleeper. Driver Barney "BB" Barton chirped to his two teamers after leaving the restaurant, "We'll be shitting bricks for a week after eating all that red meat."

Stu had seen distant pictures of the farmhouse sent by the real estate agent. Tab stared at it up close through the windshield.

"Oh, Stuart, this isn't good."

"I'm sorry, Tabitha."

"What's wrong, Mommy?"

"It's just not what I was expecting."

The farmhouse rested on a dozen cement block piers visible through the white vinyl lattice board skirting the rectangular frame.

White vinyl molding ran vertically down the middle of the end of the house, covering the seam. The double-wide mobile home looked fairly new. The metal roof appeared intact. The treated wood porch in the front of the home was recently stained. A preformed set of concrete steps leaned against the front of the porch. An obvious attempt at improving the curb appeal included a freshly cut yard of thick centipede grass.

"The key should be hanging on a nail on the back side of the mailbox post." Stu winced as he studied Tab's reaction to the new digs. He dreaded the eventual emotional firestorm. It'd be a crucifixion ala Tabitha.

Tab regrouped. Faked a smile. "I'll get them. I saw some interesting flowers in the planter box." Tab noticed the square box made with stacked railroad ties. Freshly mulched with brown pine bark. Several flowers that she recognized right off were blooming. She had seen their pictures in a Southern gardening magazine. They looked like daylilies. She longed to start flower gardening since the yard back in California was too small. It was one of the things she looked forward to with the move. She approached the planter and reached for the mailbox post.

She froze. "Oh my god!" she screamed.

Win and Stu dropped their overnight bags, running toward her. She backed up several feet, pointing at the mulch inside the planter box.

"What's the matter?" Stu yelled as he approached his trembling wife. Win stood behind his dad. They huddled together.

"There's a snake in there."

"Where?" Stu yelled again.

Win inched a little closer. "There it is, Daddy. It's huge."

A thick six-foot gray rat snake was coiled up next to the wood post. Its spindly tail vibrating in the mulch, obviously alarmed by the approaching two-leggers.

"What are we going to do?" Tab asked.

"I don't know anything about snakes here. Maybe I can find a stick or something. Get him moving."

Tab grabbed Win, backing up a bit more. Stu returned with a garden rake he found in the backyard storage shed. After a few prods, the snake slithered over a tie and crossed the road into the ditch. Win snatched the key off the post and handed it to his dad.

"Win, go check out the backyard. There's something back there you might like."

"And look out for more snakes. Don't wander off. Come right back, Win," Tab added.

Stu inserted the key into the dead bolt. As Tab entered through the doorway, she noticed the door jam. It wasn't even four inches thick. Her dad was a professional carpenter. She had helped him install countless locksets with her nimble hands during summer breaks. Ordinarily, a stud wall was at least five inches thick with the interior drywall, a three-and-a-half-inch stud, and an inch of exterior insulation and siding.

"Stu, these walls are made with half studs. I could kick this door in myself." She studied the beige living room wall. She located several poorly-mudded-in drywall screws. The wall studs were on twenty-four-foot centers, not the customary stronger sixteens. She no longer wondered why mobile homes disintegrated in high winds.

"You better think about a storm shelter. I'm not lying down in that ditch with the snakes."

"Ten four on that."

Win bounded in the door behind Tab. "Mommy, there's a four-wheeler in the backyard. I need the key."

"Hold on, feller." Tab walked to the back wall of the trailer and peered out a window. A bright-red Honda ATV was parked next to the garden shed. "Oh shit," she murmured. "Win, those things are dangerous. We'll have to get someone to show us how to operate it."

They heard the hiss of the CTC tractor trailer's parking brake. Tab stared at Stu. "We need to talk."

"Win, how about going outside and hang out with the team. Stay out of the way while they're unloading. Mommy and I need some special time."

"Okay, Daddy." Special time meant Daddy was about to get cruci-fried. Win jumped off the cement steps and ran toward the truck as the men clambered out.

"Dammit, Stu, do you realize what's going to happen next? Those men will tell everyone in the company that the Barons are living in a f——ing trailer in the middle of Alabama. Damn, I can't believe this is happening." She stared out the front window as Win high-fived the team.

"Tab, look at me. There's no way I'm going to make you live in a trailer for the rest of your life. Let's give it some time, okay? Brian says that it's common to employ a farm manager and provide a house. Maybe we can use this for the farm and see about building a real home. Please, be patient, okay?" Stu pulled his wife toward him and hugged her tightly. She nestled her face on his firm pecs, pinching him hard on his waistline. He grimaced.

"Stu, you're something else. You know that?"

"Tab, I can't do this without you. We're a team, right?"

She pinched his side again. "Come on, feller, we got a truck to unload."

*****

BB looked both ways and pulled out of the driveway onto the dirt road. "Bro, I sure hope the boss and Miss Tab are going to be okay."

Javoris Washington grabbed the truckers' atlas out of the side door pocket and dumped it on his lap. "Shee-it, man, going from a million-dollar home to a double-wide, my wife would've shot me in the balls, twice."

Willy Holmes quipped from the sleeper cab. "What you talking about, bro? My old lady would've tied my black ass up, threw me under the trailer, and set it on fire."

"Bossman's got his hands full now. Keeping the missus happy, fending off the crackers, raising two hundred acres of fish. He's gonna miss managing a fleet of psycho drivers," BB said.

"And poor Win. That boy doesn't have a clue what's coming next living around here," Willy added.

*****

Stu's Ironman beeped on the nightstand in the bright sunlit bedroom. He shucked the single bedsheet, walked over to the bedroom window, and gazed out. A catfish pond bordered the yard. He could see the aerator in the far corner throwing water several feet into the air. Several white long-legged herons lounged around on the levee. Sunlight filtered through the trees on the eastern edge of the farm. Bunches of Spanish moss, hanging off the lower branches of a bald cypress tree on the edge of the spacious yard, waved in the slight breeze. Stu smiled at the change of scenery. He was excited about his first full day on the farm. His giddiness was like waking up on a snowy Christmas morning as a youngster, marveling at the tree surrounded by brightly wrapped presents.

Tab stirred, struggling to wake up. "What time is it?"

"Well, here it's seven. Back in crazy land, it's five."

Stu disappeared into the master bath.

Tab flung the covers off, swung her legs over, and peered out the window at the expanse of rectangular ponds. A pickup truck drove slowly along the main levee. The herons took flight and regrouped further away.

"Day one, here I come," she murmured.

Stu stood in the living room, staring up at the cheap molding strip covering the gaping, ill-fitting seam in the ceiling peak where the two halves of his new home came together. He desperately craved a positive moment to placate Tab's newest anxieties about the move. One of her three suitcases remained unpacked.

Win, on the other hand, could barely contain his enthusiasm about the new digs. The Honda would be one more steep learning curve.

Fortunately, the previous owner's only farm employee, Guy Colback, graciously agreed to work the night after their arrival. He had another job lined up. He'd be working for the first time in his life

139

in air-conditioning, at the John Deere dealership, performing routine maintenance on riding mowers, weed whippers, and chainsaws.

The doorbell rang. Baron looked at his watch, 8:02. There was a middle-aged man standing outside on the front porch.

"Mr. Caine is here."

"Okay, I'll be right there." Tab was in the master bathroom wondering what a farmwife should wear when company comes. She opted for blue jeans and a loose pull-over blouse, white ankle socks, and tennis shoes. She brushed her blond mane back. A ponytail would have to do for now.

Win bounded out of his bedroom wearing soccer shorts and a UCLA T-shirt. Raring to go.

Stu opened the front door with Win at his side.

"Good morning, Stu. Who's this young man?" Brian bent slightly, extending his hand.

Win stuck his hand out, firmly shaking Mr. Caine's hand. "I'm Winchester Baron. You can call me Win."

"Okay, Win. Good to meet you. Looking forward to your first day on the farm?"

"Daddy says we need to feed the fish today. I had four goldfish. Fed them every day until they died."

"Well, maybe the catfish will do a little better." Brian grinned at Stu.

Stu laughed. "After writing that check last week, they'd better perform circus acts."

Tab appeared at the front door. "Brian, this is my wife, Tabitha."

Tab said, "Brian Caine. Good to finally meet you. Stu's always saying good things about you."

Caine nearly stuttered, momentarily stunned by the beautiful, winsome woman delicately holding his hand. If mortals could melt, this would be the closest he'd get to morphing into a mindless glob. He stammered out a reply, "Well, I hope I can make your move here as smooth as possible. Moving from California to Alabama will be a shock in more ways than one. Just wait 'til you see what we eat around here."

"Speaking of food, we have fresh cinnamon rolls. If you give me a minute, I'll find the box of coffee cups," Tab said.

"The neighbors up the road brought the rolls last night. Really nice people. They were wearing bonnets," Stu said.

"They're Mennonites. It's a religious group, similar to the Amish colonies in the Midwest. They're a little more advanced than the buggy riders. Not hooked up to cable TV yet. They have weather radios. Real friendly folks. They take their religion seriously. Have their own schools."

"Their own schools?" Tab inquired.

"Yes, ma'am. I'm not sure if they take in outsiders. Probably have to be Mennonite to attend. Next time I see their minister, I'll ask. He raises catfish too."

"Thanks, Brian. Appreciate that." Tab rubbed Win's kinky hair. "Win attended Montessori for a couple of years. He's ready for first grade."

Both men made their way to the round kitchen table. Talked about the move and the farm. Win opened the door of the refrigerator. It was almost bare. Only a six-pack of full-strength Coca-Colas remained. Left behind by Mrs. Hopkins.

Tab dug through packing boxes, looking for the cups. Mr. Coffee belched a cloud of steam, gurgled for a few seconds, and hissed as the decanter filled.

"Mommy, can I have a Coke?"

"Win, I suppose just this one time since there's no milk. Stu, we gotta get groceries today. We don't have anything for lunch. If I have to eat another cinnamon roll with Coke, I'll be looking for a fishing pole. It'll be catfish sushi for lunch, dude."

Brian smiled. "There's a grocery store in Bellevue. A Piggly Wiggly. Right on the highway on the south side of town. You can't miss it."

"Tab, I need to stay here with Brian. Can you manage by yourself?"

"Yeah, I can handle it. Win, wanna come along?"

"Aw, Mommy. I really want to stay here with Daddy. Can I please?" Win begged.

"Okay. You boys go have your fun. Don't be complaining when I come back with strange food. You had your chance."

Tab disappeared into the bedroom, wondering what one wears grocery shopping in Alabama. She looked at the round thermometer attached to the outside frame of the bedroom window. Eighty-two degrees. It was only eight thirty. She opted for a bright-yellow mid-calf sundress.

The boys finished savoring their sticky, decadently laced white cream rolls. Stu placed the cups and plates in the sink. Win put his half-empty Coke back in the refrigerator. Brian noted their tidiness. He had assumed that the family would be used to a maid waiting on them hand and foot given their wealth. The larger catfish farms employed maids. The high-end silver BMW tooling around Bellevue would be getting attention from the snooty locals.

"Well, Stu, you want to check out the farm? The keys should be in the truck."

"Sounds good. Win, you ready?" Stu turned around to face Win.

He was already headed for the door.

The farm's pickup was a crimson red 1995 Ford F250. Stu hopped behind the wheel. Win and Brian slid in the other side. Win's ankles hugged both sides of a strange rod sticking out of the floor on the transmission hump.

"What's this for?" Win pointed at the short knobby stick.

"That's your lever for the front tires. It's called four-wheel drive. You use it when it gets muddy," Brian said.

"We have six hundred trucks. Do they have four-wheel drive, Daddy?"

Stu smiled. He wondered what was going on at the office this morning. "No, Win. They don't have four-wheel drive. Our trucks don't ever get in the mud." *At least they shouldn't be.*

Brian looked at Stu. "Six hundred trucks?"

"Something like that."

A great blue heron flew across the main levee, landing on the shoreline of the first pond. The main levee separated two rows of ten ponds. The long-legged bird waded into calf-deep water and stabbed at something under the surface.

"Do they eat a lot of fish?" Stu asked.

"Well, yes, but not catfish. They may eat a fingerling or two, but they prefer trash fish like shad and green sunfish." Brian opened the air conditioning vent on his side. Stuart noticed and adjusted the AC to a lower temperature.

"They can be a problem in a way. They act like decoys for the cormorants in the fall."

"Cormorants?"

"The scourge of the earth. The Mennonites joke that they're a biblical plague pest. They arrive around October in flocks by the hundreds. One bird can eat a pound of catfish a day."

"What?" Stu stared at Brian.

"You'll spend a lot of time in the winter running birds. That's something Win can help you with. We use special firecracker pistols to scare them off.

"That sounds like fun!" Win exclaimed. "Can I ride the Honda and do it?"

"Whoa, son. We'll work into that one."

"Okay, Daddy." Win playfully bumped his dad's side.

"Stu, see that power pole with the gray box. Let's park over there. Let me give you a short course on oxygen management. Colback's leaving this morning. We need to get up to speed on oxygen until we get somebody hired."

"Yeah, dude, this learning curve is straight up now."

"Well, let's see if we can level it out some."

Stu sensed the onset of a mild anxiety attack. *Am I scared about failing? Or am I over-the-head stupid for doing this? Maybe both. What have I got myself into?* He parked the truck on the gravel levee. Stu reflected as he gazed out over the shimmering ponds. His heart beat a little harder than normal. He took a deep breath and let it out slowly. Did it again. Felt a little better. He turned to look at Win. They were already outside, standing at rear of the truck, talking excitedly. Win was full of questions.

"Win, while Mr. Caine and I are talking, I need you to do something for me." He needed to find an activity for Win during his one on one with Brian. He studied the truck's bed. There wasn't anything overtly hazardous.

"Sure, Daddy, what can I do?"

"How about putting the trashy stuff in this corner." Stu pointed to the front left corner nearest the gas cap. "And put all the good stuff, like this tool," he picked up a rusty Crescent wrench and tossed it in the opposite front corner, "over here. And the stuff you aren't sure about put it next to the tailgate, okay?"

"Okay, Daddy." Win climbed into the bed, up and over the upright tailgate.

"He's quick on his feet. Does he play sports?"

"Soccer's his game. He was the leading scorer on the team."

"We don't play soccer in Bellevue. Smackover has a league, though."

Brian retrieved a shoe-box-sized oxygen meter from the rear seat of the crew cab and placed it on the hood. "There are two critical pieces of equipment on a fish farm, the oxygen meter and the feed truck. You'll never make any money unless oxygen and feed management are mastered." He grabbed the black knob on the YSI Model 54A and switched it from Off to Red Line. The black needle darted from side to side inside the meter window.

"The Red Line is one of the diagnostic meter checks. It's really the battery checker, but Red Line sounds cooler." Brian smiled. "The needle should come to the red line. If you can't get it there by turning the knob, replace the batteries."

Stuart nodded. "Got it."

"Next is the Zero." Caine pointed to the Zero knob at twelve o'clock on the meter's gray face. "This is another built-in diagnostic check. If you can't get it to zero out, something's wrong—internal circuitry, probe, loose connection. Gotta figure it out and fix it. Can't fix it, use your backup meter."

"Where's the backup meter?"

"Should be in the shop. That'll be our next stop. We keep the feed truck there." Brian hooked his hands over the front of his belt near the buckle. "Okay, here's where we start talking some science. How much biology and chemistry have you had?"

"Dude, I majored in girls, booze, and harassing the shit out of the frat boys," Stuart whispered. "Took intro biology and chemistry. Majored in psychology. I was into the sciences. Loved statistics. Hated upper math. I have yet to use anything I learned in calculus."

"Me too. Calculus was a sheer waste of time. We got something in common." Brian grinned.

"Ended up driving a truck after I graduated."

"Well, you've done pretty good. Not many folks can write a check for a catfish farm."

Win was busy organizing. He was studying a tarnished rifle cartridge, trying to read the caliber imprinted on the bottom.

They watched an osprey fly over a pond. "Those are the good guys. They eat snakes."

"Well, he missed one yesterday. Tab turned inside out when she almost stepped on one in the front yard."

"There are 4,000 types of snakes on earth, and 3,998 of them live in Alabama," Brian quipped. Stu didn't think that was funny.

Brian added in a more serious tone, "Most of them are harmless. Very rarely see the cottonmouths in catfish ponds."

"Daddy, I found a two-two-three bullet!"

"That's good, son, find another one."

"It's a popular caliber for catfish farmers. They're good for reaching out and hitting the wiser cormorants," Brian said.

That'd be another hurdle. Getting a rifle for the farm. Stu shrugged, lost in thought for a few seconds.

"You okay?" Brian asked.

"Tab's got this thing about guns."

"Everybody has a gun in Alabama. Even the preachers are toting."

Stu chuckled.

"Okay, back to our science lesson." Brian turned the meter over. "This is a saturation chart. It tells how much oxygen is supposed to be in the water at a certain temperature. The important thing to remember is you want to calibrate the meter with air temperature, not water temperature. Water temperature is important, but this model calibrates with air temp."

"Got it. Air temp for calibration."

Brian flipped the meter back over and turned the main knob to the Temp setting. The meter needle settled on the 29 C figure on the white display face.

"Okay, the probe is at 29 C." Brian grabbed the grayish probe at the end of a twelve-foot cable attached to the side of the meter.

"Why centigrade?" Stu asked.

"Well, all the environmentalists, the scientific nerdy types, use these things. Catfish farming is a small market segment compared to all the darter chasers. I guess the meter companies haven't gotten around to making a redneck version yet."

"Those darter chasers, we breed them in California."

"Tell me about it. The fisheries department at Auburn is slap full of them. They don't see eye to eye with us aquaculturists. Not a lot of meat on a darter."

Win chunked a piece of concrete block into the water.

"If I had to design one, the meter face would have four distinct areas on the read-out. In blue, I'd have the words, 'Fish Are Okay, Go Back to Bed.' In yellow, the words, 'Better Do Something.' And in red, 'Your Fish Are Dying.' And then a small area in black, 'Your Fish Are Dead.'"

"Yeah, we're gonna go into lots of detail on those areas, right?"

"We're getting there." Brian flipped the meter over to the back side again. "We're at 29. According to this chart, the oxygen saturation should be 7.7. In other words, if the water has 7.7 oxygen, it's saturated. If we try to add any more, it'll escape into the air."

"And we can add more with the aerators, right?"

"Yeah, good. You're learning. Great."

"Daddy, I found a full beer can. Buddy wiser. Trash or keep it?"

"Find a date on it, Win. Let me know. Brian, we better hurry up, I don't know how much longer I can stall him."

"Just about done. I'll explain keeping the fish alive later." He picked the meter up off the hood.

"Okay. We're at seven point seven. Make sure the probe cap has a wet cotton ball." They both looked inside the thimble-sized plastic cap. "Calibrate the meter to seven point seven using the calibration knob, like this." Brian adjusted the last black knob on the far right of the meter face until the needle rested over the desired number. "Now, she's calibrated and ready to rock and roll." Brian grabbed the cable and the probe. "Win can help us now."

"Win, come here. Need your help."

"Coming." Win hopped over the tailgate and jumped off the rear bumper.

"Win, listen to Mr. Caine. We're going to check the oxygen."

"What's oxi-gen?"

"It's air in the water. Fish use it because they have gills instead of lungs," Brian said.

"Okay," Win said. "At home when their flappers aren't moving, we flush them down the toilet."

Both men grinned.

"Take this probe. Dangle it under the water. Move it back and forth real slow," Brian instructed.

Win took the probe and the cable out of Brian's hands. He squatted down on his heels at the edge of the pond. He lowered the probe into the water and slowly moved it back and forth. Stuart and Brian watched the meter. The needle came to a rest on the 6. Brian moved the center knob to the Temp setting and the needle stayed on 28.

"Okay, Win. Good job," Brian said, smiling at Win. He turned to Stu. "An oxygen reading of 6 and a temp of 28. That's good. No problems. Think you can do it by yourself?"

"Well, let's see." Stuart turned off the meter and started over. He performed almost all the necessary functions, tripping on not replacing the probe cap during calibration.

"Remember. Calibrate with moist air in the probe cap."

"Got it."

They hopped in the truck and headed to the shop. Stu parked in the shade of an immense live oak dripping with Spanish moss. Guy Colback was getting in his personal truck. He was on the way home for good after packing up his stuff from five years of employment.

"Guy, this is Stuart Baron and his son, Win." Stuart got out and shook hands with Colback. Win stayed in the truck and waved.

"Mr. Colback, I appreciate you looking after the farm last night. Hear you're off to greener pastures," Stu said.

"That's right. I start tomorrow. Looking forward to working in air-conditioning for once in my life. These Alabama summers are tough."

"We have four seasons: almost summer, summer, still summer, and Christmas," Brian cracked.

Stu and Win laughed. Win couldn't wait to tell Mommy.

"I underestimated this humidity. That's for sure. When does it get better?" Stu asked.

"We'll get our first break around mid-September. There'll be a morning when you debate about grabbing your windbreaker. You'll know fall is around the corner. It's like God threw a switch. Finally got tired of watching the suffer fest," Colback chuckled.

Colback reached for a lone pouch of Red Man on the dash-board. He stuck a wad in his right cheek. Win noticed, intently look-ing at the wiry man. In a few seconds, he spewed a red stream of spit out his window. Win recoiled at the sight. It looked like blood. The man was missing a few front teeth.

"Guy, you have any problems last night?" Brian asked.

"The aerator motor in pond twelve is bad. Better get it fixed today. The pond's gotta hell of an algae bloom."

"I heard that," Brian replied.

"Good luck with the farm, Mr. Stu. You're getting a pretty sweet deal. Farm's a real moneymaker. Most of the machinery isn't wore slap out yet. She's stocked full of fish." Colback spewed out another red stream. Win watched it splatter on the gravel. "Here's my card and phone number in case you have questions about anything." He handed Stu a business card. It read, "Colback Small Engine Repair. If it ain't diesel, I can fix it."

"Thanks, Mr. Colback," Stu replied.

With that, he mashed the clutch, threw his battered Datsun rice runner into gear, and drove off with a wave out the window.

"Daddy, what was that man chewing?"

"It's tobacco. Kinda like cigarettes, but you don't smoke it."

Brian looked at Win. "Makes your teeth fall out first, then your lower jaw rots off. Girls hate it when you try to kiss them."

Stu chuckled. "And if I ever catch you using it, you'll stay in your room until the paint peels."

Brian chortled.

They strolled into the cool dark shade of the cavernous equipment shed. Inside were three John Deere utility tractors, a one-ton Ford pickup with a large hopper on the bed, and an aluminum johnboat with a twenty-five horsepower Merc sitting on a rusty, crusty boat trailer. Win immediately spied the boat.

"Wow, look, Daddy, there's a boat!"

"Yeah, son, go check it out."

Win dashed to the boat. He climbed inside and moved the outboard from side to side with the tiller.

"Win loves to fish. My parents live in northern Minnesota. They have an outboard boat. We spend our vacations up there fishing for northerns and yellow perch."

"The boat's used to treat ponds. Let's make sure they didn't leave any chemicals in it," Brian said.

Stu and Brian strolled over to the boat and looked inside. A near-empty can of starting spray was next to the deep-cycle NAPA battery.

"This isn't good," Brian said, grabbing the can of ether. "Once you start using this stuff on a cranky motor, it becomes addictive. I call it engine crack."

"No need to explain that one." Stu grimaced.

"Let me show you the feed truck."

They walked around the feed truck, looking it over. The four-wheel drive diesel Ford F350 single cab sported a flat black steel-plate bed. The dually's four rear mud grip tires had nickel-deep lugs. Stu noticed there wasn't a license plate on the rear. Not even a plate holder.

"No plate?" Stu asked.

"Truck never leaves the farm. That way you can use off-road diesel. Off road is twenty cents cheaper. They put red dye in the off-road. Troopers carry long straws to check for it. Don't let them catch you on the road with red dye. Not even a hint of dye. The fine is ten grand."

"Ouch," Stu said. "What happens when I want to take it in for maintenance?"

"Be sure to run all the off road out and fill it slap full of on road. The fine for an untagged vehicle is survivable. You explain to the trooper where you're going, he'll probably let you slide the first time."

"I'm gonna get it tagged," Stu said.

Brian pointed to the fifteen horsepower Briggs and Stratton blower engine. He reached around and pulled out the oil stick. Almost-clear yellowish oil covered the hashes just below the Full mark. He stuck it back in the hole. He deftly unfurled the wingnut on the air cleaner cover and looked at the filter element. It was clean, maybe new.

"Stu, the catfish feed can be really dusty at times, so it's important to keep the oil and filters clean. These engines don't last very long. Problem's the design. When you start them up, they go to full speed without a warm-up idle, and then when you shut 'em down, they go from full speed to off. That's no way to treat an engine. I've never seen one configured differently. So preventative maintenance is very important. You might get four years out of one."

"Don't worry. I'm a firm believer in PM. I try not to lose twenty tons of Alaskan crab legs due to a clogged fuel filter," Stu deadpanned. "Unless someone has shot up my truck to hell and back with an AR-15."

"Huh?"

"Long story, let's save it for a cold beer."

"Okay then, let's hop in and feed some fish," Brian said as he got behind the wheel.

Win got in the middle again. Stu took shotgun.

Instead of sharing the middle hump with the gearshift, Win had to scrunch in next to his dad due to the floor-mounted scale console occupying most of the middle seat area. Stu put his left arm out along the top of the bench seat and reached around Win, giving him a titty squeeze. Win returned the gesture. Brian swiveled the display so Stu could see it. Brian punched a few buttons, and the display read 0000.

"I've been feeding the farm since Mrs. Hopkins left. Like we went over on the phone, only three ponds are full of harvestable fish. The rest were seined a couple of times. Just stockers and fingerlings in those. I'll feed the full ones today and let you feed the rest of the ponds."

"Sounds like a plan, Brian."

"Okay then, the hopper scale is indicating we need feed."

Brian started the truck's engine. Stu grinned at the familiar reassuring growl of a V8 sucking down diesel.

"That's music to my ears. Let's go make some money, dude," Stu said.

Brian put the lever in reverse and backed the truck. The backup alarm bell echoed off the steel walls of the shed.

Win looked at his dad. "You need to get out and look?"

Brian looked puzzled. Stu noticed.

"It's company policy that when one of our rigs is backing up, a team member gets out and directs. No exceptions, therefore no excuses. Win has ridden shotgun enough times to learn the rules. When we buy new trucks, he's usually with me when I drive a new model tractor to the locker from the dealer. Lots of accidents happen in reverse. My truckers take a lot of pride in their virgin rear bumpers."

"Daddy, what's a virgin?"

Stu and Brian smiled. "Son, that's a question for your mom. Ask her tonight at dinner when her mouth is full. I'll have my camera ready."

"Sounds like a plan," Win replied.

Brian pulled up underneath a twenty-five-ton feed bin, squinted into the bright sunlight, and centered the bin's trapdoor with the eight foot square opening of the truck's feed hopper.

"Hop out and let me show you how this works. Oh, first off, we need to double-check that the hopper is empty and the scale display is correct. Win can help."

They went to the back of the truck. Brian instructed Win to climb up the metal ladder fastened to the rear of the truck. Win quickly scampered up the steps and peered down inside the hopper.

"Anything in there, Win?" Brian asked.

"No, sir. It's empty."

"How much do you weigh?" Brian asked Win.

"Don't know."

"Stay there, I'll tell you."

Brian glanced at the digital scale console in the cab. It read 65.

"How does sixty-five sound?"

"Works for me," Win said.

"Okay, stay right there and tell me when she's full." Win hugged the top rung of the ladder, peering inside.

Brian walked to the side of the truck and tugged on a dangling steel chain attached to the bin's superstructure. A gear wheel slowly moved an attaching arm and the trapdoor at the bottom of the bin opened. Pelleted feed cascaded like a waterfall into the empty truck hopper. In just a few minutes, the hopper was almost full of half-inch-long brown pellets that smelled like frosted oat Cheerios.

"It's near the top, Mr. Caine."

"Good, you can come on down now." Win hopped down. Dad gave him a fist bump.

"Might have to put you on the payroll, son."

"Payroll more than my allowance, Daddy?"

"Might be. Depends on how many fish tolerate my stupidity."

They made their way to pond one. As the truck rounded the graveled corner of the rectangular pond, Stu noticed that the truck leaned toward the water side of the levee.

"They ever tip over?"

"No, never heard of one tipping over, but quite a few have rolled into the pond. They aren't nimble enough to check oxygen when they're full."

Brian flipped a silver toggle switch in the up position. He mashed down on a momentary push button. The dual-cylinder Briggs and Stratton rumbled to life under the hopper. The attached blower fan whirled, building up to a deafening roar, inducing a slight vibration in the cab. Despite having the windows rolled up, the men had to nearly yell.

Brian pointed to the second toggle switch. "This one controls the slide gate for the feed. Important thing to remember is it's not an instantaneous on and off. Takes a second or two to completely open or close. Feed amounts will be plus or minus ten to twenty pounds."

Win noticed the rippling pond surface. Dense ripples covered a patch of water that stretched for thirty yards along the levee. Then schools of fish suddenly appeared, their backs breaking the surface.

"Look, Daddy. Fish. Hundreds of them!"

"That's a good sign. That's fish waiting on the feed. When you see them respond like that, that means they're feeling good, no serious water quality or disease issues at the moment," Brian said.

Stu nodded. "That's so cool. Can't wait to show Tab."

"Okay, Win, push this lever down and let's feed some fish," Brian said.

Win pushed the lever down. Feed pellets hurled out of a four-foot-long metal chute, forming a cascading arc. The pellets landed in the turbulent green water. Food-size catfish boiled at the surface by the thousands, gobbling up the floating feed as fast as it hit. Brian drove the truck at walking speed along the levee. The fish followed, leaving a frothy wake.

"How do you know how much to feed them?" Stu asked.

Brian was glancing at the feed readout on the scale as he drove. "Well, that's more art than science. But I've figured out a way to flatten the learning curve."

"Man, I'm all ears."

Win glanced at his dad. *A face that was all ears.*

"Let's get these first three ponds fed. I'll let you feed the rest. Then we'll tackle the science in a quieter setting."

They finished feeding the farm three hours later. Stu managed to fill the hopper twice without banging into the bin's massive steel-legged superstructure. His truck driving skills coming in handy. Win proved to be very helpful by writing in the feed amounts for each pond on the rusty clipboard. His mastery of numbers impressed Brian.

After parking the feed truck in its corner of the shed, they strolled over to a dust-covered refrigerator next to the work bench. Inside were three chilled grape Gatorades.

Stu noticed the neatness of the tool area. He only hired former military to manage the truck service bays at the lockers. They were anal about keeping things ship shape.

Large box-end wrenches from one and a half to three quarter inches were hanging on pegboard hooks. A chest-high five-drawer red Craftsman tool chest stood at one end of the sturdy wood-planked tool bench. A heavy-duty steel vise was clamped on the other end. Coffee cans full of nuts, bolts, and washers lined the back wall of the bench. A folded greasy rag was centered on the middle of the bench.

Brian noticed Stu admiring the tidiness of the work area.

"Colback was a bit of a neat freak. Not quite OCD, but close."

"Former military?"

"Yeah. There's a funny story there. Colback finished Marine boot during the middle of Vietnam. No doubt heard the stories about the fighting. Came home before shipping out. Blew his big toe off with a deer rifle. He maintains it was an accident. Marines gave him a general discharge."

"I need to find out how much they're paying him. Figure out if I can afford to air-condition this freaking shed." Stu winced. "Just hire him to be my shop mechanic and feed fish. He could stay in air conditioning all day long."

"I think it'd be a tough sell getting him back. Fish farming takes a toll. Bad lower backs from toting aerator motors up and down pond banks, skin cancer from this relentless sun, and hearing loss from feeding fish seem to be the most common."

"Trucking's tough too. I've got a full-time person who only deals with workers' comp. Speaking of aerators, didn't Colback say there was one down?"

"Yeah, you're right. That's next. Let's tackle the feeding part now while it's fresh on our minds."

Stu glanced over at Win. Restless again, trying to pull the starter rope on the boat's motor. Stu walked over to the tool chest. He yanked out several drawers. He picked out several sockets and smaller box end wrenches. Just like he suspected, it was a mix of American standard and European metric.

"Win, come over here and help me out." Stu grabbed an empty dairy milk crate and turned it upside down. "Stand on this. Go through the drawers one by one. Take out all the tools marked mm. Put them here on the counter. We'll get a separate tool chest for the metrics. Oh, and be sure to wipe them." Stu grabbed a clean rag out of the box underneath the bench.

While Win was busy sorting and wiping tools, Stu and Brian sat on the tailgate.

"Okay, restating the number one priority when operating a cat-fish farm. Feeding catfish will make or break you. You underfeed them, you lose money. Remember, more pounds, more dollars. You overfeed, you lose too. Mother Nature's always looking over your back. Feed the ponds too much, she'll kick you in the teeth because you just tanked the water quality, stressing the fish. The goal is a decent feed conversion rate. We call it the FCR. You need a good production yield too. You need to shoot for an FCR better than two pounds of feed to one pound of gain. For yield, the Hopkins were getting seven thousand pounds per acre per year. They were in the top ten percent of production. The state average is six thousand pounds. You can make some serious moola at six thousand with a FCR of two to one, provided feed and fish prices stay where they are now. No guarantees there, though. Farming's a highly variable business. Key to surviving is controlling as many variables as possible, limiting the impact of all the shit we can't control."

"Kinda like diesel fuel and tires," Stu added, wondering how Ross was fairing in Los Angeles. Stu usually handled the shit.

"Back to feeding fish. Today was easy. I just tried to feed them what they ate yesterday. We want to minimize the yo-yo effect. Imagine a toy yo-yo. Up and down, up and down." Brian imitated holding a yo-yo in his right hand, performing the motions. Win noticed and smiled.

Stu noticed Win's diverted attention. "How's it going over there?"

"Okay, Daddy. There are a lot more m and m's."

"That makes sense," Stu said. "Between a half-inch and a five-eight's socket, you could have a thirteen, fourteen, and fifteen millimeter."

Win nodded. He liked the metric sockets more than the strange numbers with the slants. He wondered why there was a 5/8 and 7/8 but no 6/8.

"Okay, back to the art and science of feeding catfish. This is based on some really good research from Auburn."

"Auburn?"

"Auburn University. My employer. The campus is close to the Georgia line. I'm field staff for the school. Work for Extension. We take the useful research and sort it out from the crap research. Give it to the farmers so they can make some money."

"Brian, did you ever watch *Green Acres*?"

"Yeah, once in a while. Why?"

"There's some government guy on the show who never knows jack shit about anything."

"Oh yeah. What's his name? It'll come to me. We got a few of them idiots around. Some of them aren't worth the bullet. We hired a goat specialist from Tuskegee. The county has less goats now than when he started working ten years ago. Yeah, *Green Acres* is still one of my favorites. Right up there with the *Andy Griffith Show*."

"Yeah, I love to watch it with Win. He's fascinated with Opie."

"Good, well-rounded ag agents are a dying breed these days. Extension's becoming a welfare agency. Too busy telling folks that if they stopped eating so much they wouldn't get fat. The touchy-feel-ies on campus and the field agents aren't on the same page anymore. How are the farmers gonna make it if everyone goes on a diet?" Brian said, trying not to smile. Stu returned the grin.

Stu looked over at Win. He was on the bottom drawer. The half end of the work bench was nearly full.

"We better hurry up, Brian." He nodded over to Win.

"Yeah, right. Okay, back to the yo-yos. The key is avoiding big swings in feed amounts from day to day. If you stuff them full one day, chances are you knock them way off feed the next day. Research shows that if you keep them slightly hungry from day to day, you get the best yield and feed conversion rate. That sub satiation amount is eighty-five percent."

"Okay, so what you're saying is keep them slightly hungry from day to day. How do we determine that sweet spot of eighty-five percent?" Stu asked.

"It's really simple. I like Tuesdays for starting a new feed week. First off, this is a hard concept for most of the catfish farmers, feeding fish should never be considered just another farm chore. This is your only decent shot at making money on the farm. Everything else is low priority."

"That makes sense to me, Brian. That's not a hard concept to grasp."

"Well, it may make sense now, but it will dog you sometimes when you have a zillion things to do, there isn't enough time in the day, and Win's late for his soccer match."

Win glanced at the men when he heard the word *soccer*.

"Why Tuesday?" Stu asked.

"Tuesday is stuff-the-fish day. Bear with me here. You're going to stuff them full of feed on this day only. You may waste a hundred pounds or so while learning. With experience, this amount will go down."

"I'm with you. But still not clear on why you chose Tuesday."

"You'll become very familiar with Murphy's law of farming."

"I could write a book on the Murphy's law of trucking."

"Well, it may not happen on this farm. But all kinds of crap will happen over the weekend. Monday, it's gotta get fixed. When you come up for air on Tuesday, that's your designated stuff day. You can choose Wednesday instead. This farm's in pretty good shape, Tuesdays will probably work."

Brian showed Stu the feed clipboard and pointed to the daily feed amounts for the previous week.

Brian continued, "And realize, like I said, on Wednesday, they'll be off feed. They may only eat fifty percent of Tuesday's amount. But you feed them eighty-five percent of Tuesday's ration Thursday, Friday, Saturday, Sunday, and Monday. You yo-yo the ponds twice a week on Tuesday and Wednesday and flatline them the rest of the week. You'll actually save time feeding in the long haul because it takes the guess work out most of the days. You can't be in a hurry on Tuesdays. That's the key to it."

"By the way, more fish are killed Saturday and Sunday nights than any other time. I call it night man rollover." Brian lowered his voice. "That's when your night man is rolling off his old lady when he should be in the pickup checking oxygen."

"I follow you, dude."

"Oh, and try not to run out of feed. You can't afford it. Tally your total feeding every few days. A bin load is around twenty-five tons. There are only two hundred good feed days in a year. This farm is eating seven tons of feed per day. You're growing almost four tons of fish a day. Eight thousand pounds. Ten cents profit per pound. Eight hundred bucks profit a day. The feed mill's good about customer service, but they can't deliver on half a day's notice. They only have so many trucks. You being the new kid on the block means you're way down on their pecking order."

Brian looked at his watch. It was close to noon.

Stu glanced at his watch. "Damn, where did the time go?"

"Man, these catfish farms are in a different time dimension. Summer speeds by from May through September. I've never heard a catfish producer complain about how slow the summer was going. You'll come up for air in October."

"Win, let's go get some lunch."

"Sounds like a plan, Daddy." Win hopped off the dairy crate and climbed into the front seat.

"Brian, let's go see what the missus found for lunch."

"Sounds good. We'll tackle that aerator job afterwards. You'll need to change into something you can get wet in."

*****

Special Agent in Charge Jerry Feaster, now sporting a bronze tan after his week in Fiji, was in the middle of a briefing on the Bajalista cartel by Agent Adams when his administrative assistant,

Tara Packard, deep-tanned herself, walked in and interrupted their conversation. "SAC Jose Santiago in Los Angeles on line one, sir."

Sir, my ass, thought Adams. *More like, 'Please eat me again, lover boy.'*

Feaster picked up the phone. He listened for a moment. "Jose, I've got Agent Adams in my office right now. He's been monitoring the tracker. Let me put you on speaker."

"Hey, Jose, how you doing out there?" Coop asked. At first, Feaster was taken aback by the informalness of his agent speaking to another SAC like this but then he recalled the two were classmates at the academy. Santiago had steadily advanced through the agency. Adams was a rogue. His rogue. Adams's thick personnel dossier was a veritable guide on how not to get promoted in the DEA.

"Coop, doing fine, but I wish I had better news." After a palpable break, Santiago continued, "Our undercover agent, Mario Quintana, hasn't checked in for three days. We've lost track of him since the drop-off on the hill. We're stretched pretty thin right now. Was wondering if we could get you out here since you're up to speed on the Bajalistas?"

Adams waited for a reaction from Feaster. He nodded. Adams headed for the door.

"Jose, he's all yours. Good luck. Hope you find your man."

"Thanks, Jerry."

CHAPTER TWENTY-ONE

Tab was putting away groceries when the boys entered through the mudroom at the side door. She closed the refrigerator door and leaned against it, facing them.

"Let me guess. It's time for lunch."

"Mommy, we fed the fish this morning. Millions of them! Daddy let me get in our new boat!"

"Boat? Hope you were wearing a life jacket, Win. You can't swim long distances yet."

"It's sitting in the shed. A work boat. Not exactly a pleasure craft," Stu said.

"Well, I wanna see this boat. Make sure it's seaworthy," Tab said.

"Stu will have plenty of opportunities to take you boating, maybe at three in the morning, putting out hydrated lime when the fish come up because the carbon dioxide is too high."

"That sounds like loads of fun." Tab smirked.

Stu looked at Brian, slowly shaking his head. *This just keeps on going. Maybe I should change the farm's name from Nighthope to Enigma Acres.*

Tab bent over and sniffed the top of Win's head. "What's that smell?"

Stu walked over, bending down over Win. "Oh, that's feed dust. Smells like Cheerios, doesn't it?"

Brian excused himself to hit the restroom. He needed to wash the feed funk off his hands.

"Tell us about your journey into town."

"First off, what do you guys want to eat?"

"What's on the menu?" Stu asked.

"Cold cut sandwiches and chips. If you want cordon bleu Cornish hen, sautéed asparagus, and sage-infused brown rice, you'll have to drive me to Whole Paycheck in Birmingham."

"Sandwiches and chips okay with you, Brian?" Stu asked.

"Man, if the roadkill's not moving and still looks fresh, I'm game," Brian said.

Win looked in his direction, his head cocked to one side.

"Win, go wash up." Stu smiled.

As the boys devoured their cotto salami and pepper jack cheese sandwiches, Tab started with her rendition of the trip into town.

"I found the store without any problems. Gosh, I love the traffic already. No traffic lights between here and the store. The Piggly Wiggly isn't exactly Whole Foods, though."

"Brian, Whole Foods is a very upscale grocery. If you want organic cat litter, they got it. I always referred to it as Whole Paycheck. Everything's real pricey. But then in California, everything's pricey."

"You're not kidding. My last gallon of milk in LA was over four dollars. Only two and a half here."

Brian thought it was odd that folks who could write a check for a catfish farm paid attention to the price of milk. Maybe that's why. They were careful with their money.

"How about the people, Tab?" Stu asked.

"Gosh. Really friendly for the most part. They smile and say hello. The language is so funny, though." Tab sipped on her Diet Pepsi. "The cashier asked me if I would like some heeelp totin' my food out to the caar." Tab was trying hard to speak Southern. "For a moment, I thought she was speaking a different language."

Stu chuckled. "Brian, do we sound funny to you?"

"Well, not funny, but you aah definitely ain't from around heere," Brian put on his drawl thicker than normal.

"Stu, wait until you see the food. Oh my gosh, these people love their greens. I saw turnip tops but no roots. There's a big green plant called collards. Really cheap too. You can get a cart full for less than ten bucks."

"All meat and three restaurants serve collards. They call them greens around here, usually served with bacon or ham pieces and a little vinegar. Really good with Tabasco sauce," Brian said.

"And, Stu, they don't waste anything off a hog or chicken. You can get chicken feet, hog jowls, turkey necks. I saw something that looked like animal brains."

"We call that souse meat. Did you see the chitterlings?"

"I did. I had no idea what they were. The package was covered in frost. Couldn't quite make them out."

"They're also called chitlins. Pig intestines. The foulest smell in the world when cooked in a big iron pot. I run for the hills when I smell them. Some folks will die for them around here." Brian winced. "Southerners use every part of the hog but the squeal."

"Oh, and you are not going to believe this, Stu. Right next to those awful Vienna Sausages your truckers eat were pickled pig lips."

"So where are they?" Stu jokingly looked over his shoulder at the kitchen counter next to the folded stack of brown grocery bags.

"You can buy a case of them and hand them out for Christmas gag gifts at the next party," Tab deadpanned.

"That would be the ultimate gag gift for sure."

Win pretended to gag. Brian laughed at his antics.

"Win, have you ever had a Moon Pie chased down with peanuts mixed in a bottle of RC cola?"

"No, Mr. Caine."

"Well, we're going to start you off right living here in Alabama. You come to my office, and we'll get you converted over real quick like, okay?"

"Sounds like a plan."

Tab studied her boy for a second. *The South's indoctrination had begun.*

The men finished their meal. Stuart disappeared to the master bedroom. He changed out of his worn Lee's blue jeans into faded black running shorts and an old pair of white canvas Keds. The temperature was climbing into the lower nineties, and the humidity was thickening by the hour. According to Brian, they'd be getting in waist-deep water for the aerator repair. Brian was in the backyard with Win looking over the Honda. Win nodded as Brian talked. Stu stood at the bedroom's picture window, smiling at the budding friendship.

"Hey, Win," Brian said in a low voice.

"Yes, Mr. Caine?"

"In the South, it's polite to use someone's first name with the *mister*. You can call me Mister Brian, okay?"

"Cool."

Tab finished unpacking the rest of the cardboard boxes marked "Kitchen." The faux-walnut eye-level cabinets with their ill-closing doors and the musty storage space under the kitchen island would barely provide enough space. She designated the cabinet above the four-eye Kenmore for the liquor. She slid the half-empty bottle of Glenfiddich toward the back of the cabinet. It stood all by itself. She wondered if she would be lonely living on the farm.

How hard would it be making new friends?

She stared at the bottle. Alcoholism ran deep throughout her family. Both Grandpa and Dad had drinking problems. She had set limits on her daily alcohol since the photo shoot at the mansion. She pushed the memory to the back of her mind and focused on her reflection in the window. She noticed the empty bird feeder.

She remembered seeing the Walmart on the west side of Smackover after crossing the Mississippi state line.

She found a pad and pencil and wrote, "Birdseed, nectar feeder, sugar. Scotch."

She missed her hummingbirds. *How many times did they come back and check on the feeders, only to find them empty?* She hoped someone close would be feeding them. *Donny sure as hell wouldn't be. His bumper sticker, 'Try wiping your ass with a spotted owl,' summed it up.*

*****

Stu and Win met Brian at pond six in separate trucks. Brian's tool kit for aerator motor replacement was stored in the shiny aluminum box behind the rear window of his blue Silverado. The tools and supplies were in an eighteen-inch-long leather tool bag. He emptied the bag out, placing several hand-size tools and electrical supplies on the tailgate of his truck.

"In case you're wondering why I have tools for aerator motors, I'm conducting aerator research on another farm. Cheap Chinese motors are wearing my ass out," Brian said as he looked in the dark bag for his new roll of black electrical tape. "Stu, how mechanically inclined are you?"

"I suppose on a scale of one to ten, I'd give myself a seven. Lefty-loosy and righty-tighty have been mastered. I quit looking for left-handed hammers when I graduated from college."

Brian chuckled.

Win was busy using the professional-grade wire strippers. He liked how the sliding parts worked together, practicing wire stripping with short pieces of waste wire, using both hands to squeeze the handles.

"First thing we need to do is figure out which one of these beasts isn't working." Brian strolled over to the power pole and opened the cover for the two-hundred-amp panel box. He switched on the top left breaker. A pond aerator responded by rocking forward. The blades rotated, throwing water four feet in the air. He switched it off. He then flicked the breaker lever to the right for the number two aerator. The aerator hummed momentarily and then automatically threw the lever to the tripped position.

"Gotcha," Brian quipped.

The twenty-foot-long aerator was attached to the pond bank with two ten-foot-long bank arms at each end of the machine.

Brian lifted one bank arm off the square anchor post buried deep in the levee. Stu grabbed the other matching arm at the other end of the aerator and lifted it off its post. They pulled the machine to the bank.

"Okay, before we get in the water, let's shut down the power completely." Brian walked back over to the breaker box and threw the big red lever on the side of the breaker panel down to the off position. "Now we can work on it. You don't want power going in the water. We're going in. Electricity and water are a deadly combination."

Brian waded into the water and approached the motor cover. Stu was looking over Brian's shoulder, getting used to the sensation of wearing shoes submersed in murky green water.

"Stu, gotta be careful here. Snakes hide under these covers." Brian slowly lifted the hinged thin aluminum cover off the motor and peered underneath the motor. "Sure enough, there's a big one in there." Stu clambered out of the water. Brian laughed at Stu's animated antics as he exited the pond.

"Stu, get my beaver stick in the back of my truck."

"Beaver stick?"

"Yeah, it's a wooden stick about five feet long with tooth marks on both ends. I pulled it out of a beaver dam."

Stu found the stick and pointed to the sharp edges left by the cutting action of powerful beaver incisors. Win felt the edges and smiled.

"That's cool, Daddy."

Stu handed the stick to Brian. Brian took it and gingerly propped the cover all the way up. He studied the large brown three-inch-thick four-foot snake coiled up between the motor and the gearbox.

"We're okay with this one. It's a harmless Natrix."

"How can you tell?"

"Round pupils. Moccasins have vertical elliptical pupils. Can't tell by color or pattern. Moccasins around here are brown and patterned like this one. But the eyes are a dead giveaway."

"Damn, Brian, are you sure?"

Brian reached in and grabbed the snake behind the head, lifting it out.

Stu climbed back out of the water. Win was on his heels, as tight as white on rice, both scrambling back to the truck.

"Come on down, take a good look at him."

The Barons looked at each other with quizzical looks.

As Stu and Win eased toward Brian with the snake coiled around his arm, the snake's disposition changed. Probably sensing two more predators on approach, its mouth was now wide open, trying to nail Brian's other hand. "See, no fangs, just rows of little teeth."

Win touched the snake's belly. It was the first snake he had ever touched. Stu kept his distance.

"What are you going to do with him, Brian?" Stu asked.

"Can we keep him, Daddy?"

"Win, you take that home, your mother won't even bother packing."

Brian climbed out of the pond and gently tossed the snake down the other side of the levee. It slithered down the bank into the drainage ditch. "They eat fish. He'll have to eat wild ones until he figures out easier pickings are back up the hill. Let's get back to work."

Stu and Brian returned to the aerator. Win stepped out onto the two-inch-wide beached arm, momentarily balanced, and made it out to the machine, finally perching on top of the gearbox, watching the repair job.

Brian placed his canvas tool bag on the floor of the machine. He took out a socket wrench and nestled a 9 mm socket on the stub. "Stu, how about taking off the wire cover while I detach the power cable off the frame." Brian grabbed a pair of wire cutters and deftly snipped off two black zip ties. Stu ratcheted the four bolts out and pried the electrical cover plate loose with a flathead screwdriver. They peered inside the wiring box.

"Just like I suspected. Toast." Brian winced. The wire connections were scorched and partially melted. "Gotta pull the motor and replace it. Stu, go ahead and snip the wires as close to the motor connection as possible. We'll reuse most of the power cable."

Stu went to work on the three power wires and the ground wire. "Brian, how come there are three powers? I've done a fair amount of house wiring and have only seen two wires plus a ground."

"That's because the farm has three-phase power. See the power lines up there?" Brian pointed to the sky near the power pole. "You got three wires running off the transformer."

"Three phase?"

"Yeah, supposedly three phase is more economical and the motors are cheaper. I'm sorry I can't explain it better than that. Electricity wasn't one of my strongest subjects in physics."

"Does it matter which way we hook up the wires?"

"Oh, yeah, if we get one miswired, the machine will run backward. We can turn it on for a second and check it. We'll swap one of them around if we have to, and it'll be good to go."

"Now I suppose we need to remove the motor?"

"Yep, this isn't the fun part. Due to all the corrosion it can be frustrating. For Win's sake, I'll keep the cussing to a minimum."

"Win."

"Sir?"

"What's said on the pond dam, stays on the pond dam, right?"

"Ten four, Daddy. Just like that commercial for Vegas."

They managed to detach the corroded motor from the gearbox. Getting two hundred pounds of cast iron up the bank, into the back of the truck, left them winded and drenched in sweat. The strength-robbing invisible fog of humidity was so thick, Stu would have traded it for the ammonia stench in Uncle Phil's hog house. Win hunkered down in the shade of the farm's pickup.

Stu wiped the sweat off his brow with the back of his hand. "Gawd, it's hot out here."

"You'll get used to it." Brian paused for effect. "In about thirty years."

"You guys thirsty?" Stu asked.

"I could use another grape Gatorade about now. How 'bout you, Win?"

"Sounds like a plan, Mr. Brian."

"We'll get a new motor at the shed. We can grab some drinks."

"How do you know if there's a new motor in the shed?"

"Oh, man, that's a fundamental operating principle of Murphy's law of fish farming. You keep replacements for everything that revolves around keeping fish alive. Universal joints, spare tractors, emergency aerators, backup oxygen meters, electrical motors, water quality kits. I know farmers that have dual backup alarm clocks."

"Okay then."

"You need to keep at least three motors and three gearboxes on hand at all times. That should cover you for most weekends."

Stu looked out over the expanse of water. It seemed so peaceful. After listening to Brian all day, it seemed Mother Nature's version of a fomenting apocalypse could happen any moment.

"We better get going. You need to get a nap in this afternoon. Get rested before tonight. The fun starts again at eight," Brian said.

Stu was still looking out over the water, praying the learning curve would flatten out a little more. He really wanted to go for a run. The anxiety from all the unknowns was almost overwhelming.

Downing their Gatorades, worshipping the deep shade of the shed, they returned to the pond and replaced the motor. Brian used his amp meter, checking the three legs of power at the panel box. They were pulling twenty-one amps.

"Good to go now," Brian said as he secured the panel box lid shut.

He put away his tools and closed the tailgate. He looked at his watch. It read 14:45.

"Stu, you really need to knock out a three-hour nap. We should start again at eight."

"What do you mean we?"

"Oh, man, I can't turn you loose yet. I'll ride the ponds with you on your first night."

"Dude, that's kinda going beyond the call of duty for a government man, isn't it?"

"Not really. That's my job. Helping the fish industry. Fish don't punch time clocks. They'll die when they want to. Don't worry about me. I take lots of comp time in the winter. The farmers and I get pretty worthless spending time in shooting houses, drinking Jack, validating the local gossip. You'll be sitting on the beach somewhere remembering all the insane hours you clocked during the summer. You might even take up deer hunting in the winter like the rest of us rednecks."

Win looked at Brian. "Can you hunt deer with a baseball bat?"

Brian stared at Win, gauging his seriousness.

Stu sighed. "Let's save that one for a cold beer."

"We're up to two now."

*****

Brian arrived at eight sharp. He wore faded khaki chinos, a long-sleeved Magellan fishing shirt, and smelled like he performed a full-immersion baptism in a font of Deep Woods Off. Stu took the hint, changing out of his cutoff jeans and T-shirt. He would soon get acquainted with Alabama mosquitos. They weren't easily deterred by screen doors. The bloodsuckers were big enough to open them. Soon he'd be comparing them to Minnesota's version, strong enough to unzip a tent fly.

Tab was curled up on the couch with Win, watching the Discovery Channel. The Direct TV satellite dish, the new service contract signed late that afternoon, pointed southwest over Texas. Reintroducing them to the world beyond Spencer County. The microwave dinged. The essence of Orville Redenbacher wafted in the air.

"Good evening, Brian. Stu told me about your job dedication. That's very admirable. We need to clone you. Send your units off to California."

Stu grabbed his truck keys off the kitchen table. "Yeah, we could start off sending them to Cal Trans. Lazy bastards."

Win glanced up at his daddy. Tab gave her husband the look. Brian noticed the quiet messaging. Stu sought an exit. "Well, Brian, let's go check on my fishies."

"We should be back in a couple of hours. I'll need to use your dining room table for an hour or so. Need to show Stu an easy way to comprehend oxygen dynamics. You might want to sit in on it too. It'd be good for you in case you need to fill in for him. The night work on a catfish farm is critical."

"I'll be looking forward to it. Would you guys care for a fresh pot of coffee when you come back?"

"That'd be great," Stu said. They left for the ponds.

Stu cranked up the truck in the carport. The radio had just started in with Lynyrd Skynrd's *Sweet Home Alabama*. He turned it down to be polite in case Brian needed to talk.

"Man, that's a good way to get shot around here," Brian drawled. "What I'd do?"

"Don't ever turn that song down in the presence of Bama good ole boys. It's considered heresy. You'll be in for an ass whupping."

Stu concentrated on the lyrics. "Well, I heard ole Neil put her down. Well, I hope Neil Young will remember. A Southern man don't need him around."

"I see what you mean. The Alabama anthem." Stu chuckled.

"Just saved your life. You owe me now." Brian chuckled back.

They parked in front of the shed and retrieved the oxygen meter off the counter.

"Okay, let's turn her on again and do a quick battery check."

Stu turned the meter on and performed a red line check. "Looks good, dude."

"Okay, now we need the clipboard in the feed truck. Should be some blank oxygen sheets under the feed sheets," Brian said.

Stu strolled over to the feed truck and fetched the clipboard off the driver's dash.

"Good to go. Let's load up," Brian said.

Stu took the wheel of the farm pickup, and Brian slid in, riding shotgun.

"Just start here with pond number one." Brian pointed to the pond behind the shop.

"Well, that's the first thing today that makes sense."

"Park it right there behind that aerator. Kinda angle it sideways halfway down the side so you can reach the water with the stick."

Stu parked the truck several feet from the edge of the water.

"Okay, get your meter ready," Brian said.

Stu performed the calibrations flawlessly. He made sure the moisture cap had a wet sponge.

Brian grabbed the clipboard. "Okay, my man, give me an oxygen reading. Oh, this should help." He flicked a toggle switch above the center ashtray. The spotlight on the toolbox behind the rear window illuminated the side of the truck and the bank below.

"Good deal. Was wondering what that switch was for," Stu said.

"There's a handheld in the toolbox. If they get up on you and get stressed too bad, they'll be cruising the surface with their whiskers poking out of the water, waiting on you to save their lives. The grim reaper will have started the countdown. If you wanna know how many you got up, count the eyeballs and divide by two," Brian deadpanned.

"Seriously?"

"Oh, yeah. Cops, firefighters and catfish farmers have one thing in common. The pucker factor. Nothing like watching a hundred thousand pounds of fish die in a manner of minutes."

"How come you have to keep reminding me I may have bit off more than I can chew?"

Brian laughed. "Keep chewing, it'll go down eventually."

Stu removed the cap off the probe and stuck the pole out the window. He moved the probe back and forth about a foot deep in the dark green water.

They watched the meter needle settle around the eleven mark.

"We'll call it eleven even. Don't worry about the tenths until it gets less than four. Eleven parts oxygen at eight-thirty is good. What's the water temp?" Brian asked.

Stu rotated the knob and it settled on thirty-one centigrade. Without prompting from Brian, he turned the meter over and looked at the conversion chart taped to the back. "Eighty-eight degrees."

"That's almost a perfect temp for catfish. Their optimum is eighty-six. Bad news is oxygen levels can change quickly at that temperature."

"How quickly?" Stu asked.

"Quicker than a nap. Next pond, dude."

Stu and Brian made their way around the ponds, ending up at pond twenty across from pond one. The readings ranged from six to fourteen. It had taken them about an hour and twenty minutes to do the first round.

"Okay, let's go to the house. I'll give you a crash course on oxygen."

The men pulled into the gravel driveway and parked. Brian stopped by his pickup and grabbed some papers off his dash. Tab was watching the very beginning of the local news out of Birmingham. Stu walked up behind her and nipped at her neck, smelling her damp freshly shampooed hair. It smelled of coconut.

"Gosh, you smell good, girl," Stu said gently in Tab's ear, his arms wrapped around her trim waist.

"How it'd go out there?"

"I don't know. Brian's still teaching."

"You still anxious about all this?"

"Yeah, I really need to get a run-in and relieve some of this tension."

Brian was at the kitchen carport door. He knocked briefly before stepping in. Stu and Tab parted their embrace. They sat down at the round kitchen table. In the middle was a carafe of fresh coffee, a bowl of sugar, and a pint carton of Piggly Wiggly half-and-half. Three shiny yellow porcelain coffee cups adorned with the red CTC logo rested on paper napkins.

The men fixed their coffee. Tab opted for a mug of skim milk.

"Win go down okay?"

"Yeah, took him a while to wind down. He can't stop talking about that four-wheeler. You need to get him a helmet."

"You're right. Where do we go for that?" Stu asked Brian.

"I'd try the Honda dealer in Smackover."

"Brian, would you mind giving us a course on operating it?"

"No problem. I have a Kawasaki that I use for hunting. They're all basically the same in terms of driving."

"What do you hunt?" Tab asked.

"Mostly deer. I'd like to do more turkey hunting but it's too much frustration. About like golf."

"Amen to that," Stu quipped.

Tab looked intently at Brian. "Are there enough deer around to kill?"

Brian looked at her, sensing an upcoming inquisition. Stu put his hand on her knee under the table, squeezing gently. He hoped the discourse into shooting defenseless animals would be mild.

"Tab," Brian started softly, sensing the terseness in her voice, "Alabama ranks the highest in whitetail deer numbers. The state allows us to shoot a deer a day for ninety days. If the Alabama Farmers Federation had their way in Montgomery, we could harvest two deer a day. There would still be enough to maintain the population," Brian said politely with firm conviction. He wanted to allay her concerns without getting confrontational. He hoped she wasn't a rabid antihunter. At least she wasn't a vegan. They could get militant in a heartbeat. *She looked too healthy to be a vegan.*

Stu looked at his doubting wife. "Hey, girl, I've got twenty ponds of dumb fish out there depending on me right now. Brian, I'm all ears, so get me up to speed on this oxygen thing."

Tab wrapped both hands around her mug of milk. "I'm sorry we got off track. Nobody in my family ever hunted. I didn't grow up around guns."

"That's okay. No worries. I think with time you'll get more comfortable with hunting and guns. It's part of the culture here."

"Well, we'll see about that. Stu may develop an interest in all that eventually." The image of the snake flashed again. *How many more were there?*

Stu nodded. He was a galaxy closer to someday owning a real gun.

"Do I need to get a paper and pad for notes?" Tab asked.

"No, you're good. It's not complicated. Working with smart people like you two is a real pleasure. I run into some doozies."

Tab smiled.

Peace was at hand. Stu wondered what venison tasted like.

Brian removed a Gem clip from a short stack of blank graph paper. "There are three concepts you have to master with oxygen and fish ponds. First, the main consumer of oxygen is not the fish. It's the tiny green plants in the water. The algae. Fish only consume twenty percent of the oxygen.

"The second thing you need to know is, fortunately, oxygen consumption during the night is linear or, in layman's terms, predictable most of the time. Hence this graph paper. We're going to do a little exercise to get this point across."

Brian drew a line down the left side of the paper about three blocks in and then a second line across the bottom, left to right, also three blocks in. The lines met in the left-hand lower corner. "The vertical represents oxygen, and the horizontal represents time. Each block represents one part oxygen and one hour of time. Simple." Brian started numbering blocks. Stu and Tab looked intently at Brian's sketching. "I'll label from 6:00 p.m. and go out to 6:00 a.m. for the next morning.

"Now, one more important detail. The stress zone." He drew a horizontal line at the two for oxygen all the way across the graph from left to right, blackening in the area below. "That's the stress zone for the fish and the pucker factor for you."

"Pucker factor?" Tab asked.

"Taking a baseball bat to a gunfight." Stu sighed.

Tab smirked. Brian looked bewildered.

"We'll save that one for a beer too," Stu said.

"That's three. I may have to invest in a bigger beer cooler."

"Auburn let you drink during office hours?"

"It's always five o'clock somewhere, man."

They chuckled. Tab wondered where she had packed the CDs. Alabama's Jimmy Buffett was one of her favorites. She recalled that he was a native of Mobile and had attended Auburn. He lasted one semester. His English teacher had said he'd never amount to anything.

Brian continued, "Okay, this is example one. We go out there right after sunset, say eight o'clock, and the oxygen is twelve." Brian took his pencil, traced out to the corresponding hour at the bottom of the page, and made a heavy dot near the left edge of the paper. The mark indicated twelve oxygen and 8:00 p.m.

"Now, we go out again, three hours later, and check. She's dropped to ten." Brian added another dot to his graph.

"Okay, now the fun step. We connect the two dots and extend the line to the bottom of the graph." The line ended around nine the next morning.

Stu commented without prompting, "Looks like we hit the stress zone at about nine o'clock the next morning."

"Exactly, but this is good because the sun has been up, shining for a couple of hours. Photosynthesis should be kicking back on. The algae is making oxygen again, and it should be increasing by this time in the morning.

"Another example, and this one will be with worse consequences." Brian placed a dot at fifteen parts oxygen at eight o'clock and then his second dot at nine parts and eleven o clock. He turned the graph around and let Tab and Stu look at the data points.

"Draw your line, now," Brian said.

Stu drew the line. "Whoa. We hit the stress zone at 3:00 a.m. That's not good."

"Worse yet, you'll be at zero oxygen by sunrise. Hopefully you turned the aerators on way before then."

"Okay, so when do the aerators come on?" Tab asked.

"I'd say as a rule of thumb at four oxygen. This is something you learn from experience. Sometimes they gotta be switched on before it gets to four if it's going to be an hour or so before you make the next round. Let's say you have a pond going down pretty fast. It could be below four before you get back to the pond on the next round. Go ahead and turn at least one aerator on. Main thing is keeping the oxygen above two at all times."

Stu looked at the graphs and nodded. "This makes sense, Brian. Thanks."

"Well, it's just a teaching tool. I'm not expecting you to graph twenty ponds every night. If you did it for the first few nights and noted where the oxygen actually ended up before turning on the aerators, you'd be amazed at its accuracy." Brian looked at his watch again. It was slightly after eleven. "We need to get back out there. I'm a tad nervous about not knowing what's going on."

"Oh my god, if you're nervous, that means we better run to the truck."

Brian laughed. "We'll be all right. Let's get going."

The two men got up and left quickly. Tab didn't get a goodbye kiss.

After Stu got behind the wheel, he turned to Brian, "You said there were three things I needed to learn about oxygen management. Still waiting on the third."

"Fish don't read graphs," Brian said, looking into the side mirror, trying to hide his grin.

Stu's first night checking ponds was almost without a cluster. The minor cluster occurred when Stu accidently ran over an armadillo. Instinctively, the critter jumped, banging into the undercarriage when Stu dead-centered it. Dazed, no doubt, it dived into the pond. Both men were amazed they could swim that fast. Brian referred to them as possums on a half shell. Stu saved that one for Win.

Most of the aerators were turned on during the early morning hours and were still churning water at daybreak. Brian had gone on home as the first rays of sunshine filtered through the dense grove of red cedars on the eastern edge of the farm. Stu, as instructed, started turning aerators off in the ponds if the oxygen was above three.

When Stu rolled into the driveway at six fifteen, he smelled hickory-smoked bacon. Tab was in the kitchen still organizing the cabinets and taking empty boxes out to the fifty-five-gallon burn barrel in the backyard. Bushed and very hungry, the staying awake all night had burned up more than his usual amount of calories. On top of the farm work, he was still adjusting to the new time zone. The last time he could remember being so exhausted was the time he and Ross drove all night, coming back from Oregon, after delivering a load of furniture, too broke to pay for a hotel room.

CHAPTER TWENTY-TWO

Tab sat on the edge of the bed, gently nudging him awake. "Stu, an eighteen-wheeler is headed to the ponds." He mumbled for a second, squinting at her with an eye slightly open.

"Damn, what time is it?"

"It's just past one."

"That would be one in the afternoon, right?"

"Yes." Tab giggled.

"What kind of eighteen-wheeler?"

"A shiny round one like they haul milk with, but it had a long arm on the side."

"That's a screw auger. They're used to haul grains and feed. I better get down there. I don't remember arranging for fish feed."

"Did you remember to set up farm insurance?"

"Oh, yeah, our agent back in LA has a college buddy in Tuscaloosa. He set us up. I signed the paperwork back in LA. We're good to go."

Stu donned a pair of LL Bean khaki shorts and a peach-colored T-shirt. He darted into the master bath, splashing cold water on his face. The mirror confirmed the facial itch. He scratched at the three-day growth. New gray hairs in the stubble.

Tab stood beside him in the mirror. "You still think this was a good idea?"

"You know, it's a blend of insanity and space travel. Like waiting for a floating crescent wrench to take out your space shield as you're hurtling along at warp speed. That's the dream I keep having over and over anyway. Seriously, though, it's going to be a few weeks before we settle into a routine. I can see right now that I need to get some help. That's gotta be my first priority. Brian's supposed to be helping with that."

"I really like Brian. We'd be in a world of hurt right now without him," Tab said.

"Yeah, he's been a savior. Wonder how much money it'd take to get him off the government tit?"

"A pile. If he's university faculty, he's probably vested in a decent pension plan. With a liberal vacation policy to boot."

"Yeah, you're probably right." He tried plucking out the gray hairs. Vanity surrendered to pain, he frowned and gave up. "I need to get going." Stu offered Tab a kiss.

Tab handed him his toothbrush. He took the hint.

Win was sitting cross legged on the living room carpet watching Mr. Rogers on Alabama Public TV.

"Kinda hot for a sweater, isn't it?" Stu teased.

"Oh, Daddy, he always wears a sweater."

"Come on, let's go check on that truck."

He didn't need to say it again.

They drove up to the idling tractor trailer next to the feed bin. The driver unhooked a short thick black rubber bungie attached to the long arm. It kept it from banging into the long nine-foot-diameter aluminum tube.

"Good afternoon, I'm Stuart Baron. I bought the farm from Mrs. Hopkins. This is my son, Winchester."

The driver took a good look at Win, mentally processing the youngster. He stared at the close-cropped nap of kinky hair. Momentarily puzzled, he shrugged it off.

Win proudly stepped forward, warmly greeting the man. "Good to meet you, mister." Win stuck his right hand out, then realizing his mistake. He looked up at his dad.

Stu whispered, "It's okay."

"Sorry, I didn't catch your name?" Stu asked.

"Stub Ryan."

The man's right hand was missing. Win couldn't help staring at the bulbous knob at the end of the man's thin forearm.

"What'd you bring me today?" Stu asked.

Ryan looked at him funny-like. "This is what we call catfish feed."

"Okay. Anything I need to do to help? We're new at this."

"Nah, I got it," Ryan replied. He positioned the auger tube over the opening for the feed bin and threw another lever in the up position.

The feed tumbled through the tube and fell inside the bin. The truck unloaded in about fifteen minutes. Win busied himself hurling gravel into the nearest pond until his dad reminded him that the gravel was on the road for a reason and cost money.

Ryan handed Stu the delivery ticket. "That's the last load for Hopkins's feed contract. My boss says you need to make arrangements for the next load."

"Ten four. Thanks."

Stu showed it to Win as the truck pulled away. The bottom figure read "$6,160." Stu pointed at it and read it out loud. Four digit numbers were a tad difficult for Win.

"Daddy, that's a lot," Win exclaimed. "How long will it last?"

"According to Brian, less than a week."

"Daddy, are you going to spend that much every week?"

Stu still had about six hundred thousand stored in the cardboard box, fictitiously labeled *National Geographic,* on the top shelf in his bedroom closet. *Cocaine or marijuana, whatever those assholes were into, would soon become catfish.*

"Well, Daddy?" Win stared at him. Waiting on an answer. Hoping the fish wouldn't starve because his daddy ran out of money. Remembering all the goldfish flushed down the toilet.

"Yes, Win, I'll be spending that much every week." Stu grinned.

After a sumptuous late lunch of roast beef sandwiches and jalapeno-flavored potato chips, Stu called Brian at his office.

"Brian, it's two thirty. Just finished lunch. Haven't fed the fish yet."

Brian winced. "Stu, let's get 'em fed before five, okay? They don't need to go into the early morning with a stomach full of feed. Low oxygen while digesting feed isn't good."

"Ten four on that. How we coming on finding farm help?" Stu asked.

"As a matter of fact, I'm glad you called. Got a man set up for an interview tomorrow morning if you're willing."

"Shoot yes. What time?"

"That's your call."

Stu thought for a moment. "Well, I'd rather do it before I go down for my morning nap."

"Let's do a promptness test. See if he can get there by seven thirty sharp," Brian suggested.

"I like how you think, Caine."

"Okay, I'll be there around seven. Give you some pointers on hiring folks around here. Hopefully he'll show up. I drove by his house early this morning before work. Everything looked tidy. He didn't have a foreclosure sign in the front yard anyway."

"That's good starting intel, Brian. Neat and tidy without bad credit is a start. How do you feel about drug testing?"

"Well, it's not normally done around here. I don't see anything wrong with starting a trend."

"It's standard operating procedure in the trucking industry. We get insurance discounts with routine and surprise testing."

"That's your call. I think it's a great idea."

"See you tomorrow morning."

CHAPTER TWENTY-THREE

Stu and Brian sipped on some freshly ground Costa Rican peaberry at the kitchen table before the interview. Tab was wearing cobalt-blue gym shorts and a V-necked pink T-shirt. She loaded the breakfast dishes into the Kenmore. Brian barely managed to keep his glances from turning into voyeuristic stares. She finished bending over the open dishwasher door, allowing Brian to concentrate on the task at hand: preparing Stu for an Alabama job interview.

Brian recognized another attribute of Tabitha Baron, her naturalness with others. She carried herself well. She shared the same confident manner of her husband. Not the least pretentious like so many of the older Southern belles he had to contend with on the last remaining plantations. He hated traveling to the Mississippi delta, attending social functions with the wives of the industry's pioneer catfish farmers. They were always in a contest to see who could reset the snoot bar. *If you don't have an ancestor buried in a gray uniform, you better come through the back door of my house, son.* Tabitha Baron was refreshing. She made him feel comfortable and welcome in her home.

Brian politely wiped his mouth after he finished his second cup. He slid his chair back from the table and crossed his leg at the other ankle.

"I have a story about hiring folks around here. Tab, you might want to listen in. It's kinda funny."

Tab sat down opposite Brian. She picked up her cup with both hands and sipped. Stu reached over and tucked a loose curl behind her ear.

Brian started, "Before my extension job, I worked on Alabama's largest catfish farm. We had about five hundred acres. They hired me as a farm manager right out of Auburn. I started out checking oxygen at night so I could learn the ponds and then got put on days managing the crew and the hatchery. There were eight guys on payroll, mostly day laborers, a mechanic, a full-time feed man, and three on night duty. About six months in, my boss bought another hundred acres of water about seven miles away from the main farm."

"Where was this farm, Brian?"

"Over in Dallas County, near Selma."

Selma rang Tab's memory bell. She recalled the bridge incident with the troopers and the beating of the protestors from one of her American history college courses. Selma was only sixty miles away. She wondered what the town was like now, some thirty years later.

"I had to hire a night man right off or I'd be stuck doing the oxygen checking. We were already spread pretty thin, labor wise. The owner didn't want the night crew leaving the main farm."

Tab got up to turn off the dishwasher, making it easier to hear Brian's soft-spoken voice. She couldn't get over the racket of the Kenmore. It sounded like a tomcat was stuck inside, loud thumps with alternating screeching and muffled howling as it swapped cycles. Stu said it was possessed by a demonic god named Catfish Murphy and she had better not open the door in midcycle. She missed her Bosch.

"We put the word out that we were hiring. I set up an interview with a man who had worked nearby in a tire store and lost his job when the owner retired. Well, he arrived promptly, which is always a good sign. His name was Frankie DeCarter. He was a black man in his fifties, slightly pudgy, but very strong looking. His hands were the size of shovels. Heavily calloused. I knew right off he wasn't allergic to work."

Stu chuckled. "Allergic to work. Yeah, I know the type. We got them in California too. Most of them work for Cal Trans."

"I told him about the job. I said, 'Mr. Frankie, this job is checking oxygen from sunset to sunrise during the summer. You'll get a long weekend off every two weeks. From November through March, it'll be during the day helping the mechanic with winter maintenance.'"

Stu took notes on a small pad of paper, making a list of issues to cover for the interview.

Brian continued, "He was okay with the hours. Then I told him about the actual working conditions. I wanted him to know exactly what he was getting himself into. I said, 'Look, this farm's in pretty rough shape. We just bought it and plan on sprucing it up in the next few months. The snakes are as big around as your arm.'" Tab winced at the vision. "'Some of the tractors don't have decent brakes, so you're gonna have to chock the wheels with a railroad tie when you park on a pond levee. The roads don't have near enough rock. They're slicker than owl shit after a rain. It could be one cluster after another.'" Brian glanced at Tab for her reaction to his colorful terminology. He was turning red.

Tab smiled at his embarrassment. "Brian, I'm okay. I know what a cluster is. A billy goat surrounded by fifty nannies in heat."

Stu chortled. He looked at his watch. "Better hurry, Brian. The interviewers shouldn't be late for the interviewee."

Brian continued, "Mr. Frankie has been taking all this in. He asked me, 'Mr. Brian, how much you gonna pay me for all this?'"

"I said, 'I'll start you out at three hundred per week, and after a few months, I'll pay you what you're worth.'"

"Frankie looks at me with all the sincerity in the world and says, 'Mr. Brian, I can't live on what I'm worth.'" Brian let out a self-appreciating laugh, and then the Barons laughed with him.

"That's precious, Brian. Thanks for sharing. You two better get going. It's seven twenty." Brian got a hug before leaving.

They elected to interview the man under the shade of the feed bins for security reasons. Tab wasn't keen on bringing a stranger in the house. Brian didn't want anybody mentally inventorying the tools in the unlocked farm shed.

Stu wanted Brian to take the lead on the interview for the catfish questions. Stu would follow up on some basic inquiries into the man's work history.

They drove out to the mailbox at the end of the driveway. It was seven twenty-five. They sat in the pickup and gazed up the road.

"Brian, when I hire people, I try to find the ones with uncommon sense."

"Uncommon sense?"

"I usually ask a question that requires them to think on their feet. I don't want people with common sense working for me."

"Man, you're losing me."

"Obviously, you know how to think on your feet. I've picked up on that just working with you the other day. The way you handled that snake. Replacing the rusted motor on the aerator. Teaching Win about the four-wheeler. You're comfortable solving problems. You're wired that way." Stu shifted around in his seat, facing Brian. "The average person in this country, at least in California, is a freaking moron. Did you know, America ranks fourteenth in the world in terms of cognitive skills and problem-solving among technically rich countries? We are letting our kids in school slide on being able to think rationally and solve problems. In California, we don't call kids who get Ds and Fs failing. We coddle them, refer to them as emerging." Stu waved his hands, making exaggerated air quotes. "I don't want employees with common sense. I want those with extraordinary sense or uncommon sense. You follow me?"

"Yeah, that makes sense. I'm serious. Not trying to be funny." Brian nodded several times, staring out the window, looking up the road.

"Over the road trucking requires problem solving. We have to get the loads delivered in the quickest time possible. That's our competitive edge. Nobody else can touch us. I always put at least one guy on a team who is wired to solve problems. With time, this trait gets passed on to the other two."

"I'll bet your truckers have seen some crazy shit out there on the road, huh?"

"Oh, man, you wouldn't believe half of it. Our company picnics are side splitters when the stories get started. One of my favorites is about the speeding woman with bald tires." Stu shifted around in his seat and adjusted the air conditioning vent.

"One of our teams had to attend court because they had witnessed a serious accident. They got to watch several people brought before the judge for traffic citations. There was this woman cited for speeding ninety-five on the interstate in the rain. When the judge asked her why, she said the first trooper that had pulled her over said she needed to hurry home and buy new tires because her current ones were bald."

"Oh my god," Brian laughed.

"My grandfather was a pathologist for the New York City morgue. He noticed that some brains were less convoluted than others. He read up on it, and sure enough, very intelligent people have deeper convolutions, particularly the judges, doctors, and intellectual types. Some of the run-of-the-mill people had very shallow convolutions. Whenever he encountered the freaking morons, the Darwinian dead-ends, he referred to them as slickheads. Always made me laugh when he was driving in traffic and muttered, 'Damn slickheads.'"

"We got lots of them down here too." Brian checked his watch. It was seven thirty.

"How'd you hear about this guy, Brian?"

"He showed up at the airport, asking my uncle Buster if he had some work. He told him to come see me. Name's Willie Jones. He moved back from Memphis. He grew up around here. You're getting first dibs on him."

"Man, I appreciate you thinking about me, Brian."

"You can't afford to get off on the wrong foot with hired help. It can end up costing big-time. Everybody knows everybody around here. It's not hard finding out about people. Let's try not to hire one of them slickheads."

Stu and Brian chuckled.

A 1986 robin's-egg blue Cadillac Fleetwood Brougham with a heavily rusted front bumper and Tennessee plates made its way slowly down the dirt lane. It was seven thirty-one. As it approached, Stu noticed the left front tire was almost flat.

The car stopped at the driveway. A black man, in his forties, lowered the electric window on the passenger side. He asked the two men in the pickup if they knew a "Mistah Baron." It was then that the man and Brian recognized each other from their brief meeting at the office.

Stu and Brian exited the truck. They met Mr. Willie Jones in front of the Cadillac.

They shook hands. Stu noticed the man's firm handshake. Their eyes met for a good first impression. Stu appreciated this, sincere eye contact while firmly shaking. It was never a good sign if the eyes looked away during that first second. His degree in psychology and training in human resources enabled him to peg human personalities with uncanny accuracy.

After the pleasantries, Stu remarked, "Looks like your tire there could use some air."

"Mr. Stu, that tire was almost sitting on the rim at the house. I used one of those cans of tire foam. I prayed to sweet Jesus that I'd have enough air to get here. I didn't want to be late."

"Well, we'll get you fixed up so you can make it back home," Stu said.

"Mr. Willie, how about following us a little piece down the road here. We'll have our meeting and pump that tire up," Brian said.

The men got in their vehicles. Jones followed them to the shed. Stu and Brian, due to the tire emergency, elected to conduct the meeting in the shade of the shed, closer to the air hose.

Stu and Brian sat on the lowered tailgate. Willie Jones leaned against the front hood of his Cadillac.

Brian started off. Jones looked puzzled.

"Excuse me a sec, fellas. I'm confused. Who's doing the hiring, you or Mr. Baron?" Willie looked directly at Brian Caine.

Stu interrupted, "I'm sorry Mr. Jones. We should have made that clear. I'm actually the owner and will be doing the hiring. Brian's helping me out since I'm new in the catfish business."

"Okay. Just ah' wondering is all. Never been interviewed by two people before."

"Just blow smoke up his dress, not mine," quipped Brian as he nodded toward Stu.

They shared smiles.

Brian continued, "Mr. Willie, this is a catfish farm with about two hundred acres of water. Mr. Baron here is looking for a night man to begin with. He'll eventually hire a day man. So right now, we're interviewing for a nighttime oxygen checker."

"Before we go any further, you got any objections to working at night?" Stu asked.

"Fellas, I drove a cab in Memphis for fifteen years from ten o'clock to six in the morning. I prefer working nights. I like to fish in the morning. Allows me wind down after work."

Stu and Brian let this soak in. *Good longtime history of working. One employer for fifteen years. Night guy too. Not afraid of touching a damned fish.*

"Let me explain what oxygen checking entails," Brian said.

"That's okay, Mr. Brian. My daddy checked fish for Mr. Mueller down in Safford for twenty years. On weekend nights, sometimes I would ride with him and write down the numbers. We worked a place where the cottonmouths were as big around as your arm."

Brian was almost grinning ear to ear. It was time to pin him down on the honesty issue.

"He worked for the Mueller's, huh? Which one?"

"I believe it was Mr. Neal. Harry had passed. Daddy couldn't work with the bees though. He was allergic. Carried around one of those injector sticks."

Brian was familiar with the farm. The Muellers were big honey producers. Now out of the bee business due to the mite plague.

Mr. Willie had passed the honesty test. The basic facts matched up.

"Mr. Willie, tell me a little about your past work history, and why you want to work on a catfish farm?" Stu asked.

"Mr. Stu, like I said, I worked for a taxi company in Memphis. I was fired for violating company policy. I was one of the crazy ones that worked the southeast side."

"That's not my favorite part of Memphis, for sure," Brian winced.

"Tell me about it. Hookers, drug dealers, gangbangers, place was like the south side of Chicago. You couldn't pull a shift without hearing gunfire. About my second week in, I started packing heat. Had a shoulder holster with a forty-five Colt auto. Real good for drawing while seated. I served in the Army for six years. Made it to sergeant. Forty-fives were standard issue for sergeants at the time. I heard they went to 9 mm Berettas. Too much gun for the ladies."

"Thank you for your service," Stu said.

"Appreciate it. Never left stateside. My MOS involved operating heavy machinery. I was in transportation. Had to pack heat because I transported payrolls and special dispatches between bases."

"That involve anything with eighteen wheels?" Stu asked.

"No, sir. All they let me drive in the army was basically straight frame shit. Mostly deuce and a halves, you know, the six-by-sixes. I was qualified for the M1088s, the armored tank haulers, but since I stayed stateside, there wasn't much demand for moving tanks around."

Stu grinned. Brian was thinking the same. *This guy might do. Little fifty-five horsepower tractor isn't going to intimidate him.*

"Well, you're probably going to call my old boss, so here's what happened. They let me go 'cause I ended up shooting two gangbangers in self-defense. Violated company policy carrying a gun."

Brian was stunned. He stared intently at Willie. Being face-to-face with someone who had actually shot a person was a novel experience.

"You kill them, Willie?" Stu asked without missing a beat. The news didn't stun Baron. He had witnessed human carnage only thirty feet away. Several of his teams had been involved in similar situations. Per company policy, his truckers could carry if they had concealed gun permits in their home states. You could forget about getting one in California unless you were related to Kit Carson.

"Yeah, one died damn quick like. The other one bled out in about five minutes. They shot me first. Grazed my collarbone. Asshole was probably aiming at the back of my head."

"Did the investigation prove all this?" Stu asked matter-of-factly. Brian was still mesmerized.

"Cops called it a good shoot. Never heard that phrase before." Willie kicked at the gravel. "The kid that shot me with the twenty-five cal. died right after I shot him in the head. The kid shooting the thirty-eight missed me completely. I was laying low with my arm extended over the front seat, spraying and praying with my forty-five. I put one in his femoral artery. Fortunately, he ran outta bullets before I did."

"I'm sorry you had to go through all that, Willie," Stu said, grabbing Willie on his shoulder and giving him a light shake. Stu's long experience of running a league of truckers had polished his empathic button.

"Well, my immediate boss, Mr. Mask, hated to let me go. Said I was one of his best drivers. Nobody ever called in a complaint on me. But it was company policy."

Brian spoke up, "It still isn't right. Assholes shot first. You gotta right to defend yourself."

"Willie, you get your gun back?" Stu asked.

"Not yet."

"Damn, that sucks," Brian said.

"Yeah, well, the worst part was the gang's price on my head. Cops told me it'd be best if I left town. So here I am looking for something to do."

"Mr. Willie, you get another gun?" Brian asked. He was going to need one working nights with the varmints and the fish poachers.

"Hell yeah. Got me one of those Dirty Harry specials. A forty-four Magnum. Blow a head clean off," a very black Willie said, trying his best to imitate a very white Clint Eastwood.

Brian and Stu laughed. Everybody starting kicking gravel, relieving the tension. Bonds among men started to form.

"Mr. Willie, you got any questions?"

"How many hours per week and what's the pay?"

"First off, it's a salaried job. The paycheck will come from my company in Los Angeles."

"What company is that?"

"Coast to Coast Trucking."

"Really? I used to see your trucks all the time at the Love's in south Memphis right off interstate fifty-five. Sometimes half a dozen at a time. Crazy drivers were always walking fast like they were in a race or something."

Stu grinned. "Yeah, we're called the NASCAR of trucking. You should see one of my teams change a flat tire."

"Salaried?"

"Yeah, like my truckers, I put everyone on a three-tier salary system. Apprentice at twenty-five, yeoman at thirty, and master at thirty-five thousand. That's just base. We have merit incentives that almost doubles the base. Since this isn't a trucking job, the merit incentive here will be a yearly bonus based on pounds produced. Brian and I think the bonus could be as high as fifteen thousand. The base starting out will be twenty-five a year."

"I was making that a year in Memphis, but tips amounted to about two hundred a week."

"So that's about an extra ten grand tax free?" Stu calculated.

"Sounds about right."

"So we're in the ballpark. Tell you what, I'll make your bonus in cash too? How about that?"

"I can live with that. Bonus in December?"

"Yep."

"Okay, hours then?" Willie asked.

"Here's the bugger part. I need a nightman to work eleven days straight, Monday to Monday plus Tuesday, Wednesday, and Thursday morning. Then you get a long weekend off, Thursday night, Friday, Saturday, and Sunday. You come in at seven and leave at seven, provided all the fish are okay in the morning. That's just from April through October. From November to April, you only have to work mornings from eight to noon, no weekends. That should compensate for the weekend work twice a month." Stu looked at Brian. Brian nodded.

"What would I be doing those morning hours?"

"Mainly helping me or the day man with PM."

"PM?"

"Preventative maintenance. Aeration repair, sandblasting and painting, tractor cleaning, detailing trucks."

"Well, I know a lot about maintenance. My stint in the Army. You ever drive a Crown Vic with five hundred thousand miles on it?"

"Damn, that's a lot of mileage. I thought I was doing good putting three hundred on my pickup," Brian said

"Hell, we'll easily put two million on a Peterbilt. We're firm believers in PM."

"Okay, then. Mr. Willie whatcha' thinking? You still interested?" Brian asked.

"Yeah, I'd like a shot at it."

"Hope it doesn't come to that," Stu said.

Willie looked at Mr. Baron. Then realized the irony in his choice of words.

"Hopefully, the only thing you'll be shooting around here are snakes and cormorants," Brian added.

"I still need to check with your former employer. What was the name of the taxi company?"

"Kwik Cab of Memphis. K-W-I-K. Mr. Paulie Mask was my supervisor. He only works the night shift."

"I assume you were honorably discharged?" Stu asked.

"Yes, sir. Got my DD-214 at the house. A service commendation medal to boot."

"Pass a drug test?"

"Sir, I don't even drink."

"Okay. Now let's see about this tire."

Stu passed on asking Mr. Willie a question confirming if he had uncommon sense. Capping the two gangbangers sufficed.

That evening, between pond checks, Stu called Mr. Paulie Mask at the cab company and inquired about Willie Jones.

"Best damn cabdriver we ever had. Can't shoot worth a damn. Put five holes in my back seat. Only hit the punks twice. You're getting a good man, Mr. Baron."

CHAPTER TWENTY-FOUR

Win knocked on the bedroom door.

"Come in." Tab sat up in bed. He didn't look good. "What's wrong?"

"My head and neck hurt, Mommy."

Win walked to the edge of the bed. She threw open the covers and swung her legs around. Facing Win, she could see slight swelling below his ears. She felt his forehead. He was feverish. She remembered seeing this in the emergency pediatric admitting room at LA General during her volunteer stint.

"Oh, Win, poor thing, you've got the mumps. I'm sorry." Tab had scheduled his follow-up MMR shot before he was to enter first grade at HIldago Elementary. "Bad news is it's going to last a few days, but the good news is you get to eat lots of ice cream." Tab hugged on Win.

"Here, buddy, climb into bed. Daddy should be home soon."

Tab tucked Win in, but before she could slip into her slippers, Win tossed the sheet off.

"Mommy, I'm too hot."

"Want the fan on?" Tab pointed to the ceiling fan above the bed.

"Yes, Mommy."

Tab flicked the switch. The Chinese fan wobbled fiercely on its highest setting. She trimmed it back to low. She hoped it was firmly fastened to the ceiling. It dawned on her several days ago that craftsmanship in the home was severely lacking. The rocking toilet bowl required a nasty trip down to eye level on the bathroom floor. Armed with a Crescent wrench, she had tightened the rusted anchor bolts.

Tab walked over to the bedroom window, looking outside at the ponds in the early rays of dawn. Stu was making his way back down the main levee toward the house.

"I'll get you some ice water, Win."

As she filled his plastic tumbler with ice, Stu walked in the mudroom door and kicked off his shoes. They were caked with dark mud.

"What'cha doing up this early, girl?"

"Win has the mumps."

"Damn. Weren't we supposed to get him vaccinated before school started? Do we need to get him to a doctor?"

"No, not unless there's complications. Too high of a fever or trouble breathing. One of those childhood tribulations. Chicken pox might be next."

"Tomorrow's the deadline for signing him up for that private school in Bellevue. You thought anymore about homeschooling?"

"Let's see how the school works out first."

"I guess we better see about finding a babysitter then. We both should be there for the visit with the headmaster."

"You know, those church ladies that came by might know a babysitter. Maybe I could bake a cake and ask our neighbors. I saw some teenagers standing out in their front yard."

"I'm going to check on my little man." Stu walked down the hallway. Tab followed with the water. Win was sound asleep.

"Poor kid. Today we were going to practice driving the four-wheeler. I bought him a helmet."

Stu bent over the bed, peering at his son. He could see the swelling. "He couldn't wear the helmet if he wanted to. The chin strap would pinch him below his ears. How long will this last, Tab?"

"At least three days."

"Better get some more ice cream, huh?" Stu asked.

"Yep."

Stu snuggled in behind Tab while they stood looking at Win sleep.

"Missed you last night. You should ride with me out on the ponds. We could do it in the back of the pickup," Stu whispered.

"Just what I need. Mosquito bites on my butt."

CHAPTER TWENTY-FIVE

The fifteen-year-old Mennonite arrived promptly at ten o'clock on her two-speed Schwinn. Her shiny dark brunette hair was partially tucked under a satin white bonnet. The bright-yellow homemade dress, ordinary-looking black shoes, and white ankle socks adorned the tall trim lithesome young woman. Absent any makeup, her breathtaking natural beauty and innocent nature reminded Stu of a girl he had dated in high school. He remembered the bed of glowing embers in the hearth of his parents' log cabin, nestled in the deep woods of northern Minnesota. Their first kiss. The girl radiated the same angelic innocence.

Win immediately took to Tessa Koehn. They settled down on the living room floor for a game of chess. The girl occasionally eyed the blank television, biting her lip, seemingly silently praying, resisting the temptation to venture into the world of the heathens.

As Stu and Tab left the driveway in their silver BMW, Stu commented on the girl's curiosity about the television.

"Tab, did you see her looking at the television?"

"Yeah, I did. I almost turned it on for her."

"I told Win they don't have televisions, radios, Playstations, Nintendos, and all that kind of stuff."

"What he'd say to that?"

"He said, 'Maybe they play outside a lot.'" Stu checked both lanes for oncoming traffic before he turned north off of Nighthope Farm Lane.

"He's probably right. I haven't seen a chunky one yet."

Tab's and Stu's first impression of Robert E. Lee Academy wasn't good. The extensively potholed parking lot combined with twenty or so rusted air conditioners hanging at various angles in dingy double-pane windows along the side of a gray steel building, built in the midsixties, indicated that the school might be struggling to stay open.

They glanced at each with looks suggesting they should keep on driving around the school and head back home.

"What'cha thinking, Tab?"

"Let's just see. They may be spending the money on the teachers. It still beats the one classroom out on the prairie."

"Barely." He parked the car and gapped the windows.

Tab grabbed the manila folder containing Win's graduate certificate from Montessori Kindergarten and the recommendation letter from the director.

As they walked toward the front double doors under a freshly painted red and white canopy, Stu noticed the football field. Dark-green grass, freshly cut, sported a dozen raised sprinkler heads. He heard the *tush, tush, tush* as the water sprayed and misted over the lush turf. He caught a whiff of tap chlorine coming from the field. A US and a state of Alabama flag hung motionless in the humid air. A newer-looking building, about the size of a typical fire station, sat kitty-cornered to the main building. Above the double door in the distance, a sign read "Rebel Athletics Department."

Stu and Tab entered the main lobby. The floors were recently waxed. Glistening glass doors on the seven-foot-tall trophy case were temporarily free of hand smudges from passing kindergartners. The trophies were dated back to the late eighties. The school's football reign evidently ended a decade ago. And no hint of a soccer program.

Two old flags, faded and lightly tinged with dust, buttressed the sides of the trophy case. The one on the left was the US flag. A brass plaque indicated it had flown for a ceremonial minute over the Capitol back in the fifties. It had forty-eight stars. The red flag with the starred blue cross of the Confederacy stood on the right.

They entered the reception room off to the side of the lobby and faced a mid-chest-high counter. The counter was high enough to completely obscure most kids in grades K through four. It could stop emboldened parents unless they were Olympic hurdlers. A sign-in clipboard for visitors and a tray of outgoing mail rested at opposite ends.

A pleasant-looking lady in her early forties, Jessica Mason, stood up from her desk. Not recognizing the two newcomers, she introduced herself.

"Good morning, I'm Stuart Baron, and this is my wife, Tabitha. We just moved from California and would like to enroll our son, Winchester. He'll be a first-grader."

"Well, Mr. and Ms. Baron, we'd love to enroll him. Did you bring him with you?" Mason leaned against the stout counter and peered over the edge.

"No, Winchester's home with the mumps. We moved here last week. Probably picked up the infection in one of those spotless truck stops," Tab said, looking directly at her husband. Mason caught the sarcasm in her voice and smiled.

Stu preferred truck stops over rest areas. He liked surprising his teams. Nothing like the boss suddenly appearing next to a team member while taking a piss.

"Well, Mr. Sonny Wright, our headmaster, would like to meet you. He interviews all our parents before enrollment. Let me check and see if he's free. Be right back."

"Sure." The Barons glanced around. Everything in the office seemed to be tidy and well-kept. The cubby holes for the teachers were currently empty except for the football coach's. Stuffed full, mostly junk mail. Stu had read an article in the *Journal of Human Resources* about the high percentage of professional athletes diagnosed with ADD. He surmised that the football coach probably didn't have the patience to tackle mundane correspondence.

Mrs. Mason returned. Stu asked if the school had a football coach, nodding at the stuffed cubby hole.

"Oh, yeah, he's around. I pull that stuff out and throw it in a box when I need to put his paycheck in there. He's got stuff in this box," she kicked at something by her feet, "dating back to hula hoops." Mason smirked.

"Mr. Wright would love to meet you. Come on through." Mason unlatched and lifted the heavy hinged top with both hands. Stu and Tab wiggled through.

Sonny Wright stood up behind his desk and firmly shook Stu's and lightly grasped Tab's soft hand. He, like most men, was momentarily stunned by her beauty. She was wearing a white satiny blouse tucked into a fashionable pair of tight blue jeans. He recognized her Spade handbag. His wife possessed the same fashionable taste for designer purses.

"Please have a seat, folks." Wright gestured toward two well-worn faux leather chairs. The armrests looked much older than the rest of the chair. The walnut stain had rubbed off long ago, revealing the bare white poplar wood. They were scratched with telltale finger-nail marks, left by students enduring the headmaster's wrath.

Wright was tall, lean, and sported fading tattoos of military service, maybe Navy or the Marines. A blurry anchor blotched the top side of his forearm. He was slightly muscular and sat ramrod straight. His long, ruddy face and thinning hair piled over his crowning bald spot indicated he was in his late fifties. He was missing part of his lower-left earlobe. Several dark-brown blotches around his neck and under his other ear indicated a current struggle with melanoma. Stu guessed his naval service and maybe a passion for the water was taking a toll.

"Mrs. Mason tells me you have a son ready for the first grade. That's great because that class has fifteen moving up from our kindergarten and three newcomers. We try to hold our classes to no more than twenty."

"That's good. Our son Winchester's very outgoing in group settings. He's never disruptive," Stu replied.

"Win's well-mannered. We have a letter of recommendation from the director of his Montessori academy. They loved him almost to death." Tab beamed. She fished out the letter and handed it to Wright. He cursorily looked it over. He noted that they were from California.

He performed a little mental reprogramming as he sat studying the two in front of him. Without stereotyping the Californians to the extreme, he wondered if they were aware of the nondiverse student and faculty makeup of Lee Academy.

"Well, he certainly sounds like a good candidate for our school. I see you are from California. What brings you to Alabama?"

"We bought a catfish farm. Finally tired of the rat race in Los Angeles. It was getting way too wild for us," Stu said.

This tidbit about being too wild was the desired harbinger he needed for *The Doctrine of Lee Academy*.

"Well, unlike the public schools here in town, we have a zero tolerance for wildness. Our discipline policy includes light corporal punishment." Wright nodded at the short canoe paddle with numerous quarter-sized holes in the blade, standing in the opposite corner. "Most school districts don't administer corporal punishment."

The Barons stared intently for a second at the paddle. Tab sat straight up in her seat and leaned forward. Stu clutched the armrests. Wright noticed their alarmed reaction. He hit nerves. An epidural in the wrong spot.

"Better explain that policy to the letter, Mr. Wright," Stu said.

"Well, we always notify the parents beforehand. They're asked to be present for the administration of a light paddling. I assure you we don't lay into them and leave marks. It's more of an attitude adjustment rather than a painful experience. They learn rules have to be followed. If the kid is a constant problem, requiring more than two corporal punishments in a semester, then we start taking steps to expel."

"And who makes that decision?" Tab asked.

"The teacher and I get together. We then compile a case report for the school's board of directors. Each board member, there're nine of them, casts a secret vote, and if a majority rules in favor of expulsion, then the student is expelled. Then I suppose it's off to public school. He probably ends up being one step ahead of the jailer the rest of his life."

Stu looked seriously at Tab. She grabbed his hand. They looked at each other. The thought of Win being paddled by a stranger was unsettling.

Stu cleared his throat. "You never paddle until the parents have been notified and have a chance to be present?"

"Absolutely. In the event you can't make it in to school right away, the student is placed in detention, which is that hard steel chair out there in the reception area. He or she can sit there all day long. If the parents don't come in that day, then the student is suspended until the parents come in. Also, the parents can elect to forgo the paddling and then the student receives an out-of-school suspension. The length of suspension depends on the severity of the infraction."

Tab looked at Stu. "Win's never going to face this situation. You know how well-mannered he is."

"Yeah, I know," Stu replied. He turned and faced the headmaster.

"Mr. Wright, you gotta understand. Our Win's like Opie Taylor's clone. If he messes up, he's gonna have a good reason. It'll be a doozy."

"We shouldn't have any problems then." Wright smiled.

Tab and Stu filled out the requisite papers for enrollment. Stu whipped out his personal checkbook and filled in nine predated checks for each month of the school year for five hundred and fifty dollars. The first check for two thousand dollars covered the onetime family foundation fee.

Tab asked Mrs. Mason where she could get Win vaccinated before school started. She recommended a doc in the box in Smackover. He gave discounts to Lee Academy students since he was an alumnus.

Before leaving, Mason showed them the first-grade classroom and provided a list of required school supplies.

Tab and Stu exited the air-conditioned building. The humidity felt like an invisible wall. The heat, hammering, relentless. The blazing sun was directly overhead. The blinding glare off the galvanized siding, reflecting on the white graveled parking lot, searing their eyes. They donned their Ray-Bans. Wavy heat mirages lingered over the car roofs. Egg-frying hot.

"Gawd, I underestimated this freaking heat." Stu winced.

Tab looked over at the football field. She recalled her cheerleading days in high school and at UCLA. "Can you imagine playing football in this heat?"

Stu punched several controls on the dash to get the max A/C going. He slowly pulled out of the driveway, dodging several more potholes.

"Well, Tab, now what'cha thinking?"

"Wright lays a hand on my kid, I'll shove that paddle up his skinny ass."

Stu stared at her, squarely hitting the last pothole. She rarely swore.

"Other than that, you going to be okay with sending him here?"

"Well, we'll have to see. If he or we can't deal with it, I'll home-school him."

They had already checked out M.L. King Elementary. The school, built in the fifties and renamed in the seventies, had been neglected for years. A large crack in the red brick wall stair-stepped its way from the footing to the eave. The posts holding up the entrance canopy were deeply pitted and rusted. The dingy gray concrete walk out front was buckling. It hadn't been power washed since it was poured.

They didn't bother to go inside. It looked so depressing. They couldn't imagine dropping Win off there every morning. Especially after experiencing two uplifting years at Montessori.

As they drove through the southern edge of town, they spotted the local café Brian had mentioned as serving a meat and three. The Stallion Diner sported a large wooden-lettered sign above the door, "Hot Food, Cheap Gas." A waist-high folding sandwich board on the sidewalk read "We Got Worms." There were two gas pumps directly in front of the main double glass doors. One pump sold ethanol-free, and the other, eighty-five octane infused with ten percent gasket-eating corn alcohol. A lone pump on the side of the building offered kerosene.

Stu looked at the digital clock display. It read 11:35. "Let's get some lunch."

"What about Win?"

"We'll get him a burger and fries to go. He may not feel like eating."

"I bet Tessa will. She could use a little meat on those bones."

The parking lot was full. That was always a good sign. Several farm pickups were scrunched alongside the gutter on the city's narrow main drag. A lean Catahoula cur with one blue eye panted while lying on the aluminum toolbox behind the rear window of a Dodge Ram. It was parked under a massive live oak, still growing despite the numerous embedded lead Minnie balls. Courtesy of a Yankee regiment from years past. It dripped with luxuriant growths of chigger-laden gray Spanish moss and lime-green mistletoe, providing shady respite from the broiling sun. The decal on the dented rear bumper read, "My Australian Shepherd Is Smarter Than Your Public School Honor Student."

A sheriff's patrol cruiser, a standard-issue Crown Vic, was also parked in the shade, its CB radio constantly chattering, the conversations hardly amounting to anything vitally important.

"Damn, that makes all the sense in the world," Stu said.

"What?" Tab asked.

"CB radios for the farm. Distance will never be more than a mile, usually line of sight. I could get a base station for the house and put mobiles in all the trucks. Perfect."

"Yeah, but where are you going to get them around here?"

"Girl, we've got Midlands in every truck. I make the call. They'll be here by the end of the week."

"Yah, suh. Sounds like a plan." Tab smirked, practicing her Southern drawl.

As the outsiders opened the diner's creaky door, the lively banter faded as those fortunate to be facing the door noticed the arrival of the new faces. Most were focused on Tabitha Baron. Even the two waitresses, Heather Cobbs and Amy Herron, both unmarried, took notice and stood stock still, eyeing the new feminine competition. Being married didn't matter much in Bellevue. The town's wife-swapping clique rivaled free agent signing day in the Majors.

Stuart subconsciously checked to make sure his zipper was up. The patrons with their backs to the front door twisted around, wondering why their table partners suddenly lost interest in who was screwing whom.

Tab whispered, "Stu, what's wrong? They're all looking at us."

"Let's grab that booth in the back." Stu nodded to an empty booth along the front picture window.

As they sat down, the banter grew back to its normal volume. A few men were still mesmerized.

Tab sat down right next to Stu, leaving the opposite seat vacant. She sensed insecurity and, like Stu, felt safer facing the lobby's front door.

Tab whispered again, "What's up with these people?"

Stu whispered back, "I don't know. It kinda reminds me of a *Twilight Zone* episode." Stu made up a title to put a little funny scare into Tab. "The Strangers. Next Week's Gumbo at the Diner."

"Cut it out. Be serious for once."

"I think it's just that we're fresh faces. This town's off the beaten path. It's on the road to nowhere. The interstate is a good thirty miles away. If you aren't local, you're lost."

"Okay then. Hand me that menu."

Stu grabbed the two glossy laminated menus. An index card handwritten with today's special was Gem-clipped in the corner. The card read "Chicken-Fried Steak, mashed potatoes and gravy, collards, and cornbread. $5.99."

"Tab, is this chicken or steak?" Stu pointed to the card.

"I don't know. Ask the waitress."

"I'd rather take your lipstick and write *stupid* on my forehead."

Amy Herron, the younger waitress, came around to their booth with pad in hand. She was in her late twenties. The purple lace tattoos around her ankles and studs in each nostril reminded Stu of all the girls he didn't hire. Her black hair was tied up in a tight bun. A faint hint of a moustache could be seen above her upper lip. She kinda took to Margo back in LA without the tats and body armor. Not the kind that would look good in an evening gown. More fitting would be stroking the gear knob of a turbo-charged Cummins.

"Can I get you something to drink?" Herron asked.

"Yes, we'll take two Diet Pepsis," Stu replied.

"Diet Coke be okay?'

Tab shifted slightly in her seat. She preferred Pepsi. Stu regrouped.

"Tell you what, we'll try some of that tea." Stu looked over at a pitcher of tea on the service table.

"Sweet or unsweet?"

"Two unsweets," Stu answered.

Amy returned with two tall plastic glasses of iced tea. Stu and Tab looked for sweetener packets in the small tray on their table. Not seeing any, they looked around at the other tables for the telltale pink packets.

When Herron returned to take their order, Tab asked very nicely if they had any sweetener besides sugar.

"No, ma'am. Heard that stuff causes cancer."

"Miss, we're from California. Everything causes cancer out there. But only in California." Stu grinned.

Herron grinned back, breaking the ice.

They ordered three cheeseburgers, two all the way with fries. Tab ordered hers without mayo and onion. Stu asked for a takeout box for the third one.

Across the room in the furthest corner of the café was the big table. Around it sat half a dozen men ranging in age from forty to sixty. Most were dressed in outdoor work clothes, blue jeans, not ratty or faded, two were wearing cargo shorts, and one was dressed for business sans tie and sport coat. His long sleeves pulled up and neatly folded midforearm. They were about to embark on another story of Larry Honlon's, a fiftyish-looking man in loose coveralls and a white T-shirt. He had a good nature about him, smiling and chuckling. He spoke with plenty of animation, waving his hands almost constantly. He was a polished storyteller. Some had suggested that he could do well in Vegas as a stand-up comedian.

Local attorney William Pippert, the man in the business attire, smiled occasionally, maintaining his professional dourness. All but one man listened intently to Larry Honlon as he continued sharing a recent story about living the life of a good ole boy.

203

Bip Dolen sat stock still, upright with perfect posture, hands folded in front of his empty plate. He spent most of the lunch hour peering at the woman by the window. It wasn't a total stare down as he would catch himself and look away, if either Tab or Stu glanced in his direction. He had wide shoulders, a narrower waist, and was firmly built. His handsome face belied his age. Stuart noticed his lingering glances. He caught several good looks at the man's frontal and side profile. He also noticed the man's wrinkled neck and very small throat wattles. To Stu, the recent face job was obvious. And it was a poor one at that. The plastic docs in California would have offered a partial refund. Dolen was the de facto ringleader of the wife-swapping clique in Bellevue.

"You all know about the new women's federal prison opening up over in Pickens County, right?" Honlon chirped, breaking for a moment to sip his sweet tea. "The feds spent forty million on it."

"Yeah, how come Pickens County landed it and we didn't," Gabe Holder, a local welder, asked no one in particular.

"Because we only got one motel in this town, and they charge by the hour," replied Gary Shanek, the county's former coroner. "Damn dotheads aren't the least bit interested in improving it. And you got a probate judge that's perfectly content sitting on his ass collecting a hundred grand a year when he should be heading up the Chamber of Commerce finding new business for Spencer County instead of screwing all that river trash down at his camp house."

"Well, we all know who you voted for in the primary," Gabe quipped.

"Look, you gotta give Judge Abbott some credit. He finally got that road to his camp house paved and then stiffed that Birmingham road contractor to boot. Didn't cost the county a dime. He's looking after our county funds all the time," Pippert chimed in with a shit-eating grin.

Larry took another swig of ice tea and continued, "Okay, so it's Friday afternoon, and my two, Jermaine and Quincy, are talking about all the beer and girl chasing they got lined up for the weekend."

Everybody but Dolen was listening intently. They realize this was going to be another classic Jermaine and Quincy story for the ages. Five of the six men were leaning back, grinning at one another, hanging on the next story line from Larry. Deputy Ken Feats reached down to his gun belt, damping down the volume on his radio.

"Well, I see the opportunity to get them off on another wild-goose chase. I say to Jermaine and Quincy, 'Hey, have you heard about the new part-time federal job at the new female prison?' Jermaine says, 'Nah, what part-time job?' His running buddy, Quincy, is all ears. My two are always hitting me up for spending money in between paychecks."

"Aren't they all?" Donny Grater, the owner of the local fish sein-ing company, chimed in. He had to recruit hungover men hanging out at the local quick gyp so he could get enough workers for the day. "I've got more W-2s than Disney World." He shrugs. The others chuckle and swig more tea.

Honlon continues, "So I say, 'Fellas, it's a part-time job ser-vicing the female inmates. The ones that earn good behavior points during the week get privileges with the male stud service. Employees have to service three females in one eight-hour shift.'"

Everybody's snickering at the table. A few are shaking their heads, grinning at Larry.

"Jermaine and Quincy are thinking so hard now, I'm waiting on smoke to come out of their ears.

"Jermaine turns to Quincy, 'Three times, bro, when's the last time you did that?'

"'Shooting blanks count?' Quincy asks me. 'The Feds gonna provide the rubbers? No tellin' what you can pick up in a prison,' Jermaine says. I told them, 'Government issue. Heavy duty for sure. Thicker than a bike tube.' 'All this going down inside the prison?' Quincy asks. Yep, they got beds in special rooms just for it, I said."

"My sheriff's going to flip out when he hears this," Deputy Feats said to no one in particular.

"Now, boys, they're studying me so hard, my face is hurtin'. It's all I can do, ya know, look serious. Quincy asks, 'Boss, where do we sign up?' So now I got Jermaine and Quincy hook, line and sinker." Larry looked over his shoulder to make sure there weren't any women within earshot. "All they can think about is getting paid for pussy." Larry gulped his tea. The whole table is chuckling.

"I tell them they got to get in line by six in the morning at the guard shack at the main gate. They'll be handing out job apps."

"Tell us you reeled them in before they punched out Friday," intoned Gabe.

"Oh, hell no. I was going fishing that morning at the lock. I usually drive past the prison at six. I just knew Jer and Q would be waiting in line at the gate, all jacked up about their new job prospects."

"You are so bad," Pippert piped in, shaking his head, his thumbs locked behind his suspenders.

"Okay, so I'm sitting about a hundred yards away, across the highway in a private drive, tucked back in the trees at about five minutes to six. Then this freaking caravan shows up. About a dozen cars full of Jermaine's and Quincy's buddies pull off the highway, headed to the main gate. The two guards pile out with shotguns, probably expecting a dawn prison break. Q gets out first, hands up in the air, waving. He gets within five yards of the guard shack. He and one of the guards gets in an animated conversation. The guards finally wave him off.

"His hands go down and he shoves them in his pockets and turns away. Quincy walks back toward his car, stops for a moment at Jermaine's car, says something to Jermaine. They both do a one eighty. I suppose they start telling everyone in the procession that they ain't taking no applications for no jobs. Well, now I'm thinking, if they see me sitting here, I'm a dead man. So I back up some more, back into the trees. They're ripping out of there like their momma's houses are on fire."

"What happened Monday morning when they showed up for work?" Gabe asked.

"They actually took it pretty well. Said I got 'em good that time. Jermaine was talking about writing a letter to the warden. Maybe selling the idea to him.

"I said he could use my office and type it out. I'd pay for the stamp."

"Well, the government's done crazier shit then that. I hear we're selling guns to those Mexican drug runners now," Pippert commiserated.

"Someone pass me the damned tea," Gabe said.

Bip Dolen fantasized about the woman sitting at the front window. He made a subtle dick adjustment, his middle leg sporting a mind of its own. He had barely paid attention to Larry's story.

"Damn, I've seen her before," he said to himself.

"What'd you say, Bip?" Pippert asked.

"Oh, just trying to place where I've seen her before," nodding toward the woman.

"She's a looker all right. Think she's a candidate for the Club?"

The Club was a local euphemism for the wife-swapping clique. Tabitha Baron would easily make the top of the list. Deputy Feats was ready to sign up. His wife now outweighed him. He was double dosing on the purple pills. The side effects and dull headaches still weren't worth it. She had entered the twelve-pack zone. A former hooker with a past due date.

"Don't know. Need to find out if they're just passing through or newcomers," Dolen replied.

Brian Caine walked in. He automatically, out of habit, headed to the big table after spying an empty chair at its end. As he made his way across the room, he bumped into Herron.

"You want the special today, Brian?"

"Yeah, sure." He noticed the familiar faces sitting in the booth by the window and made his way through the crowded diner to Stu and Tab's booth.

"Hey, good to see you ventured into town. This is where the sun sets and rises. Those fellas over there think they could run the country if you gave them a shot at it," Brian said.

Stu and Tab looked over at the table. They looked back at the couple. "Yeah, we noticed them on the way in. At first we thought we were in a private club or something. Folks didn't look very inviting. I guess you don't get many new faces around here, huh?"

"Not really. What brings you to town?"

"We signed Win up for school at the academy."

Brian grimaced. "How'd that go?"

"Pretty good actually."

Brian Caine was a handful of brain cells away from shell shock. "Where's Win?"

"We couldn't bring him today for the signup. He's got the mumps."

Something was worrying Brian. He couldn't hide it. Stu keyed in on the strong nonverbals.

"Something wrong, Brian?"

"Oh, no, nothing's wrong. I just know how different Win is. And well," he stammered for a second, "our schools may not be up to par with what you're expecting."

"We plan on filling in the blank spaces for sure. Right, Tab?"

"Oh, for sure."

Win's enthusiasm for learning was about to get tested big-time, Brian thought.

"Well, I see y'all are about finished. I'll go have lunch over there with the tribunal. Have a good afternoon. Tell Win I hope he gets to feeling better."

"Looking forward to my night off. Willie starts tonight."

"Great, but it won't hurt to check on him during the night."

"Ten four on that."

Brian moved out of the way and extended a friendly hand to Tab as she extracted herself from the bench seat. She gave Brian a tight hug and a kiss on his cheek. Brian felt her firm breasts on his chest. He blushed as he made his way to the big table. This got their attention.

Tab savored the moment. *Now they've got something to talk about.*

Caine spent the next few minutes telling the chieftains about the new strangers in town. He left out the part about Win. The insurrection could wait.

Bip Dolen paid his lunch tab, drove straight home, and dashed into his double-bay garage. He dropped several cardboard storage boxes off the top shelf to the spotless cement floor.

He never threw anything away, including his old *Playboys.*

"California girl, you're in here somewhere," he muttered. His photographic memory was almost as sharp as the scalpel the surgeon used last week performing his butt lift.

CHAPTER TWENTY-SIX

Murphy's law was conceived on Provo's salt flats in the pursuit of breaking the land speed barrier. Stuart and Ross had revisited the unwritten compendium of all-time clusters after buying their first truck. While watching the cantankerous '79 Mack get crushed at the salvage yard as they split a six pack of Olympia, Stu hoped it would forever close another sordid chapter on the unpredictable relationship between man and machine. Ross gleefully worshipped the final demise of the beast. After the magnetron dumped it on a temple of smashed road carcasses, he said, "That was better than a Mayan sacrifice."

The vagaries of catfish farming yields no quarter to Murphy's law. Stuart Baron was about to reckon with the third coming of Mr. Murphy.

As Stu backed up to the feed bin, Willie pulled up in Nighthope's new oxygen checking truck, a dark-blue 1998 F-150 with oversize Goodrich catfish tires. Brian had advised Stuart to trade the standard highway tires that came with the truck and get the catfish tires that "everyone was using." They were heavy duty, seven plies thick, with deep mud lugs. When overinflated with ten pounds of air, the radials took on a squared-up posture, eliminating the vulnerable sidewall bulge. This kept the sharp dorsal spines from the catfish carcasses from ruining the tire. The "endangered-protected-supposedly-al-most-extinct-now-too-numerous-to-count wood storks," Brian had ranted, constantly drug the carcasses up on the levees. The spines could puncture a bulging sidewall. Stu already knew that punctures in the sidewalls couldn't be fixed. That open road anomaly cost him tens of thousands. Fish spines would be another learning curve. Brian showed him how to fix a tire with a quick plug on the spot. He took every chance he could to educate Stu on the eventual appearance of Murphy.

"How'd it go last night, Willie?"

"No problems. All the aerators are working. My lowest oxygen is in number seven—it's two point five. Got 'em all off except that one. Everything else is above a four."

"Great. I'll hold off feeding seven then. I'll feed it last."

"Where's Win?" Win usually rode shotgun, writing down the numbers for Mr. Stu.

"Today's the first day of school at Robert Lee. Tab's taking him."

"Robert Lee?" Willie said as he tucked his chin into his neck, his eyes gazing over the top of his sunglasses.

"Problem?" Stu asked.

Willie thought for a second, looking away. "No problem, boss."

He looked at his watch. It read 7:45. *History in the making.* He noted the time again for posterity's sake. He momentarily debated writing it down on the oxygen sheet.

Stu had gotten a similar reaction from Brian. This reaction from Willie made him wonder a little bit more.

"Okay, go home and get some rest. I'll see you tonight."

"Sure thing, boss. Be safe."

Stu finished backing up to the feed bin. He walked over to the plastic mail box fastened to the support leg. There was another delivery ticket. Somehow, the feed truck had snuck by. He retraced the morning in his head.

Must have been distracted by Win and Tab getting ready for the first day of school.

It dawned on him that he needed a yard dog. He hadn't had a dog since high school in Minnesota. He never owned a dog in California. Dogs weren't allowed to act like dogs. No way was he going to tote dog shit home in a plastic bag. Peeing on a hydrant was a damned citation. He thought about what kind of dog would be good on a catfish farm.

A Lab would be nice with all the water. Win would have fun throwing sticks in the ponds, playing fetch. A German shepherd would be good too. They were fiercely loyal and protective. Tab seemed a little apprehensive about not having close neighbors. The isolation at night was a little spooky for her. His sarcastic retort about the best line in the movie *Aliens* "In space no one can hear you scream" almost landed him on the couch.

He pulled on the chain for the sliding trapdoor on the bottom of the bin. The trapdoor opened about an inch and seized in the flanged track. Feed pellets fell through the narrow gap into the hopper. He gave it a good yank. It slid to the full open position with a shrill click. The cheap Chinese quick link attaching the chain to the welded half hackle on the trapdoor had snapped in half. Feed was quickly filling the truck's hopper. There was no way to close the trapdoor with the chain mechanism.

Baron yelled, "Oh, shit!"

In five seconds, two tons of feed filled the truck's hopper. The third ton heaped on top and started overflowing. The next twenty-one tons would swallow the feed truck.

Baron scrambled up the ladder. He stuck his arms through the torrential river of falling feed. Pellets stung his face. He tried to get a better grip on the trapdoor so he could pull it shut with his hands. It wouldn't bulge. Feed overflowed onto the ground all around the truck. Over the cab's roof onto the front hood. Waves of feed advanced toward all four support legs on the concrete pad.

It took two minutes for the twenty-five tons of feed to completely empty. He watched the feed truck completely disappear in a perfectly shaped conical mound of brown pellets. As the last few pellets dropped out, he sat on his haunches, contemplating his next move.

He was the consummate problem solver. Almost relishing the frequent clusters at the company. Taking pride in figuring out workable solutions. He never entered the panic mode. Panic clouded the thinking process. Benson was always preaching to the teams, "Panic paralyzes, fear energizes."

He took several deep breaths while he studied the completely buried truck. He'd need a shovel to dig the truck out. He recalled seeing one in the garden shed behind the house.

He wondered if maybe it would be best to go to the house, put on his running clothes, and go for a run. He always thought clearer during his runs. He hadn't run in weeks.

"Yep, that's what I'm going to do. Go for a damned run."

Stu started at a slow jog at the end of the driveway, heading west down the red dirt road. He had never been past his mailbox. He was looking forward to the mini adventure. The near-crotch-length Nike polyester shorts, supportive running briefs, and white performance ankle socks tucked inside the New Balance 990s had been stored in a separate moving box. He forgot to pack his collection of special polyester running shirts. An ordinary cotton T-shirt would be too hot, so he elected to go shirtless. *Hell, I'm losing my beach tan anyway.*

It was the first time anybody ran down Nighthope Farm Lane for the hell of it.

Even though the road was fairly level, he quickly became reacquainted with the sapping effect of Alabama's unrelenting summer humidity. It was rare for the humidity to get much higher than fifty in Southern California unless it was raining. He had no idea how high the humidity was, but it was like running inside a wet sponge. About a mile down the road, he cried uncle and shifted down into a brisk walk, wiping the profuse amounts of salty sweat as it poured off his forehead. His eyes stung. His bare chest and arms dripped with sweat. He then realized he hadn't drunk enough fluids that morning. He was operating on two cups of coffee and a bowl of instant oatmeal and milk. He decided to knock out another ten minutes and turn around. He picked up his pace to an easy gait, trying his best to fight through the discomforting conditions. The heat index, a new concept he would start paying attention to, was a hundred degrees.

He passed a well-kept white frame house surrounded by an immaculately maintained front yard. A long row of mulched roses bordered the right of way. A woman in her seventies, still in her nightgown, raked dry pine needles away from the towering loblolly pine in the center of the yard. Stu waved. She stared at him and then retreated to her front door and stepped inside. The screen door slammed shut behind her.

He came to the end of the road. On his right was a hanging sign for the P. B. Shiloh Church. One of the eyebolts had come loose from the horizontal arm, and the sign dangled downward, held by the other eyebolt. The sign's paint was peeling. The one-room church was tucked under the shade of several massive live oaks. Stu walked around the church on the sparsely graveled circle driveway, worshipping the bountiful shade.

He noticed a bare concrete slab where the air-conditioning units should have been and the sawed-off conduit cables. A meter was missing in the power box. One of the windows was broken. Shards of glass littered the area below.

As he rounded the driveway back onto the road, he noticed the thick expanse of leafy, long-vined plants filling the deep ditch opposite the church. He stopped to study the distinct palm-sized, lobed leaves. The luxuriant green growth was obviously thriving. Pencil-thick green tendrils snaked across the road. He surmised it was probably kudzu. Ross had referred to the invasive plant. It wasn't hard imagining, with enough time, that the church could disappear inside a living green mountain.

On his way back, he thought about the feed bin debacle. The feed needed salvaging. It was worth about six thousand dollars, and more pressing was putting it up somewhere so rain wouldn't ruin it. Alabama's weather pattern, according to the bald guy in the suspenders on the Birmingham station, was now into "the typical pop-up late-afternoon thunderstorm pattern." It hadn't rained a lick since they had arrived, but he heard thunder in the distance the other day.

He needed to get the feed off the ground into shelter. He thought about his brother-in-law. He was constantly scooping pig shit and moving it outside the parlors with front-end buckets on small tractors.

"That's it," he said to himself, "all I need is a front-end scoop."

Now where am I gonna store it? No way I can put it back in the bin.

"I got it," Stu exclaimed out loud. "I can store it in the shed in the corner where the boat is now. Build a temporary wall of cinder blocks about as wide as the tractor scoop. And then drop scoops of feed into the truck hopper." Stuart picked up his pace, excited about figuring out a solution. *You the man with the plan.*

As he turned into his driveway, he thought, *Now I need to find a front-end scoop.* He'd call Colback at the John Deere dealership after his shower. All the tractors on the farm were Deeres and probably came from the dealership. They could get him set up. Surely he could find a use for the scoop for other chores. *Probably come in handy lifting those freaking heavy aerator motors.*

He checked his mailbox. Several flyers from the local grocery stores and Tractor Supply were folded inside, addressed to occupant. An approaching vehicle, a sheriff's patrol car, a brown dusty Crown Vic, pulled into his driveway. The young deputy studied Stuart Baron. He rolled down his window.

"Morning, sir."

"Good morning, Officer."

"Take it you live here." The deputy winked at the mail in Stu's hands.

"Yep, just moved here from California. Bought the farm so to speak."

"You meet Ms. Torne this morning?"

"Ms. Torne?"

"Yeah, your neighbor lady about a half mile down the road. Probably in her nightgown. No dentures and wrinkled tits."

"She wasn't very friendly. I waved at her, and she dashed inside."

"That's her. She's our local nutjob. We get called out here every other week or so. She thinks there are aliens living under her house."

"She call again this morning?"

"Well," the deputy shot out a stream of tobacco juice, "she reported a man wearing only underwear running down the middle of the road." The deputy winked again at Stu's very short running shorts.

"Oh god. Officer, I'm sorry."

"It's okay. At least I don't have to check her crawlspace."

The deputy moved the lever from park into rear and checked his rearview.

"Have a good day, sir. Might want to get some longer shorts, though. She's got a shotgun."

"Ten four on that."

He pulled out and slowly cruised toward Ms. Torne's.

"Damn crazy woman," the deputy muttered. He was the youngest deputy on the force. Always getting stuck with the mentals. *'Bout time the sheriff hired some more men.* He recalled the last staff meeting. The deputies assigned to night shift put in their notices. They were jumping ship. Headed to Tuscaloosa County. The sheriff announced that until more officers were hired, everyone left would be rotating on-call duty after midnight. The county would no longer be actively patrolled 24-7. For the citizens of Spencer County, it was now SPD. Shoot first. Pray you have enough ammo. Dial 911.

CHAPTER TWENTY-SEVEN

Win tightly clutched his daypack as he sat in the right front seat. He looked out the darkly tinted window as they made a left-hand turn, off the city's main boulevard, and then a quick right into the parking lot of Robert E. Lee Academy. It was seven fifty-five. Their vehicle was fifth in line from the drop-off zone marked with white-hashed diagonal lines. The parking lot was further away. Kids of all ages were piling out of car doors and dashing for the front door. Several adults stood around directing traffic, admonishing the juniors and seniors driving their own cars to slow down. They were limited to using the far outside left lane, well away from the drop-off zone.

"Win, I can park and go inside with you."

"No, that's all right. I got this."

"You sure, Win?"

"Got it."

"Love you."

"Love you too, Mom."

Win had never used the word *mom* before. It was always *mommy*.

Tab harbored second thoughts about letting him do this without her. She bit her lower lip. His small hands yanked at the door handle without any hesitation. She noticed other similar-aged children bounding toward the front door. The car behind her beeped. Tab wanted to say something to Win, but he was gone.

Win strolled up to the double-glassed doors. Sonny Wright was stationed outside.

Smiling, he approached the tall man and said very proudly, "Good morning. My name is Winchester Baron. I'm starting first grade."

The man stared down at the black Opie Taylor.

Wright's perception of time momentarily froze. Forty years of privileged education in the land of Dixie just spocked into an unwritten *Star Trek* episode. He fought off the enveloping tunnel vision. The shift into warp speed. Wright pushed down on the horizontal bar handle. The door unlatched. And the once functionless second hand on his battered gold Rolex ticked forward.

Wright smiled at the polite boy. "Win, follow me."

As the door closed behind them, the pandemonium in the parking lot commenced.

Lynn Noler, the academy's youngest board member, rammed her brand-new Audi smack into the rear of Jen Ashworth's almost-new Land Rover, hitting it hard enough to explode the passenger side front air bag. Fortunately, her spoiled-to-the-core daughter had already disembarked. She piled out of the vehicle, coughing from the powdery fumes of the dusty explosion.

Darrell Gavins bumped into the rear of Bart Henderson's rusted out Dodge Ram pickup, almost dislodging his double-barreled shotgun in the rear window rack.

The drivers bailed out of their vehicles. After cursory looks at their respective damages, they met in the middle of the drop-off zone.

"Did you see that? He just walked through the front door. Wright let him in too," Gavins said.

"Since when did we start letting them into our school?" Henderson asked.

"Damn, news to me," Ashworth said.

"Well, Noler, you're on the damn board. What the hell's going on?" Gavins asked.

"I don't know anything about this. We've got a board meeting tonight. You can bet it's gonna come up."

Win followed Mr. Wright to his classroom at the very end of the hall. Several dozen kids were putting things away in their lockers. They turned around and gawked at the boy as they went down the hallway. Win offered smiles, oblivious to the growing consternation among the nondiverse denizens of Lee Academy.

His teacher, Abigail Pickens, was at the door. Her smile turned into a brief frown and then back to a forced smile. She stared holes through Wright's skull as he approached.

"Ms. Pickens, this is Winchester Baron. Where would you like him to sit?"

Pickens looked long and hard at the new kid. "Baron, you're in the front row. There's a name card on your desk."

"Thank you, ma'am," Win said, looking straight up into her blue eyes. She returned another forced smile. Pickens and Wright watched Win find his seat.

As Win sat down, the other kids stared at him. Win was already studying the front board and found his name in cut out letters. His classmates had all gone through kindergarten together except for three other new faces.

"Mr. Sonny, I would've appreciated a heads-up on this."

"Ms. Pickens, my heads-up on this started two minutes ago. His parents are white. He must be adopted. I didn't have a clue."

"What are we going to do?"

"We're gonna join the rest of the country and move forward. That's what we're going to do."

"Jesus, why me?" Pickens shrugged. She walked in, closed her door, and looked over her new flock. Most were still gawking at Win's short-cropped afro.

Win beamed. He was currently entranced with the aquarium by the window. A fancy long-tailed goldfish with bulbous eyes gobbled down the pelleted ration for the day. It looked healthy and happy.

*****

Head Football Coach Jason Whitt was parked behind his gray steel desk, propped ankles crossed. Reclined all the way back in the rusted steel swivel chair, the cracked vinyl seat a mere two loose bolts away from biting the concrete floor. Whitt was built like a fire hydrant with legs. Stocky, a short stump of a neck with a torso almost as thick as he was wide. He held a sheet of paper, searching for new names on the class rosters in the elementary grades. They hadn't had a winning season in the peewee football league for the past five years. At the varsity level, the past four state championship runs had been thwarted by their nemesis, Bessemer Academy, in the playoffs. Bessemer had started admitting blacks several years ago. The lack of speed in his running backs and receivers was Robert Lee's Achilles' heel. His farm boys were slow as shit compared to the inner-city kids. No one doubted Coach Whitt's ability in motivating his kids to be strong and talented in their positions. They always placed first at the state weight lifting championship in Aliceville.

But you couldn't coach speed. Either you got it or you don't.

Assistant Coach Steve Cooke darted in the head coach's office. Cooke was his defensive coordinator. He had played for Alabama's Gene Stallings as a linebacker on the scout team. He was still lean and trim, unmarried, and still in full rut. He had testosterone to spare.

"Did you hear, Coach?"

"What now?"

"We got a new black kid."

"No way."

"Hell yeah, he's sitting in first grade right now."

"Damn. Let's go look at him."

Coaches Whitt and Cooke peered through the postcard-sized mesh-reinforced glass window in the door of Ms. Pickens's classroom.

"Look at him. Boy, he looks fast. When does she have playground break?" Whitt asked.

Cooke had the hots for Abigail Pickens. She was single and the same age. He already had her daily schedule memorized.

"Ten thirty-five to ten-fifty," Cooke replied without missing a beat.

Coach Whitt whispered, "You get a piece of ass yet?"

"Heck no. I think she's a virgin," Cooke whispered back.

"Don't give up, man. She needs it. I can hear her clock ticking from here."

Coach Cooke gave Abigail Pickens one long last look. Her long, slender, toned legs lacked pantyhose in the above-the-knee yellow sundress.

"When you get done drooling, Cooke, we'll get back to work."

The two met Headmaster Wright in the lobby on their way back to the athletic office.

"Sonny, we just got a look at the new brother in first grade. How the hell did that happen?"

"Damn, I was completely blindsided. I just finished looking at the admittance papers. Figured out what happened. I only interviewed the parents. They didn't bring the kid along for some reason. I assumed he was white." He scratched his head. "Now I've got an insurrection brewing. We have our first board meeting tonight. I may be packing my bags."

"No way. We'll be there backing you up. You go, I go. The only way I'm gonna get any speed is getting some of that on our teams. The board wants a state championship. They need to get more open-minded around here. It's about time."

"Kid's kinda young for varsity." Sonny grinned.

"I know that. But it's the precedent we're setting. Opens up future recruiting. We could steal some local speed from the public school with scholarships."

"Board meeting's at six. Wear a flak jacket." Sonny winced.

"Don't worry, Sonny. I got your six."

*****

At exactly ten thirty-seven, Ms. Pickens showed up at the pine bark-mulched playground with the new monkey bars and slide. Assistant Coach Cooke was waiting with a kickball.

"Abby, I was wondering if I could teach your kids a new game. We need to go over to the softball field."

"Yeah, sure." She purred at the tall, lanky Cooke. Maybe they'd get to first base on the next date. She wondered what the holdup was. *He was so shy. Probably still a virgin.*

"Kids, listen up. Coach Cooke wants to teach us a new game."

Winchester Baron was off by himself. On the monkey bars. He nailed all twelve bars, turned around, and did it again. He hit the ground on two feet, looking for something else more challenging.

He noticed his classmates and Ms. Pickens turning around and following a man wearing a whistle around his neck. He was toting a soccer-sized ball.

Win caught up and stood in the back, listening to the man.

"Okay, kids, this is kinda like softball, but instead of hitting a ball with a bat, we roll the ball from the pitcher's mound and you kick it. After you kick it, you run the bases like softball."

"Everybody understand?" Ms. Pickens asked.

"Okay, we don't have a lot of time. Everyone out in the field, some of you gotta cover the bases. I'll pitch," Cooke said.

Win grabbed third base. The rest of the class filled in the infield and a few hit the outfield.

Coach Cooke looked around. "Okay, we need a kicker. You, on third base, you get to kick first." Win ran to home plate.

Ms. Pickens was in the catcher position, but due to her wardrobe, she wasn't about to give Cooke a free look squatting behind the plate. She hoped the kickers only needed one pitch.

Coach Cooke rolled the ball toward Win. Win took two steps and kicked the ball over Cooke's head, past the nearest outfielder. Three more outfielders chased after it as it rolled toward the back fence. Win turned it into a triple.

"Damn," Coach Whitt said, his right foot perched on his truck's bumper in the parking lot.

Coach Cooke turned to look at his head coach. He gave a thumbs-up.

As the class piled through the field gate back to the school building, Coach Whitt met Cooke outside at the door of the athletic office.

"What'cha think, Coach?" Cooke asked.

"I'm thinking peewee quarterback. Got any idea how smart he is?"

"Didn't really get a read on that. He's attentive, though."

"I hope he can hang in there. The next few days isn't going to be easy for him."

"Us either."

"I know, bud." Coach Whitt winced. "Damn this county and all these die-hard rednecks. You suppose Alabama could have won twelve national championships without a little color thrown in?"

"Hell no."

*****

Tab was first in line waiting on the three-o'clock bell. K through three would be dismissed first, then four through six, and then the rest of the savvier, traffic-aware kids would follow. Sure enough, Win flew across the parking lot the second he saw his mom's car. He popped in the passenger seat and tossed his daypack behind him.

"Well, how was your first day at school?"

"The teacher, Ms. Pickens, is really nice. She put me in charge of feeding General Forrest."

Tab looked at Win. "Who is General Forrest?"

"That's our class pet, a fancy-tailed goldfish."

"That's a strange name for a fish."

"There's a big poster of him in the hallway. He was in the war. He liked the letters KKK too."

Tab squarely hit a deep pothole. An ice cube in her tall UCLA tumbler, nestled in the cup holder, flipped out. Win picked it up off his floorboard and chunked it out the window.

"Okay, what else?"

"Rosalind Colton, the girl that sits next to me, said I was famous." Win looked out the side window as he slid it back up. They drove past an old black man selling sweet potatoes in the Texaco parking lot.

"Her big brother told her I was the first nigger that ever went to Robert Lee."

Tab looked at Win. "Oh, Win, I'm sorry you had to hear that."

"Mom, what's a nigger?"

Tab clenched the wheel. Her palms were sweating. She debated about making a U-turn, returning to the school. The mama bear in her fought any attempt at logical reasoning. She wanted to maul somebody. Didn't know whom to start with. The traffic light changed to green. The SYSCO delivery truck behind her laid on the horn. She didn't move.

"Mom?"

She looked straight ahead. Her eyes misted over. She wiped at a tear. Took a deep breath.

The light turned yellow. Pissed off changed into sadness. She wanted to cry. Fought it back.

She struggled for words, finally catching her voice. "Win, that's a word I didn't think I'd ever hear again. I heard it back when I was in college. Was hoping things had changed. This is the South. I guess things change a little slower down here. From now on, we're going to call it the n-word, okay?"

"Yes, Mom, but I still don't know what it means."

"It's just a really bad word for acting black."

"I guess I don't know much about acting black."

*****

The board meeting was tumultuous, as expected. Coaches Whitt and Cooke along with Sonny Wright held their ground, sitting at the head of the table, admonishing the nine board members that it was time to face reality.

Chairman of the board, Mr. Charlie "Red" Burris, asked Wright, "Just who are these people?"

"They own Coast to Coast Trucking in California. They bought Mrs. Hopkins's farm after the accident," Wright said.

Jake Owens, owner of a six-truck fleet that delivered empty plastic milk jugs to all the creameries in the southeast, stared at Wright. His top plate almost dropped out of his near toothless mouth. Forty years of Skoal wintergreen had stained his four bottom teeth a dull green.

"Did you say Coast to Coast?"

"Yes, Coast to Coast Trucking. Los Angeles, I believe."

Owens, sitting at the opposite end of the long board table, looked from his right to his left.

"People, this man spends more money on oil filters than we spend on payroll." He dabbed his stained green index finger on a Xeroxed handout.

They all had the year's budget in front of them. Unless tuition was raised another 5 percent, they'd have to start cutting programs. The drama team would go first. Private schools got absolutely no state support despite lightening the load on the public schools. Everyone realized there was no way in hell Robert E. Lee Academy would get a dime out of state or local coffers. The fifty-year-old fire hydrant out front, rusted shut, was solid proof.

Tyrone Mullins, the oldest board member with two twin girls graduating in the spring, took his parting shot before adjournment. "Sonny, I hope in the future, you check out applicants a little more thoroughly." He looked at Coaches Whitt and Cooke. "I don't really care how fast they are if they start molesting our girls."

Coach Whitt retorted as he stood up, "I'm sorry. I wasn't aware of a single football player in my thirty years here ever being accused of impregnating a girl. However, I can think of several on the drama team. Kinda makes you wonder what the hell happens on those field trips, huh?" With that, he left the room. His sidekick, Coach Cooke, was on his heels as tight as white on rice.

Wendy McNeil blushed. She was the drama coach and not exactly on good terms with the other real coach. After-hour shenanigans had occurred during the last drama competition in Montgomery. As an English major in college, former editor for the University of Alabama's *Crimson White*, and now editor for the local paper, the term *missing a period* had taken on a whole new meaning.

Someone moved to adjourn on that note. It was not recorded in the official minutes.

CHAPTER TWENTY-EIGHT

Rosalind Colton's daddy, Chester, was the meanest man in town. He killed two people in self-defense under dubious circumstances in unrelated incidents. There were no witnesses. Traceable weapons with the victims. The poorly departed also resided on the same side of the tracks as the Coltons. The sheriff hated renewing Chester's annual pistol permit, but he had no defensible clause for its denial. Folks in town avoided looking directly at Chester Colton if he was pumping gas or waiting at the parts counter at the local NAPA. The wrong glance or a misunderstood attempt at humor could get one a thump on the nose or a punch in the gut.

He was the only man in the county permitted to excrete raw sewage out of a four-inch PVC pipe into the woods behind his trailer. He threatened to rape the inspector's sister if he was forced to comply with the local septic ordinance. The spineless inspector, a result of Spencer County courthouse nepotism, was afraid of his own shadow. He signed off on Colton's septic system inspection report after Colton had showed up on his front porch asking about his sister.

The Coltons lived on a dead-end road north of the city. If the State Tourism Department decided to erect a tourist marker depicting an example of authentic Alabama white trash, the Coltons would be prime candidates for the stellar recognition. In the middle of a postage stamp fenced-in yard was their thirty-year-old single wide trailer. They owned a herd of yappy, wormy beagles, their rabbitless challenge in life yelping at the mailman. The Colton kids spent their bare-footed toddler years stepping in dog shit. The neighbors wondered whether the kids or the dogs had more worms.

Besides for the dented mailbox plastered with Roll Tide stickers, the only other yard adornment was a pile of yellow-stained mattresses serving as a white trash version of a trampoline. The Colton brood hadn't jumped on them in the past five years. The pile served as a sleeping pad for nine incestuous, inbred beagles.

Chester and Isabel conceived all four kids in their fourteen-by-sixty-foot trailer. The master bed's thumping headboard against the uninsulated wall could be heard clear down in the kitchen at the opposite end of the home. When the two were drinking and screwing, Henry Lee, seventeen; Amber, fifteen; Courtney, thirteen; and leaky-condom kid, Rosalind, six; huddled in the kitchen and waited for them to pass out.

Isabel didn't work. Her quart of gin a day habit kept her from holding down a minimum wage job. Clocking in for work at eight o'clock sharp for the Southern Pride catfish processing plant wasn't her cup of tea.

Chester had three jobs. He worked days pouring melted plastic into molds at the milk jug factory. He then worked part-time until about midnight as a bouncer at Club 28, the local honky-tonk, on the western edge of town.

Chester's third livelihood allowed him to send all four kids to Robert E. Lee, much to the chagrin of the school's treasurer. The board had intentionally set the fees on the high side in hopes of eliminating the white trash. Evidently they weren't steep enough. And the Coltons always paid in cash. At least the treasurer didn't have to worry about bounced checks from the Coltons. Annual tuition was five thousand dollars per kid, no quantity discounts. The Coltons finally figured out that after number four, quality rubbers were cheaper than the book and lab fees.

Public school wasn't an option. Chester Colton wasn't sending Amber and Courtney to school with a "bunch of horny niggers."

Only Isabel knew why he was headed up to the National Forest. Chester's late Saturday afternoons hardly varied from April through September. His weekly trips started at the conclusion of spring turkey season and stopped two weeks before deer bow season.

He always stopped at the Valley Junction store and picked up a six-pack of Milwaukee's Best about an hour before sunset. The game officers and forest rangers would be headed home. They might get called out for a night hunting complaint after midnight. Colton would be long gone. The fishing in nearby Payne Lake sucked, so the valley locals surmised he wasn't up there wasting his time.

The store's owner took his five-dollar bill and slid the six-pack across the counter, not having the guts to ask him what he was up to. If one was brave enough to look in his truck, one might see several boxes of pint Ziplocs tucked under the seat and a couple of Black Diamond headlamps resting in the center console. A cheap box of Walgreens double AAs for backup were on the passenger seat.

The Forest Service folks loved their longleaf pines. They planted the slow-growing straight pines mostly for posterity's sake. The lumber industry preferred the faster growing, more profitable loblollies. The longleafs also provided a niche habitat for the nearly extinct red-cockaded woodpecker. Evidently, a loblolly pine wasn't good enough for them. The feds even going to the extreme of carving out two-story-high cavities for nesting boxes. Avian public housing. Shiny cones of aluminum at the base of the trees kept the gray rat snakes from stealing their eggs, a federally subsidized crime prevention program to boot.

The rangers would come along with their drip torches filled with diesel, gasoline, and used motor oil and commence with the religion, worshipping the god of fire. The longleafs thrived on burned ecosystems, their fire-resistant bark harmlessly charring while the struggling young sweet gums, oaks, and cedars succumbed to the waist-high flames. The cycle would be repeated every few years, leaving vast groves of straight pines reaching for the open sky.

Chester avoided the roadside longleaf stands with the woodpecker condos. Too many damned bird lovers wanting to add another one to their lists. He had his areas picked out, far away from the nearest roads. He'd hoof it a mile or so, but the load coming back out never amounted to more than two or three pounds.

Chester's new plot had been burned off in a prescribed burn back in March, which made for perfect planting and growing conditions. The government arsonists wouldn't get around to doing it again for another five years. The Hawaiian was spaced every ten feet or so to reduce the telltale off-brilliant green.

He planted just inside the drip lines of the twenty-year-old longleafs. Just enough sunshine but out of direct sight from above. The shadows of the pines dampened their signature green brilliance. Always planted on a southern slope, the dope thrived in the red sandy soil, laced with a ritualized cup of agricultural lime, a tablespoon each of triple eight, and bomb-grade ammonium fertilizer.

Chester was stooped over plant number twenty-seven. It was waist-high, brimming with thimble-sized buds wrapped tightly with delicate red hair-like filaments, a trait of high-dollar Kona Red. The current market price, down in the Footwash Community at the very southern edge of Spencer County, was a hundred and fifteen an ounce.

The sun dipped behind the forested horizon. The shadows coalesced into an enveloping darkness. Great horned owls cater-wauled in the distance. Colton flipped on his headlamp.

He snipped off the buds with a pair of kitchen shears and stuffed them into the pint Ziplocs. Each bag could hold about two ounces. By time he harvested plant thirty-four, he had sixteen bags slam full. Nearly four g's worth. It would easily cover next month's tuition for his four. *Not bad for a few hours work.*

Chester made his way back to his truck. He gathered up the empty beer cans in the cab, placing them into a plastic grocery bag. He'd chunk it in a ditch on the way out of the forest. He shoved the full Ziplocs inside the deflated spare tire and popped the undersized rim into the center. The Spencer County Sheriff's Department didn't have a drug dog. This transport method so far had escaped detection at the Saturday night DUI checkpoints. He made sure the unused Ziplocs were hidden from sight. Wary cops could key in on them. They were considered drug paraphernalia. He tossed his pack of Zig-Zag Orange into the glove compartment. Deputies would alert to visible rolling papers if a pouch of tobacco wasn't in plain view.

The drive from the northern extreme of Spencer County to the Footwash community took almost an hour. His faithful buyer was eagerly awaiting the delivery. Snake Jackson, the local purveyor of sin, sold tax-free bootleg cigarettes, the best Tennessee Valley moonshine, California mushrooms, Mexican crack and coke, homebrew meth, and sometimes, depending on his bro in Montgomery, AK-47s. All one had to do was ask. Colton was his sole supplier for weed for three months a year. Baja could fill orders the rest of the year.

Chester rolled into his driveway a little after ten. He spied Henry Lee, for the first time in two days, sitting on the front stoop, sneaking a smoke. His mom had climbed into a bottle of gin again, passing out at the kitchen table. He had helped Amber and Courtney carry her to the bedroom. Chester's work schedule, the boy's school-time, and football practice didn't allow for much quality father-son time during the school year. Friday-night football games were the exception. He never missed a home game when number 55 would be starting as middle linebacker.

Chester and Henry Lee had a pact. If he sacked the quarterback, ten bucks would be added to his weekly allowance. If the quarterback needed help getting to his feet, he got a twenty. Henry Lee never ran out of beer money after a game.

"Hey, Daddy, did you hear about the new nigger at school?"

"That's all they're talking about at the club, son. Hella of a note, huh?"

"I guess." Henry Lee shrugged.

"What I want to know is…why he's still there?" Chester stared at Henry Lee. "If I wanted you and your sisters to go to school with niggers, I'd quit working so damned hard and send your butts off to Martin Looser King." Chester disappeared inside. The screen door slammed shut behind him.

Henry Lee took the hint. Being the school bully was second nature. He had the best role model in the county.

CHAPTER TWENTY-NINE

Win held on to his favorite soccer ball as he rode to school with Mom.

"What's up with the soccer ball?"

"Coach Cooke wants me to show him some soccer stuff."

"Cool. Tell me about him." She enjoyed this quality time with Win. Life back on the farm was more hectic than she had planned on. Stu's rat race had morphed into a fish race. He seemed to be going ninety miles an hour all the time. *He was happy and content, at least for now.*

"Coach Cooke's really nice. He hangs around when we have our fun breaks. He likes Ms. Pickens. That's all the girls in the class talk about. Win hummed, 'Pickens and Cooke sitting in a tree...'"

"You getting along okay with your classmates?"

Winchester rubbed at a green grass stain on his black-and-white Wilson.

"Some of them can't tie their shoes. Ms. Pickens won't do it for them. Says they need to learn that at home." Win flipped the ball over in his lap. "I tie lots of shoes."

"You need to show them one time and that's it, Win. Otherwise, they'll never learn. That's probably what your teacher thinks too."

"I suppose."

Tab smiled. She checked her rear mirror. Her golden-blond mane needed trimming. *Maybe those ladies down the road knew a hairdresser.*

They pulled into the drop-off zone. "Okay, have a good one. Give me a kiss." Win bussed her on her right cheek.

Win bounded out of the Beemer in the drop-off zone. He gave Mr. Sonny a high-five as he darted through the door.

Sonny waved at her. *God, she was cute.*

Win was a tad late getting to his classroom door. He had three pairs of shoes to tie on the way, Bubba Long's, Macky Smith's, and Sylvester MacBeth's.

A big kid appeared as he finished MacBeth's.

"Hey, how 'bout tying mine." It was more an order than a question.

Win looked up, still on his knees. He was ginormous. His game jersey indicated he was number 55. A stubble of dark chin hair and a big oozing zit on his Adam's apple suggested he might be one of those seniors his classmates had told him to avoid no matter what.

Win hesitated but figured, *What the heck, I'm down here anyway.*

He snatched the loosely tied shoelaces on the black Keds, snugging them up in a perfect bowtie.

"How's that?" Win asked.

The big kid looked up and down the hallway.

"Show me which one of these is yours." The kid pointed at a row of lockers next to Win's classroom door.

"Number three there." Win pointed.

Henry Lee Colton snatched Winchester Baron by his belt and the neck collar of his new cotton Polo shirt. He forcefully walked Win over to the lockers. He pushed him against locker four and opened 3, forcing Win inside. Colton latched it shut and hustled down the hallway.

Win noticed right off that lockers didn't have inside escape latches. Dad had showed him the latch in his mom's car.

It was spooky quiet inside the locker. He could see light coming through the five horizontal slats near the top. He remembered his poor goldfish in the funny-shaped bowl on the kitchen counter back in California. At least they could turn around. The soccer ball at his feet was in the way.

Ms. Pickens looked up from her desk at her assembled classroom after the late bell. She noticed her star pupil was missing.

"Anybody seen Win this morning?"

"Ma'am, he was right outside the door before the bell," Bubba said.

Everybody looked at Ms. Pickens except Rosalind Colton. She harbored the necessary intel. The five years of knife carvings on her wood desktop merited her undivided attention.

Pickens walked over to the door, peering out in the hallway. It was empty.

Fortunately, it was annual fire inspection day for Mr. Sonny and Fire Chief Scotty Hallmond. A fire drill was planned for later that morning.

Sonny and Chief Hallmond checked the pressure level in the fire extinguisher in the elementary hall. They heard a faint rapping noise just past Pickens's door.

"Chief, I better check that out." Sonny sighed.

They centered in front of the number three 3 and looked at each other. It sounded like a finger drumming slowly against the thin aluminum. Sonny Wright reached down and slid the stainless steel latch up and slowly opened the door, expecting a furry pet to scamper out. There stood Winchester Baron, smiling somewhat with a perplexed look, glad he had been rescued but worried about not being able to feed General Forrest before class.

"Win, what are you doing in this locker?" Wright asked.

"Nothing, sir. It's really too small to do anything."

Fire Chief Hallmond chuckled at the innocent retort.

"Okay. Why are you in here?"

"Don't know that either, sir."

"Okay then. How did you get in there, and who locked you inside?"

"A big kid. Don't know his name. He was wearing a number 55 shirt."

Wright thought for a moment. *Fifty-five, Henry Lee Colton. Yeah, that figures.*

"Win, you can get back to class now." Sonny opened the classroom door and winked at Ms. Pickens.

She smiled back. Win sat down and looked at General Forrest. He was doing fine. *Probably a little hungry.*

When the fire chief left, clipboard in hand, and all smiles from a near-perfect report except for the rusted-out fire plug in the front, Sonny Wright darted over to the athletic building.

"Coach, we got a problem."

Whitt looked up from his annual requisition list for the Booster Club. His headmaster was in front of his desk, staring intently at him with his hands on his bony hips.

"Now what?"

"Colton crammed Baron inside his locker. Poor kid spent ten minutes in there. It's a wonder he wasn't scared to death."

Whitt stood up and tossed his reading glasses down on his desk. "How is he?"

"He seems okay. Wait 'til his parents hear about this shit."

"Sonny, I got this. When I get done with Colton, little Winchester Baron's going to have his own yard monkey for the rest of the school year."

Coach Whitt strategically waited until Henry Lee Colton was finished eating. He had made a pig of himself again, two trips to the salad bar and three peanut butter and jelly sandwiches.

Coach Whitt walked up to Colton while he was seated at the senior table in the lunchroom. "I need you out on the field in five minutes. Bring Footes, Decker, Wyatt, Bonds, and Hoggle with you."

"Coach, we have history class at one."

"Screw your class at one. You got four minutes now."

Coach Whitt was standing in the north end zone when the starting seniors on his football team arrived in their street clothes.

He gathered them up except for Henry Lee Colton. "Go get the Igloos. Fill them with ice water and bring them back here." Colton and Whitt watched them trot off to the commercial icemaker in the athletic building.

"Colton, how bad do you want to stay on the team?"

"Coach, you know Alabama's looking at me, right?"

"Guess that would make you the first in your family ever to finish high school and go to college, huh?"

"Well, yeah. If I get a scholarship."

"Reckon the university has any blacks going to school playing football?"

"Come again, Coach?" Colton struggled with the rhetorical question.

"We're going to see how bad you want to play football for Alabama. Start running."

"Say what?" Colton was wearing black Levi jeans and a navy-blue cotton T-shirt, leaving his game jersey in his locker due to the heat. All the school's ancient air conditioners were set to max, struggling and losing to the unrelenting heat. His homeroom, on the far western end, was stifling. Still, he wasn't in running attire for ninety-five degrees, 80 percent humidity, and a cloudless sky. The blazing sun, directly overhead.

Coach Whitt pointed toward the south end zone.

He yelled in Colton's face like a Marine DI in his former life, "When you get there, drop down and give me twenty. You get back here in more than two minutes, you'll do it again. Understand, boy?"

"Yes, sir."

"Run, you son of a bitch!"

As Henry Lee Colton took off, Coach Cooke stepped out from the tight shadow of the end zone stand. He waited with more wrath.

Colton reached the far end zone. Coach Cooke yelled, "Drop down! Give me twenty! Better make 'em good too, or I'll make you do 'em again!"

Colton got down on his knees and stretched out for his first push-up. He was already winded.

Cooke screamed, "Get your damned ass out of my sky! You look like a fricking camel!"

Colton flattened out. The last one hurt. His arms trembled. He struggled to his feet.

"Better run, boy. You got fifteen seconds to get down there." Cooke looked at his stopwatch.

Colton looked at the other end zone. Coach Whitt was looking at his stopwatch too.

Colton took off.

"Kid's slow as shit." Whitt grimaced. "'No way he's going to play for Alabama at this rate."

Colton's five teammates showed up with the water coolers.

"Damn. What did Henry Lee do now?" Footes Garris, quarterback, asked the others.

"You didn't hear him bragging at lunch how he locked that new kid up in the locker?" fullback Decker Colbeck said.

"The black kid?" Footes asked.

"Yep."

"Put those coolers down. Go sit on the stands at the fifty. You all watch this redneck exorcism. Take some damn notes for your history class," Coach Whitt snickered.

"Yes, sir," Footes said.

Colton made it back to the end zone in two minutes and twenty seconds.

He fell to his knees, heaving. His lunch spurting out into a glistening pile on the dark-green turf. The hefty helping of Thousand Island gave it a nice pink sheen. Sweating buckets, clothes soaked to the skin. The hand-me-down light-tan leather belt dark on the top edge.

"Get up, Colton. Do it again. You're slow as shit, boy!" Whitt screamed. He stood over Colton, still on his hands and knees, his face inches from the turf, waiting on the next heave.

Coach Cooke heard Whitt clear across the field. He reset his stopwatch. He grinned. It brought back memories of his days practicing against the starters at Alabama. He had gotten his licks in. Leveled some prima donnas. Made them humble again. The coach had patted him on his back. He'd start against Auburn.

Rufus Wyatt said, "Coach's going to kill him. Shee-it, man, it's a hundred degrees out here. You know Henry Lee hates to run."

"Well, he should have thought of that before he put the little kid in the locker, huh," receiver and Eagle Scout Homer Bonds said.

"You all know what a bully he is. Fuck. Didn't he know Coach Cooke liked the little kid?" Booger Hoggle said, spewing out a stream of Red Man.

Colton grimaced at his teammates as he ran past. They returned anguished looks. He was completely gassed, nearly stumbling over his own feet. At the twenty-yard line, Colton tripped. He hit the turf facedown. The blow almost knocked out his wind. The little wind he had. He couldn't suck it in fast enough.

Coach Cooke trotted over to the spot where Colton had tripped. He plucked out a single blade of grass and threw it out of the way. This would be his attempt at drama for the day.

Coach Whitt enjoyed the animated theatrics. *Coach Cooke had potential.*

"Get up, boy. Clock's running. You don't make it this time, I'm calling Coach Dubose. Gonna tell him you couldn't outrun your grandmother. You can kiss that scholarship goodbye!" Cooke yelled.

Colton struggled to his feet. Tears welling. If he went home and told his daddy he wasn't going to play for the Tide, he may as well move out and start robbing Dollar Generals with his uncle Lester. He started running. It was more of a hobble.

He dropped down in Cooke's end zone. His body felt like molten lead. His mop of red hair soaked to the skull. His arms trembled on the fifth push-up. At nine, they gave out. He bit into the turf.

Colton cried, "I can't do anymore. Please let me rest." He rested his gut on the ground.

Coach Cooke bent over. "You better get going, boy. Time's a burning. Coach Whitt's down there, looking at his stopwatch, shaking his head."

It took Colton thirty precious seconds to knock out the last eleven push-ups.

He hobbled down the field toward Coach Whitt on his fourth one-hundred-yard lap. He gripped his left rear hamstring. It was in a full spasm. His calf muscles were burning knots. His front quads quivered.

Coach Whitt looked at his stopwatch, 2:45. The kid was toast. Colton wobbled the last five yards, nearly fainted, and then crashed to the ground in a heap of humbled humanity at Coach Whitt's feet.

He rolled over on his back, his tucked knees swaying from side to side. In between deep, gut-sucking heaves, Henry Lee Colton whimpered, "Coach...I'm...sorry."

Coach Whitt got down on one knee. He looked Colton in the eyes. Blades of grass and black dirt stuck to his oozing zits. A sheen of salty sweat covered his face. Colton looked up into the blazing sun, trying to focus on Whitt's snickering face.

"From now on, if anybody as so much makes Win Baron frown, you'll be back out here doing this shit again. Understand, boy?"

"Yes, sir," Colton cried.

Colton didn't look so hot. Well, actually, he looked really hot. He had stopped sweating. Appeared to be a tad clammy. Rolling over, he retched again. His midmorning snack, a cheese Danish and a can of Mountain Dew, soaked into the thirsty turf. Coach Whitt straightened up, motioning for Colton's teammates to come.

"Douse him before he burns up," Whitt ordered gruffly and walked away.

They unscrewed the lids off their Igloos and covered Henry Lee with thirty-five gallons of ice and water from head to toes. Standard procedure for heat exhaustion. Eagle Scout Bonds took Colton's wrist and checked his pulse. It was racing but steady.

Booger Hoggle looked worried. "Is he gonna live?"

Bonds grimaced. "I think he'll make it." The other boys were hanging on Bonds's prognosis. He was going to be a doctor someday. Probably gynecology.

"Let's get the dumb son of a bitch out of this sun," noseguard Andrew Wyatt said.

They got Colton to his feet and dragged him half-conscious to the shade of the concession stand.

Headmaster Sonny Wright had watched the ordeal from his office window. He needed one more thing out of Henry Lee Colton: an apology to Winchester Baron. From now on, Colton would be tying Baron's shoes.

CHAPTER THIRTY

Stu heard the rumbling diesel feed truck from the kitchen as it made its way back out his main farm road. The trailer had that distinctive sound of being empty. As it rocked from starboard to port in response to the uneven roadway, he heard the twisting and creaking of the cavernous aluminum tube. When it was full, the tractor trailer scrunched down on the gravel, the tires squeegeeing stones off the belly of the tube.

He grabbed the stuffed, business-sized envelope off the top of the refrigerator, slipped on his Tommy Bahamas, and flip-flopped down the driveway.

As he flagged down the driver, he noticed it was Stub. The truck rolled to a stop. Stub pulled out the parking brake knob. The trailer hissed. He rolled down the Freightliner's window. Stu climbed up on the running board and handed Stub the bulging envelope. The seams were reinforced with Scotch tape to keep from busting open. It contained fifty-five one-hundred-crisp-dollar bills.

"What's this?" Stub asked.

"My feed payment for the previous load."

"Mr. Stu, we aren't supposed to take cash for feed deliveries."

"That's okay. I trust you."

"Yeah, but I don't trust myself. I got enough fuel to get to the casino over in Mississippi."

Stu chuckled. "You'll be all right. I'm sure you got more catfish that need feed today." Stu hopped off the running board and waved goodbye.

Stub shrugged, tossing the envelope on the passenger seat. He rolled up his window, slowly shaking his head. *This California dude's something else.*

Pulling away, he watched Baron flip-flop back to the house in his left rearview mirror. He glanced at the envelope. His month's house mortgage, two vehicle payments, the booster dues at Robert Lee, his boy's past due football uniform payment, his daughter's upcoming orthodontist bill, the secret-from-the-wife-new hunting rifle with on-store credit could all be covered.

Shit, keep driving to the mill, man.

Stub tossed the envelope on the plant manager's cluttered desk. Butch Nabors had his daily issue of *The Wall Street Journal* open to the commodities section. All the feed ingredients that go into making catfish chow were highlighted—soybean meal, chopped corn, wheat mids, bone meal, and distillers grain solubles. Trying to predict prices for the next few months was a crapshoot. Prices could fluctuate for any damned reason. Now there was a prediction of a bean shortage in Brazil because they couldn't be delivered due to a truckers' strike. But that wouldn't happen if the Brazilian president was finally impeached. Meanwhile, the bean price in the States shot up despite an actual shortage never occurring in the first place. The international trade domino effect—someone farts in Chile over anchovy meal and the price of menhaden meal peaks in Pascagoula.

"What's this?" Nabors asked.

"That's the California dude's feed payment."

"You're shitting me?"

"'Fraid not."

Nabors sliced the envelope open with his folding Buck knife and dumped out the crisp bills.

"Boss, if he keeps doing this, and I think he is, you gotta give me a different route. I don't trust myself."

"I feel your pain, Stub. We'll give it to Graham. He's still a scoutmaster, right?"

"Yeah, thanks." Stub left the office.

Butch stared at the money. He hit the phone intercom on his desk. "Tammy, get me Andrew at Hamilton Bank."

"Andrew Whitt, Hamilton Bank." Whitt was the president of Hamilton Bank of Bellevue.

"Andrew, how ya doing? Missed you at the Lions Golf Tournament."

"Oh man, had to bury my dog, Brute, that morning. Butch don't ever get a Great Pyrenees. Damned hole's too big. It was freaking ninety degrees by nine that morning."

"Sorry about your dog. Yeah, it was a warm one. Glad it was just nine holes. The fan on my golf cart quit working."

"Heh, what's going on?" Andrew asked while gazing at a pile of papers requiring perfunctory signatures.

"One of our catfish farmers paid in cash this morning. Fifty-five hundred. Stub seems to think he's going to make a habit out of it."

"Mind telling me who it was?" Whitt asked.

"The Barons. Nighthope Farm."

The Barons were new customers and had opened a personal checking account several days ago. Andrew thought it strange he didn't open a business checking account. Of course, he couldn't share any of this with Butch. It would be a severe infraction of privacy banking laws—both state and federal.

"Yeah, I know Mr. Baron. I met him out in the lobby the other day. He seems like a straight shooter. Real pleasant and polite. Educated."

"The other day you were telling me about a new banking reg. Something about taking in large amounts of cash?"

"Yes, thanks to the so-called war on drugs, banks are supposed to flag transactions of regular large cash deposits."

"Well, we might have a problem. You know we don't normally do cash business here at the mill."

"Definitely. I see the problem. The feds are going to follow the bread crumbs. They'll ask you why suddenly you're making large cash deposits. Then they follow the crumbs to the Baron's, which should get you off the hook. Now your customer is in the spotlight."

"You reckon they're involved in drugs?" Butch asked.

"Man, I hope not. The talk at the diner says he's got a legitimate business back in California. Owns a huge trucking firm. Coast to Coast, I think."

"Yeah, that's the rumor down here too," Butch replied.

"Sounds like you need to have lunch with him and figure out a workable solution."

"Look, Butch, I'd be willing to go with you and pay him a visit. I'd like to see about starting a business account with them. Man like that could be an asset to the bank if he's indeed legitimate."

"What'cha doing for lunch today?" Butch asked.

"No plans, bud."

"I'll pick you up at eleven thirty and we'll drop in on Nighthope Farm."

Stu and Tab were sitting down to lunch when the new crimson-red 1998 GMC Sierra pulled into their driveway. Stu thought he recognized both men but couldn't place them right off.

The doorbell rang as Stu and Tab made it to the front door.

Stu opened the door wide and smiled at his distinguished-looking visitors. One man was attired in a business suit with a loosened tie, and the other was wearing pressed chinos and a crimson red polo shirt. A pissed-off white elephant was embroidered above the left pocket. Both middle-aged men were trim and jaunty. Lady-killing types one might belly up to at the Flora Bama bar on the coast.

"Mr. Baron, I think we've met before. I'm Butch Nabors with South Country Catfish Feed, and this is Andrew Whitt, president of Hamilton Bank in Bellevue."

"Good to see both of you again," Stu said. "This is my wife, Tabitha."

Tab stepped forward into the doorway and smiled, her untrimmed blond curls gracing her cute cheek dimples. Both men shook her hand lightly.

"It's indeed a pleasure meeting you, Mrs. Baron," Butch nearly stammered.

All Whitt could think was, *Okay, what movie have I seen her in?*

"You can call me Tab. Mrs. Baron lives in Northern Minnesota." With a grin, she purposely enunciated Min-ne-sootah like William Macy from the *Fargo* movie.

"We're sorry if we're interrupting your lunch. Our schedules for traveling together are pretty much limited to around noon," Nabors said.

"Oh, that's okay. We were just eating cold-cut sandwiches. No big deal. Would you like to join us for lunch?"

"No, that's all right. You could talk us into something cold to drink though," Whitt said.

"We've got diet Pepsi, Purple Power Kool-Aid, Piggly Wiggly orange juice, and crystal-clear well water," Tab said with a smirk aimed at Stu.

"I'll take a diet Pepsi," Whitt replied.

"That works for me too," Nabors added.

They gathered at the dining room table. Stu took his usual seat. His lunch plate had one bite missing out of a hefty cold-cut sandwich next to a heaping pile of nacho-flavored Doritos. Butch and Andrew got up from their seats when Tab returned with their drinks. Courtesy among gentlemen was still alive and well in the South. Stu took another bite out of his sandwich.

Tab delicately tucked her curls behind her ears and looked at the two men opposite her. "You sure you don't want anything to eat?"

"Oh no, we're good. Really. We won't be long. Go ahead and eat," Butch said.

Whitt couldn't help but notice the choice of condiments on the table. Most of it was store-brand stuff. Piggly Wiggly mustard, pickles, and mayonnaise. The only high-end item was the birdseed-riddled organic twenty-one-grain bread. He noticed the stained purple plastic mug with an oversized handle. "Win" was in bold letters on the side. There were two Coast to Coast coffee cups on the kitchen counter.

"I'm looking at those coffee cups on your counter there. Coast to Coast. Is that your company, Mr. Baron?" Whitt asked, breaking the ice.

"You can call me Stu, guys. Mr. Baron lives up in the frozen tundra with Mrs. Baron. Good luck running into him. Probably wearing his arm out trying to catch a musky as we speak."

Tab added, "Stu and his partner, Ross Whitestone, own Coast to Coast Trucking in Los Angeles. They have over six hundred trucks."

Whitt was good with numbers. Six hundred times eighty thousand came to nearly fifty million dollars. *About the net worth of the bank.* He stared at the cheap paper napkins on the table.

"I gotta ask. What got you interested in catfish farming?" Nabors asked.

Tab played with Stu. "Go ahead. Explain that one. I'm still wondering."

Stu smiled. "I saw this billboard on the highway in Los Angeles advertising farm-raised catfish. It had been a really bad day. I decided there, and then I wasn't going to spend the rest of my life parked on a freeway."

Tab smirked. "That's his current short version for a midlife crisis."

Andrew and Butch chuckled.

"Stu, most folks just get a tattoo and buy a Harley," Butch quipped.

"That would have been fine with me. Stu, is it too late?" Tab asked, feigning seriousness.

"You going to let Win ride on the Harley with me?"

"Heck, no."

"Then I guess we're stuck with this fish farm." Stu reached over and gave his wife a half hug.

Butch cleared his throat. "Stu, we need to chat with you about that cash payment this morning."

"Oh boy, that sounds intense. I've got empty bird feeders, and my hummers are out of nectar. I'll excuse myself. Let you boys take it from here."

Butch and Andrew watched Tab get up and disappear into the mudroom.

Stu noticed their admiring eyes and waited for them to refocus. Her white terry cloth gym shorts and tight pink tank top got their attention. He was enjoying the frequent nooners with his new lifestyle.

"Guys, let's go sit in the living room," Stu said.

Butch and Andrew sat down on the sofa. Stu settled into his La-Z-Boy. The living room fan wobbled fiercely.

"That thing going to stay put?" Butch asked.

"The one in the bedroom came loose the other day. Before it crashed, the power wires held for a few seconds. That'll give you time to scoot if it comes loose."

Both men studied some more on the fan. Andrew scrunched to the far side of the sofa out of the drop zone. Butch took the opposite end.

"Okay, guys, what's on your mind?" Stu was ready to conduct business and get back to the endless chores.

"Stu, we're having issues with your recent cash payment for the feed this morning." Butch started. "My driver seems to think you may make a habit of it."

Andrew added, "Seems the federales are serious about this war on drugs. The Department of the Treasury is involved now, and that includes banking policy."

"Large cash transactions raise red flags for everybody," Butch winced.

Stu sensed that these two men were uncomfortably nervous. He was still good at reading faces, gaging the nonverbals. Andrew loosened his tie and fidgeted with his shiny chrome pen, clicking it on and off.

Butch rotated the chrome fake Movado on his wrist. Beads of sweat appeared on his forehead. Stu recalled a scene from the *Godfather* movies. It was like they were waiting on Stu to finish them off with the imaginary .44 Magnum under his seat cushion.

"Guys, relax, okay? I'm not a drug trafficker or mobster. If the feds come a-knocking, they can turn this place upside down. They won't find anything stronger than eight-hundred-milligram ibuprofens. I've got nothing to hide. They can't put anyone in jail for paying for stuff in cash."

Andrew got back on track. "Stu, how much you plan on spending on feed this year?"

"I'll need a thousand tons to finish out this year's stocking."

Andrew turned to Butch. "What's that worth, bud?"

"If he books today at two hundred forty a ton, that's two hundred forty thousand, not counting discounts and patronage rebates."

"I can bring in the cash tomorrow. We can set up a business account. Butch, you got autowithdrawal with Andrew's bank?" Stu asked.

"Sure do. You set up autowithdrawal and you get another 2 percent discount right off the bat," Butch said.

"That comes to a rebate of forty-eight hundred. Enough to pay your lawyer when you sue the feds for trashing your place looking for that pain medicine." Andrew smirked.

"You got that right." Stu retorted.

"You bring in a quarter mill in cash. We may have to give my head teller CPR."

"You okay with that, Stu?" Butch asked.

"Is she pretty?"

Andrew laughed. "Very."

PART THREE

CHAPTER THIRTY-ONE

Tijuana, Mexico

El Diablo supervised the packaging of another hundred kilos of cocaine in the dimly lit warehouse. Staying out of earshot, the workers surrounding the large work table referred to him as *Senor Muy Feo*, Mr. Very Ugly, after he returned from the States with another version of a nose.

Stacks of old newspapers and brown paper grocery bags were positioned at both ends of the table as half a dozen men wrapped cellophane bricks of pure cocaine with newspaper, followed with a single wrap of brown paper. The bricks would be placed in the middle of one-hundred-fifty-pound burlap bags of unroasted green coffee beans. About fifty or so coffee sacks without the drugs would be packed last nearest the rear door. The rearward sacks would then be sprayed with female dog-in-heat urine. The United States Customs Border Patrol Labradors would go bananas, getting woodies over the coffee bags. Upon inspection, these sacks would be cleared. The bricks of cocaine, hidden inside coffee sacks along the front wall of the trailer, would be forty feet away. The truck would show up at the border exactly one hour before the shift change for customs. Getting to the front of the trailer would require the border agents to manhandle over ten tons of coffee, sack by sack. The multimillion-dollar ruse would work for three months until a fresh anal-retentive agent with uncommon sense transferred to the border.

Diablo was perched on a stool, next to a stack of newspapers, overseeing the wrapping process. He noticed a particular photo on the front page of the *El Sol de Tijuana*. A worker grabbed the front page with the photo.

"*Alto, dame ese!*" Diablo shouted at the startled man.

Diablo snatched the front page out of the *manejo*'s hands. He shrugged and grabbed another sheet. The others continued to wrap, occasionally looking at Diablo as he studied the front page.

Diablo swore loudly in Spanish.

The worker at the end of the table worked on the translation. He was practicing his English for his eventual home in Chicago. "He's got you now, motherfucker."

Diablo stared at the photo. It was the same man on Yucca Hill. *Stuart Baron, Pueblo de Hildago, Hero, bate de beisbol.*

He'd get this shipment loaded out. He'd be returning to the States.

*****

Cooper Adams bought a city map at one of the Los Angeles International Airport gift shops. He picked up his rental from National. It was a new 1998 Pontiac Sunfire sedan. He could have opted for a luxury-size Crown Vic but figured he'd be doing quite a bit of surveillance. Unmarked Crown Vics looked like cop cars. He stomped on the gas pedal at the beginning of the freeway ramp. The four gerbils under the hood screamed bloody murder.

Adams winced. *Shooting the sequel to* Bullitt *wasn't happening in this piece of shit.*

He looked for the La Quinta on the interstate billboards as he approached the exits for Hildago. Adams made a mental note to call Special Agent in Charge Jose Santiago in the Los Angeles District DEA office when he got to his room. The local office would be conducting a briefing to get everyone on the same page.

Santiago was his roommate at the academy in Quantico. He fondly recalled the bar fight with the pompous FBI recruits. At that time, DEA and FBI shared the same facility for recruit training. Jose

Santiago grew up on the mean streets of Spanish Harlem. After the brawl, some of the FBI nerds had to be carried back to their dorm. Santiago, despite his street smarts, learned how to kiss the right asses as he made his way through the agency. He was promoted to SAC with only seven years under his belt.

Adams plopped down on the king bed. He tried to dial an outside line to his home office in Virginia, but the line was locked. He called the front desk requesting an unlock. Using the unsecured motel line would be a risk. He'd talk in partial code with Agent Junkins. He was still monitoring the stash via satellite.

"Hello, Junkins."

"Hey, Coop. How was your flight?" Junkins knew from past experience that Cooper usually attracted the shit in airports. Flying with him was atypical. For a DEA agent, Coop had a hard time keeping his head down. He could be discrete getting through airport security, armed to the teeth, but when he got on board, he could turn into a long horn steer in a chandelier shop.

"Acted like an air marshal again. We had a drunk and belligerent SOB on my flight. When are these airlines gonna learn, booze and pissed-off passengers are never a good mix. This guy was merciless on the stewardesses. After they cut him off, he dog cussed the crew."

"Coop, you couldn't just sit there, right?"

"Hell no. I waited for a few minutes for a hero to show up. The asshole grabbed a stewardess by the arm. Had to do it. Decked him with one punch, right hook under the ear."

"Jesus, Coop. Maybe you should transfer to the air marshals."

"Ended up hog-tying him with restraint zips in the rear pantry. Shoved a dirty dishrag in his yapper. Duct-taped his mouth shut somewhere over Nebraska. He's got a good case of carpet burn on his ass. LAPD dragged his sorry butt all the way down the center aisle to the front exit door. By the time they got him to the side hatch, his shorts were around his ankles. Bunch of damn ragheads spit on him on the way by. Got belligerent again on the tarmac. They painted him with pepper before pulling his shorts up. Everybody on the left side of the plane got to see it. By time they loaded him up, he was bawling like a baby."

"Glad to hear LAPD doesn't mess around. Those pansies up in San Fran could learn a few things hanging out with them. Betcha half of them couldn't pass a drug test." His first rookie field assignment was in San Francisco, chasing pot growers through the Mendocino National Forest."

"How's the package?" Adams asked.

"Still there, hasn't moved since you left."

"The house still under surveillance since it moved off the hill?" Adams asked.

"Oh, yeah. Your SAC buddy moved on it right away." Junkins scratched his shoulder under his holster strap. "By the way, the docs cleared me for field duty. Recommended I stay off my Harley for a while, though."

"That's great, man." Adams unholstered his Glock and laid it on the nightstand. "Okay, if the package moves, let me know. I'm at the LQ. I'm going to check out the location tonight. Don't know if the bad guys know where it is yet."

Junkins glanced at the blinking green dot on his monitor. "Be safe, Coop. Bye."

Cooper Adams undressed and hit the shower. A professed night owl, he could spend the night on his feet or sitting in a car, no problem. He hardly ever had problems with jet lag. His adrenals had a faulty valve. He was amped up most of the time. The agency's psych doc diagnosed a slight touch of ADD after the shooting, suggesting small doses of Adderall. Medium doses worked a lot better.

*****

El Diablo was worn out. The lonely trek through the dank three-mile narrow tunnel with the shoebox-sized rats and hairy wolf spiders put him on edge. He could gut a man in a heartbeat, but a spider web wrapped around his face would turn his ass inside out. To make matters worse, his old beater, a 1976 Chevy Impala with a hellish 454 V8, at the tunnel warehouse in Imperial Beach was missing. The sweaty trek in ninety-degree heat to the car detailing shop down the block pissed him off even more.

He stole an immaculate yacht-sized white 1980 Lincoln Town Car. The front license plate read "ButtDoc." The keys still in the ignition. They should have put a sign in the windshield, "Steal me." The detail shop's employees were on their afternoon siesta. The car's owner and detail foreman wouldn't miss it until five that afternoon.

Diablo got a rise from stubbing out his El Dragones in the virgin ashtray. The newly perfumed, luxurious, deep upholstery soaked up the lingering smoke. The three-hour drive up I-15 would be boring as hell, but coming back with some of the money and Baron's bloody fingers would be worth the trip. His boss would appreciate the effort.

When he arrived in Hildago, he ditched the hot Ford and bought a beater for five hundred in cash at a used-car lot. The 1985 Toyota Corolla spewed blue smoke. The doors rattled nonstop. It'd get him back to Imperial Beach.

He pulled into a Waffle House. Spying an outside Pacific Bell phone rack and a tattered, weathered phone book hanging under the counter, he flipped through the white pages and found the section for Hildago.

"S and T Baron. 3131 Montezuma Circle."

Someone had already ripped out the street map. An empty taxi cab was parked in front. Diablo walked into the restaurant. He waited on the taxi driver to finish his meal and return to his car. He'd ask him for directions to Montezuma Circle. As he waited in the corner booth toward the rear of the restaurant, he noticed the first crescent of the moon breach Yucca Hill. His shoulders still ached. He looked forward to the retribution.

Diablo ignored the "*No fumar*" sign posted on the window. He lit up another El Dragone. The assistant manager noticed the plume and headed down the aisle. She looked at him, from about three booths away, shuddered, and decided to let the manager handle it.

She turned around, murmuring, "Damn wetbacks."

Diablo tossed a dime on his table and left when the driver approached the taxi. The cul-de-sac was only three blocks away. He figured on hitting the house around midnight and settled in for a nap in the front seat of the Toyota. His new Llama tucked in between the front bucket seats. He'd be ready if someone came along and tried to mess with him.

*****

Cooper Adams parked down the street from Montezuma Circle. He noticed the fiber optic cable van parked with the engine running, probably running the AC on max, burning unlimited government gas.

He walked around the car, hopped on the sidewalk, and strolled up to the side passenger door. He knocked on the window. A young agent, fresh meat out of the academy, looked at him. Adams flashed his DEA badge. The agent lowered the window.

"Special Agent Cooper Adams."

"Special Agent Clyde Long." He pointed to the driver. "That's Agent Maxwell Henry."

"You guys need a break? I can get this tonight."

"Our SAC said you'd be showing up. Yeah, you can have it, man. Nothing going on here but tomcats making more tomcats. Oh, the family that lived here. Dude, they moved out. Reefer truck showed up, and they left. Man, woman, and one child. No furniture as far as we could tell. Just boxes of clothes."

"Reefer truck?" Coop inquired.

"One of those Coast to Coast rigs," Long replied. "Oh, and the tracker is still in the house. Guess that's why we're still here."

Henry started the van and moved the lever into D.

"Don't forget your cones."

"Huh? Oh, yeah, almost forgot. We've already backed over them twice. Tough little suckers."

"Damn rookies," Adams muttered on the way back to his car.

He could see the Baron house out the right side of his windshield over the row of waist-high Chinese privet in the neighbor's immaculately manicured yard. The streetlight in the island hummed for a few seconds, finally illuminating the cul-de-sac. Four residential driveways were evenly spaced around the circle. The Baron driveway was directly behind the planted island.

A neighbor exited his house next to the Barons. He carried several rolled-up newspapers and a bundle of mail. He stopped at the corner of Baron's garage, looked around, acting nonchalant. He reached for a corner brick above his head, grabbing something small. The neighbor looked around again with his same faked, unexcited expression, and ambled over to the front door of the Baron house. He inserted a key in the dead bolt and opened the door.

"At least the damned key wasn't under the doormat." Adams winced.

The neighbor wasn't inside but for a few seconds. He came back out empty-handed. He stopped again at the corner of the garage, looked around like a chump, and put the key back up on the brick.

Adams scratched his chin, feeling his two-day old stubble. *Okay, the neighbor's taking in the mail. Nobody's home. And he thinks he's an actor.*

He pulled out a cigarette-pack-sized homing unit from his inside sport jacket pocket. He turned it on and gently pulled out the three-inch chrome antenna. One of the five green LEDs started blinking.

"I'll be damned. It works."

He turned it off. The IT guy back at headquarters told him it would eat batteries. Adams waited. He watched the neighbor's house. The downstairs light was on. Probably watching television in the living room.

Several hours went by. The downstairs light went off, a light in the upstairs came on, and then a light in a small frosted window.

Probably a bathroom.

It went off in about five minutes.

Long enough to brush and floss. Maybe flex the pecks in the mirror.

Fifteen minutes later the upstairs went dark. He could make out a blue glow. It was ten thirty.

Watching Leno.

Ten forty. *Okay, Jay, finish your monologue.*

The blue glow disappeared. He looked at his watch, 10:44. He'd give the neighbor two hours to fall into a deep slumber. The neighborhood was surprisingly quiet—no barking dogs, no teenagers racing up and down the street. Not even a moonlight stroller. Moths gathered at the streetlight. An overweight cat pounced on something in the island.

It was almost midnight when Adams woke up from his short nap.

He exited the rental. Stretched his back. Shook his legs one at a time. He tightly retied his black Rocky tacticals, remembering the advice of his field training officer: "You'll never know in advance when to run for your life."

Of all the federal law enforcement agencies and the elite military units, only DEA recruits were required to run a timed three-hundred-yard sprint. They were expected to run from shit or run down the shit. He lightly caressed the knurled grip of his Glock, firmly seated in the Alien Gear waist holster on his right hip. He wasn't expecting trouble in the vacant house, but out of caution, shifted into the be-ready-for-the-shit mode. The mental preprogramming could save a precious second in a flight-or-fight reaction.

He made his way to the cul-de-sac, briskly walking up the sidewalk in front of the Baron house. He reached in his pocket, retrieving the homing unit. Turned it on. Two green lights blinked in unison.

This is gonna be in and out. Adams worried about a patrol unit driving by, noticing the only car parked on the street. Running the tag. They'd figure out National owned it. Maybe keep on going. Maybe not.

He darted to the corner of the garage and found the key. Adams was in the house in less than a minute.

Damn that was easy. Illegal as hell, but who's gonna know?

He reached in his back pocket and stretched on a pair of latex gloves. Leaving fingerprints would be a no-no. His prints were logged on the federal database in the good-guy file. DEA agents were supposed to be discrete. His SAC back in Virginia was constantly admonishing, "Dammit, Adams. Stay off the radar screen."

Staring upward at the staircase in the front lobby, he darted up the stairs, stopping midway. The unit indicated three dots. He took two steps at a time. Made it to the landing. Looked again. Three solid dots, and the fourth one was dim. There were four open doors at the top foyer. He stood in the doorway of a kid's bedroom. A life-size poster of Catu, Brazil's famous soccer player, hung on the wall. He looked at the unit. The fourth was still dim.

Disney character night-lights in the wall sockets illuminated the upstairs foyer. He appreciated the lighting effect, just enough where one might see a human form in front of the glowing green Trijicons on his Glock. He stepped in the doorway of another room.

"Bingo." The fourth light was solid green, and the fifth LED was dim. He dashed toward the closet. The walk-in was almost bare. On the clothespole hung a few faded shirts, very outdated, and one pair of tie-dyed bell bottoms.

Seriously? Adams winced.

Six pairs of worn-out Nikes in an almost-perfect row rested on the bottom shelf. A couple pairs of faded pink walking shoes were on the other end.

He looked at the unit. All five LEDs were solid and glowing brightly. There it was. A green military duffel bag on the very top shelf. He fished out his Streamlight from his jacket pocket and looked inside the bag.

Well, it was almost empty.

Left was a lone stack of one-hundred-dollar bills wrapped with a five thousand dollar paper band. Adams took his notepad out and started writing down serial numbers of the bills.

He heard it distinctly. There was no doubt about the sound.

Breaking glass.

Cooper reached for his holster, pulled out his 10 mm Glock, and slightly tugged on the slide. A shiny brass cartridge was already chambered. He held the pistol in his right hand, cupping his Streamlight in his left, holding it shoulder high. It would stay off until he identified the faint image of a target. He eased around the corner of the top foyer. Peering down the staircase into the front foyer, he could hear someone downstairs opening and closing cabinets and drawers.

El Diablo's eyes adjusted to the dimness of the kitchen. A Mickey Mouse night-light allowed him to slowly rummage through a stack of papers under the wall phone. He had already ascertained whether anyone was home by peering in the windows of the empty garage. He had another confirmation: the refrigerator was empty and unplugged.

In the stack of papers, he found a glossy flyer from a real estate firm in Smackover, Alabama. On the front page a name was circled, "Nighthope Farm. Bellevue, Alabama."

Now he had to find the money. Apparently, the house wasn't wired for security, so he could take his time. The seclusion of the back patio and the head-high fence hid his arrival. He doubted anyone heard the shattering of the small glass pane next to the doorknob in the french door.

As he rounded the corner of the kitchen, leading to the front foyer, a blur of a hand hammered him squarely in the face. Adams followed up with another straight left arm punch. The Streamlight serving as additional weight, his fist squarely landed on the tip of an already messed-up half nose.

Diablo staggered backward. He reached futilely for the Llama loosely tucked in his rear waistband. It was too late. He had never practiced a quick draw from that position. His shirt was in the way.

Adams continued his advance. He dropped him to the floor with a sideways arcing kick to the upper out seam of Diablo's pants, shocking the center nerve plexus in the middle of Diablo's thigh. His left leg collapsed. He toppled sideways to the kitchen floor.

Adams pounced on top of the paralyzed man. Diablo was still dazed from the initial punches. He didn't offer any resistance as Adams rolled him over on his stomach. Adams sat squarely on the man's lower back, his knees straddling Diablo's torso. He grabbed a handful of greasy hair with his left hand and wrenched the man's neck straight back to a painful angle. Diablo's hands reached around, grabbing Adams's wrist. Adams pulled back more on the man's head.

Diablo's grip tightened on Adams's wrist.

"Who the hell are you?" Adams yelled.

"Who the fuck are you?" Diablo screamed.

With his right hand, Adams upholstered his Glock and yanked out his pair of Hiatts. He deftly cuffed Diablo, cinching down on the stainless steel hoops. They dug into Diablo's meaty wrists. He slammed Diablo's face on the tile floor. Fresh blood clots broke loose and blood flowed again out of Diablo's nose. Adams leaned his upper torso toward Diablo's head, mashing the man's face into the stone floor with all his strength and weight.

"You're a fucking cop!" Diablo screamed.

Adams groped behind his back with his other hand, trying to find a wallet or some form of identification. He found the .45 tucked near Diablo's ass crack. He pushed the mag release lever, dropped the mag on the tile floor, and performed a one-handed tactical breech clearing using the edge of the kitchen counter. A shiny brass cartridge hit the floor and rolled away. He continued looking for identification in all the pockets. He pulled out a pair of Fiskars pruning shears, the blades locked, and a pair of car keys from his left front pocket.

"One more time, who the hell are you?" Adams asked.

"Your worst nightmare, gringo."

"Tough guy, huh?"

Adams reached around again, rolled Diablo slightly on his side and groped at Diablo's belt buckle. He unbuckled it and snatched his belt off. He turned around on Diablo's waist and sat on his ass as he cinched the belt around the ankles. Fortunately, it was one of those belts with convenient holes the entire length of the belt. One could go from being morbidly obese to a POW survivor and still get utility out of the same belt. It was standard issue for streetwise plainclothes cops. They made good tourniquets. Drug traffickers liked them for the same reason.

The hog-tied man squirmed on the kitchen floor. A dark pool of blood from Diablo's mouth and nose was smeared in all directions.

Adams stood up and looked at the man's backside. *Time to get a good look.*

He rolled the man over. "You must be the ugliest damn goat-fucker this side of the Rio Grande."

"I'm going to kill you someday, bitch."

"Looking forward to the day you try that, asshole."

Coop stared at the man, taking in all his facial features. Screwed-up bloody half nose. A deep scar from the left ear to the right ear. Screwy eyes. They didn't match up. One looking straight ahead, and the other, skewed. Greasy, straight, shoulder-length black hair. Cleft chin. Two gold teeth in the front. One now loose.

Surely, if he was in the national database, his mug shot would be the all-time digital hit. The NCIS computer would sing like a thousand-dollar payout from a penny slot machine.

He pulled out a kitchen stool from underneath the kitchen counter and sat down, keeping an eye on Diablo. Now he had to contemplate his next move. He couldn't formally arrest him because he, too, had breached the house. The wetback wasn't talking. He shined his Streamlight over at the patio entrance and found the broken window with the intense beam. He flicked it off. He pulled the .45 auto out of his waistband and gazed at it. He jotted down the serial number in his pocket notebook below the four entries for the hundred-dollar bills.

Adams scratched the stubble on his chin. He walked over to the kitchen counter under the wall phone and pulled it open.

"Bingo. The junk drawer."

He rifled through it and found a roll of packaging tape and brown sisal cord. Luckily the beginning edge of the clear tape had been folded over slightly, keeping him for squinting for the invisible edge. He walked over to Diablo, rolled him back over on his stomach, and taped his wrists. He unlocked the cuffs with the pin key on his key ring and hooked them on his belt. He wrapped Diablo's ankles with several feet of tape just for good measure. Adams made several loops of cord around Diablo's ankles and tied another loop around his neck, bending his legs skyward with his toes pointing to the ceiling. Diablo would have to keep his feet lined up with the back of his head if he didn't want to strangle himself with the makeshift garrote.

"Last chance, asshole. Who are you? What the hell are you doing here?"

"Fuck you."

"You know what I should do? Dunk your head in the toilet after I take a good dump. You'd talk eventually."

"You're a fed."

"You don't talk, I don't talk."

"You'll be doing the talking when I find you again, asshole. Yelling for your mama right before you die."

"I bet your momma's a whore in Tijuana, huh, tough guy."

"Bitch, you gonna pay for that."

Adams sneered.

He darted upstairs, retrieved the bag with the bundled bills, and dropped it on the kitchen floor. He rewrapped the man's hands with packing tape, thoroughly covering up his fingers and thumbs. Adams put the mag back in Diablo's pistol and stuck it back, deeper this time in Diablo's ass crack. He then snatched the cordless phone off the wall. He noticed the answering machine next to the phone. It indicated eleven messages were pending.

Adams was surprised to hear a dial tone after finding the shears on Diablo.

"Hey, goatfucker, you forget to cut the phone line?"

Diablo sneered back. "I'm gonna to cut your balls off and watch you choke."

Adams punched three numbers.

"Nine one one, what's your emergency?"

"I want to report a burglary at 3131 Montezuma Circle. Man broke in the back door, and he's inside the house now."

"Your name, sir?"

Coop hung up. He smiled at Diablo.

"Have fun with the LAPD, asshole."

He pushed the eject button on the answering machine, removing the tiny cassette, pocketing it deep inside his front pants pocket.

On the way out, Coop wiped the front doorknobs and returned the key to the hiding spot. He sprinted for his car.

As he approached the Waffle House, two units, running in silent mode, with flashing blues, raced by. Coop grinned as he pulled into the restaurant. He was famished.

CHAPTER THIRTY-TWO

Donny Jones woke up at 1:00 a.m. to flashing blue lights circling around and around his bedroom. He threw his bathrobe on and slipped into his loafers with the deftness of a firefighter. Only thing missing in the routine was the shiny brass pole in the middle of the floor.

Just as he stepped onto the Barons' front yard, El Diablo was hustled out of the house by two uniformed cops. A third officer, a burly sergeant in his early fifties, brought up the rear. Jones and Diablo exchanged angry glances.

Damn, that wetback's butt ugly. What the hell happened to his face?

"Sarge, what's going on?" Jones asked.

"You know who lives here?"

"The Barons. Stuart and Tabitha, and their little boy, Winchester. They just moved to Alabama."

As the younger cop placed his gloved palm on the top of the perp's greasy head at the rear cruiser door, Diablo glanced at Jones when he said Alabama. He remembered the brochure on the countertop.

Nighthope Farm. Bellevue, Alabama. His mind was a steel trap.

"Looks like a burglary. You sure the residents are away?"

"Yeah, I called them three days ago at their new home in Alabama. Told Mr. Baron they were still getting mail. He forgot to tell the post office to stop delivery. I'm taking it in for them."

The sergeant made some notes in his pocket notebook. "Can you get me his phone number?"

"Sure, it's in my house."

Jones left to retrieve the phone number. He returned and found the sergeant in the Baron's kitchen. Jones noticed the dark pool of blood on the floor. "Sarge, I was with the LAFD for twenty years. Firefighter and finished out as a paramedic. Retired two years ago. Don't believe we ever met officially."

"Sergeant Dave Bruno."

"Donny Jones."

"I recognize you from somewhere. Must have been a mutual assistance call. Hope you're enjoying retirement."

"Loving every day of it. Hear it's a lot crazier now. This drug war's getting out of hand."

"No end in sight either." Bruno winced.

"What the hell happened here?" Jones figured he'd ask given they used to be on the same side. Bruno could shrug the question off, keeping the former first responder in the dark.

"I don't understand it. Found a loaded gun on him. The window over there's broken, so it appears to be forceful entry. Found a duffel bag and some money next to him too."

"What's not to understand then?" Jones asked.

Bruno looked Jones in his eyes, measuring his reaction. He was a seasoned investigator. He could gauge complicity or innocence with consistent accuracy.

"Perp was tied up when we got here. Someone made the 911 call from this house."

Jones stared at the sergeant, trying to comprehend what he'd just said.

"Come again, Sarge?"

Bruno cracked a smile. Content with the innocent response.

"Either the perp had a partner who took most of the cash and valuables or two independent burglars were here at the same time. The one who called it in had a sense of humor."

"How often does that happen?"

"In my thirty years, it would be my first."

"Sarge, here's that PX for the Barons." Jones looked at the pool of blood. "Guess I better clean this up."

"Dude, be careful. Probably got spic Ebola. I'd nuke it with Chlorox. Still got some gloves?"

"Nah, I don't."

"Here, use these." Bruno reached into a back pouch on his gun belt, tugged at the Velcro latch, and pulled out a pair of thick purple latex gloves. "You're not allergic to latex, are you?"

"Shit, man, I'd rather drink Benadryl the rest of my life before I screw around with hep C and HIV." Jones winced.

"Well, we'll leave it with you then."

"You guys done here? Not gonna process the scene anymore?"

"No. We got a busted window. A badass with a gun. A tote bag with five grand. He won't be squirming out of this one."

"Okay then. Be safe, Sarge. Let me know if I can help."

Sergeant Bruno left, stepping over the broken glass at the rear patio door. *Damn French doors. Putting a pane of glass right next to the lock. Must have been some convict in France who came up with that idea.*

Jones stared at the broken glass and the coagulated pool of dark blood. "I'll come back in the morning," he said to himself. He checked the front door to make sure it was locked.

Sergeant Bruno was getting in his unit when rookie officer Don Baker walked up to his window.

"What now, Baker?" Bruno changed into his usual gruff, be-a-hard-ass-supervisor demeanor. The fresh meat coming out of the academy left a lot to be desired. Standards were softening.

"Sarge, when I unwrapped all that tape, I noticed bruise lines on his wrists. Like he'd just been recently cuffed. Real hard too. Just thought you'd want to know."

Bruno stared at Officer Baker. Baker was an overeducated college grad lacking instinctive street sense. Anal about details, though. He'd make a good investigator someday, if he survived his probationary period without any new orifices.

"Okay, Baker. I can't wait to hear his story during questioning. This one's not making sense."

*****

Cooper arrived at his La Quinta just after three. He was about to punch the pillow when the phone rang.

"Coop?"

"What's up, Junkins? Shit fire, what time is it out there?"

"It's right after six. Time to rise and shine, man. Your package sprouted legs. Headed downtown. It's booking too."

Coop thought for several seconds. *The package was probably in the trunk of a patrol unit.* Cops never paid attention to speed limits unless they were running radar. First thing they taught in the academy: speed limits were for civilians. It was balls-to-the-wall mode from now on, boys and girls. His mom refused to ride with him if he was behind the wheel. It scared the crap out of her. She called it offensive driving.

"Thanks, Junkins. Call me back when you get a more permanent fix on it."

Coop already surmised where it was headed. The evidence room, make that, warehouse, for the LAPD. As far as he was concerned, the freaking batteries could die. The money was with the Barons, wherever in the hell they moved too. It was the cartel's money. The homing chip was back in government possession. The bean counters at Quantico and Los Angeles Metro could fight over it now.

As Coop stared up at the ceiling, watching the green LED flash on the ceiling's smoke detector, he wondered how much money might have been in the bag. He needed to confirm there wasn't any nefarious collusion going on between the cartel and the Barons. If not, Baron might end up atoning to the IRS. He hoped not. Finders keepers, losers weepers. He made a mental note to listen to the cassette tape. He dozed off into a deep slumber, finally dreaming about pulling back his Hoyt on a trophy bull.

CHAPTER THIRTY-THREE

Coop woke at 10:00 a.m. his time. LA time was seven. He enjoyed the free hot breakfast in the sparkling, marble-floored lobby. It was a hell of a lot better than the customary tightfisted camel-rider breakfasts on the east coast. He detested the stale cake donuts, mealy-tasting apples, and cheap coffee that looked like tea. *Damned sheep fuckers from Yemen were the worst coffee makers.*

He loved LQ's beefy gravy and fresh, hot biscuits. The offering of exotic fruit—the mangos, papayas, and pomegranates—made up for the absence of Southern-style grits, a Virginian staple. The morning's coffee was especially good, a robust dark roast, brewed by someone who actually drank coffee. The world, according to Cooper Adams, should pay more attention to the traveler's adage, "People who don't drink coffee should be barred from making coffee."

Coop took a fresh cup back to his room. He packed just in case. He didn't know if he'd be staying another night. He looked at the message cassette lying among his pocket change and his spare 10 mm bullet. He picked up his proverbial last round and put it in his left front pants pocket. It would be his final solution if he ever ran out of ammo in a firefight. He had sworn to himself that he'd never let a cartel take him hostage. He put the tape and the change in his right pocket, grabbed his tactical duffel bag, and headed for the door.

The DEA's Division Headquarters was on the seventeenth floor of the Roybal Federal Building in downtown LA. The division's jurisdiction included the state of Nevada. San Diego and San Francisco were given to other divisions. Washington figured the efforts directed toward the drug smuggling near the border and the hassling of the pot growers in northern California deserved their own districts. LA could deal with the Nevada mafia distributing blow out the back doors of their casinos.

As Coop entered the lobby of the granite shrine, he snatched out his badge wallet and flashed it at the federal guard stationed at the metal detector. The guard hit the mute switch just as Coop waltzed thorough the machine. The lights on the overhead threshold lit up like the Christmas tree on the First Lawn.

The ride to the seventeenth floor felt almost motionless. The door opened to a bustling lobby full of men and women in various modes of dress. Most were wearing polo shirts with holstered weapons, a few in poorly tailored sports suits, and the Rambos still in their full-black tactical attire, sans knee and elbow guards, just back from a mission. They were still amped on adrenaline, ready to throw down a belligerent purely for shits and giggles.

Coop spied the large corner office with the picture window in the very back. The largest office didn't need a sign. It was always assigned to the SAC. On both sides of this office were the assistant SACs.

The sign read, "Jose Santiago, Special Agent in Charge."

A huge black glass desk was completely bare except for a multi-line phone. No family photos, no legal pads, not even a pen. Jose Santiago's broad shoulders were turned to the door. He gazed out the picture window at the San Gabriel's on the northeast horizon, deep in thought. Coop knocked on the doorframe. The man rotated around in his plush office chair and smiled.

"Cooper Adams. How in the hell are you?"

"Mending new orifices, buddy."

"Yeah, I heard you took one for the team. You okay?"

"Oh, yeah, the agency shrink thinks I'm a nutjob."

"Coop, you've always been a nutjob." Santiago grinned.

"So what's going on with you, Jose?"

"Still not married. Been dating a nice woman for four years. I just can't commit. Sometimes I think she's scared to death for me. Don't think she's cut out to be a cop's wife. Between our paranoia about not trusting people and the cynicism that gets coded into our DNA, she wonders how I get through the day. Sometimes the relationship goes platonic for months on end. Carnal urges finally surface. She'll wear me out on weekends. She calls it fucking the demons out."

"Man, I'm in the same boat. Somebody needs to start a dating service for women that understand cops. Takes a special breed of woman to put up with our shit. Marrying a cop isn't the answer. We need soft, cuddly, innocent. Not programmed to shoot holes at the shadows haunting us every waking minute."

"Sounds like we need to belly up to a bar. Pontificate over a pitcher or two," Santiago said with his hands folded on top of each other in his lap.

"That sounds good. Let's do it soon, bud."

"The staff briefing on Agosto's Bajalista Cartel is in ten minutes. ASAC Wilkins is in charge."

"Let me hit the head before we get started." Coop walked around the desk, giving his old roommate a shoulder bump. "Good to see you again, Jose."

Coop exited the office and headed to the restroom. Assistant SAC Wilkins popped his head in Santiago's office. "Boss, the briefing's at eight thirty. You gonna make it?"

"I'll be there."

"Hey, who was that guy in your office?" Wilkins asked.

"Agent Cooper Adams from Quantico. My old roommate at the academy. He's been watching your stash blip in Arlington while recovering from a bullet."

"Well, speaking of the blip, it isn't at the house we've had under surveillance. Our team got there this morning at daybreak, no blip and no sign of Adams."

"Seriously?"

"Yeah, your man there," Wilkins said, pointing in the general direction of the restroom, "took over surveillance last night."

"Relax Wilkins, I'm sure he's got an explanation."

"Well, I'm dying to hear it." Wilkins left abruptly.

That was a poor choice of words, Wilkins. Santiago winced. Wilkins had never popped a cherry. Adams already had five bad guys nourishing earthworms in his seven years. His fearless reputation was well-known through the ranks. East coast tactical teams sought him out. He'd get in Wilkins's face faster than a grizzly bear downwind of a freshly opened can of chunky tuna.

The briefing room was standard layout for DEA. Two dozen swivel chairs circled a rectangular conference table. The table was big enough to perform a NASCAR-style tire change. At one end of the table were several rows of folding chairs reserved for the newbies. The ones fresh out of the academy. It was also the firing line for the typical cop banter before the official briefings. The older seasoned agents could get merciless on the rookies.

Adams hesitated for a moment on where he should sit. He sure as hell didn't want to piss off an administrator right out of the gate. He'd have plenty of opportunities to do that later. He figured the seat at the top of the table was for the SAC and the two on either side were for the ASACS. Unwritten SOP.

He chose the third chair away from the SAC. He pulled it out from the table.

"Dude, I wouldn't sit there," a voice quipped from the coffee service island. A young, handsome Italian, dressed in pressed chinos and a wrinkle-free bright white shirt with a bright-peachy-colored tie was standing sideways to Adams, stirring the indissoluble clods of *Shur-Fine* creamer in a Styrofoam cup. "That's the Mormon's chair."

"The Mormon's?"

"Yeah, that's what we call him. He's from Salt Lake. We doubt he's a practicing Mormon. He's got more cherries than a cherry tree. Did five years working with the spooks in East Berlin. Took down the Russian mob. We don't mess around with him. Better not sit in his chair."

Adams plopped down in the Mormon's chair.

"Okay then. Bart Naples. Been here two years. Transferred from Jersey."

"Cooper Adams. Temporarily assigned to LA from Quantico. Out here to help locate the kingpin for the Bajalistas."

"Thee Cooper Adams?"

Adams looked quizzically at Naples. "Something I don't know?"

"Hell, you're a living legend. We heard how you double-tapped and put one in between the eyes of the guy after he shot you."

"Yeah. Saved the government hundreds of thousands in court costs and prison time. Still waiting for the bump in salary."

Naples chuckled. "Well, most of the field agents think what you did should become SOP. Perps shoot back. They die. End of story."

"Look, if you can stand up to the endless reaming from the Office of Professional Responsibility and the psych analysis, go for it." Adams grimaced.

The rest of the LA team trickled in. Most carried their own brews in tall stainless tumblers. A few opted for the lobby's Starbucks.

Adams stayed in his chosen seat. Naples sat next to him. He appreciated the gesture with a nod. Nice knowing someone already took a shining to him. He liked Naples. Easygoing. No pretensions. Confident. Good foxhole material.

The table seats filled up. Half a dozen younger faces found their seats in the folding metal chairs. The pecking order was in place. Two athletic-looking female agents sat side by side at the end of the table. Gazing at them, Adams recalled his early days of the academy. At first, he was embarrassed by his male counterparts when the off-color, often sexist banter started rolling. After the second day, the females were holding their own. Girls entering the realm of law enforcement, typically were not the pampered sorority chicks he had chased at Virginia State. They were tough. Survivors from the inner city. At ease knee-capping the perverts in the balls, riding the subways. Growing up in a middle-class suburb was an unwritten ding on an academy application. Adams served on the academy's applicant selection committee.

"Hey, Wop," the grizzled agent said loudly from the other end of the table. Nicknamed Moose due to his north woods Maine background and hirsute qualities, he pointed at Agent Naples, lamenting, "I think you need to change the batteries out on that tie. When you gonna learn how to pick out a decent tie?"

Naples grinned. "I don't know, man. Your wife picked it out for me this morning."

Moose chuckled at the well-deserved retort. He turned around suddenly. A young rookie was laughing at his expense. *Big fucking mistake.*

"Hey, you with the two-inch mini Ruger. Don't you know you aren't supposed to carry anything bigger than your dick?" Moose said.

Adams grinned. The two female agents giggled. The other veteran agents chortled. The rookie in question turned beet red.

The banter continued mercilessly, frequently centered on the weekly screwups by the rookies. Adams was eating it up. Good times. He started to relax.

A lanky, well-proportioned agent in his early forties entered the room. The room quieted down. Eyes fixed on the new man sitting at the table.

Naples whispered to Adams, "That's the Mormon. Agent Ethan McMullin."

McMullin looked askance at Adams sitting in his chair. He walked to the other side of the table, sitting down opposite Adams. They exchanged momentary icy stares. The Mormon opened his newspaper, raising it up to his face. Began reading.

Naples whispered in Adams ear, "He's pissed. He always reads the paper like that when he's pissed."

Coop smiled. He didn't mind pissing people off.

Jose Santiago would be a little late for the meeting on purpose. He realized the ritualistic bantering was part of the process building team comradery. It was a fundamental step for the rookies. Take heat under pressure. Learn the pecking order. Figure out who the power or influence brokers were in the department. Kiss the necessary ass. Kick the rest. When he stepped in the room, the bantering would stop. It'd get serious. Only the veterans close to retirement would still levy a few shots as he took his seat. They knew that a fleeting smile from the boss would be the signal for getting down to the deadly business at hand.

As Santiago neared his doorway, his desk phone rang. He looked at the display. It was a direct line coming from outside the building, by-passing his administrative assistant. He shrugged. He looked at his watch. He had to take it. Less than ten people knew his direct number. Most of them were higher-ups. His mother in Eagle Pass was the only civilian who knew. And she rarely called.

"Special Agent in Charge Santiago."

"Jose, this is Max. I've got bad news." Max was the field director for the FBI in San Francisco. "Your missing agent, Mario Quintana, was murdered."

Jose Santiago's shoulders slumped. Quintana was in deep cover with the Los Serpientes, the narco-trafficking bike gang. He had gone off the radar screen several days ago.

"Damn, who all knows?"

"Besides for forensics downstairs, just you and me."

"What happened?"

"Gangbanger on a moto threw a package on the steps of the federal courthouse this morning. Got him on the cams. Federal security opened it up. Ziploc bag with four severed fingers. Ran the prints. Came back to Quintana."

"Dude held out for four before they killed him." Santiago winced.

"I read his bio. He's a former SEAL."

"I know, Max."

"Sorry, man, I know it's tough losing one of your own."

"I've got a staff briefing right now. I'll break the news."

"You gonna call the Navy at Coronado?" Max asked.

"Yes, I will. I'll take care of next of kin too." Santiago groaned.

"What happens when a SEAL is murdered?"

"It ain't pretty. There's always retribution. No quarter. It's a black op."

"The end of the Serpienties, huh?"

"Let me know what happens up there."

"Sorry about your man, Jose. FBI will be in contact to start the investigation. You got a point man on this?"

"I'll let you know after the staff meeting. It's probably going to be his case contact."

"Okay, Jose. Again, I'm sorry."

"Bye, Max." Santiago lowered the receiver down on the cradle gently. He straightened up and gazed out the window. The spackled line of brownish-yellow pigeon shit on the window ledge summed up how he was feeling. Mario Quintana had a new, pregnant bride at home. This was going to be tough day for everyone.

Santiago entered the room. His somberness sucked out the air. His two ASACs knew something dreadful was fixing to land on everyone in the room. Adams was already steeled. Santiago looked at him. Their eyes met and locked. The anguish was palpable. They were brothers. Had shared the fear in their first gun battle. Seen the horror of innocent death.

The room went quiet. Everyone was seated and rock still except Santiago.

"Special Agent Mario Quintana was killed in the line of duty. He was tortured."

Gasps filled the room. By their reaction, Cooper surmised Agent Quintana was a loyal and devoted member of the team.

Santiago let the news sink in before getting into the details. The two female agents dabbed at their eyes. The Mormon said a silent prayer. Moose snapped his pencil in half. Others looked at Santiago, waiting on his next word.

"FBI received a package this morning with four severed fingers. Prints came back to Quintana. We all know severed fingers are a calling card for the Bajalistas. The Los Serpientes are their current drug couriers. He's been undercover with them for the past month."

"Damn. Held out for four fingers," Moose said.

"Hell. He was a SEAL," Naples added.

Special Agent Norm Glass cleared his throat. "I was his contact during the insertion. He stopped calling in three days ago. Of course, I notified ASAC Wilkins."

ASAC Wilkins nodded in the affirmative.

"Last thing Mario told me was there was a guy from the cartel hanging around. They called him the devil, El Diablo. We checked on all the known lieutenants for Agosto by the name of El Diablo. It was a dead end."

Cooper Adams feigned a cough. Santiago took the hint.

"This is Special Agent Cooper Adams. Just arrived from headquarters. Adams has been tapped into an NSA sat feed in Arlington.

He's been watching our tracker left behind by the cartel on the hill. Also been restricted to desk duty for the past thirty days recuperating from a bullet. Evidently, the tracker moved from the hill to a residence nearby and recently disappeared from said residence. Agent Adams will now bring us up to speed." Santiago looked at Adams.

"Thank you, Special Agent in Charge Santiago. First off, I'm sorry to hear about the death of Agent Quintana. I wish I could have arrived under brighter circumstances. Thanks to Quintana, we were able to insert that tracker in the payment supposed to go to the cartel somewhere in Baja. By tracking the payment, we could locate tunnels, routes through Mexico, method of transport, handlers, and ultimately, the final destination. Kingpin Agosto's a hard one to locate. We know he likes the beach on the Baja coast, but we can't pinpoint an exact address. The tracker dead-ended at a residence owned by Stuart and Tabitha Baron in Hildago. We watched it move off the hill into their home—"

Wilkins interrupted. "I hope you're going to shed light on the current tracker location."

Adams returned the stare to ASAC Wilkins. "I'm getting there, Wilkins."

Adams continued, "I took over visual surveillance from your team last night. Upon watching a neighbor open and secure the house with a hidden key, I entered the vacant residence likewise, conducting a brief search for the tracker."

Wilkins gasped. "You didn't? No freaking warrant. And you entered a residence?"

Adams returned another stare, icier than the first. He glanced at Santiago.

Santiago lifted his palm slightly, a gentle admonishment directed at both of them. "Wilkins, feel free to make a notation in the record that Special Agent Cooper Adams willfully and illegally entered a private residence without a warrant."

Santiago knew Adams had probably performed the mental acrobatics standing in front of the residence. Quantico could file it in Adam's personnel folder not yet named Shit Happens.

Wilkins looked around the room. Everyone at the table seemed to be daring him with I'd-like-to-kick-your-ass stares if he grabbed his pencil and started writing. The rookies in the back sat motionless, watching the drama between grizzled, streetwise agents and the one administrative geek that no one liked.

Adams continued, "After locating the tracker in the residence, I confronted a burglar, restrained him, and then called the LAPD. I left the residence before the party started. My partner back in Arlington reported later that said tracker was headed downtown. Probably LAPD. I haven't confirmed that."

"Damn. This is incredible. You're in town, for what, less than twenty-four hours, and you just happen to stop a burglary in progress in a home under surveillance for a freaking month," Wilkins said.

"What did this burglar look like?" Santiago asked Adams.

"Definitely Hispanic. The ugliest man I've ever seen. Big scar running cheek to cheek, screwed-up nose, mismatched eyes."

"You get anything out of him?" Santiago asked.

"Nothing. I wish I'd had more time to force something out."

Wilkins realized he was dealing with the roguest of the rogues.

The rookies stared at their new hero.

The other ASAC, Stan Baker, asked, "You reckon he was really a burglar or linked to the cartel?"

"You know, come to think of it, he accused me of being a fed after I threatened to dunk his head in the crapper."

Wilkins's mouth popped open. A pigeon could have landed in it.

The rookies were on the edge of their seats, needing more space to get on their knees and chant in reverence to their new savior, Saint Cooper.

Santiago fought back a smirk.

"Adams, we need you to check out some pictures. Someone get the damned lights," Baker said. A rookie shook off his trance. He flicked off the wall switch for the overhead fluorescents.

Baker fired up the computer in the corner of the room. After the mouse arrow darted around for a few seconds, he found the Powerpoint file labeled Yucca Hill. "These are pictures taken during our faked bust with the Los Serpientes and the cartel. We purposely let them get away. Like Adams said, our intention was to track the payment to Agosto. We needed pictures of the Serpientes and the Bajalistas together in a swap. We didn't anticipate the mule dropping the money with the tracker on the hill."

He opened the first slide.

"There's Special Agent Quintana on his moto." Baker aimed at the deceased agent with a laser pointer.

Adams vaguely recalled seeing his face at an academy commencement. He had made a point of picking him out in the program because of his SEAL training.

"These are the mules in Agosto's Bajalista cartel."

He slowly clicked the mouse. The pictures changed.

He got to the man coming down the hill with the black sawed-off shotgun confronting the jogger. The bad guy was pointing the gun at the helo. They had a full-frontal picture of him.

"Damn. That's him." Adams winced. "The burglar in the Baron house."

The revelation sank in. The older agents realized the implications. This particular battle in the war might involve collateral damage.

"The cartel's found the money. Civilians are at risk now," Santiago said.

"It gets worse, people," Adams said under his breath.

"How so?" Baker asked.

Adams looked at Santiago. "Quintana's fingers were severed?"

"Yes, forensics seems to think it was some kind of shears rather than a knife."

"I found a pair of pruning shears on him. LAPD may have Quintana's killer and the weapon downtown in holding."

Baker stood up abruptly and said, "I'm calling LAPD. Agent Adams, come with me in case I need more details."

Baker made the call and got the booking sergeant on the line. He mentioned the residence in Hildago and the approximate time of the arrest. Adams described the suspect and the shears. He handed the phone back to Baker.

Baker winced as the officer filled him in on the latest developments. He hung up after repeating his name and giving his contact information. LAPD detectives would be arriving shortly. They'd get the shears to the FBI in San Francisco following the proper chain of custody.

"Let's go back to the meeting, Agent Adams."

The two reentered the room. The banter subsided. The under-the-breath, heated one-way conversation between an animated Wilkins and a stoic Santiago about Cooper Adams abruptly ended. Everyone in the room waited for the ASAC's update.

"Our suspect put an LAPD officer in the hospital last night. He escaped custody en route to central booking. He was last seen running down the middle of the river."

Adams turned slightly in his seat, looking directly at Baker.

Baker returned the look. "The Los Angeles River, the mother of all concrete ditches."

Santiago asked, "Who is this guy?"

Baker continued, "Sounds like a pro. Probably a key guy in the cartel. I'll bet he's former military, police, or a mercenary. The officer's going to live. He was able to write out a few details before undergoing surgery. The suspect feigned positional asphyxiation. The officer, still in his probationary period, fell for it. Officer opens rear door, bends over, undoes the suspect's seat belt. He was going to lay him down facedown on the seat and add another cuff when the suspect head butted him in the temple, knocking him unconscious. Suspect took the officer's cuff key and his service weapon, a .40-cal. Beretta. Suspect shot him in the back of the head, nearly blowing off the officer's lower jaw."

*****

The man, soaked in sweat, approached the clerk at the bullet-proof ticket window at the Greyhound Bus Station in downtown Los Angeles. The clerk gasped. There was a dime-sized blood clot stuck in the man's half nose. The clerk tried to track the man's left and right eyeballs, finally settling on the straight ahead, left one.

"*Quireo un ticketa a Alabama.*"

"Mobile, Tuscaloosa, Birmingham, or Montgomery?"

"Mobile." The man remembered his boss occasionally smuggled drugs into Mobile Bay on the banana freighters. It'd be his way home.

"One way or round trip?"

"*Una via. Cuanto questa?*"

"*Dos ciento y cinco.*"

The man peeled off two Franklins and a Lincoln from his tightly wound roll. No longer sequestered alongside his blistered dick.

"*Cuantos dias a Mobile?*" Diablo asked.

"*Tres dias.*"

The man snatched the ticket out of the clerk's hands, disappearing in the crowded station.

The clerk grabbed his bottle of antibacterial hand gel, removed the nozzle, and dumped it liberally on his hands and forearms, vigorously rubbing it in. He then smeared the rest of the bottle all over the counter. He hoped his next customer wasn't smoking.

CHAPTER THIRTY-FOUR

Agent Adams knocked on Donny Jones's front door.

Jones opened the door slightly, the brass chain at shoulder height stretched tight. He was wearing a blue bath robe and slippers. A thumb-thick unlit Cohiba poked out of the side of his mouth. The gold label read "Havana, Cuba."

"Good morning. I'm Special Agent Cooper Adams with the Drug Enforcement Agency. Like to ask you a few questions about your neighbors, the Barons."

Jones yanked the contraband out of his face, placing it in the front pocket of his bathrobe. "You know, their place was broken into last night."

"Yeah, I know. Was wondering if I could look around a bit. Understand you're looking after the place in their absence."

"How come the DEA is involved? The Barons are good people. I can assure you they aren't involved in drugs."

"I don't think they are either, Mr. Jones. The burglar may be involved in trafficking narcotics. I'm trying to figure out how he ended up here."

"Okay, give me a minute to change. There's lots of broken glass. I was just getting around to cleaning up the damned mess. Need to get my boots with the blood and all. You can get in through the back door. Damned wetback broke out a glass panel. Guess I better call a glass guy, huh?"

"You're a good neighbor, Mr. Jones."

Cooper made his way to the patio and entered the kitchen. If he could figure out where the Barons went and if the burglar come across the same information, he could get on the trail. As he walked to the counter, he saw the tiny cover still open on the phone answering machine. He needed to find a microcassette player. He recalled seeing a Radio Shack near the Waffle House.

He looked at the printed materials on the counter under the wall phone. A glossy brochure from a real estate company in Smackover, Alabama, had a highlighted circle drawn around a farm named Nighthope in Bellevue, Alabama.

He rummaged through some more papers in the stack. A new yard services contract with Spiffy Lawn indicated the yard was to be fertilized once a month and cut three times a month if needed. *What a racket,* Cooper thought. *Stop fertilizing and you probably don't need to cut it as much.* A pest control contract indicated that indoor control was no longer needed. House-perimeter spray only. A letter appreciating the Baron's recent donation of five thousand dollars to the Greater UCLA Boosters rested on the bottom of the stack.

Jones reappeared in a faded blue paramedic uniform with shin-high rubber boots.

"Mr. Jones, do you know where the Barons moved to?"

"Sure do, there was a brochure here somewhere with a picture of the farm they bought. I remember Mrs. Baron showing it to me." He looked at the pile under the phone. "Here it is. Nighthope Farm. It's a catfish farm in Alabama."

Adams held it up to the lights and squinted at it up close. He looked for prints, remembering the man's greasy hair. He could make out some faint smudges. "I need to hold on to this. Might be something we could use."

"Sure, whatever you need. I should call the Barons and let them know about this."

"Yeah, that'd be a good idea. Can you get me their phone number too?"

"Sure, I'll be right back."

While Jones went to retrieve the number, Adams closed his eyes and sequenced the previous night in his head. How did the man track the money down? Something was missing. Did the cartel have their own homing devices? Was there a leak in the agency? His cop paranoia was reaching in. An icy hand palming his skull. Or were the

Barons involved in the cartel? Maybe the cassette would reveal some pertinent information.

Back at the hotel, Cooper inserted the cassette into his new microcassette handheld recorder and pushed Play. Messages one and two were hang-ups. The third was a dothead bitching about talking to a machine.

Message four. "Tab, Abby here. Girl, my kitchen looks fabulous. Fab-u-lous. Can't wait to show you." The woman sounded excited, young, and sophisticated.

Message five. "Stu, got the results of the last random drug test. All four teams came back clean. You too! We're still laughing on how the boss's number came up. Dude, you can stop sweating over those poppy seed muffins."

Man's worried about eating poppy seeds. Failing a drug test. Yeah, we got ourselves a confirmed drug trafficker here. Adams smiled.

Message six. "Don't forget to leave your house key in our usual spot before you leave. Good luck to all of you." The voice sounded like the neighbor.

Message seven. "This is the IRS. You will be arrested in three days if we don't receive payment for back taxes by 5:00 p.m. today. Call 202-759-4765. We accept all major credit cards."

Assholes. Adams winced.

Message eight. "This is June Spree with the Hildago Water Department. We'll swing by and turn the water off at the street box next week. I'm waiving the monthly service fee until you resume service. Hope you enjoy living in Alabama, Mr. Baron. Thanks for the football tickets. Roll tide."

The local wheel getting greased. Good for you, Baron.

Message nine. "This is Gorman Zippa with the Zippa Law Firm. On behalf of our client, Hector Sanchez, the man you viciously assaulted in front of the liquor store, we're requesting a civil compensation award of twenty thousand dollars to cover his pain and suffering. Our office is located at 529 Samaritan Drive."

What the hell? Adams scratched his head. He listened to message nine again.

Message ten. "Hey, Stu and Tab, Ken here. We told that grease bag Zippa that if he bothers you again, we'd publicize his five attempts at passing the bar. Put the scores on a freaking billboard. I doubt you'll be hearing from him again. Let me know if you do."

Gotta love these attorneys.

Message eleven. "Hey, Stu, this is Brian in Alabama. Mrs. Hopkins left the house key on the back of the mailbox post. Safe travels on your trip here."

"End of messages."

Adams called Jose on his direct line. After he hung up, he packed his bag for Alabama. The DEA's Gulfstream was rolling out of the hangar.

PART FOUR

CHAPTER THIRTY-FIVE

Bellevue, Alabama

Brian Caine scratched his chin as he studied the cluttered garage. The wife was with her girlfriends at a daylily farm. *Jesus, how many damned daylilies does she need anyway?* At last count, she had over a hundred. The neighbors marveled at their beautiful yard. If it wasn't for her, they never would have believed he was an ag agent for the university. He had a wet thumb, not a green one. He couldn't keep a cactus alive if his life depended on it.

He promised Sally he'd clean the garage. He wanted to surprise her. Let her park the car inside for the first time since they had purchased the ranch house.

The packed garage was a chronological assortment of crap starting at the door and ending at the back wall. Near the overhead door was a table saw with an odd-size blade he bought at a garage sale last month. He didn't even know if it worked. Behind that was his fifteen-horsepower Johnson outboard his fishing buddy had dunked in the lake last year. It was deader than a doornail. Behind that was a cardboard box full of old computer stuff. A Tandy "Trash 80" desktop, the one with the keyboard and monitor molded together, was surrounded by thick cables with obsolete plugs. The relic was so damned slow he could fetch a cup of coffee while it was thinking.

And against the wall was an old Boy Scout project, his prized snake cage. He had built it for his Reptile and Amphibian Merit Badge. It had housed several large rat snakes. The local cosmetics laboratory had provided the baby rabbits after tormenting them with the latest facial cremes.

I should give that to Win. His keen interest in farm wildlife had developed into a fascination with snakes. A pet box turtle was staying in the mudroom. Mrs. B drew a firm line about bringing snakes in the house. Brian backed his pickup outside the door. He chunked the no-longer-sentimental shit into the bed. He'd go to the landfill first and hit the Barons on the way home. *Maybe Stu and I could catch up on those beers.*

*****

Win loved Saturday mornings on the farm. His dad had adjusted the four-wheeler significantly limiting its speed. Until he learned how to swim a complete lap in a catfish pond, he was forbidden from riding around the ponds unless under parental supervision. And he better not even sit on it unless he was wearing a helmet with a snapped-in chin strap. After school he could ride out to the feed bin. Sometimes he'd check on Stub while he unloaded, careful to stay out of his way if he was in one of his moods. Stub had poked him in his shoulder with his arm knob last time. *That felt weird.*

Stu flagged Win down as he drove the pickup toward the ponds.

"Hey, Win, you wanna go fishing?"

"Sure, Dad. What about Red?"

"Turn that thing around and follow me. We're going to pond eight. Be careful."

"Yes, sir." Win loved riding the ponds. He practiced dodging the catfish skulls and their sharp dorsal spines. They had already punctured two tires. Dad could usually fix them with the tire poker, a plug, and the smelly glue.

Stu lowered the tailgate and grabbed the casting rod with the closed face Zebco 888. He opened a plastic Folgers can, fishing out one of the raisins coated with catfish blood bait. To Win, it smelled horrible. He hated putting the nasty raisins on the hook. Dad didn't allow wussies on his farm. He held his breath as he baited the hook.

Win casted it out about twenty feet. In a few seconds, the red-and-white plastic bobber disappeared in a swirl of water. The line tightened. Win gave it a good yank, and the heavy action pole bent slightly.

"Gotcha!" Win exclaimed.

"Bring him in, son. I'll get the cooler."

As Win looked at the four, pound catfish laying on a bed of ice in the cooler, his dad handed him a tropical punch Gatorade. Stu picked up the cooler and pushed it forward into the bed of the truck.

"That's gonna be our supper tonight."

"You know how to clean them?"

"I imagine it's about the same as a Minnesota bullhead. Only bigger."

"Yeah, I reckon so."

"Reckon so? Win, you're starting to talk like a Southerner."

Win shrugged his shoulders. "*Que sera sera.*" He had learned a little French in Montessori.

Stu laughed. "I prefer Southern over French, son."

"*Pues!*" Win exclaimed, throwing his arms up.

"Okay, Espanol will do fine too." Stu popped Win in the shoulder. "How's school going?"

"I'm not tying shoes anymore. This big kid in twelfth grade told everyone to tie their own shoes or he was gonna stuff them all into a locker."

"How about that unfriendly girl in your class?" Stu recalled the pillow chat with Tab about a redhead using the n-word.

"Oh, she's okay. She told me I can be her secret friend when her Daddy ain't around."

"Ain't? When we get home, I want you to show me that word in the dictionary."

Stu remembered one of his teachers going into a memorable rant about the word. She made the offending student write down the entire dictionary definition on the chalkboard. She had waved a new piece of yellow chalk like a mini sword and underlined the last admonition. "Ain't has no place in formal speech and writing.

Its nonstandard use is the sign of an illiterate person." Stu doubted if Win would receive the same scolding at Robert E. Lee Academy.

Brian met Win and Stu on the main levee road. They rolled their windows down and threw the trucks into Park.

"What are you doing out here on your day off, Brian?" Stu asked.

"Cleaning out the garage today. Took some stuff to the landfill. Thought I'd drop by. Got something for Mr. Win too."

"What you got, Mr. Brian?"

"A snake cage. Big enough for a gator."

"I gotta see this," Stu said.

They hopped out. The snake cage was as long as the width of the bed. The treated wood frame and steel chicken wire appeared to made by a craftsman. The joints were mitered. The top had a framed square door about two feet by two feet with heavy duty hasps. "My uncle Wallace helped me make it back when I was in the Scouts."

"Your uncle did a good job. I'm impressed."

"Well, he builds houses for a living." Stu hung on that statement for a second or so.

"Wow, Dad. We can put a bunch of snakes in there!"

"Thanks, Brian. Let's take it up to the shed. No way Tab's gonna want it anywhere near the house."

"Stu, I got a box of eight-track tapes. Def Leppard, Metallica, Motley Crue, AC/DC, U2. You want them? I couldn't toss 'em, man. Too many memories."

"Brian, the last time I saw an eight-track was in my very first truck. Turned that sucker into a square cube of steel. Don't need that memory."

"Sounds like another beer," Brian said.

"Dude, let's find a spot for this snake cage. Then I can get started on what I owe you."

"Sounds like a plan. See you at the shed."

*****

The light-blue shiny Gulfstream jet with an American flag decal on the tail fin touched down at the Bellevue Airport. Two agents from the Atlanta office were waiting on Special Agent Cooper Adams. They brought him a confiscated Dodge Dually crew cab with Florida Dade County plates. After exchanging pleasantries with the crop duster crew and their pet billy goat, they loaded into the black Crown Vic, its A/C running at max, and headed back to Atlanta.

Cooper hopped in the truck. It was a behemoth. He cranked up the eight-liter Magnum V-10. The custom glass packs rattled the loose change in the cup holder. The Atlanta agent advised him to turn the engine off when he was at the gas pump. No freaking way the pump would keep up. It was the first pickup Adams had ever driven. He loved the roominess of the interior. *I could get used to this.* A US Government gas card was in the clean ashtray. *Good to go.*

Laying in the back seat, as he requested, was a hard-cased Smith and Wesson Military and Police AR-15. An ammo box full of pre-loaded twenty-round mags and an unopened case of 77 grain 5.56 mm Black Hills FMJs rested on the rear floorboard. Enough to start a war with Baja California.

An Alabama road atlas rested on the front passenger seat. Each county meriting its own page. Every pig trail in the county of Spencer was listed. He located Nighthope Road just off of Highway 25 south of Bellevue. It dead-ended at the P. B. Shiloh Church. He wondered what P. B. stood for. He supposed "poor black."

As he drove through the county, he was struck by how much it reminded him of southern Wisconsin. His grandparents ran a dairy farm near Beloit. Missing were the dairy cows, replaced with the stouter, low slung, and more meatier versions, mostly black Angus and cinnamon-red, white-headed Herefords with short, stubby horns. The sudden hankering for a medium-rare porterhouse made him touch his SOG tactical knife, clipped inside his right front pants pocket.

He spotted a lone Texas longhorn on top of a ridge. He surmised it was probably there for shits and giggles by a generational farmer bored with raising the same old breeds.

The land was gently rolling. Ponds filled in most of the valleys. Strange-looking machinery with blades on horizontal drums floated near the dams of every pond. *Must be catfish ponds.* He had never seen a catfish up close. His only exposure to fishing was an impromptu deep-sea fishing charter put together by his classmates after academy commencement. The upchucked beer and pizza made good shark chum. He had been awarded Top Gun, making him the official badass of the group, but spent most of that afternoon gripping the chrome handrails, belching into the three-foot swells.

Coop turned off the highway, driving slowly down the red dirt lane. He lowered the front deeply tinted electric windows. A residence on the right, a single-wide trailer, was centered in an immaculately trimmed yard. A young woman in a bonnet and light-blue calf-length dress was wearing out a whining weed whipper, trimming the grass around the front porch. A fat blond Labrador panted in the shade of a sprawling magnolia tree out front. The steel gray mailbox read 50 Nighthope Lane. A wooden sign under the mailbox read, "Jesus Loves You."

He waved at the young woman. She took her hand off the throttle handle, waving back with a smile. *That's good. We got friendlies.*

He continued on down the lane. Coming up on his left was a beat-up, old mailbox, its half-rotten four-by-four post listing toward the roadway. It read simply 113. The number 3 was barely stuck to the dusty flap door. The single wide skirt-less trailer squatted on rusted twin axles. The hubs were almost hidden in the knee-high weeds. The trailer was supported on each end with numerous piers of well-weathered concrete blocks. Another pile of blocks served as a half-ass makeshift staircase to the battered front door. Out front was a large roan-colored pit bull, nearly skin and bones, tethered to a stout log chain. It was missing most of one ear.

A young white man, also nearly skin and bones, sat in a hot pink plastic chair under a gnarly hackberry tree, smoking an unfiltered Camel. Beer cans littered the area in front of him. Adams tried a wave. The man watched the truck go on by, taking another draw on his cancer stick, too damned lazy to blow the smoke out of his face.

It wafted around his cauliflower ears. He scratched at imaginary bugs crawling under his skin.

Okay, got our neighborhood meth head. Save a bullet for him. Might need two. He remembered the dog.

About a mile further down, he passed 1200 Nighthope Lane on the right. A planter box of flowering yucca and various daylilies surrounded the freshly painted mailbox post. Ruby-throated emerald-green hummingbirds darted in and out of the flowers. He slowly passed by. In the yard was a red Honda four-wheeler with a kid-sized bucket on the black seat. The yard had been freshly mowed. Grass clippings were scattered on the graveled driveway. Behind the house was a large expanse of rectangular ponds, two rows separated by a crowned gravel lane. Coop continued on down the dirt road, taking in the surroundings. Gathering intel.

He came to the end of the road. The P. B. Shiloh Church and a fenced cemetery was surrounded by a jungle of kudzu. A heaping pile of faded plastic flowers marked the corner of the far edge of the cemetery. He circled around the church. He guessed the local meth head was probably responsible for the missing copper wires and the A/C unit. He headed back up the road.

As he drove faster down the bumpy road, he felt a new sensation on his chest. He clutched at his left breast area with his free right hand. His man boobs jiggled.

"Damn. What in the hell?" he said to himself.

He hadn't visited his local gym in two months. Maintaining elite fitness had always been a priority. Adams was a proven warrior. His self-confidence was firmly rooted, due in part to the extensive training in tactics, exacting practice and applied field experiences in life-and-death situations. Gym time was a vital component of maintaining the warrior's edge.

The need to get back in shape now overwhelmed him. At this rate, he could end up failing his semiannual PT test. His SAC would bench him if he didn't qualify.

As he drove back toward the Nighthope Farm, he thought about what he would tell the Barons. Sitting somewhere in the weeds conducting surveillance, waiting on the ugly one to show up, would make him a sitting duck. He was dealing with a professional who'd also be casing out the Barons. The better plan would be serving as a covert bodyguard. Stay in Baron's shadow. Dress like a farm worker. Maybe Baron needed some farm help. Get a little exercise and cancel the Mexican's Christmas to boot. Surprise the asshole. Two birds, one stone.

He knocked on the door.

Tabitha Baron answered.

The covert bodyguard idea seemed like a good plan so far. Even her shadow was nice.

"Mrs. Baron?"

"Yes, can I help you?" she replied.

The man standing on her front stoop looked out of place. He was definitely good-looking, trim, and well-built, standing very erect. He had a very confident way about him. When he shook her hand, he gazed into her eyes, like he was trying to read a bio on her corneas. The handshake, sincere and gentle. His sports jacket was in dire need of dry cleaning. Wrinkled khaki pants. His footwear too stout compared to the rest of his attire. She doubted right off he was a salesman. A confusing first impression.

"Special Agent Cooper Adams, Drug Enforcement Agency." Coop showed her his gold badge in the black leather billfold. His photo ID was opposite the badge inside a clear vinyl flap.

Tab took a deep breath. Her mind raced. She looked at the man hard.

"Are we in trouble?"

"Ma'am, is your husband home?"

"Yes, he is. I'll go get him. He's in the bathroom."

"Mind if I come inside?" Adams shifted into officer survival mode. He didn't need the front door opening and end up staring at the working end of a shotgun.

"Oh, sure. Come on in, Officer."

Tab disappeared down the hallway. Adams stood in the living room and took it in. Everything was very neat and tidy. No ashtrays, no MJ leaves or seeds scattered under the table in front of the couch, no bong on the highest shelf of the bookcase. Family photos adorned about every level spot in the house. Lots of smiling faces, full of orthodontic teeth. No meth mouths.

Win entered through the back door carrying an empty, moldy hummingbird feeder. He noticed the stranger standing in the living room. He placed the feeder in the empty kitchen sink and came around the sofa, walking up to the man.

"Hi, I'm Winchester Baron. You can call me Win."

"Hello, Win. I'm Cooper Adams. You can call me Coop."

Coop shook hands with the young boy. His mind reprogrammed to meet his black father.

"I better call you Mr. Coop. My mom and dad won't like it if I call you by your first name without the mister."

Coop chuckled while he kept a wary eye on the hallway entrance.

*****

"There's a DEA agent in our living room."

Stu stared at Tab. The blood drained out of his face. He clutched the edge of the bathroom counter. "Oh god."

"Stu, don't you pass out on me now." He had been feeling faint lately due to the long hours and hitting too much caffeine.

"What does he want?"

"I don't know. He wants to speak to you."

"Damn." Stu took a long, forced breath.

Stu and Tab entered the living room. Win was showing the man his pet box turtle named Humpy. Stu walked toward the man and extended his hand.

"Hello. I'm Stuart Baron."

"Special Agent Cooper Adams. Drug Enforcement Agency."

Win gawked at the man, digesting the words *special agent. That's really cool.*

Coop smiled at the boy and winked at his parents. "Could we go somewhere private?"

Tab and Stu took the hint.

"Win, it's time you get to that room of yours. Clean it up. I need all your dirty clothes. And don't put clean ones in with them because you don't want to put them back in the dresser. Pick up your toys. Put 'em in the closet. I need to vacuum."

"Okay, Mom. Nice meeting you, Mr. Coop."

"Nice meeting you too, Win."

Win put Humpy back in the cardboard box by the mudroom door and disappeared down the hallway.

"Mr. and Mrs. Baron, I'm going to come right out and say it. You may be in danger."

Coop let that soak in for a minute, gauging their reaction. Tab inched closer to Stu and grabbed his sweaty hand. The blood drained out of his face again.

"Folks, why don't we sit down," Coop suggested.

Stu shrugged at the front door. "Agent Adams, could we take this outside on the front porch?"

"Sure, I understand. By the way, I'm impressed with your boy. He's well-mannered and polite."

"Thank you, Officer. We just moved here. It's a challenge for us at times, but he's eating it up," Stu said.

Stu hit the switch for the overhead porch fan. It responded with the is-it-going-to-stay-attached-to-the-ceiling wobble like all the other unbalanced Chinese fans. Coop studied the fan for a moment. He moved the rocking chair.

"Mr. and Mrs. Baron, we know about the money. I'm not here for it. What you do with it doesn't concern us. But I wouldn't be surprised if the IRS eventually gets curious somehow."

Tab looked at Stu. "I told you this might happen."

Stu sighed. "I'm sorry."

Agent Adams continued, "We had a tracking device in the canvas bag. We were tracking it back to a Mexican drug cartel. The cartel went looking for it on that hill in Hildago. Somehow, they ended up tracking it to your house."

"Our neighbor called this morning about the break-in and a federal agent investigating. I suppose that was you?" Stu asked.

"Yes, sir. It was."

"Damn, how'd you get here so fast?" Stu asked.

"Used the agency's jet. Sucker flies nearly six hundred miles an hour. Impressed the hell out of the guys at your local airport."

Stu and Tab warmed up to the federal agent. Despite the threatening news, they were comforted by the man's sincerity. Stu particularly liked his aura of self-confidence.

"Folks, I need to slip out of this jacket." He stood up.

Adams took off his jacket, folded, and drooped it over the back of the rocker. Stu and Tab stared at the huge black handgun nestled in the nylon holster next to another badge. Adams was sweating profusely in the stifling afternoon humidity. Semicircles of sweat soaked the area below his armpits.

"Agent Adams, can I get you a drink? I just made some iced tea."

"Mrs. Baron, that would be great. Thanks."

While Tab went to get drinks, both men leaned forward, talking in lowered voices.

"Mr. Baron, we think there may be a higher-up in the cartel, we call them lieutenants for some damned reason, that may have learned about your new digs here. He was in your house probably looking for the money and may have learned about this farm. He was arrested on the scene by LAPD and, during transport, escaped after shooting a police officer. We think he's a professional killer. We also suspect he killed an undercover agent. These are very bad people. I'm here to protect you. Get him if he shows up."

Tab returned with the iced tea in a tall tumbler.

"Tab, the burglar they caught in our house escaped from custody. Agent Adams thinks he may show up here looking for the money."

"What are we supposed to do?"

"Well, my first choice would be for you and your son to leave until he's in custody. Mr. Baron needs to stick around for bait, so to speak."

Tab stared at Agent Adams. "Are you alone? Do you have help?"

"For now, it's just me. My next stop is the local sheriff. I didn't want to make a cold call on him until I gathered some intel. Sometimes we gotta be careful with the locals. They can be uncooperative for nefarious reasons. I'll put a call into the attorney general's office in Montgomery."

"Well, I'm not leaving my husband. Win's on total lockdown in the house until this is over with."

Stu smiled at his faithful wife. Tab was good at getting her way. She could get a pothole fixed in a New York minute.

"Agent Adams, could I get my chief of security on the way to help us out?"

"Chief of security?"

"Name's Terry Benson. When Tab and my partner's wife go overseas on vacation, he serves as their bodyguard. He's a Vietnam war vet. Extracted SEALs. Seen his share of shit. After the war, he worked as a contractor for Blackwater, did a short stint for the Department of State, and then headed up a mercenary outfit in Latin America. Let's just say he has unique ways of doing things. I use him mostly to check out new employees, keep track of company assets, and keep the Teamsters at bay."

Adams was nodding until he tripped over the mention of the Teamsters.

"Teamsters?"

Tab added, "We own a trucking company in Los Angeles. Stu and his partner manage about two thousand truckers. They're proudly nonunion, which causes the Teamsters lots of consternation. Benson's been known to put their recruiters in the hospital. Like Stu said, he has unique skills."

"I wouldn't be surprised if he knew the whereabouts of Jimmy Hoffa," Stu quipped.

"Sounds like a useful guy. How soon can you get him here?"

Stu looked at his watch. "Before midnight."

"Make the call. I could use the help."

Win dashed into the living room as his parents and Mr. Coop came through the front door. He noticed the gold badge and the humongous black gun on Coop's belt.

"Wow! You really are a special agent."

"Win, Mr. Adams will be staying with us for a while. He's helping Daddy with business. While he's here, you need to stay in the house. Understand?"

"Yes, Mom. Ten four." Win wasn't about to leave Special Agent Coop alone anyway.

"Win, you play checkers?" Coop asked.

"Checkers? That's for little kids. Chess is better."

Coop smiled. "Okay, Win, you can teach me."

"Stu, we need to talk," Tab said, her voice low but not quite a whisper. "Let's go in the back behind the shed."

That brought back memories for Stu. His dad had a shed. He didn't like sheds.

"Okay." Stu winced.

Tab told Win that they were going outside for some special time. Coop watched them through the kitchen window. He could tell from Mrs. Baron's rigid walking, hands on hips, that Mr. Baron was about to get an earful.

Win piped up, "Special time means Dad's fixing to get it good."

"Yeah, that's kinda what I figured."

Tab laid in, "This is not what I had in mind. Now we got an armed federal agent living with us. Jesus. We need to let Ross and Abby know that the DEA knows about the cash."

Stu nodded. "You're right. You gonna call Ab?" Letting Tab know she was right, right off the bat might reduce the flaying.

"You know, the way I see it, I got screwed on this deal. First off, our boy is called the damned n-word on the first day of school. Fortunately, Win isn't traumatized for life. For now, anyway. Who knows what happens next around here."

Stu shoved his hands in his front pockets. "I'm sorry, Tab."

"You get a catfish farm. Ross gets a new yacht. Abby gets a new kitchen. What do I get? A used double-wide in fucking Alabama."

Stu winced. He could count the number of times she'd dropped the f-bomb on one hand. Most of those came after someone creased her rear bumper. He steeled himself for another crucifixion.

"Oh, and now a cartel wants the money back. What? You gonna tell 'em it's out there swimming around now?" She waved at the expanse of ponds.

"Tab, look. Special Agent Adams looks capable of doing his job. Terry will be on the way. Let's take this one day at a time. Things don't work out, I promised we'd go back home."

Tab looked into Stu's eyes. He gazed back at her for an instant and looked at his feet. Feeling like a whipped dog, he shuffled his feet, kicked at a mole hill. She shoved him in the shoulder.

"Come on, dude, let's get through this. We're a team." She gave him a quick hug. "You're something else, you know. Jesus, I hope this is your last midlife crisis. I don't think you can cap this one."

"Working on it, girl."

"Better not. I'll shoot you myself."

Coop looked out the window as the Baron's parted the quick embrace.

"Looks like you still have a dad," Adams chuckled.

"Oh, yeah. Crucifixions can't stop my dad, either," Win said as he concentrated on setting up the chess board.

CHAPTER THIRTY-SIX

Tab had a house full of men armed to the teeth with those god-awful guns, a curious six-year-old, and they were hungry. She stood over the Kenmore waiting on the pancakes to bubble. The coffee pot finished hissing. She poured herself a cup, wrapped her fingers around the mug, and gazed out into the backyard. She sensed the need for more sleep. She'd be operating on caffeine for the time being. Waiting on the bad guy to arrive didn't allow for much sleep last night. Every noise outside had deserved a second thought. Willie had come in on his weekend off to run the ponds so Stu could stay in the house. He was also apprised of the situation. Now he was packing. The damned farm had turned into an armed camp.

Willie made his way to the house after his final check. They had invited him for breakfast. Benson was in Win's room. Win had slept with her and Stu in their king. Poor Coop was on the sofa sleeper, nearer the doors as he requested. She hoped he'd be able to stand up without grimacing. Sofa sleepers weren't known for comfortable sleeping. He was in the hallway bath. She could hear the shower running. She wondered how buff he was. She noticed the taut sinews in his neck and his thick formidable wrists. She knew his type. Gym rat. He had the thighs of a running back. A natural athletic swagger that reminded her of her favorite celeb athlete and heartthrob, Joe Montana.

Willie knocked lightly on the mudroom's entrance door and entered.

"Good morning, Ms. Tab."

"Good morning Willie. How'd it go last night?"

"Nothing major. After I picked up Mr. Terry at the airport, pond number eight acted up, but it's doing okay now. Got a tractor in it. I'll check on it after a while."

"Appreciate you coming in on your weekend off, Willie. We're all kinda stressed out."

"Everything's going to work out fine, Ms. Tab." Willie had his chrome-plated Smith and Wesson .44 Magnum slung in a shoulder holster, the pistol near his left armpit. Two speedloaders were nestled in a leather pouch near his right pit.

Adams hadn't met Willie yet. He came around the hallway corner and saw the armed black man sitting at the table. Tab just finished pouring the man a cup of coffee with steady hands. He assumed he was a friendly and introduced himself.

"Special Agent Cooper Adams, DEA."

"Catfish security. Willie Jones. Nighthope Farm."

Tab smiled at Willie's attempt at levity.

Cooper noticed the cannon strapped on Jones's chest. "That a .44 Mag?"

"Yessiree."

"You gonna warn me before you touch it off?"

Willie smiled back. "I'll try to remember."

Tab looked puzzled.

While Adams and Jones acquainted themselves and talked about guns and war stories, Tab left the kitchen to rouse the rest of the boys. The pancakes were getting cold.

After the filling breakfast, Terry and Coop planned out the day with Tab and Stu. They avoided talking about a confrontation while Win was present. Willie left to go home and get some sleep before the evening's night shift.

"Look, guys, I have to run to the grocery store if you want to keep eating around here. Who's going with me?" She looked intently at Terry and Coop.

"Mom, I want to stay with Dad, okay?"

They looked at Win, enjoying the innocent remark.

"Win, that'd be great." Tab rubbed on Win's frizzy afro.

"I need to stay with Stu. Terry, you okay with taking Tab?"

"No problem, Agent Adams."

"Okay then. Give me about thirty minutes to make out a list and get ready. Any food allergies I need to know about?"

"I'm allergic to anything that's supposedly healthy to eat," Adams deadpanned.

"Tab, you know me, if it isn't twitching, I'll eat it," Benson added.

"How about grilled catfish?" Stu asked.

"We just had catfish the other night," Tab said.

"Yeah, but it was fried. I've been wanting to grill it for a change."

"Stuart, let's practice grilling fish when we don't have company," Tab asserted.

When the missus used his full first name in open conversation, it was matrimonial code for "You aren't going to win this one. Back down, homeboy."

"Okay, you win. Steaks?" Stu asked.

"Now you're talking." Tab smiled.

Coop realized she was tougher and smarter than his first impression. She could hold her own. Independent. Not the least bit subservient. He'd better think things through before issuing a tactical command. She wasn't about to act like a new recruit arriving at boot camp at four in the morning, jumping at the commands of a raging drill instructor. She was one of those authority questioners. There'd be hesitation on her part if he started barking out orders. He'd have to establish street cred with her. Let her realize, on her own, that he knew what he was doing. He hoped there'd be enough time to develop this relationship. He'd have to factor this in if the shit hit the fan sooner than later. Her golden-blond roots radiated brilliance in more ways than one.

CHAPTER THIRTY-SEVEN

As Tab made her way through the aisles of Piggly Wiggly, Terry Benson gave her ample space. He kept a wary eye on the large windows in the front of the store. He posted himself in Tab's aisle at the end near the front doors. Adams had described the cartel man. He said be on the lookout for the ugliest damn taco on earth.

He didn't pay much attention to the middle-aged man fondling the firm cantaloupes as Tab picked out some sweet potatoes. *Idiot thought he was God's gift to women.*

Bip Dolen had finally picked her out on the cover of an old *Playboy*. Miss March of 1983. She was standing right in front of him, the former Tabitha Fuller. She hadn't changed much in the twenty years since her wild college days at UCLA. Still perky, trim, a golden-blond mane of hair just past her muscled shoulders. Her teal-blue eyes radiating a delightful combination of mischief and innocence. Different though was a honed aura of confidence. She moved with deliberation. Dolen was focused on the set of feminine attributes that had merited several glossy pages in front of a glowing fire place on a plush bright red carpet in a California mansion.

As Tab picked out an assortment of salad dressings, Bip Dolen shot around the corner and waltzed right up to her. She took a step backward. The man's back faced Terry Benson. He alerted to the violation of personal space and Tab's reaction.

"Well, hello. If it isn't Miss March herself."

"Excuse me? Do I know you?"

"Not yet, but I'm willing to change that."

"How's that?" Tab frowned. She had been through this ordeal more times than she could count. It had been a while.

"You want to keep that photo shoot a secret in this town? We can keep it between the two of us. Just you and me at my camp house on the river."

"Are you nuts? I'm a married woman." Tab put her hands up in front of her chest. Took a bladed stance.

Good girl. Benson was closing in.

"Oh, come on. A woman like you. You don't fool around anymore?"

"No. If you don't leave me alone right now, you're going to be in a world of hurt." She looked over his shoulder at Benson. He was rapidly advancing with his right hand stuck inside the left flap of his sleeveless khaki vest.

"Right now" was code. Shit dangled in front of a fan.

"How so?" Dolen grabbed her right bicep and attempted to pull her.

Bip Dolen's life passed in front of his eyes. Someone had grabbed his nut sack from behind. His testicles were being squeezed against each other. His jewels morphed from golf balls into mini footballs. Going commando that morning was turning into a huge mistake. Another hand grabbed a fistful of his Bryll-creamed hair, bending his head all the way back nearly to the middle of his shoulder blades. His neck was an inch away from snapping. Pain seared through every fiber of his body. His eyes teared. He was close to passing out. That bowling ball of a kidney stone he passed last week was nothing compared to this. He'd rather pass a porcupine. Pain at a six on a scale of one to five.

Tears continued to pour out of his eyes. Air sucked out of his lungs. He couldn't scream. All he could do was gasp as sheets of pain racked his body.

"Come on, asshole, you're going with me," the deep-voiced man said behind him.

"Terry, don't kill him." Those would be the last words he would hear from Miss March's mouth. And he would remember them for the rest of his life.

Benson pushed him toward the double swaying doors to the meat department in the back of the store. He relaxed his pull on

Dolen's head and used his recently improved face for a door opener. As the pair made their way past the bloody meat counter, Dolen made another near-fatal mistake: he grabbed for the meat cleaver.

Benson responded by squeezing his balls together with all his strength. Dolen dropped the cleaver to the floor. Both hands went instinctively to his groin. Benson body-slammed him into the stainless steel freezer door. The handle hit Dolen in his solar plexus, sending his diaphragm into a paralyzing spasm. Benson let him hit the floor. He curled up into a fetal position, still clutching his jewels, wheezing for what little air he could suck in. He passed out and appeared lifeless.

"Okay, Terry, that's enough," Tab whimpered from behind.

Terry turned around. "You okay, Tab?"

"I'm all right. What about him?"

"He'll live. He'll wish he was dead for the next few days."

The meat department's crew returned after their lunch break. They found the groaner still curled up on the floor, his hands cradling his swollen nut sack. When the police arrived, Dolen could not physically describe his attacker. He conveniently forgot to mention the woman. Adultery was still listed in the Alabama code book. The imposed penalty being a little worse than spitting on the sidewalk on Sunday in Opelika. But he preferred not to give his estranged wife any more ammo. The first two divorce attorneys had reamed him out during their civil colonoscopies.

*****

After the sumptuous dinner of perfectly cooked rib eyes, salad, and baked sweet potatoes, Stu and Tab went on a walk to the feed bin. Terry and Coop stayed back about twenty yards, giving them some privacy. Win pestered Coop with questions about being a special agent man.

Tab took a deep breath. "Terry and I had a situation at the grocery store this morning."

"Oh boy. Now what?" Situations with Terry Benson were usually climatic. He wasn't one to hold back on the reins.

"I was accosted by a stranger in the store, and well…Terry, saw it go down."

"Another creep?" Stu asked.

"Yeah, it's been awhile. Guy must have a photographic memory. He even recognized me down to the month. Idiot grabbed my arm."

"Is he going to live?"

"Yeah, the family jewels are a little worse for wear, though. He won't be doing it for a while," she snickered.

"The old neck pull and nut sack move?"

"Yep, his all-time favorite."

They continued walking, escaping into their own worlds.

Stu remembered the time when he and Tab were on a beach in the Dominican Republic. Benson was positioned about twenty yards away. A private security guard patrolled the beach. The guard accosted a poor man selling trinkets to the tourists. Without a verbal warning to get lost, the guard hit the old man on his collarbone with his night stick, breaking the bone. The man hollered in gut-wrenching screams. As the guard wound up for another blow, Benson appeared, grabbed the baton from behind, and dislocated both of the guard's shoulders. He then hurled the man's sidearm into the surf, telling him to find another job in perfect Spanish.

He hired Benson because of the threats when his company decided to go nonunion. The Teamsters sent their thugs. And Tab's past notoriety surfaced at times. Her baggage never got completely unpacked. There was always a smelly sock hidden under the suitcase liner. A creep in every city.

Stu stopped walking. "I'm sorry, Tab."

"Hey, that one's on me. The booze. Needing the money at the time. The creeps will die out eventually." She grabbed his hand, and they continued walking. "Let's not worry about the past. We need to focus on this drug thing."

"Girl, how in the hell is he going to find us here in Alabama?"

"I've been thinking about that too. Reckon Coop knows?" Tab asked.

"I think Coop knows a lot more than he's willing to share. It may be for our own good, though. The waiting around is bad enough. What's Win saying?"

"He's in his own little innocent world. He thinks it's all about CTC. Doesn't have a clue." They turned around and looked at the three. Win was in between Coop and Terry. They were swinging Win back and forth, playing human swing set.

"I want to show you something. Brian loaned it to me." Stu reached in his back pocket and pulled out a small black pistol.

"Oh, Stu, not you too?"

"Relax, it's a bird banger launcher. It can't shoot bullets. It's for scaring birds. Brian says they're showing up early this year."

"What kind of birds?"

"Cormorants. They come in flocks of hundreds. Each one can eat a pound of fish."

"Jeepers, that can get expensive. I thought it was bad with the nectar. Do you realize I'm going through a quart a day? We have dozens of them."

"We'll stop at the feed bins. I'll give everyone a demonstration."

Tab and Stu waited in the shade of the feed bin. Win noticed the gun in his daddy's hand.

"Daddy, you got a gun too?"

"No, Win. It's really a firecracker shooter. Let me show you." Stu reached into his front T-shirt pocket and pulled out a circular plastic container that looked like something snuff would come in. He popped the red lid off and plucked out a BB-sized copper plug. He pulled back the hammer and nestled it in the breech hole. Terry and Coop watched intently. Stu reached deep in his cargo shorts front pocket, pulled out a shotgun-sized cartridge, inserting it into the other end of the barrel.

"This little copper plug is the primer. It ignites the cartridge. Okay, everyone, stand behind me."

Stu aimed the pistol into the sky at about one o'clock and pulled the trigger. The cartridge flew out with a sharp bang, screamed into the sky, and blew up with a report much louder than a M-80.

"That's cool, Daddy. Can I try it?"

Stu looked at Tab. She nodded.

"I get it next, please, please, please," Terry said like a kid. Tab playfully punched him in the shoulder.

Tab managed to shoot off a few rounds. To the neighbors, it must have sounded like the Fourth of July. Coop hit a bucket-sized fire ant hill with his first shot. The hill exploded, leveling the mound, and scattering tens of thousands of pissed-off worker ants. They were now on individual warpaths, looking for something to sting.

"Might be a good time to go back to the house," Terry muttered.

As the sun began to set behind the tree-lined horizon and the last rays of sunshine glanced off the quiet ponds, Willie showed up for the night shift. He was loaded for bear.

CHAPTER THIRTY-EIGHT

As Willie, Coop, Terry, and Win ate french toast and apple-wood-smoked bacon, Stu attempted to call Brian at work. He had a question about the weed problem in pond seven. It was next in line for harvesting. The fish were ready, but the fish procurement man at the processing plant said the submersed weeds had to be removed before they could seine the pond. Destiny said Brian was on vacation and wouldn't be back for a week.

Stu hung up after talking to Destiny for a few more minutes. She thought it sounded like a good idea.

"Coop, can you help me with a little chore this morning?"

"Sure, what you got in mind?"

"I want to pull up some weeds in one of the ponds. Was wondering if I could get you to pull one end of a cable with your monster truck. It's got a CB radio, right?"

"I reckon that's what that big antenna is for." Coop was referring to a ten-foot-long whip antenna attached behind the rear window on the top edge of the truck bed. He recalled seeing a radio with a microphone mounted on the hump.

"Great. I found a steel cable, looks to be about two hundred feet long. We'll drag it through the pond and tear out the weeds. Figure we could use two pickups and communicate with the CBs."

"Sounds like a plan," Coop replied.

Win got ready for school. Terry and Tab decided to wait on Win in the school's library while he was in class. Five people in the two-bedroom house was feeling crowded. Tab was stressing out. Vastly outnumbered by men, the damned guns, cooking for an army, endless cleaning, keeping up with Win and his boundless energy. She craved peace and quiet. The call ahead to the headmaster was appreciated. Sonny Wright planned on spending quality time in the library sharing naval war stories with Benson. He would make sure Mrs. Baron was comfortable.

Benson ignored the decal on the front door. It depicted a red line drawn through an old-fashioned revolver. He interpreted that as meaning "No revolvers allowed." His semiauto Sig was therefore exempt.

When the criminals pay attention to the signs, then I'll play by the rules too.

*****

Coop and Stu started at the shallow end of the pond farthest from the steel riser pipe at the deep end. They planned on disconnecting when they reached the drain pipe. Most of the weeds were in the shallow end and along the edges. They couldn't grow in the deeper water.

They selected channel fifteen out of the twenty-three CB channels to communicate and coordinate the pulling.

As the trucks inched down the opposite levees, the cable worked like a charm. Mats of thick green leafy southern naiad floated to the surface. The water muddied slightly as the cable sliced through several inches of muck.

Almost halfway down the levee, a woman, obviously very Southern, her drawl greatly exaggerated, sounded off on the radio. Channel fifteen was evidently her niche for the interstate corridor in the adjoining county. She was drumming up business. Her male suitors were scattered along the four lanes of the super slab between Meridian and Tuscaloosa.

"Come in, Big Stick. This is Honey Hole."

Stu chuckled as he listened to the chatter. His memories with Ross, listening to the other truckers on the radio as they ventured out of California headed east, flooded his mind.

He hoped the woman would go away if Big Stick failed to answer.

She tried another radio acquaintance. "Come in, Rough Rider. This is Honey Hole."

Streetwise Coop had figured out exactly what was going down: there was a hooker at an interstate rest stop.

"Hello, Honey Hole. Long time no see. This is Rough Rider coming atcha from Merry City."

Coop broke in. "What say you two find another channel?"

Honey Hole came back. "Who's dat?"

Rough Rider chimed in. "Sounds like we needs to teach him some manners."

The hair on Coop's neck stood out. It was on. "This is Long Hard Steel. Get off my damned channel."

Honey Hole shot back. "Long Hard Steel my ass. I betcha you got one smaller than my pinkie."

Stu grimaced. This was going south fast. Both trucks were approaching the last one-third of the pond. Coop was not paying attention to the task at hand, paying more attention to the show-down at the CB corral.

Stu tried to get on the channel, but Honey Hole, Rough Rider, and Long Hard Steel continued to exchange heated barbs. Every time he pushed the mike to speak, they walked all over him. Their verbal audience was growing as the bleed over from the other channels dialed into the drama on channel fifteen.

"Soft Steel, you ain't from around here. We hear that Virginia accent. Nothing good ever comes out of Virginia but government queers. Everyone be on the lookout for a faggot with Virginia plates. We'll teach him some manners in deep Dixie."

"Tell me what rest stop and I'll whip your asses!" Coop yelled into his mic.

"Listen to that little pecker," Honey Hole howled. "I bet my mama could stomp his ass."

"If your mama is half the whore you are, I bet she's got blisters on her pussy make the Rocky Mountains look like anthills," Coop howled back.

"I'll cap you for that one, bitch!" Honey Hole screamed.

Stu stopped abreast of the riser pipe. The cable was still moving toward the vertical eighteen-inch-diameter steel pipe sticking about one foot above the pond's surface. It was anchored in three yards of concrete at the bottom of the pond. It wasn't going anywhere short of a nuclear explosion. Coop was still pulling. The cable rubbed against the pipe and created a small ripple at the surface as it vibrated. Stu felt the tug on the rear bumper and then the rear of his truck inched sideways, scrunching the gravel under his tires, toward the pond. He was practically standing on the brake pedal, but his locked tires couldn't fight the strength of Coop's truck.

Stu yelled into the mic, "Coop, hold up. You're pulling me into the pond!"

The message went unanswered. Rough Rider's illegal signal booster walked all over Stu's transmission as he went into another rant about teaching Soft Steel, now renamed Little Pecker, some Alabama manners.

Stu's rear bumper headed down the levee inches from the edge of the water. Stu laid on the horn. Coop's windows were rolled up, the A/C fan was on max, and the constant squawking from the CB drowned out the blaring horn. Coop was totally oblivious to Stu's plight.

Coop was well past the riser pipe and almost abreast of the last levee. He was still animated about the disparaging chatter. His manhood was in question. Some lowlife had just defamed all the Virginians before him—Washington, Jefferson, Monroe, Madison, and his all-time favorite hero, the undaunted courageous warrior Meriwether Lewis.

He also sensed his truck wasn't pulling very hard anymore, like something had come loose. He looked for Stu's truck. Stu was standing on the opposite bank, truckless, glaring back at Coop. The truck was floating out in the pond. They both watched as the bed slowly filled with water and, like the Titanic, saluted with a tail dive and disappeared into the green water. Stu's favorite beaver stick popped to the surface.

Coop reached over to the radio, turned it off, and gripped the steering wheel with both hands. He stared straight ahead.

Stu briskly walked over to Coop's truck. "Well, was all that worth it?"

Coop grimaced. "I'll trade you a dry Dodge for a soaked Ford."

"Thought this was government property?"

"Shit, man, this belongs to the DEA. We sell guns to the bad guys. Think they give a flying shit about a damned truck?"

Stu shook his head. "Coop, you're a piece of work."

"Yeah, my boss tells me that all the time."

"Well, I reckon we need to pull her on out. I'll unhook you. Turn it around, we'll hook it back up, and then you head back down this side. She should come out over there in the shallow corner, hopefully right side up."

"Sounds like a plan."

The soaked truck came on out, wheels down. Several two-pound catfish flopped around in the bed of the truck. Stu tossed them back into the pond. Out of curiosity's sake, Stu reached in and turned the key. Not even a whimper. The on-board computer was dead as a doornail. The truck was totaled. His next call would be to the farm's insurance agent. He hoped submersion was covered.

Stu got in on Coop's passenger side. They rode back to the house.

"This is a nice truck." Stu liked the leather interior and roominess of the crew cab.

"Yeah, these duallies are popular with the drug cartels that operate out of Miami. You see a Hispanic down there wearing a lot of gold bling and driving a dually, even the K9s get woodies. We always find traces of narcotics in them."

"Maybe I could buy it when it goes up for auction."

"I don't know exactly how that works. We're confiscating vehicles all the time, tractor trailers, boats, Ferraris, Ski-Doos, even airplanes. I guess it all gets auctioned off at some time."

"Well, when all this is over, let me know."

"Stu, I promise. When I get back, it'll be a while before I turn in the paperwork. Consider the truck on indefinite loan."

Coop was impressed by Baron's reaction to the farm mishap. After all, the man owned a fleet of several hundred trucks. He couldn't fathom all the challenges of keeping a fleet like that running from day to day. *It had to be one cluster after another.*

They pulled into the driveway. Coop took a deep breath. He feigned struggling with words, stammering, "I'm…I'm…" He thunked the back of his head with his palm, "I'm sorry."

Stu chuckled at Coop's antics. "No worries, dude. I didn't like the paint color anyway. What's up with all this crimson red anyway?"

*****

Win bounded out of Tab's car and ran inside the house. He was in a hurry to change out of his school clothes and help Dad and special agent man Mr. Coop.

Stu came out of the master bedroom. He almost bumped into Win in the hallway.

"Whoa, boy, where's the fire?"

"Hey, where's your truck? Where's Coop? Thought you were out on the farm. Mom said I could ride Red out there."

"Coop's in the bathroom getting washed up. We had an accident with my truck. Coop and I put it in a pond."

"No way, Dad. Really?"

"Yeah, really. It floated about ten seconds, and then it sank."

"Did you get it out?"

"Oh, yeah, it's sitting in the shed. Figured we could get it running again maybe this winter. I'd give it to you when you get a little older."

"Cool!"

"Win, don't get your hopes up. Sometimes they won't run again. Right now it's dead as a doornail." CTC had a history of truck submersions. Some good. Some bad. Some really bad.

Tab and Terry came through the mudroom door.

"Hey, Stu, where's your truck?" Tab asked.

"Daddy put it in a pond!"

"What? Are you okay?"

"Oh, I'm fine. Coop's feeling a little bad, though. He's had a rough morning."

Coop showed up and heard the last part of the conversation.

"What happened?" Terry asked Coop.

"I sacrificed Stu's truck in honor of Virginia's patriots." Coop grimaced.

"This sounds like the making of a good story. We got any beer?" Terry asked.

"Let's save the beer for later. We still have a mission to complete," Coop replied.

CHAPTER THIRTY-NINE

"Nighthope Two to Base. Nighthope Two to Base." The base radio on the nightstand awoke Stu and Tab. Win, sound asleep in the middle, barely stirred.

Stu pushed down on the button for the pedestal microphone, speaking softly, "Go ahead, Nighthope Two."

"Need help. I've got fish up in pond nine. Looks like the bloom died off. Need another tractor."

Tab was fully awake. "You want me to go with you?"

"No, you stay here with Win."

"You sure? I don't mind."

Stu whispered back, "No, we don't need Win waking up and not finding either one of us here."

Stu dressed into some old clothes at the foot of the bed and stepped into the hallway. He noticed the hallway bath light was on. He heard Coop snoring out in the living room.

Terry emerged from the bathroom. He saw Stu in the hallway. "What's up, boss?"

"My damned fish are up. Wanna help?" Stu figured he'd let Coop go on and sleep. Take Terry with him.

"Sure, give me a minute. Let me get a few things together."

"Hurry, this isn't a drill. I got money out there fixing to die."

Terry and Stu stopped at the shed. Stu hopped on a John Deere 5105 utility tractor. The power-take-off shaft was already attached to a portable emergency aerator. Terry followed him in Coop's G-ride down the main levee. Willie's truck was at the far end of the last pond on the farm.

*****

GREGORY N. WHITIS

Diablo inched his way around the house, peering in the windows. He had seen the two men leave the house as he hid behind the garden shed. He saw the woman and the kid asleep in the rear bedroom. The man on the sofa bed also appeared to be asleep. He squinted in the dimness and noticed the pistol and a set of cuffs on the end table next to the couch. He would have to take care of the guard first, and then he could mess with the woman. It had been awhile. Raping the woman behind the Subway in San Francisco after killing the agent had relieved some pent-up tension.

He eased around the carport. He tried the knob on the mudroom door. Surprised it was unlocked. He quietly slipped in, making his way slowly through the kitchen, into the living room and around the couch. The man was snoring. He picked up the Glock and shoved it in behind his belt. Taking the cuffs, he pushed on one loop, muffling the ratcheting clicks with his other palm. He bent down, placed the open loop around the top rail of the bed frame, and quickly snatched the other loop around the sleeping man's wrist. He recognized the man. He cinched down hard.

Coop, startled awake by the biting pain around his wrist, immediately recognized the man standing over him. Diablo sneered. Coop yanked at the cuffs, reached over with his other hand, pulling with all his might on the bed frame, groping for his Glock.

"Now I get to kill you."

"You son of a bitch. You killed Quintana."

"Asshole was tougher than you. He held out for four fingers before he admitted to being DEA. How long you going to hold out?" Diablo reached in his back pocket and pulled out a pair of pruning shears.

"I'll be calling your mama a whore for each one, asshole." Adams grimaced.

Tab woke up to the loud voices coming from the living room. She hopped out of bed and cracked open the door. There was a new voice coming from the living room. Hispanic. "Oh my god," she gasped. "He's here!"

She ran to the base radio and pushed down on the mic button.

"Stuart, the bad man is here. Please hurry."

316

There was no answer. Stu, Terry, and Willie were busy placing the emergency aerator in the corner of the pond. They couldn't hear the radio due to the roaring of the tractor.

Tab waited for a reply. The voices in the living room grew louder. Pitched with emotion. Win stirred, rubbing his eyes.

She looked around the room for a way to protect herself. Win's baseball bat was in the corner. She eyed the bird banger pistol on the dresser.

"Mom, what's wrong?" Win sat up in bed. He heard a strange voice from the hallway.

"Win, help me with this." She picked up the pistol.

"Why?"

"A bad man is here. Coop needs our help."

Tab's hands shook. She couldn't load the tiny brass primer in the breech. She was losing her fine motor skills as her body flushed with adrenaline. The dexterity she needed to load it had vanished.

"Let me have it, Mom."

Win took the pistol, loaded the primer, and grabbed a red banger shell, inserting it into the pistol barrel. He then cocked the hammer all the way back. "Take it. It's ready. Aim and pull the trigger."

She wanted to signal the men on the farm by shooting out the window. She couldn't raise it up. It wouldn't budge. She heard loud thumping and yelling in the living room. It sounded like a full-on fight.

Coop exited the bed on the opposite side to get in a more defensive posture. He crouched down on his feet, bending at the waist, with one arm still cuffed to the frame. Diablo ran around the sofa and kicked Coop in the head. Coop, dazed from the blow, fell to his knees. Diablo climbed on top of his back, riding Coop down to the floor. He placed Coop's cuffed pinkie finger in the shears.

Coop let out a blood curdling scream. Tab and Win rushed down the hallway. Coop screamed again. His pinkie finger squirted bright-red blood.

Tab took aim and fired.

The blast was deafening. The banger round entered Diablo's open shirt and lodged under his left armpit. It exploded, tearing off a

CD-sized patch of skin. The burning hot propellant melted the shirt's polyester fabric onto his skin. More debilitating was the shock wave to his heart. It seized. Diablo dropped like a sack of coffee. Coop had seen it happen before. It was like a one-in-a-million, bone-crunching tackle that kills a teenage quarterback in his tracks.

At that same instant, Willie was momentarily looking toward the house. He saw the bright flash of light in the kitchen window.

"What in the hell was that?"

The cavalry was on the way.

Diablo, barely conscious, clutched at his heart.

"Win, get my keys!" Coop yelled.

Win grabbed the pile of keys by the reading lamp. He threw them to Coop's extended left hand. A perfect throw.

Coop uncuffed himself. He cuffed Diablo behind his back. He snatched his Glock and a 9 mm Beretta out of Diablo's belt. His finger, profusely bleeding, had a deep gash all the way to the bone, nearly all the way around. Arterial blood spurted out in rhythm with his racing heartbeat. Tab ran to the mudroom, grabbing the first aid kit off the wall.

Diablo appeared lifeless. There was still smoke coming out of his armpit.

Win stared at the man lying on the carpet. "Is he dead?"

Coop took a deep breath. "Give me a sec, Win. I gotta focus. Damn this hurts." He grimaced, staring at his finger.

"Coop, let me get that bandaged."

"Tab, hold on. I gotta keep this guy alive."

Coop rolled him over, checking for a pulse. None. He wasn't breathing either.

"I can't believe I'm going to do this."

"What?" Tab screamed.

"Give this son of a bitch CPR."

Coop knelt beside him, thumped on his chest twice, and started doing deep heart compressions with kneaded, bloody hands. He heard and felt the man's ribs crack. Diablo coughed. He was coming back.

The locked front door flew off the hinges. Benson entered first, gun drawn, scanning the room, his eyes following the arc of his semi-auto Sig as it went from one side of the room to the other. Willie entered with his .44 Mag in both hands, a little lower, fanning out on Terry's left side. Stu dashed in with his favorite beaver stick, fanning right.

Coop ducked as the arc of Willie's .44 Mag went over his head.

The men gathered around the downed man.

"Holy fuck, he's an ugly bastard," Terry said.

"Tab, get Win back in the bedroom. Let them handle this from here." Stu winced.

"Should I call the police?" Tab asked.

Coop looked at her. "No. Not yet." He looked at Terry. Terry nodded. Things had already been planned out in advance. Specific skill sets would be in play.

"What about your finger, Coop?" Tab asked. It was still spurting blood. Tab clutched the first aid kit to her chest.

"Tab, let me have that. I've patched up a few guys back in the day." Terry took the first aid kit. "You all go back in the bedroom now. We got this, okay?"

Stu, Tab, and Win left for the bedroom. Diablo moaned. He struggled with the cuffs slicing into his wrists.

Stu turned around as he entered the hallway and looked at Willie. "Hey, man, don't forget about my fish."

At the moment, Stu really didn't give a fuck about his fish. He kinda knew what was in store for the man. Terry and Coop were about to go all out. Tom Clancy style. *Willie didn't need to be around as a witness.*

"Roger that, boss," Willie replied.

"Willie, there's a black gym bag up on the top shelf in Win's room. Mind getting that for me?" Terry asked.

Willie left the living room. Terry squirted betadine all over Coop's finger. It dribbled on the carpet, mixing in with the pool of blood at Coop's feet.

"Ms. Tab's going to need a new carpet." Coop grimaced. He looked at the door laying in the living room. "New door too."

"Stu needs something better than a stick," Terry deadpanned.

Diablo moaned again. They both stared down at him.

"We need to do it somewhere else and without Willie," Coop said while Terry wrapped adhesive tape around the sterile gauze.

"Willie's got fish to take care of," Terry replied.

Willie returned with the black gym bag. Terry took it from him.

"Hey, Willie." Terry paused. "Coop and I need to get some information out of him before we turn him over to the authorities. It's best you not be around for the party. Understand you served in the Army?"

"Yes, I did. Six years. Shit happens. You two do what you have to. Tell him that if he ever comes back, he's going home in a box."

"Ten four on that," Coop said.

Willie left.

Terry reached in the bag and removed a thimble-sized glass vial of ketamine IM and a hypodermic syringe. He loaded it with five cc, thumped the side of the thick needle, and plunged it deep into Diablo's thigh. He slowly pushed down on the plunger. Diablo exhaled deeply one time and stopped moving.

Terry looked up at Coop. "We got thirty minutes to get him ready for the fun and games."

CHAPTER FORTY

Diablo began to stir. He fought his way out of his slowly lifting brain fog. He wanted to wipe the crud out of his eyes, but his hands were still cuffed behind his back. His ankles ached. They were cuffed also. The loops bit into the joints above his feet.

He heard a ratcheting sound. His ankles lifted off the ground, then his legs, next his waist, and now his torso. In less than a minute, he was suspended upside down. The pain at his ankles intensified. He was hanging from a game gambrel used to butcher whitetails. The twin-link chain of the cuffs grated against the lower bar of the gambrel, sliding back and forth as his body swayed above the concrete floor.

The pain at his ankles was similar to driving a blunt iron peg through both feet. Or perhaps losing four fingers.

Benson locked down the release lever for the winch. It was bolted to a steel post supporting a girder for the shed. It had been used for hanging and cleaning deer by the previous farm owner. Diablo's head was four feet off the concrete floor. Coop grabbed Diablo by the hair, tilting his face up. As Diablo's eyes focused, he saw a man grab his shears off the counter.

Adams said, "We got all night for this, you ugly bastard. My friend here doesn't work for the government. He doesn't give a rip about your constitutional rights. Since you're in the country illegally, no one knows you're here, right? You could disappear, and no one would know. That's the good part about you assholes sneaking across the border."

Benson unlocked the shears, wiped off Adam's blood with a shop rag, and slid his index finger along the blade.

Adams continued, "I know how sadistic the cartels are." Adams wrenched Diablo's head up more. "Problem is, I never made it past the Old Testament. Kept reading the best part over and over, an eye for an eye and a tooth for a tooth. Didn't see much sense in reading any further."

"Go to hell," Diablo said in perfect English.

"You gonna have to deal with us there too," Benson snickered.

Coop looked at Benson. *Good one. He was on the same page.*

"How's that feeling right now?" Benson said as he looked up at Diablo's ankles. They were turning blue from the bruising.

Diablo didn't answer. Benson approached Diablo with the shears.

"You need to start talking," Coop admonished. "Like I said, we got all night."

"Fuck you."

"Tough guy, huh?" Adams had ruled out snipping fingers. *The wetback probably had hep and HIV.* Decided he wasn't worth the risk. They hoped the pain from hanging upside down would have elicited some cooperation.

Adams spied Win's snake cage in the corner of the shed. He motioned to Benson. They strolled over to the cage. Inside were five four-foot-long thick brown snakes.

Terry whispered, "Are they cottonmouths?"

"Nah, the Virginia swamps are full of these. Just harmless water snakes, but they look like cottonmouths, don't they?"

"He won't know the difference," Benson whispered back with a smirk.

"Hell no. A snake's a snake to those assholes."

They dragged the cage across the floor and placed it under Diablo's head.

Adams unlatched the hasps and swung open the square access hatch.

Benson walked over to the winch, unlocked the spool, and slowly backed it off. He lowered the man down toward the cage and stopped when Diablo's head disappeared in the hole.

The snakes slithered around inches from Diablo's face. He frantically moved his head back and forth, his neck bouncing off the edges of the hatch.

Adams kicked the cage for the desired effect. An agitated snake struck Diablo in the nose. The toothy jaws locked down on the lip of his remaining nostril. Needle-sharp teeth latched and stuck to the rearranged cartilage. The snake violently writhed in an effort to fight loose. Diablo screamed. The snake released and dropped back down into the cage. Tiny pores filled with blood on Diablo's nose. The blood trickled into his eyes. He continued screaming.

Willie heard the screaming out on the ponds. He shut his truck windows. He prayed the Barons couldn't hear it. He didn't pray for the man.

Benson stood at the winch. He slowly winched Diablo out of the cage. *Click. Click. Click.*

"What do you want to know?" Diablo cried.

"Who the hell are you?" Coop asked.

"Manuel de Avarez Castillo."

"Who you working for?"

Diablo hesitated answering. He looked hard at Coop. *I want to kill you.*

"Answer the question or back down." Adams looked over at Benson.

Click.

"Jose Agosto."

Coop recognized the name. It was good intel. *Screw those libtards. Torture does work.* Agosto was the kingpin for the Bajalistas. Now he needed a location.

"Good answer. Need a location and a phone number."

"I tell you that, you might as well kill me 'cause I'll end up dead anyway."

"Yeah, but my friend here is really good at this. Probably better than you. I could leave right now. Leave it all up to him." Adams picked up the shears and waved them in front of Diablo's face.

"He lives in a town in Baja on the coast. San Peter. We call it La Casa de Roja. Only house on Caballo Loco Avenida.

"Phone number?"

"527-444-690-504."

Coop spied the shop phone on the wall. "You sure about the number?"

"*Si.*"

Coop fished out his international calling card from his wallet. He entered a link to some post office in Montana, now closed, but the telephone service still activated just for this purpose. The phone call from the farm couldn't be traced. He waited for a ring tone.

Coop dialed the operator. "Need to make an international call. Mexico. Number is 444-690-504."

It was ringing.

"*Hola,*" a female voice said on the other end.

Coop switched to his fluent Spanish. "*Manuel Castillo. Quero hablar con el Senor Agosto.*" I want to talk with Mr. Agosto.

"*Esta ocupado.*" He's busy. "*Dejele un mensaje.*" Give me a message.

"*Tengo el dinero en Alabama.*" I have the money in Alabama.

"*Un minuto.*"

Adams could hear footsteps in the background, distant talking, and then someone picked up another phone.

"*Manuel? Como va?*" Jose Agosto asked.

Coop hung up and smiled. He had a fix on Agosto.

Diablo closed his eyes. He was close to passing out. Pressure was building up behind his eyes. His eardrums throbbed. His ankles felt like they were going to pop.

Coop placed a call to SAC Santiago. He was on the phone for several minutes, nodding occasionally at Terry.

A van would be arriving from the Pensacola Naval Station in several hours.

Coop grabbed Diablo by his hair and wrenched his head up. Diablo stared at Adams with a blank expression. "Good news and bad news. We're done with you here. That's obviously the good news. Bad news is there's a SEAL team on the way. The agent you killed in San Francisco, former SEAL. Welcome to Hell." Adams dropped Diablos head.

Benson jabbed him again with a full syringe. The next time he woke up, he'd be feeding intel to hungry SEALs about the floor layout of Casa de Roja, its security details, and the number of inhabitants. Their love sessions with ice-cold water and soaked towels over his face wouldn't stop until all his answers matched up. They'd return him to Mexico in strict accordance with SEAL immigration policy. He'd get his first free lesson in high-altitude skydiving over the Gulf of Mexico. They promised him that they'd teach him how to properly pack a parachute for the second lesson. From twenty thousand feet, Diablo would have two minutes to figure out what he did wrong on the first lesson.

CHAPTER FORTY-ONE

The Baron household returned to normal. Stu arranged for CTC One to return Coop to Virginia and then fly Benson down to Jacksonville. One of the truckers had to be let go gently due to substance abuse issues. He had failed the company's random drug test. If he could pass the next one, Coast to Coast might rehire him as a warehouse loader. He'd never get behind another rig. Maybe Benson's exit interview would scare him straight.

Stu continued driving Adam's G-ride for a few weeks until a flatbed showed up and hauled it away. He bought a new Ford F-150. Dark blue with orange pinstripes. Brian had helped him pick it out. The personalized license plate read "Low Tide."

The weather in late September finally turned the corner from the blistering hot and unrelenting, stifling humidity to tolerably cooler and dryer. The afternoons still heated up. Early mornings elicited mental debates on whether a light jacket was needed. Pond temperatures were maxing out in the upper seventies, and the fish slipped a little in their daily feedings. Stu was finally at ease leaving the farm and venturing into town with Tab and Win, taking him to school. He enjoyed being a part of their morning ritual.

Stu smiled as Win high-fived several classmates entering the academy's front door. The headmaster waved excitedly at Tab. She waved back, playfully imitating his excitement.

"He always do that?" Stu asked.

"Yeah, some mornings I think he's going to dislocate his shoulder."

"Something going on between you and the headmaster I should know about?"

"He mentioned something the other day about working as a substitute teacher. Told him I'd pray on it."

"You do remember how merciless we were on substitute teachers? It was like a contest. Who was going to turn her into a raving lunatic first?"

"I don't think a private school would be that bad. They run things pretty tight around here. Win says no one messes with Mr. Sonny."

"Frankly, I think it would be a good thing for you, Tab. You'd be able to get out of the house and meet people. I love the isolation on the farm, but you've always been more of a socialite."

Tab waved to a couple other mothers in the lot. "We haven't been to the diner in a while. How about a biscuit and some coffee?"

"That sounds good." Stu looked at his watch. He had a man coming to the farm at ten that morning. He wanted to keep it a surprise.

Tab and Stu entered the diner and sat at a window booth.

They noticed that about half a dozen men and one woman were dressed in full camo. Even their knee boots were in Mossy Oak.

Stu asked Heather, the waitress, if it was hunting season.

"Yeah, today's the first day of fall turkey season. Normally it's in the spring. This year they're trying it in the fall. Guess there are plenty of turkeys."

Stu and Tab enjoyed their biscuits and fresh piping hot coffee as the working class of Bellevue filtered in and out of the diner. Many had a first-name basis with the diner staff. A few had credit accounts with the cashier. It was a friendly atmosphere. Stu and Tab relaxed, relishing the hometown comradery as it unfolded.

Several men at the big table were also dressed in camo. A gentleman, in his early seventies, entered the diner and strolled straight to the table. He walked with a slight limp, slightly stooped from a Korean war wound in his lower back. He was on veteran's disability in addition to his Social Security.

"Y'all ain't going to believe the size of the turkey I got this morning. Sucker is nearly six foot tall!" Vern Hopper exclaimed. He said it loud enough for everyone in the crowded diner.

"No way, Vern. You been drinking this early in the morning?" Larry Honlon asked jokingly.

Everybody knew Vern didn't drink. He was the oldest deacon at First Baptist. He lived to hunt and fish. He did it mainly to save on groceries.

"I was in my shooting house down in my best green field. He stepped on out of the fog with about ten hens. He was ah' eatin' and ah peckin' at bugs just like the hens. I shot him at about fifty yards."

"You say it's nearly six foot tall, Vern?" Honlon asked again, winking at the others at the table.

"It's out in the truck, fellas. I'm fixing to take it up to Water and Woods up in T-town. Enter it in the Big Bird Contest. Might fetch the five-hundred-dollar grand prize," Vern said as he hooked his thumbs in the sides of his camo overalls.

"Well, I ain't ever seen a six-foot-tall turkey." Honlon got up and made his way to the door. The rest of the table followed.

Stu looked at Tab. "You ever seen a turkey that big?"

Tab shook her head no.

"Let's go look at it," Stu said.

They finished their coffee. Stu laid a ten-dollar bill on the table, amply covering the meal with a generous tip.

The men crowded around Vern's battered red Ford Ranger. The tailgate was down. Vern held a scaly bird leg up in the air. He was pointing at the long sharp spurs. Tab couldn't see over the men. As her Chanel No. Five wafted in the air, the men turned around and parted like a wave to let her see inside the bed. She looked at the dead bird, nodded and smiled, and turned around to find Stu.

"Did you see it?" Tab asked.

Stu sighed, whispering, "Tab, that poor man shot an emu."

"Well, at first I thought it was an ostrich, but an emu makes sense."

"My uncle used to raise them on his turkey farm. They made good guardians for his outdoor flocks. They can get mean. Phil said the spurs on their feet can cut you up pretty bad," Stu said.

Stu and Tab headed back to her car.

"I read that the emu farmers went bust raising them. They turned them loose in the woods 'cause the market dried up." Stu winked at the group still huddled around the bed of the pickup. "That one there probably just took up with a wild flock of turkeys."

"Stu, that poor man's going to drive all the way to Tuscaloosa. Someone up there's bound to know it's an emu. Somebody's going to bust his balloon. He's counting on that five hundred dollars."

They watched the men continue to ogle the dead bird.

"Yeah, he's probably already got his heart set on the prize money," Stu said.

"He seems like a nice man too," Tab added.

"Tab, I got an idea. Hop in."

Tab and Stu waited until the man got in his truck. They headed north on Highway 69 toward T-town. As he approached the police jurisdiction sign, Stu flashed his headlights several times. Vern Hopper noticed them in his rearview mirror and braked. Stu waved his arm out the window. They pulled over into the public high school parking lot. Stu got out and walked up to Hopper's door.

"Problem, mister?" Hopper asked.

"Hey, man, I saw your bird at the diner."

Vern Hopper grinned. "Yeah, I'm on my way to enter him in the big bird contest."

"You realize that isn't a turkey, right?"

"Say what?"

"Sir, that's an emu. They're kinda related to an ostrich. Folks used to raise them but turned them loose. Couldn't make any money."

"Shoot, I thought the stupid thing had a skin infection and was just losing his feathers. Put him out of his misery before winter got here. He was sure acting like a turkey. Did you see the spurs on him?"

"Yeah, I did. Just like a wild turkey, too."

"An emu, huh?"

"Anyway, I'll give you five hundred dollars for him. I'd like to get him stuffed and mounted. Put him in my man cave."

"You sure he's an emu?"

"Pretty sure, sir. You go ahead and take him up there, maybe he'll qualify as a big bird anyway. Here's my card." Stu fished out a new Nighthope Farm business card. And his very last five hundred Mexican dollars.

The man looked at the five crisp C-notes. He wiped a tear from his eye.

"I appreciate it. What's your name?"

"Stuart Baron."

"You ain't from around here, are ya?"

"No, sir, but looks like I might be here awhile." He was thinking about the meeting with the man at ten.

"Tell you what, Mr. Stuart, let me get on to Tuscaloosa. I'll bring him right back and drop him off at Richey's Taxidermy on Avery Lane."

"Sounds like a plan. What was your name?"

"Vern Hopper. I've lived here my whole life. Except for Korea and a few train stations along the way, I haven't ever been anywhere else."

"Mr. Vernon, good luck in Tuscaloosa. Give me a call when you get back to Bellevue after dropping it off at the taxidermy. I'll make the arrangements this morning. You can come to the farm and look at it when it's done."

"Sounds good. See ya later."

Hopper drove off. Baron smiled. He knew he'd see the man again. That was how life worked in Alabama. A man's word was good enough. Didn't need a phalanx of lawyers trying to outsmart each other. And he was finally out of bad money. A weight had lifted off his shoulders.

He told Tab he had finally spent the last of the stash on a stuffed bird.

"What are you going to do with a six-foot stuffed bird?"

"We're going to put it in my and Win's man cave."

"What man cave?"

"The man cave attached to your honking big new she shed."

Stu reached around behind Tab's seat and put a Barnes and Noble shopping bag on her lap. Inside was a book, *100 of the Best Ranch Home Designs*.

"Man coming at ten o'clock is a local home builder. I wanted you to meet him. You got a week to pick out a home plan."

Tab gazed at Stu. "I love you."

"Hope you still love me after we get our first custom home built. I've been told marriages get tested."

"Dude, after shooting El Taco with a bird banger, I think I can handle it." Tab smirked.

"Hey, I would have got him with my beaver stick." Stu grinned.

"You realize that's the second time this year you showed up with a stick to a gunfight?"

"Maybe it's time I trade in the stick for a gun?"

"Well, let's think on that some more."

"Hey, you want hear something funny?" Stu asked.

"Sure?"

"I went to the courthouse the other day getting a heads-up on what it takes to build a house here. You know, in terms of permits and codes and what-not."

"Yeah, I remember the nightmares in California. Remember that time you put floodlights in the attic? The building inspector had to inspect it twice after we wired it up." Tab winced.

"I took out my checkbook. Put it on the counter in the probate office. I asked the clerk what it takes to build a house in the country. The clerk looked at me funny-like. 'Mister, all yah needs are a hammarh, nails and some lumbah.'"

Tab laughed.

Stu looked down the highway in both directions. He had the whole road to himself. There wasn't another vehicle within a mile. He smiled as a tear rolled down his right cheek. Stu checked his left-view rear mirror one more time. The coast was clear. He made a U-turn. Headed back to Bellevue.

Tab gazed at her husband, wiping the tear off his cheek with her soft thumb.

"You gonna be okay?" she asked.

Stu glanced at Tabitha and nodded. He gazed straight ahead, giving in to more happy tears.

He could start living again.

The End

ABOUT THE AUTHOR

Gregory N. Whitis was born in Gainesville, Florida, moved to Dubuque, Iowa, before the fifth grade, graduated from Iowa State University, and earned a master's at Auburn University studying fish. After marrying Karen Joan Schimek, a tall blue-eyed blond from Milwaukee, they resided for a short time in Ankeny, Iowa, and discovered he couldn't make any money growing fish in the arctic. He landed a job as a farm manager on Alabama's largest catfish farm. He made his first attempt at floating a pickup truck there. He then was hired by Auburn University as an extension specialist so he could advise catfish farmers about the floating characteristics of pickups. He then met his writing mentor, Aileen K. Henderson, of Brookwood, Alabama, and she suggested that perhaps he should write a novel about sinking trucks. In the meantime, at the age of forty-four, he suffered a major midlife crisis, proudly graduating fourth in his class at the Tuscaloosa Police Academy. He served ten years as a Hale County deputy sheriff.

He's run in sixteen half marathons, two triathlons, and two Warrior Dashes. His doctor still says he's too fat. Most of his writing epiphanies sprout between bouts of boredom while running. Now retired, he spends his nonwriting time turning his pine acreage into OCD Park, violating every known forestry management guideline in the book. He says his chainsaws won't run properly in eighty percent humidity. The old refrigerator in the garage still keeps his beer cool. His fan club has an open invitation to drop in. Critics are shown the dewberry patch. The chiggers are free.

CPSIA information can be obtained
at www.ICGtesting.com
Printed in the USA
LVHW090806110321
681210LV00001B/76

9 781662 424045